D0377366

PENGUIN BOOKS

THE AMNESIAC

Sam Taylor was born in 1970 and is the former pop culture correspondent for the *Observer* (UK). He lives in France with his young family.

THE AMNESIAC

SAM TAYLOR

PENGUIN BOOKS

PENGUIN BOOKS

Published by the Penguin Group

Penguin Group (USA) Inc., 375 Hudson Street, New York, New York 10014, U.S.A.

Penguin Group (Canada), 90 Eglinton Avenue East, Suite 700, Toronto,
Ontario, Canada M4P 2Y3 (a division of Pearson Penguin Canada Inc.)

Penguin Books Ltd, 80 Strand, London WC2R 0RL, England

Penguin Ireland, 25 St Stephen's Green, Dublin 2, Ireland (a division of Penguin Books Ltd)

Penguin Group (Australia), 250 Camberwell Road, Camberwell,
Victoria 3124, Australia (a division of Pearson Australia Group Pty Ltd)

Penguin Books India Pvt Ltd, 11 Community Centre, Panchsheel Park, New Delhi – 110 017, India

Penguin Group (NZ), 67 Apollo Drive, Rosedale, North Shore 0632,
New Zealand (a division of Pearson New Zealand Ltd)

Penguin Books (South Africa) (Pty) Ltd, 24 Sturdee Avenue,
Rosebank, Johannesburg 2196, South Africa

Penguin Books Ltd, Registered Offices:
80 Strand, London WC2R 0RL, England

First published in Great Britain by Faber and Faber Limited 2007
Published in Penguin Books 2008

1 3 5 7 9 10 8 6 4 2

Any resemblance to actual persons living or dead is entirely coincidental. Yeah, right. What a stupid phrase that is. *Actual persons* are entirely coincidental! Life is entirely coincidental! What you want to know is: are you reading a work of fiction or a true story? Well, let's put it this way. There is no such thing as a true story. These are, you might say, the memoirs of an amnesiac, but so are all memoirs. I could write my life story a thousand times and it would never be the same and it would never be "true to life." Why? Because memory itself is a fiction: we are, second by second, in every moment of reflection, self-editing, reinventing, making ourselves up. On the other hand, if *I* write it, then it is by definition my story. It may not be wholly "true," but it cannot be wholly false either. No work of fiction has yet been written which contains not a glimpse, a reflection (however distorted) of the author's life and experiences. All novels are, to some extent, *romans-à-clef;* only, in most cases, the key does not quite fit the lock, or the door is double-bolted, or it opens on to a corridor full of other, locked doors. Or, to use a different metaphor, a fiction is not a web of lies, with the truth, still squirming and alive, at its center; in a fiction, truth and lies are spun together, inseparable, in the same slender thread of silk. What the web catches is a matter of chance.

ISBN 978-0-571-23353-3
ISBN 978-0-14-311340-9
CIP data available

Printed in the United States of America

for Odile

Contents

A man's memory is not a summation; it is a chaos of vague possibilities.
    Jorge Luis Borges

But he forgot all this as he grew older.
    Philip Larkin

THE AMNESIAC

For the briefest of instants, his mind was a blank. He knew the details of the present moment: he was climbing a dark, narrow staircase; the air was warm and close, sour-smelling; his right temple ached. But none of these facts gave him any clue to where or when this was happening, or even to his own identity.

He stood still, breathing heavily, and a hundred vague staircases swam together in his memory. Had he been here before? It looked familiar, but then a staircase was a staircase. That smell reminded him of something, though. What was it? Rotten vegetables, he thought. Uncollected refuse. Human faeces. He listened closely and heard the faint hum of traffic; someone coughing from behind a door.

Suddenly, unbidden, a series of quick, hazy images flashed through his mind. Seconds later, they had vanished, and he was left with no remembrance of them except for one: the vague, half-turned-away face of a dark-haired girl. As far as he could tell, she looked young and beautiful, but he had no idea who she was, or why she had entered his mind. He felt sure he had never seen her before. For some reason, however, the sight of her face filled him with a strange emotion. It was, he thought, an emotion without a name: whatever it is that exists on the border between hope and fear.

For a moment he was breathless, suspended in time, and then a drop of sweat trickled down his forehead and into his eye. It stang. He blinked. And, in the second that it took for his eyes to close and reopen, it all came back to him.

Reality. The present. His self.

His name was James Purdew. He lived in Amsterdam, in an apartment he shared with his Dutch girlfriend, Ingrid. He had just come back from work to make himself a sandwich. It was lunchtime on Monday 7 July; the day before his thirtieth birthday.

Relieved, he began climbing the stairs again. All in all, the blackout could not have lasted more than a few seconds. He had no idea what had brought it on – a momentary break in the supply of oxygen to his brain? – but he felt sure it was nothing to worry about.

Halfway up the stairs, he heard a harsh, urgent, familiar sound. He started to run, taking the steps two at a time. Near the top of the third flight, he missed his footing, slipped, and felt a small crack. Still the sound continued, high-pitched and imperative. The pain was horrific, but he managed to climb the last few steps, unlock the door of the apartment and crawl towards the telephone. It had stopped ringing by then, of course. All he could hear was the recent memory of its ringing, like a disturbance in the air.

Even now he remembers vividly the thirty-nine seconds he spent crawling across the sitting-room floor, though naturally it seemed to him to take much longer than that. He remembers sweat dripping from his forehead on to the smooth, pale floorboards, and resting there in perfect little pools. He remembers the sound of blood beating in the veins inside his eardrums. He remembers how strange and distant the ceiling appeared from his position on the floor. Or, at least, he remembers remembering these details; the pictures themselves quickly faded, as all such pictures do, and he is forced to reimagine them – to invent them anew – whenever he tries to bring to mind the events of that fateful day.

The first thing he did when he reached the telephone was to check the answer machine. One message. He played it: nothing but a staticky hiss followed by a long beep. He listened to the message again, searching for clues, then he dialled 9293, but the caller had suppressed their number. With an odd feeling of guilt, he erased the message.

Only then did he call for an ambulance.

I
THE PLASTERCAST

The doctor said James had broken a small bone in his right ankle and would have to spend six weeks in plaster. This was the summer of the great heatwave. It was so hot during the day that the tomatoes in the windowbox were already cooked when he picked them from the vine. James kept the blinds closed and the windows open, but he could feel the furnace heat breathing against the thin strips of grey metal. Whenever a rare gust of wind moved the blinds, it was like staring into the mouth of hell.

He didn't wear clothes during those six weeks: there was no point. Most of the time he was naked except for a pair of boxer shorts and the plastercast. His girlfriend was working, so he spent the hottest part of each day alone. He sat in the leather reclining chair, which he covered with a towel to soak up his sweat. On the left arm of the chair he kept the remote control for the television; on the right the remote for the stereo. The telephone was on the table next to the chair. It rang so seldom that he kept checking the wires at the back, thinking they must have come loose.

He also kept a collection of flyswatters to hand. They were doubly useful. With the head of one he would murder insects; with the handle of another he would scratch at the dead, flaking skin inside his cast.

Ingrid kept the fridge stocked with fresh fruit, chocolate, beer and mineral water, and the freezer full of ice-cubes and ice-cream. Every hour or so James would hobble over to put something cold in his mouth or on his forehead. Other than that, he barely moved at all.

There were plenty of books in the apartment, but he found he couldn't read. His head was too full of noise; a kind of formless buzzing. And the greater the silence in the flat, the louder his head buzzed. For this reason, he usually kept something 'on': TV, CD, DVD. And the electric fan, of course. He was lucky there were no blackouts that summer. Without electricity, he would have gone crazy.

This was a nightmarish time for James, but it had some interesting side-effects. He felt so trapped, helpless, bored, so suffocatingly alone, that he started doing something he hadn't done for a long time.

He started thinking.

In the evenings, when it cooled and the streets were shaded by the tall apartment blocks, James would cautiously hop downstairs, clinging to the banister. During the first two weeks Ingrid would help, carrying his crutches with one hand and supporting his body with the other. Once she'd gone, he had to do it alone.

Coming from the stale apartment, the city air, for all its toxins, smelled like a mountain breeze to James. He would walk as far and as fast as he could. To start with, even going to the next canal and back would leave him sweating and in pain. But as the days passed he became used to swinging himself forward with the crutches, always straight ahead, letting the other pedestrians move out of his way.

After the walk, he went to Harry's Bar, at the end of the block. The waiter saved his table, overlooking the canal, and brought out a tall beer, a ham sandwich, a green salad, a plate of chips and a dish of homemade mayonnaise. Harry would wave from the bar, and James would wave back. He would eat and drink and watch the tourists, the sky, the canal. From where he sat the water glimmered pink, orange, silver, gold, black . . . it flickered like fire in the slowly gathering darkness.

Even when Ingrid and James were together, the two of them didn't talk much. Ingrid had said all she had to say, and she knew James had a lot on his mind. After the first drink she would kiss him goodbye and go off to do whatever she felt like doing: cinema, yoga, Spanish nightclass. Then, around midnight, she would come and collect him, and help him up the stairs to her apartment. During the final four weeks, James had to manage this on his own. He was usually quite drunk by then, which made it both easier and more dangerous.

Even with the windows open, even with the fan on full speed, the air in the apartment would still be warm and thick. Ingrid, exhausted by work, usually fell asleep quickly, but James never did. Sometimes he sat out on the balcony and watched the drunks and nightwalkers in Liebestraat. Sometimes he listened to music on headphones. Sometimes he watched a blue movie on television.

James and Ingrid had sex together only twice after he broke his ankle, and both times occurred the very next morning, on his birthday. Their celibacy, I should add, was nothing to do with the plastercast. It was to do with the thoughts in his head.

On the morning of James's birthday, Ingrid woke him early and they made love before the sun came up. Afterwards he opened his presents: a shirt, a power-drill, and a CD. He was happy with all his presents: the shirt was orange and silk, expensively made but not too flashy; and the drill was a ten-speed Mikomi, a more versatile and powerful model than his old Fürcht. But it was the CD that excited him most. It was *16 Lovers Lane* by The Go-Betweens.

Ingrid put it on the stereo and moved the leather chair to the balcony. James sat with his cast balanced on the railing, drinking black coffee and watching the suited workers scurry both ways across the bridge over the canal. He thought they looked like ants, frantic and pointless, and he smiled, happy in the knowledge that he had so far escaped their fate; that he was thirty years old and still free.

The music was breezily romantic and the air had not yet lost its morning freshness. James breathed deep and, the next time Ingrid came past, he grabbed her round the waist and pulled her on to his lap. She was wearing only a thin cotton nightshirt. '*Again?*' she said, mock-weary, her smile giving her away.

Ingrid left for work at nine, closing all the blinds before she went. James's parents rang to wish him happy birthday, and the manager of the construction agency called to ask how his leg was. James explained he would be out of action for a couple of months.

He went back to bed and dozed in the darkness, listening to The Go-Betweens. It wasn't the first time he had heard the album. He'd owned it on vinyl when he was younger, but somewhere along the way he had lost his copy. It probably belonged to an ex-girlfriend now, he thought, or had been sold for a few pounds to a second-hand store. It reminded him of the room he'd had during his first year at university, in a big house on Lough Street. There had been subsidence in the area, so the floor of his room sloped down towards the street. In James's memories it was always grey and raining outside and he was lying on the narrow bed, hungover, drinking tea, listening to 'Love Is A Sign', and feeling happy-sad.

Listening to it now, in Ingrid's double bed, he felt pretty much the same way. Happy-sad. Bittersweet. He thought about that lost record, all the lost girlfriends who might have ended up with it, all the time lost since that first year at university. He had been eighteen then and now he was thirty. 'You Can't Say No Forever' came on. He wondered what it all meant. All that past, all those memories.

This was, he decided, why he liked The Go-Betweens so much. That feeling: of happiness, of being young and alive and in the moment, and yet with an undercurrent of melancholy, regret, some unnameable fear. Like the way the canal made him feel when he watched it change colour in the twilight.

James spent a lot of time that morning thinking about his new age. Thirty. At the beginning of his thirty-first year. He counted the years off, one by one, trying to remember what had happened to him in each of them. He could have looked in the boxes under the bed, of course, but it seemed too big a step to take; they had been there so long, untouched, that he felt afraid to disturb them.

The counting of the years was not too difficult between the ages of four and eighteen (the first three years, though he had no memory of them, were undoubtedly momentous: emerged from the womb; learned to walk; learned to talk), but after that he had trouble distinguishing between one year and another. In his twenty-first year he had graduated from university. In his twenty-fifth he had met Ingrid. Otherwise the time seemed to have passed so quickly, so glibly, that he was at a loss to recall anything significant at all. In retrospect, it seemed to James that he had been *willing* the time to pass quickly. As though, second by second and year by year, his only ambition had been to distract himself from something . . . something he was afraid to think about.

Lying on Ingrid's bed, these thoughts seemed to swarm around him. In the darkness he couldn't see them, but he could hear them buzzing, and the sound made him feel sick. He closed his eyes, but sleep would not come. James remembered a poem he had once studied at school: 'Aubade' by Philip Larkin. It was about Larkin's fear of death, which always reared up most strongly in the early morning, in the dark hours before dawn. James couldn't remember the words of the poem, but he remembered its mood, and how it had made him feel, sitting in that grey classroom.

He sat up, his heart pounding, and tried to see. The only source of light in the room came from the holes in the blinds, but they illuminated nothing. Indeed, they were so bright that they made everything else look even darker. Suddenly James became aware that he could not see his own body. Even with his hand in front of his eyes, it was invisible. Was that it? James wondered. Was that the thing he had been afraid to think about? His death. His mortality. He considered this for quite some time, breathing slowly and deliberately. But no, on reflection, he didn't believe that was it. The thing he had been afraid to think about, the buzzing sound; that came not from his future, but from somewhere in his past ... .

He must have fallen asleep because the next thing he knew he was covered in sweat and he felt hungry. He hobbled over to the fridge and filled a plate with a Caesar salad that Ingrid had made the day before. He put the TV on and ate the salad, watching the Tour de France. The riders were in the Pyrenees. The pine trees were dark green; the sun was shining; he could see snow on some of the higher peaks. It looked so light and cool, so solid. James wished he could have been there, instead of where he was.

Ingrid came back around seven. She asked him about his day. He said it had been fine, a bit dull. He didn't tell her about his dark thoughts; now that she was home again, he felt ashamed of himself for being so morbid. In any case, she seemed impatient to tell him about *her* day. She began to explain about a man who had taken her out to lunch. James thought for a moment she was about to tell him she was having an affair, but it turned out the man was a headhunter from a rival company. He wanted Ingrid to manage a new office they were opening. 'And guess where the office is?'

'I don't know,' said James.

'Guess,' Ingrid urged.

'Madrid? Barcelona? Paris?'

'No,' she said. 'Better than any of them. Well, I think so anyway.'

James shrugged. 'Where?'

'Waterland.'

Waterland was a suburb, north of Amsterdam, where Ingrid had grown up. Her parents still lived there now. It was a quiet, pretty, safe place, full of trees and fields, double garages and playgrounds.

James faked a smile. He could see how thrilled she was and he didn't want to ruin the moment for her. She told him she had put a bottle of champagne in the freezer. She hadn't accepted yet, she said, because she wanted to discuss it with him first. She thought they could talk, drink the champagne, then maybe go out to a restaurant.

In fact, they never left the flat that evening. Ingrid had a shower, lit a few candles, poured the champagne, and told James how she imagined their future together. She saw them in a large, modern house with a garden, not too far from her parents. She would run her office, he would work for her dad's direct-mail company (her dad was prepared to offer James an executive post, despite his lack of experience). After a year or so, when they felt settled, they would try for their first child. They would both work part-time and share parenting duties. If they wanted to go out to a restaurant, her mother would look after the baby. On weekends they would go for long walks in the countryside, invite friends to barbecues in the garden. It would be wonderful.

'So,' she said finally, 'what do you think?'

James didn't know what to say. He couldn't explain why the idea of this life frightened him so much. It was how most people lived, after all. There was nothing specifically wrong with it. He just felt shocked that he had reached this point without even being aware that it was coming: the infinite possibilities of youth suddenly over, the future mapped out in straight grey lines, the end visible. He felt like he must have been sleepwalking through the years, and only now had he woken.

But he couldn't say that to Ingrid. So in the end he said simply, 'Listen, Ingrid, you're free to do what you want. If you want to accept the job, then you should. I understand why you think it would be a good move for you. But I don't want to live in Waterland. I don't want to work for your father's firm. I'm sorry, but I don't feel ready for . . . what you're talking about.'

Ingrid's eyes grew wide with surprised pain, and then she began to cry.

They argued until early morning, getting nowhere. They said bad things. They hurt one another. Around three o'clock, Ingrid went to bed and James sat on the concrete floor of the balcony, his plastercast poking through between two railings, smoking a cigar. The cigars had been a Christmas present from Ingrid's father. James normally never smoked, but right now he felt like doing something with his hands and mouth; something suggestive of deep thought. He sat on the balcony, blowing smoke into the night sky, and listening to Ingrid sob herself to sleep. As he sat there, James wondered what was going to happen to his life.

It was nearly ten when James woke the next day. The bedroom was hot and Ingrid had already gone to work. His throat felt dry from the cigars, so he drank a whole bottle of water, then ate some cereal and milk and a few grapes. He used his inhaler and remembered to take an anti-allergy pill; he had missed several doses and felt guilty about it, but at least he didn't seem to be ill. Afterwards, still tired, slightly nauseous and unsure what to do with himself, he reclined the leather chair, put *16 Lovers Lane* on repeat, and lay there listening to it.

He must have listened to it five or six times that day. He knew all the songs, of course, and they were pretty much as he remembered. The sound was a bit thinner, but that might just have been the difference between vinyl and CD. Yet there was something else . . . something missing. A couple of times – in the verse of one song, the chorus of another – James thought he heard a fragment of what he was searching for. But it couldn't have been. It must, he realised, have been another song altogether; a song that he'd imagined was on this album, but wasn't.

James could recall hardly anything about this 'missing' song. Not the tune, nor its title, nor who had sung it. All he had was the memory of a feeling – happy-sad – and the warm sound of acoustic guitars, and a low-pitched, male voice. The vaguest echo of a melody.

It conjured up an image too, though he had no idea why: of a long street of terraced houses, seen from above. In the image it was night-time, everything stained blue. A girl and a boy – or a man and a woman, he couldn't tell – were walking, hand in hand, along the pavement. She rested her head on his shoulder, tenderly. Under a streetlamp, two policemen stood watching them. James saw the image in a kind of flashback, like the memory of a dream, but that was all; there was nothing before or after. Only this brief scene, and the music that accompanied it.

Where had he heard this song that he could no longer quite remember? He had been so sure it was on this album; that was why he had asked Ingrid to buy the CD for his birthday. And yet, now he had the album, he discovered the song was not part of it. So what did that mean? From where had the memory of the song come? Why did its absence bother him so much?

For the rest of the morning, James flicked between Channel X and CNN; between meaningless sex and meaningless violence. He drank iced water and scratched inside his cast with a flyswatter. He ate soft black olives and spat the stones into the bin. He tried not to think about the song. It was there, though, like a trapped fly, buzzing around the back of his mind.

At least, he *thought* it was the song that was bothering him. But the longer he listened to its faint remembrance in the silence of the flat, the less sure he became that it was a piece of music at all. It was like listening to a radio station slowly fading out of range. As the hours passed, the song became swallowed up, distorted, by a kind of tuneless static . . . the buzzing sound that James had heard for the first time the day before.

What was it, that sound? At first he had taken it to be the tinnitus of modernity, or the echo of it in his head: the subterranean clatter of city train wheels . . . the insectoid fizz of neon striplights . . . the sickening moan of power lines . . . the insidious hum of sleeping computers . . . the same white noise that everyone hears, and to which we all grow deaf. But the closer he listened, the more he could discern something familiar, something private, something already known to him, but forgotten. And James began to suspect that it had been there all along, this sound. It was just that, before, he couldn't hear it.

Those other noises must have drowned it out. What *was* it, that sound?

James closed his eyes and tried to concentrate. There was, he sensed, some memory or insight just beyond the radar of his mind, some thought that when he discovered it would make him sit up and shout, with horror or euphoria, 'Oh God oh God oh God', and his life would be changed for ever. But the thought remained hidden, and in the end he gave up and went over to the fridge to see what he could find to eat.

In the afternoon he ate a tub of ice-cream and watched the Tour de France. Then he went back to bed and dozed. He dreamt that he went to see the doctor to have his cast removed. But in the dream it wasn't a hard plastercast: it was soft bandage, and the doctor had to unravel it. Round and round went his hands; longer and longer grew the bandage. It trailed all over the floor of the surgery. Finally it came to an end. '*There you go!*' cried the doctor, triumphantly. James looked down: the bandage had been peeled away to reveal . . . nothing at all. His lower leg had vanished. In the dream this seemed completely normal. He paid the doctor and walked, on crutches, out of his office.

When James woke up, it was evening. He had a cold shower and opened the blinds; to his relief, the heat of the day had faded and there was even a slight breeze. He sat on the balcony and waited for Ingrid to come home.

She came back late that evening. She did this occasionally – stopping after work for a few drinks with her colleagues – but usually she rang to let him know. James made cous-cous with fried chicken breasts and roasted vegetables for dinner, then ate his portion alone at nine o'clock. He began to worry about the state of mind Ingrid would be in when she came back, then he began to worry that she would not come back at all.

In fact she arrived just after ten and seemed quite happy. He could tell she was a little drunk from the way her voice wavered and her eyes shone. She inquired about his day. Reluctantly he told her about the song that he couldn't remember, and she asked him to sing it. But the hint of melody he had remembered earlier was gone now. Or rather, he could hear it, faintly, inside his head, but he couldn't bring it past the threshold of his mouth. It got lost, or blocked, somewhere on the journey from mind to tongue.

'Sorry,' he said finally, 'I can't.'

'Never mind,' said Ingrid. 'I'm sure it'll come back to you.'

She was quiet for a few minutes while she ate. He asked her where she'd gone after work. She mentioned the name of a bar, and the name of a friend. 'It was good,' she smiled. 'We talked things over. I realised that I probably came on a bit heavy last night, so I'm sorry.'

'It's all right,' he said, 'I do understand. It's just that –'

'Relax, no more arguments, OK? Listen James, I want to say something . . .' She came and knelt on the floor next to the leather chair, her hand resting on the cast. Her tone was calm and businesslike. James felt a wave of apprehension move over him. 'I've accepted the job in Waterland. I think it's a good move for me. You're free to do what you want. If you want to come with me, that's great. If you want to go somewhere else, that's fine too. I've handed in my resignation, and they said I can work out two weeks' notice. After that, I'll move my stuff out of the flat. I'm going to Waterland to stay with my parents and find a house. I start my new job the week after.'

'Wow,' James said. 'That was quick.'

Ingrid smiled and stood up. 'The rent on the flat is paid until the end of August. I've given notice that I won't be renewing after that. You're welcome to stay here till then. It'll give you time to think over what you want to do with your life. I hope that's all OK with you.'

He nodded, speechless.

'Good. Then, whatever happens, let's try and be friends for the time we've got left.'

'Of course.'

'Do you fancy going for a walk? It's lovely and cool outside now. We could have a drink at Harry's afterwards.'

Thus began the simple routine which sustained him for the next six weeks. Down the stairs, evening walk, Harry's Bar, back up the stairs.

Ingrid, true to her word, never again mentioned her imminent departure. When they talked, they talked of small things; things belonging entirely to the present. Quite often, they didn't talk at all. This didn't feel awkward or tense. Ingrid and James were comfortable in each other's company. They were physically affectionate. They still kissed. To any passing observer, they must have looked like a long-married couple: calm, content, perhaps slightly complacent.

It was only a façade. For most of that time James was away with his thoughts. He sat in the chair next to hers, drinking beer and watching the colours in the canal, but his mind was elsewhere: another place, another time. It was as though his body was existing on autopilot while his mind retreated ever further into its own slowly gathering darkness.

James had a lot of strange dreams that summer. The plastercast dream was unusual, in that he remembered it clearly. Most of them faded as soon as he woke. There was another dream, though, that he half-remembered. It was a recurring dream.

In this dream he was walking through a dark tunnel, following a thread. Behind him, when he turned around, he could see a point of light. He knew he ought to go back to the light, but he didn't. The tunnel sloped gently downwards. It was easy to keep walking down the slope; much harder to turn around and climb it. And he wanted to see where the thread would take him.

There were little holes in the wall of the tunnel, and occasionally James would pause and look through them. What he saw through those holes attracted and disturbed him. They were images from his past; dark flashes of memory. He saw the faces of people he hadn't seen or thought about in years. He saw alleys and houses and pubs he had forgotten even existed.

When he woke in the mornings, he could never remember

the details of the dream. The faces, the places . . . they were lost the moment he opened his eyes. All he remembered was the fact of having remembered, and a complicated, lingering emotion.

James isn't sure if he ever mentioned his dreams to Ingrid. A couple of times, she told him he'd been talking in his sleep, and she looked almost sorrowful when she said it. He asked her what he'd talked about. Ingrid said it was nothing she could understand.

Their last evening together was like all the others. They sat by the canal, eating chips and mayonnaise, and drinking beer. There were German and American tourists at the tables nearby. Ingrid was reading a magazine with a beautiful, half-naked woman on the cover; the woman looked unbelievably happy. Nothing was said. Occasionally Ingrid would stroke James's hand and he would look up at the familiar whirl of people and colours without really seeing them. James was miles away. He was in a world of his own.

All that distinguishes the night in his memory is that Ingrid asked him a strange question. 'James,' she said, in a casual voice, 'why were you running up the stairs that day?'

He blinked at her. 'What day?'

'The day you broke your ankle. What made you run?'

He thought about her question. 'The phone was ringing.'

'Yes, but . . . why did that matter? The answer machine was on.'

'I know it was.'

'So why did you run?'

'What do you mean?'

'Who did you think it was?'

'Who did I think what was?'

'The person who was calling.'

'Oh. I don't know. It could have been anyone.'

'So what made you run?'

He drank his beer, frowning at the canal, trying to remember. He saw again the door to Ingrid's apartment, heard again the muffled, shrill call of the telephone, felt the pain in his ankle as he missed the step. What had made him run?

'I don't know,' he said finally. 'I can't think of a reason. I just ran. I wanted to get there before the answer machine picked it up, I suppose.' There was a pause. 'Why do you ask?'

She shrugged, and looked away. 'I was just wondering.'

Then she went back to her magazine, and he went back to his beer, and his thoughts.

He woke around noon the next day. It was a Thursday; the first cloudy day in weeks. There was a note from Ingrid on the pillow. It said that she didn't want to wake him, and she didn't want to cry, so it was better that she leave like this. Mostly, the note was just information – lots of phone numbers and the arrangements for the removal of her things (her brother would come the next day with a hire truck) – but it ended with the words: 'Whatever you decide, I hope you will be happy. I wish you a good life. Get better soon, James. I miss you very much.'

James read the note three times. He wondered what she meant by 'get better': was she referring to his ankle or to something else? He even wondered if there was any significance in her use of the present tense in the last sentence – how could she already be missing him when she wrote the letter? – but in the end he decided it was probably just her foreigner's English.

After that, he didn't know what to do. He limped restlessly around the apartment. He went to the fridge but there was nothing he wanted to eat. He skimmed through the rack of CDs but there was nothing he wanted to hear. He switched on the television but there was nothing he wanted to watch. Finally he had a bath, then fell asleep in bed. He kept the note under his pillow.

Ingrid's brother was called Frank. He was the same age as James, and the two had always got on well. Frank called on Friday morning to say he'd be coming round at six that afternoon. But James had no desire to watch the apartment being stripped of Ingrid's presence, so at half-past five he went downstairs and set off on a long walk.

Despite the overcast sky, it was still hot; after two blocks he gave up and sat in a cool, empty bar called De Stijl. He had a few drinks and talked to the barmaid, who was wearing a T-shirt that revealed her pierced navel. She was friendly and they chatted for half an hour or so, but then the bar started filling up, so James said goodbye and swung his way towards the city centre. He found a Thai restaurant in a backstreet and ate a green curry with a bottle of white wine. When he came out it was turning dark. He was sure Frank would have finished by now, but he didn't feel like returning to an empty flat so he found another bar, where he talked to a middle-aged Frenchman about fate and free will. He went to lots of bars after that; he doesn't know how many. It must have been around midnight when he heard the song.

He was walking through one of the narrow shopping streets which lead on to the Melkplaan. The bars were still open, the street busy, the sky a weird purple; he could smell fast food, aftershave, urine. He was drunk, but his senses were sharp. The music was coming from a ghetto-blaster that someone was carrying, though James didn't realise that until after they'd passed him, when he saw the silver speakers disappear into the crowd. He tried to follow, but it was difficult executing a sharp turn on crutches with so many people around, and by the time he was facing the right way he could no longer hear the music.

Afterwards he wondered whether it truly had been *the* song that he had heard, but at the time he was in no doubt. It was *his* song. The 'missing' song. In any case, the bridge between verse and chorus was now echoing in his memory. Four chords and seven words:

> Part of my heart
> Will always beat . . .

It was still only a fragment, but he felt so relieved. That song

24

had been driving him mad. Singing it over and over to himself so that it wouldn't slip his mind, James went straight home and figured out the chords on his guitar. Exhilarated, he wrote them down in his black notebook, then returned to De Stijl and told the barmaid the story of the song. He even sang it to her, but she only shrugged and continued washing glasses. It was nearly closing time: the barmaid couldn't be bothered to flirt with customers any more. James got back to the apartment just as the sky was turning light.

He awoke with a hangover. For a while he lay there, frowning at the bare wall, wondering why he felt so happy. Then, slowly, the memory of the previous night came back to him. It had a remote, unreal quality, but when he looked in the notebook, he found the chords and words written there. He put the notebook down and picked up his guitar, and spent a few minutes singing the words, trying to make the leap to the next line; but each time it ended in mid-sentence, in a pause between two chords.

Part of my heart
Will always beat . . .

Ellipsis. Lacuna. And then . . . the chorus. Something big and obvious, he was sure. He was so close now; at the border of remembrance. But then, just as he was thinking this, James noticed a strange smell, and his concentration was broken. He sat for a while, trying to recall what the smell was. Finally it came to him: it was the smell of Ingrid. The scent she used. James put the guitar down.

The rest of the day was spent staring at the pale rectangles on the walls and floor where Ingrid's pictures and rugs had been. The bookshelves were empty but for balls of dust and one single book, which Frank must have missed. James picked it up and looked at it: the title was in Spanish and the writer's name was Borges. But he felt too tired to read stories in a foreign language, so he spent the afternoon drinking tea and listening to The Go-Betweens, and went to bed before dark.

*

After that, the days grew long and heavy. It was an odd thing with days, James thought, that an empty one was heavier than a full one. Slowly he drifted into a semi-nocturnal rhythm. By the middle of August he was spending hours each night wandering the streets on crutches. The man in the hot-dog kiosk outside the train station would say hello to him; prostitutes blew him kisses from behind windows as he swung past, his distorted reflection moving across their bare flesh.

Where were all of James's friends during this time? What happened to them? I suppose the truth is that most of them were Ingrid's friends, not his. James didn't know what she had said to them, but they made no great effort to stay in touch. One of them called, a few days after Ingrid left, but James didn't feel like talking to her, and after two or three minutes of one-way conversation she said goodbye and hung up. One evening he saw another friend, a man, while he was out walking. The man caught his eye and waved, but for a reason James couldn't articulate, he felt embarrassed. He stared through the man as though he were invisible and continued swinging past on his crutches.

Each night he ate and drank at Harry's Bar, but he never spoke to anyone. The order, always the same, arrived without a word from James. His greeting to Harry was a silent wave; his thank you to the waiter a smile or a nod.

With Ingrid no longer there, James began taking his black notebook to the table at Harry's; instead of staring into space and thinking, he would stare into space and think and then write down his thoughts. His strongest memory of this period is of watching his biro leave its trail of strange black squiggles, of focusing so intently on the page – golden with evening sunlight and grey with the long shadows of his moving hand – and the words he was writing, and the things they described, that when he looked up, cross-eyed, at the surrounding scene, he could not make out any outlines or forms at all; the canal and the tourists and the glasses of beer and the red-and-white awning and the chained bicycles and the advertising posters and the waiter and the bricks of the apartment building were all merged into a single dazzling blur. Sometimes he had to close and open his eyes several times before he regained his perspective.

James had kept a diary since he was fourteen; it was a ritual, and for a long time it had been little more than that. But now, as the flotsam of his life disappeared downriver, his notebook became a piece of driftwood; something to cling to. He wrote thousands of words each day. What he wrote was no longer a report of daily events, but a kind of fragmented autobiography. Try as he might, James could not bring any shape or definition to his thoughts. The sentences followed no logical order; they made sense, grammatically, but they were *inconsequential*; they led nowhere. His words were a labyrinth, full of wrong turnings, blind alleys. Sometimes he felt he was writing in a kind of spiral, though whether his words were spiralling out, towards calm, or in on themselves, towards a vortex, he could never tell. Or perhaps they were merely circling, endlessly. If only I could give the words some structure, some order, he thought, perhaps I would be able to break the spiral, to find my way out of the labyrinth.

Often he thought about the boxes under the bed, and wondered if the time had come to open them.

There were three boxes, all made of thick grey cardboard, with neatly fitting lids. James pulled them out, one by one, and wiped away the coating of dust. The boxes were heavy. On the first box, in black felt pen on a white label, it said, '88–91'; on the second, '95–99'; and on the third, '00– '. There was a fourth, smaller box, further under the bed, but James didn't see the point in removing that. It was late in the morning, a week after Ingrid's departure.

The boxes contained his diaries. These were his most valuable possessions, not because they held any astonishing secrets, but because without them he feared he would cease to be the same person. James did not trust his memory. He relied on the diaries to do the remembering for him. They were the ropes that moored him to his self.

He opened the first box and took out all four books. They were vinyl-bound A4 diaries in different colours: black, blue, red and green. He hadn't looked at them for a long time. Nervously he opened the 1988 diary – the blue one – and began to read.

James was astonished at what he found. References to Jung and Kafka and *The Communist Manifesto*; to poems and songs he had written himself; to the political situation in Nicaragua and the Middle East. How serious he had been! Now, foreign news and politics meant nothing to him, all he ever wrote was his own diary, and he couldn't even remember the last novel he had read; probably some airport thriller on a beach in Spain the previous summer. What struck him was how strange he had become to himself. That fourteen-year-old James was someone he hardly recognised. If that was *me*, he thought, then who am *I*?

Over the following days, he read through the whole of 1989, 1990 and 1991. The final three months of this last diary were blank. That brought him to the end of the first box. The second box began in 1995. He opened the first page of the diary for that year and began reading. It was all strangely bland and unrevealing, written in the present tense and studded with the names and initials of people he hardly knew. At the foot of each page was what looked like a mathematical equation. After flicking through the first few weeks, James realised it was a running account of money spent and earned.

He put the '91 and '95 diaries side by side and studied them. The handwriting was the same, more or less; the later entries were less neat, due to lack of time, but the basic calligraphy was unchanged. In terms of content, however, a casual reader probably wouldn't have guessed that they were written by the same person. The circumstances of his life had altered dramatically, of course: he had left the womblike world of full-time education and entered the harsh world of work, with all its chaos and insecurity. Even so, James found it hard to understand what had happened to him.

People change, he thought – it's a truism – but *how*? Our life is confined to days, after all: Sunday to Monday, dawn to dusk. What great alterations can take place in someone between breakfast and lunch? Is it possible to wake up as one person and fall asleep as another?

James had no idea. All he knew was that when he traced the arc of his existence from child to man, he found, each time, a massive blip in the graph. From earliest memories to the end of adolescence, the line ran more or less smoothly. There were fluctuations and reversals, but nothing unaccountable. Then came a moment of missing data and, when the line resumed, it was somewhere else completely. How did that child become this man? Which of them was the impostor?

There was only one way to find the answers to these questions. Unable to sleep, James went out on his crutches at two in the morning and by the time he came back he had made his decision. He crawled under the bed and pulled out the fourth box.

Like the first three boxes, it was cardboard, with a lid. But the fourth box was smaller and heavier than the others, and it was not labelled. He removed the lid. Inside the box was another box; or, to be more precise, a safe, made not of cardboard, but of black metal. Inside this box, James knew, were three diaries. They covered the period October 1991 to October 1994, when he had been at university in the city of H.

James didn't know where or when or how he had lost the key that opened this box. He had no idea at all. In fact – and he felt a kind of choking shame and panic as he remembered this – that whole era was a blank. Three years of his life, and . . . nothing.

Well, that was not quite true. He could picture places, sometimes quite vividly: his room in the house on Lough Street, for example, and the lounge of a pub called The Polar Bear. But events, people, emotions, any sort of chronology . . . he was clueless.

And his diaries – the only written record of this time – were locked in a safe.

And he had lost the key.

Staring at the little black box, James felt physically sick. Was *this* the dark something he had been trying not to think about? At that moment, it seemed far more hideous, more unbearable, than the knowledge of his mortality. He considered throwing the box out of the window. Perhaps it would smash open on the pavement, revealing his secrets? But just then he remembered the salesman's guarantee: only an explosive could break that lock. And if he exploded the safe . . . the past really would go up in smoke.

James stared and stared at the black box. The more he

thought about it, the angrier he got. Part of *me* is locked in there, he thought: three years of my life.

Something had happened to him in that time; he felt sure of it. Something important had happened. Afterwards he had no longer been the same person.

With trembling hands, James put the lid back on the cardboard box and slid it under the bed. Then he got undressed and lay down in the darkness. It took him a long time to fall asleep.

James decided to write the story of his life. He doesn't remember exactly how or why he came to this decision, but he remembers the relief and euphoria he felt after the decision had been made.

He had spent the day in bed: sleeping, thinking, remembering, and failing to remember. For more than fifteen hours his body did not move at all, but his mind wandered all over. Afterwards he could not retrace the train of thought that led to his epiphany, but the first inkling came with a half-remembered quotation from Thomas de Quincey about the idea of the human mind as a palimpsest. After half an hour of searching in the store cupboard, where James had long ago piled all his old books, he had found the sentence in his copy of De Quincey's *Writings*, the page marked and the words underlined:

What else than a natural and mighty palimpsest is the human brain? . . . Everlasting layers of ideas, images, feelings have fallen upon your brain softly as light. Each succession has seemed to bury all that went before. And yet, in reality, not one has been extinguished. All-powerful memory is able to exhume any impression, no matter how momentary it might have been, if given sufficient stimulus.

James's own memory felt anything but all-powerful – he couldn't even recall having underlined this passage before – but he was comforted by the idea that the truth must be in there somewhere; that it had not vanished, but was only hidden, at the centre of some tortuous labyrinth.

He sat up and stared into the darkness. An image came to his mind: of the curving, sloping tunnel with eyeholes, through which he walked every night in his dreams.

That must be it, James thought. I am trapped inside a labyrinth, and I have lost hold of the thread that once guided me through it. The only way to rediscover the thread is to start again at the beginning.

The story of his life. It would be a detective story: in search of lost time. He would write from memory. Perhaps, James thought, if I close my eyes and really concentrate, it will all come back. Perhaps I will find the key to open that little black box.

As soon as he had made the decision, James got dressed and went out to the shops to buy a new notebook. He chose a 150-page notebook, bound in white vinyl. It was half-past seven by the time he got back from the shops, so he went to Harry's Bar with his new purchase and had begun writing before the first glass of beer arrived.

First of all he signed his name on the inside cover. He was going to write his address and telephone number until it occurred to him that these were temporary – in three weeks' time he would be living somewhere else – so instead of that he tried to think of a title. He wrote and crossed out half a dozen before settling on the one he liked best. It was a weak joke, perhaps, but it made him smile. The title was *Memoirs of an Amnesiac*.

At the top of the next page James wrote 'Chapter 1' and then he tried to think of an opening line.

'My name is . . .'

'I was born on . . .'

'My earliest memory is . . .'

It was no good. James's earliest memory eluded him, and the other options seemed too obvious, too banal. He stared at the blank page until his chips arrived. Then he sat back in the metal chair, frowning at the canal and trying to recall his childhood. But the images in his head were as ungraspable, as indescribable as the water that flowed past in the twilight: changing its colour, appearing and disappearing at every second, and yet, in its essence, only and always water. What changes, he thought, is not the colour of the canal, but the perspective of the person who looks at it.

That struck him as quite a profound metaphor, so he wrote it down. He read it twice and smiled. He had a first line! Happy and tired after this exertion, James drank a long, cold draught of beer and then ate the chips, dipping them, two or three at a time, into the thick, firm mayonnaise. They were delicious. He looked around at the laughing, smiling people, and breathed deeply. Life was good. He leaned back with his eyes closed. Childhood . . . what could he remember?

The first image that came to his mind was of walking up Commercial Drive, the road on which his parents' house had been located, to the playgroup at the top; of entering the playgroup and kicking down a tower of building bricks constructed by his friend Philip Bates. Yet the more James thought about this, the less sure he became that it was, truly, a memory. The walk up Commercial Drive he could recall in great detail, but that was because he had lived there, and walked that road every day, for fifteen years. Perhaps he only thought he remembered the first part of the memory because he knew, from later experience, the geography of the playgroup? He decided to eliminate the walk up Commercial Drive; that left the second part of the memory, when he had entered the playgroup and kicked down Philip Bates's tower. But the more he tried to concentrate on this memory, the hazier it grew. Had it really been Philip Bates's tower that he had kicked down, or some other child's? Was there truly a picture in his mind of the interior of the playgroup, or was he confusing it with the infant school? Did James actually remember anything at all or did he just *imagine* he remembered it?

34

On reflection he decided not to include this memory in his memoirs. And yet, wasn't this omission a form of lying? And what if all his other childhood memories turned out like this one? What if none of them were reliable or significant? Where would that leave him? Disillusioned, James finished his glass of beer and stared at the single sentence that he had written.

What changes is not the colour of the canal, but the perspective of the person who looks at it.

Whatever I write afterwards, he told himself, will have to reflect and give meaning to that sentence. Yet the more he thought about it, the more it seemed simply an expression of the impossibility of ever writing a book of memoirs. The past was deep water, constantly refreshing itself, always in motion, yet all he saw was its surface, reflecting whatever light there was at that moment.

He closed the notebook and looked again at the water in the canal; it was purplish-black now, with streaks and splashes of yellow where the streetlamps were mirrored. 'Water under the bridge,' people said, about something they wished to forget; but what if they wished to remember? If only James could halt the water's flow, or reverse it. If only he could re-enter his past . . . dive in and swim through it. If only he could taste it on his tongue and swallow it. But the past was not a canal; that was just a metaphor. The past did not exist, beyond the confines of his mind. And how could he dive into his own mind?

James's toes were going numb so he put his cast up on the metal chair facing him – the chair in which, until a week ago, Ingrid had always sat – and suddenly her absence hit him. Ingrid was gone. A chapter of his life was ending. For a moment James felt merely sad, but then he had an idea.

My childhood, he thought, is too distant. I was someone else then. That is the reason I am struggling to write the beginning of my story: because I am starting in the wrong place. I should begin with the recent past. I should begin with Ingrid. I should write my life story *backwards*.

'Yes,' James whispered.

It was the first word to come from his mouth in what felt like a very long time. The waiter, who was passing, looked at James curiously. To cover his embarrassment, James ordered another beer. Then he picked up his biro, opened the white notebook, crossed out the sentence he had written, and changed the '1' to a '5'. There was no particular reason why his life story should have five chapters; it just seemed a good number. James began to write.

Memoirs of an Amnesiac

Chapter 5

I lived with Ingrid for nearly five years. During that time I loved her, and thought about her, more than anyone else in the world. We slept together every night, side by side and naked. Each day, she was the first and the last person I saw; some days, she was the only person. Now she is gone from my life and I will probably never see her again. How does this make me feel? I don't know. I'm not sure I feel anything at all.

The last time I saw her, she was sitting across from me at this very table. That was ten days ago; already the memory is faded. If I try really hard, I can summon the faintest ghost of her on to the metal chair opposite, but she is far less real to me now than the lamplight reflected from the chrome tabletop, the shushing sound that the canal makes, the taste of cold beer in my mouth. She is in the past, and that is a distant land. An unreachable land.

The last time I saw her, it must have been gone midnight, her face erased by darkness as the waiter extinguished the oil lamp at our table. I don't remember that. Nor do I remember walking with her to our apartment, or climbing the stairs, or going to bed. I don't recall her saying goodbye or even goodnight. All these little events, which I know must have happened, are too clouded and vague to be counted as memories. Nine days ago, eight days ago, perhaps even seven days ago, I might have remembered them; now they are fog. Thus goes almost all of life. Into the fog.

Yet I do remember the first time I saw her. My vision was obscured, but the memory is still vivid. I was on a squash court, about to serve. My opponent looked exhausted; I was on the verge of winning the match. It was the nineteenth of September 1998 and I had been in Amsterdam for four days. My life had more or less collapsed that summer, but I had begun to sense, in the week or two before this, that the collapse had been necessary, and that it might even turn out to be for the best. At that moment, however, I was not thinking about anything other than the small green ball in my left hand, the slender-necked racket in my right, and the dimensions of the court in which I stood.

As I swung my racket arm behind and above my head, I glanced – involuntarily, momentarily – towards the back wall, which was made of tinted glass. And there she was: standing alone, her hands on her hips, watching me. I would love to say it was her eyes (those windows to the soul) that made me react as I did; but we are talking milliseconds here, and a distance of at least two metres; we are talking dark glass. No, it wasn't her eyes.

It was her body. Of course it was. The shape of her body, the shortness of her skirt, the position in which she was standing. It was lust that made me miss my serve. It was self-consciousness that made me lose the game. And it was anger – as I watched a tall man I vaguely recognised bring her a drink and lead her away – that made me go on to win the match. Nine–one, in the final game. 'Jesus,' said Leon, my friend and opponent, as I finished wiping the floor with him, 'what got into you?'

In the showers, I asked Leon who she was. He told me her name. 'She's engaged to Robert Meijer: you know him, don't you? Works on the Options Exchange. He's a friend of Jorrit's.' The memory came back to me. Robert. Tall. Athletic. Handsome. Rich. Arrogant. He'd beaten me at squash two years ago, I recalled, when I was here on holiday. I had disliked him.

Dried and dressed, Leon and I went to the bar. There were about a dozen people sitting around three tables, which had been pushed together. Some were friends of mine; the rest were friends of friends. Leon and I shook the hands or kissed the cheeks of everyone there. Ingrid was the last in line.

Up close, I could see she was pretty, rather than beautiful; a creature of dawn, not dusk. She had dark blonde, shoulder-length hair, pulled back into a ponytail. Small features, like a child's, and perfect skin, still tanned from the summer. Her skin had a kind of taut ripeness, a nectarine bloom, that made you want to touch her. She was wearing a bright, tight top (red, I think, though it may have been pink or orange) that revealed the muscles in her shoulders and upper arms and also the firm swell of her breasts. My first impression, I realised, had not been wrong. I really did want to have sex with her.

She asked us who won. 'He killed me,' said Leon. Ingrid looked at me, her eyebrows raised, as I bent down to kiss her. 'Really?' My lips brushed her cheeks; they were soft and warm and smelled of summer fruit. 'No, it was close,' I said. 'Do you play?'

Robert came over then; he must have been listening. 'Ingrid's nationally ranked,' he said. 'She'd slaughter you.' He shook my hand as he said this, and smiled. I smiled too. Ingrid, I noticed, did not. 'That's not true,' she said. 'You hit the ball really well. You just need a bit more patience.'

'More patience?'

It was at this point I noticed her eyes: a deep, chocolate brown, naked-looking; their gaze calm and direct. Perhaps I noticed a slight swelling in her pupils as the two of us stared at each other, or perhaps I'm only remembering what I wished to see? 'Well, I wasn't able to watch you very long, but it seemed to me that you were trying to win the points too quickly.' Her voice was low and earnest, slightly husky, with that curiously lilting accent in which the Dutch pronounce English. 'I think you just need to slow down, relax . . . let your opponent make the faults.'

I took her advice. For the next hour, I smiled and nodded as Robert dominated the conversation. He kept one hand on Ingrid's body all the time – her shoulder, her forearm, her knee – as though worried that if he stopped touching her for an instant she would float away, like a fairground balloon.

My patience was rewarded. As we walked from the bar to a restaurant nearby, Robert said goodbye to us. He had a meeting

39

in the morning and he didn't want to be tired and hungover. 'Some of us live in the real world,' he said to me. Before he left he whispered something in Ingrid's ear, then kissed her, possessively, on the mouth. She told me that night what he'd said: 'Don't get drunk.' Ingrid wasn't happy about this; she didn't like being told what to do. In some way, I have Robert to thank for what happened; those three words opened a door that might otherwise have remained shut.

We sat next to each other at dinner. This was, I suppose, partly chance and partly choice. Desire makes its own luck. I sat at the end of the table; on the other side of Ingrid was a loud, drunken man whom neither of us liked. As the evening went on, he said more and more stupid things, and the two of us smiled complicitly.

'Who is that guy?' I asked her, when he went to the toilet.

'I don't know his name. He's a friend of Robert's.' She seemed to blush slightly.

I said nothing, only nodded.

It was a small, dark restaurant, lit mostly by candles. The food and music were Ethiopian. The wine was French. Ingrid drank white and I drank red. After the main course, she turned towards me and crossed her legs. I would have liked to spend more time admiring her thighs, but I couldn't because her eyes were on mine. She was wearing nylon tights and I was wearing cotton trousers and I could feel the thin forcefield of static electricity each time she leaned forward and our calves touched. In the candlelight our faces smiled and talked, politely flirting . . . but in the unseen depths below, we were already half-merged, already intimate.

We talked about squash, about friends in common, about Holland and England, about her job (she worked for the personnel department of a large computer firm), and about my current situation. I had, in the previous three months, quit my job, vacated my flat, bought a van, and emptied my bank account. My money was now in travellers' cheques and my possessions were in a rucksack. I was, I told her, going to explore the world, and I began listing the cities and countries and continents where I wanted to go.

She stared at me rapturously as I spoke. 'God, I'm so jealous.'

'Come with me if you like.'

I said it lightly – not passionately, not seriously – but Ingrid didn't laugh. She stared into my eyes for what seemed an age. 'Don't tempt me,' she said quietly, looking away.

Her face was turned towards the nearest candle; I could see its flame reflected in her eyes. The flickering looked like a hint of tears.

'Why not?'

I noticed she was fiddling with her engagement ring.

'Because I might say yes.'

And then she looked at me and smiled, and I knew she would never do anything so madly impulsive.

'When do you leave?' she asked.

'I don't know. Maybe tomorrow.'

'Tomorrow.'

'Maybe.'

The others took cabs, but Ingrid said she was happy to walk home. It was a cool, clear night and her apartment wasn't far. I was meant to be staying at Leon's that evening, and his flat was only a few streets from hers. I said I would see her to the door.

We walked in silence. This bothered me at the time, because I felt I was losing the momentum we had built up in the restaurant. I cast about my mind for things to say, but each time I opened my mouth to speak, I would look at Ingrid and she would smile, and whatever I was about to say would seem suddenly pointless, idiotic, wrong. (Afterwards I learned that she had already made up her mind to sleep with me by this point, that she was simply enjoying the moment: the taste of the night air; the sweet tension that precedes the first touch.)

When we reached her apartment, I sighed and said, 'Well . . .' Either she didn't hear me or she pretended she hadn't heard me. She unlocked the front door, entered, and left it open. After staring at it in stupefaction for a few seconds, I followed her upstairs. By the time I got up to her apartment and closed the door behind me, she was already bare-legged (she had removed her tights and – unknown to me – her knickers) and was bending over in the kitchen, pouring a bowl of milk for the cat. For one strange moment, I wasn't even sure that she knew I was there.

Nervously, I said her name. She turned around and came towards me, a smile on her slightly parted lips.

———

Of course this is all too neat to be true. What I am recounting is not what happened, but a story about what happened; a story I have told (to myself and others) many times before. In reality, for want of a better word, I cannot be sure of the exact sequence of events, never mind the precise words that were used in our dialogues. As for those little details – such as Ingrid playing with her engagement ring – well, they are, if not quite inventions, certainly embellishments. Ingrid did (does?) have a habit of playing with her jewellery, and she was, presumably, wearing the engagement ring that evening. But I have no memory of her playing with that particular ring on that particular evening, and certainly not at that particular moment in that particular conversation, if indeed it ever took place. So why, you may ask, use that detail? Because it's a symbol, a shorthand for what seems (at this moment, from this viewpoint) a more general truth. And, if I'm honest, because it's the kind of detail that you always find in written memoirs. Because it's the kind of thing people expect you to remember.

———

Ingrid and I had sex that night. Three times. In the morning she asked me what time I was going. I said I didn't know. 'Well,' she said, 'if you're still in Amsterdam this evening, why don't you give me a call?' And then she went to work, leaving me to sleep in.

I was still there when she got back. I had cleaned the apartment and made dinner. She laughed at the sight of me, and we started kissing. I told her I'd been thinking and I didn't want to go away without her. 'Oh,' she said, looking very serious. 'What are you going to do then?'

'I thought I might kidnap you. Take you away in my rucksack.'

'It doesn't sound very comfortable.'

'No. Well, maybe I could stay here, then?'

'Uh-huh. And what about my fiancé?'

'Tell him the wedding's off.'

She laughed. 'Are you serious?'

'Yes,' I said.

'Oh.' A longish pause, while she looked at me curiously. 'All right then.'

And that was it.

My life had changed in a day. I woke up as one person and went to bed as another.

For a few weeks I was floating, and then slowly, without pain or disappointment, I glided back down to earth.

———

What did I do in those first weeks? Not much, I suppose. Ingrid was at work during the days, so I spent a lot of time on my own. Mostly I explored the city, and savoured my happiness. The weather was good, I remember. On a typical day I would wake up early and make love with Ingrid, and then we would have breakfast together before she went to work and I went back to sleep. I adored those lazy mornings: the sweetly fucked-out sore spots on my body; the smell of Ingrid on the pillows and in the sheets; the taste of toast and coffee in my mouth; the stripes of sunlight painted on the walls and ceiling.

Late in the morning I would get up and have a shower, then pack myself a picnic and go out. I could have used Ingrid's bicycle, but I preferred to walk. Even with a map, I still got lost. (Amsterdam is a strange city, built in concentric circles. In *The Fall*, Camus suggests it is modelled on hell, but back then I found it closer to the other place. From the beginning I felt at home here: something in the tallness of the houses, the width of the streets, the gentle, country-like flow of the canals seemed to welcome me. Only now do I wonder if Camus was right . . . or perhaps we both were? Perhaps heaven and hell are the same place, and the name you give it depends upon the way you look at it.)

I visited tourist sites as and when I found them, but usually I just wandered randomly, stopping off at cafés and bars, reading the *Herald Tribune*, daydreaming of Ingrid, and making notes in my diary. Most afternoons I wound up in the Vondelpark, among the nude sunbathers and potsmokers. I watched them with sympathy and amusement. Personally, I didn't need to take anything to get high; every breath of air left me quietly euphoric. I couldn't believe how beautiful the world was, and how few people seemed to notice this. I couldn't believe I would ever not be happy again.

At the same time, I became increasingly aware, as the days passed, that I could not continue like this indefinitely. I felt no personal need to work, and Ingrid never complained about paying for me, but deep down I felt the situation was unsustainable. Just one more day, I told myself, and then I'll start looking for a job. And then, the next day, I said the same thing. While the good weather held and Ingrid continued to seem happy, I simply prevaricated. I rode my luck. Thus it was the third week of October before I finally turned my attention to the matter of earning money.

I discussed it with Ingrid and we made a list of the different kinds of jobs I might look for. Like everything else, we turned this into a game. Journalism was out because all the local newspapers were in Dutch, and anyway I had no desire to re-enter that door, with all the half-forgotten horrors that lay behind it. I considered being a postman or a tram driver or a park attendant, but such work was sought-after and unlikely to go to a foreigner. I also thought of shop and pub and factory jobs, but these I had done before and hated. What I wanted was something simple and undemanding, but not so dumbly repetitive that I would be bored out of my brains and paid a pittance. Finally Ingrid mentioned her uncle Johann, who co-owned a small building company. I met up with him the next evening. After a couple of beers and a lengthy discussion about football, he agreed to take me on for a three-month trial.

After that, the days passed more quickly and less strangely. I picked up some Dutch, mostly swear words and names of tools. I wrote to my parents and a few friends, giving them my new address. I joined a local five-a-side football team and played every Friday in a nearby leisure centre. I began to enjoy the subtle differences between life in London and in Amsterdam: breakfasts of chocolate and cheese; pubs that didn't close until dawn; the way strangers sometimes smiled at you in the street.

The job was not much more than company dogsbody – I made the coffee in the morning and afternoon; did some heavy lifting; held things in place while others measured and sawed and drilled – until one day, halfway through my trial period, I was given a roller, a brush and several tins of white emulsion, and told to paint a wall. It was a leaning wall, with exposed beams; the inside of a large attic flat. Though this was not the most difficult of jobs, my colleagues were impressed with how well I did it. It turned out I had a talent for painting walls. Not only that, but I enjoyed it. Indeed, this is one of my clearest and happiest memories: the first attic that I painted white. I was on my own; the rest of the crew were working on the lower floors. It was a dry, blue-skied November, and the attic had two huge velux windows, facing south. I remember the dazzling light in there; the heat of the sun through glass on the back of my neck; the faintly intoxicating smell of emulsion; the sound of an Amsterdam pop station coming from the little paint-flecked transistor radio. (Certain songs, on heavy rotation at the time, take me back in an instant to that attic: 'Right Here Right Now' by Fatboy Slim and 'Believe' by Cher are the ones that come to mind.) I remember how physically tired I felt at the end of each working day; how wonderful a cold beer tasted at six o'clock; how much I loved kissing Ingrid and stripping off her work clothes; how well we slept, the two of us, after sex, as if we'd been drugged.

This was a time of absolute optimism for me. I thought about the present and felt happy. I thought about the future and my mind was as blank and light as the walls that I painted. I never, ever thought about the past. As far as I was concerned, the past was done and dusted. It didn't exist.

At Christmas I went back to England, filled the van with my belongings, and took the ferry to Amsterdam. I celebrated New Year with Ingrid, and after that an impossible whim turned slowly into normal life.

Time passed, as it does. Monday to Sunday, sunrise to sunset. Spring – Summer – Autumn – Winter – Spring. Eat and drink, fuck and sleep, earn and spend, shit and piss. In one end and out the other.

————

I read somewhere that everybody has their own basic level of happiness, like a pulse rate, which remains more or less constant throughout their life. You can boost it by falling in love and depress it by falling out of love; increase it through success and lower it through failure. But in the end it always finds its level. A few days or weeks or months after whatever it is has happened, your life returns to the everyday, the inbetween, that gently undulating, unmemorable quality that people have in mind when they say they are 'fine'.

For the next four years, that's how my life was. Fine. I was happy enough, most of the time; probably the happiest I've ever been. But what do I have to show for all that happiness? Vague memories; no more.

And what is happiness, anyway? Of what does it consist? Is happiness nothing more than the sum of its absent negatives? Not being frightened, not being sad, not being cold or hungry or ill or in pain; not suffering from insomnia or depression or addiction; not feeling lonely or trapped; not dwelling on the past or worrying about the future. Is that *it*?

I'll tell you the problem with being happy. Because you cannot conceive of ways to make your life better than it already is, you end up repeating yourself: today is a facsimile of yesterday, and tomor-

46

row of today. Slowly, inevitably, the image loses its sharpness. The decline is so predictable, you could chart it mathematically.

$$\text{Euphoria} + \text{Time} = \text{Happiness}$$
$$\text{Happiness} + \text{Time} = \text{Contentment}$$
$$\text{Contentment} + \text{Time} = \text{Complacency}$$
$$\text{Complacency} + \text{Time} = \text{Boredom}$$

But of course, this is only how I see it now. For example, I might ask myself whether my dissatisfaction, my withdrawal from the present, was gradual. It bloomed in the heat, festered under the plastercast, I can see that; but was it there before, as a tiny seed, a slowly spreading virus? Did vague malcontent turn by increments to disgust? Perhaps, but to be honest I don't remember. Doubtless I could look back and isolate incidents which proved such a theory, and I could do so without lying, without being wrong. But, had I said yes to Ingrid, had I moved with her to Waterland, had we made children together, then I believe I would equally have been able to look back on the same nearly five years and see in its mists the signs of my growing certainty, our deepening love. And, again, without lying or being wrong. Because this is how it is: the past always reflects the present. The past is like a fortune-teller; it tells you what you want to hear.

As for documentary evidence ... my diaries reveal nothing. Or rather they reveal only facts. The names of the places where we went on holiday; the objects we gave each other at birthdays; the furniture we bought; the movies we saw; the meals we ate; the magazines we read; the music we listened to; the squash games we played; the family gatherings and drinks with friends; the floors I planked and the doors I hung. Only facts.

I suppose a few things happened, over the years, that I should mention. In my first full year, I took an evening course in electrical engineering and started earning more money. In the second year, my friend Leon went to live in Chile; Ingrid got promoted and started working longer hours. In the third year, Ingrid's sister had a miscarriage; Johann's firm went bankrupt, and I joined a large construction agency. In the fourth year, my father went to hospital to have one of his testicles removed; Ingrid and I became friendly with Harry, who ran the bar at the end of our block. This year, my last in Amsterdam, there was a heatwave; I broke my ankle; Ingrid got a new job in Waterland.

———

So that's the story: beginning, middle, end. Reading it back, I realise that what I have written is little more than a gigantic list. A list of lists. Consecutive or descriptive, it makes no difference. Life cannot be written in the form of a list. Lists are for death, for afterwards.

I also notice something else: the limitations of the first-person narrator. The single I. Try looking through one eye: you can still see perfectly, but everything is surface; you have no perspective. It is the same when you look through one I. This chapter is the story of two people, but one of them is conspicuous by her absence. I mean Ingrid, of course. What were those years like for her?

I am tempted to say, 'the same'. Why not? We were together most of the time, weren't we? We ate the same food, breathed the same air. We went to bed together and woke up together. But sharing a bed is not sharing a dream; those cannot be shared. What is together but the plural of alone? We may as well have taken a mirror to bed. Each of us projected their own desires on to the image of the other for so long that they dreamed up another person altogether. I think of us now not as two people, but four: Ingrid and James, and the boyfriend and girlfriend that Ingrid and James invented.

So who was the real Ingrid? Can I conjure her up through words? Through the stories she told me about her childhood, the look on her face when she slept? I could try – I could describe her scent, her mannerisms, the contents of her wardrobe – but unless there were some way to steal her memories, or to spy on her dreams, I can never know what I meant to her. Perhaps even then, I wouldn't be able to scale the walls of hindsight. The Ingrid who loved me is gone, if she ever existed. She is in the past. Lost in time. All that remains is my memory of her double; and, perhaps, her memory of mine.

On reflection, I even feel a little jealous towards my double; after all, it was him that Ingrid fell for, not me. What was I to her, in the end? A bitter disappointment. The worm in the flesh of the fruit. A faceless being, wearing the mask of the man she loved, and tearing it off at the final, crucial moment.

———

For most of my adult life, I have been haunted by the suspicion that I am, in fact, nobody. Most of the time this feeling has lain dormant, but on certain nights it rears up, cold and enormous and undeniable.

Now, more than ever.

Since Ingrid left, it's as though this feeling – this fear – has taken her place. It's in my bed, it's in the air, it's in my head. It colours all my memories and thoughts of the future. I look back at the thousands of days through which I have lived, and feel awed by their inconsequentiality. My life resembles the writing in my diary (or perhaps it's the other way round): the days, like the sentences, each making a kind of superficial sense on their own, but in the context of the surrounding sentences and days, creating not a narrative or a meaning, but the very opposite: a riddle without solutions, a labyrinth without exits. A chaos.

Looking back at the pages of my diary, I seem to have written nothing. Looking back at the days of my life, I seem to have gone nowhere. What keeps me awake at night is the terror of slipping through the whole of my life in this way: tracelessly, pointlessly.

Yet I wasn't always like this. I wasn't always a nobody. Once upon a time I had dreams and hopes and plans. I am sure of that. I *remember* it.

What happened to that young man, that boy? Somewhere along the way I must have taken the wrong road. Something must have happened to me . . .

———

What changes is not the colour of the canal, but the perspective of the person who looks at it. Midnight, and I stare into the water. It is almost black and I can see the bright-lit outline of my head: the face a blank, the edges rippling and undefined. One question comes bubbling up recurrently to the surface. One mystery, simple and unanswerable.

Who am I?

It took James four days to write Chapter 5. When it was finished, he put it in a drawer and forgot about it. He didn't know if it was any good, but he felt better for having written it. He felt lighter.

Five days later the doctor removed his plastercast. He used a small circular saw, which tickled James's skin. James had been worrying about this moment for a long time, imagining his calf to be fleshless, or scarred, or seething with maggots, or vanished to nothing. In fact, it was only a little pale and thin. It didn't even smell too bad.

When he first walked on it, he felt stiff and unsteady, but within a couple of days it was fine. The hardest thing to get used to, he found, was moving without crutches; he had become so practised in that rhythmic swing that normal walking felt oddly slow and awkward.

On Wednesday 27 August there was a big thunderstorm. The heavens opened and the temperature dropped twelve degrees overnight. The next day was grey and misty. James unchained his bicycle and rode around the city streets for hours, breathing the cool damp air and thinking about the future.

His head was cleared, and he began to make plans. He went to check on his van, which he kept in a lock-up garage on the outskirts of the city; he renewed the insurance and had the van serviced. He emptied his bank account and converted most of the euros to pounds. He rang the manager of the construction agency and explained that he was leaving the country. He bought a ferry ticket for Monday 1 September. He packed his possessions into boxes.

While he was packing, James came across the white notebook. He sat down on the bare floor and re-read Chapter 5. He found it disappointing and slightly disturbing. The tone was so melodramatic, so relentlessly negative. It was strange to think that he had written it only two weeks before. James concluded that he had not been himself at the time; the heat and the plastercast must have been affecting him more than he realised. He thought of ripping out the offending pages and burning them, but decided in the end that he didn't want to damage his notebook.

So instead he bought a bottle of whitener and painted over his words. When the liquid had dried, the pages were almost as good as new: rough and cracked in places, with hints of letter shapes showing through, but essentially blank. James looked at the white pages with satisfaction. Now he could forget Chapter 5 and begin again, later, with Chapter 4.

He had a wonderful time that final Sunday, dusting the apartment and singing along to The Go-Betweens. There was a breeze coming through the open, unshuttered windows. When he'd finished, he took a cold beer out to the balcony and gazed down at the streets, the canal, the people, all of them bathed in the same golden, late-afternoon glow. Then he turned around to look at the empty flat. He felt like he had shed a skin.

That evening he was sitting in Harry's Bar when Ingrid's brother Frank happened to ride past on his bike. That was how Frank explained it, anyway. They shared a pitcher of beer and, after some small talk, Frank asked him what he was planning to do. James showed him the ferry ticket.

'How long do you think you'll be gone for?' Frank asked.

James shrugged. 'I don't know.'

Frank was looking at him curiously. There was a moment when James thought he was going to say something, but he poured them both some more beer and avoided his friend's eye. He didn't want a scene. Frank seemed to understand this, and they talked about other things while they finished the beer. At the end they shook hands. Frank got on his bike and was about to leave, when he suddenly leaned towards James, his face serious, and whispered, 'Ingrid says she hopes you can get things sorted out with Anna.'

'With who?' said James, but Frank had already started to pedal. He waved, then joined the traffic. James could see his head bobbing above the crowd for a long time after his bicycle had vanished.

'Anna,' James said to himself, as he lay in bed that night. That *was* the name Frank had said, wasn't it? James supposed he might have misheard; that Frank might actually have said Hannah or Diana or Joanna. But no, none of those names meant anything to him. The name 'Anna' was different.

It conjured a picture in his mind of a dark-haired girl. The picture was blurred, hazy, but he had seen this girl before, he felt sure. And then he remembered: that brief blackout he had suffered, on the stairs, just before he broke his ankle; he had seen her then, and felt some strange emotion. James also suspected she was someone he had seen in his dreams. That must be how Ingrid had learned her name, he thought; I must have said it in my sleep.

For some reason he thought of the song of which he could remember only a fragment. He thought of the long blue-stained row of terraced houses . . . the boy and the girl walking . . . the watching policemen. These memories circled his head, that last night of summer, in those black spiralling seconds before he fell asleep.

You may wonder how I can possibly know all this; how I can see all the quicksilver, gossamer visions that flicker inside James Purdew's mind, how I can feel every heart-swell and nerve-twitch in his body. But that, for the moment, must remain my little secret.

II
THE SCENE OF THE CRIME

James went up on deck and watched the harbour grow larger and clearer through the mist. He was exhausted from lack of sleep, but the smell of the sea awoke him. There is something about the odour of salt, he thought, that snaps you into the present tense, into tangible reality. The effect was helpful, because at that moment James was having trouble adjusting to the idea that this was really happening; that he was actually here.

The dislocation he felt was due partly to the fact that he had spent half the night reading a book in Spanish. It was the book by Jorge Luis Borges that Frank had forgotten to take when he moved Ingrid's possessions from the flat. James had intended to send it on to Ingrid, but that would have required him to write a letter, and he hadn't known what to say. All in all, it had seemed simpler to hold on to the book for a while.

It was a book of short stories and the title was *Laberintos*, which James was fairly sure meant 'labyrinths'. His Spanish wasn't good, so he read very slowly, and even then he only understood half the words. The stories enchanted him none the less. He had read two during the voyage: 'El Otro', about a man meeting a younger version of himself, apparently in some kind of dream, and 'La Memoria de Shakespeare', about a man who comes into possession of Shakespeare's memory. James had emerged from the netherworld of this foreign text to discover that the night had passed. He had numbly eaten breakfast to a soundtrack of crying babies, and then taken the stairs up to the deck. And now here he was . . . and there *it* was.

He gripped the metal railing and stared at the approaching city of H. It was years since he had been here, and for a moment he could almost believe that he was travelling not through space but through time; that the shape on the horizon was truly that 'unreachable land' of the past. In the dawn light, the distant buildings shone mysteriously. All kinds of thoughts and images crowded James's mind as he stood there, regarding this silverish vision of a city that was at once familiar and strange, old and new.

As the sun rose and the ferry moved closer, the banal details of the port revealed themselves – cranes, lorries, advertising billboards; the mingled stench of diesel and hops – and James felt simultaneously relieved and disappointed. The sense of going back in time had, he realised, been merely a trick of his mind, intoxicated by the stories he'd read and by his tiredness and the early-morning light. The place was only a place, after all.

And then, as these emotions faded and he thought of the memories he had lost in this city, he felt something else: a physical nervousness; a hollow thrum in his chest. James recognised this feeling. It was the same emotion he had felt on Ingrid's staircase, when he saw the face of the dark-haired girl: neither hope nor fear, but something nameless in between.

An hour later, he drove out of the bowels of the ferry and through several vast car parks. A customs officer stopped him and spent a long time inspecting his passport, while other uniformed men searched the van. The customs officer held the photograph next to James's face, and squinted from one to the other. 'James Purdew – is that you?' he asked suspiciously. James, feeling obscurely guilty, said it was. The other men signalled that the van was clear. The customs officer waved him through.

The drive from the port was grey and uneventful. James was struck only by the number of roundabouts and roadworks, by the sullen anger of other drivers. But when he crossed the great bridge into the city itself, he felt it: that unmistakable sensation of déjà vu: the feeling that each building and road sign and tree had an extra dimension, a deepened physical presence; that each existed here and now and, at the same time, in his memory.

And yet, somehow, it was the startling realness of it all that most affected him. This was true not only of the parts that fitted with his memory, but even more so of the parts that didn't, the tiny details he could never have foreseen: an abandoned crisp packet dancing along the pavement in a gust of wind; dark-skirted schoolgirls standing in line at a bus stop; a wrecking ball demolishing the remains of an apartment block. All these realities are new, he thought; they have happened without me. Those schoolgirls would have been toddlers the last time I was here. Someone would have been looking out from that apartment block: an old lady, perhaps, watering the plants on her balcony. Somehow the changes were a comfort to James. People lived here. Random events occurred here. The city *existed*. It was not merely something he had dreamed up.

He drove through the city centre, unconsciously looking away as he passed the train station, then took a left down Haight Road. Past The Polar Bear – he waved to its brown, expressionless façade – and right into Green Avenue. To his right he saw the city park, and to his left those endless-seeming Victorian streets flashed past, their names a litany: Cathedral Street, Hayes Street, Lough Street, Moone Street, Bach Street. He felt a rush of unfocused memories.

He parked the van at the side of the road and entered the park. It was still early, but the mist had already cleared. Above, the sky was a limpid, pale blue. Below, the grass was pearled with dew. All around, dogs barked, ducks splashed, mothers pushed prams along tree-shaded paths.

There were clues here, James felt sure, hiding behind trees

and beneath shadows. The air was thick with clues. His past, present and future all converged at this point. Somewhere here he would find the thread that would guide him through the maze.

I am a detective now, he thought. I am a private investigator. I am a detective and this is the scene of the crime.

The van was illegally parked, so James drove to campus and left it behind the library. The university car parks were empty, campus silent. He went to the student accommodation office, hoping to find a cheap room for the four weeks before the start of term, but it didn't open until ten, so he killed time in a café on University Road.

He sat near the window and ordered black coffee. Someone had left a tabloid newspaper on the table. It was a local weekly. James flicked past news of unknown celebrities and vague bomb threats until he reached the games page. The crossword had already been filled. He read the cartoons, then glanced at the astrology column. This is what it said for his sign:

CANCER 21 June–22 July. Congratulations – you've made a clean break. But what now? What is going to happen to your life? Why are you here and what are you searching for? Under the influence of Mars, confusion reigns and your questions won't be answered this week, but at least you are on the right track. Good news comes from the letter M and the number 21.

It was unbelievable: the astrologer had described his current position exactly. James was so surprised, he read the paragraph again, then looked around suspiciously, wondering if it might be some elaborate hoax. But the only other people in the café were the woman who was serving behind the counter and two policemen smoking and muttering at another table. None of them took any notice of James.

He looked at the astrology column again. 'YOUR STARS

for the week ahead,' it said, 'by Adam Golightly'. There was a small photograph next to the name: a bald or shaven-headed man with a small beard and penetrating eyes. It was impossible to guess his age.

James finished his coffee and thought about the astrologer's predictions. It was all coincidence, of course, he reasoned; if you write five non-specific sentences, they are bound to seem relevant to *some* of your readers. But despite his scepticism, James took it as a good omen. Staring absentmindedly through the window, past the blue painted letters (TSAFKAERB YAD-LLA) at the busy road and, beyond it, the pale grey buildings and neatly mown lawns of campus, he felt a welling excitement. Even if it meant nothing, he felt sure the astrologer was right. He *had* made a clean break. He *was* on the right track.

At ten he went back to the student accommodation office. The woman who worked there was middle-aged, with a plump, friendly face. 'Hello!' she called cheerfully when James put his face round the door. She seemed so pleased to see him, he thought she must be someone from his past, but then she asked for his name and he guessed she was simply in a good mood. James took a seat. The nameplate on the woman's desk informed him she was called Mrs Quigley. She asked if he was a student; James said he was a graduate.

'Back here visiting?'

'Yeah . . . well, I might live here for a while.'

'Oh, so you're not looking *specifically* for short-term accommodation?'

Could that be a problem, he wondered? 'I just thought it'd be good to have a base while I looked for somewhere more permanent.'

There was a pause while the woman nodded, and looked at some papers on the desk. She glanced up at him and said, 'You don't happen to be any good at DIY, do you?'

The question caught him off guard. 'I'm a builder,' he said. 'It's my job.'

'*Really?*' The woman seemed so excited, James began to wonder if he was in the right office. 'I might just have the perfect thing for you. I can't give you the details myself, because it's not registered here, but it sounds like an amazing deal.'

'What does?'

She laughed. 'Oh sorry . . . I'm not being very clear, am I? I've just heard about it, you see. Apparently it's an ex-student house, needs lots of work, I can't remember the address . . . but anyway, it's owned by this famous person – an artist or a writer or a singer or something – and he's offering free accommodation and all expenses paid for a year if someone will live there and renovate it. Plus you get half the profit when he sells the house afterwards.'

James laughed. 'Sounds too good to be true.'

Mrs Quigley didn't seem to notice the irony in his voice. 'It does, doesn't it? Especially for you, with your particular needs and . . . skills.' She was writing something now, her face flushed. 'Here you go . . . that's the address of the office. You can tell them I sent you.'

James thanked her and stood up to leave.

'You're very welcome,' she grinned. 'And do let me know how it goes. Apparently he's quite well known, the man who owns the house. That's what I was told, anyway. I'd never heard of him myself.'

'What's his name?' James asked.

The woman froze, her face blank for a second or two, and then relaxed. 'Sorry, it's gone. Oh, isn't that ridiculous? I only heard it ten minutes ago. Now, come on, what *was* it? Does it begin with M or . . .?' She looked like she was in pain. The phone started ringing. She ignored it. James began to feel anxious.

'You should answer that,' he said. 'Don't worry about the name, I can ask at the other office.'

'You could, but they won't tell you.' She smiled knowingly, her hand poised over the receiver.

'Why not?'

'It's been withheld,' she said. 'All very mysterious. I only know about it because one of my friends has been temping there.' She picked up the phone. 'Hello? Student accommodation?'

James waved goodbye to Mrs Quigley. She waved back, still listening to the phone.

Deciding he needed some exercise, James took his bicycle from the back of the van and rode into the city centre. It took him a while to locate the office. It was in a backstreet in the old town; a private-looking door with a small nameplate above the buzzer: HARRISON LETTINGS. He rang the bell and the door clicked open.

The office was on the third floor and James had the feeling that he'd been there before, though he couldn't have said when or why. There were three desks in the room, which was windowless, overwarm and crowded with filing cabinets, but only one of them was occupied – by a young man in a suit and tie. He was on the phone, sounding polite but harrassed. He had shaving burns on one cheek. James could smell his sweat: it was nervous sweat, which always smells worse. The man's eyes flicked up at James briefly when he entered, but there was no welcome or acknowledgment. He lowered his voice. James sat down in the chair opposite him. The man put one hand, visor-like, in front of his eyes, and stared down at some papers on his desk. James closed his eyes, feeling suddenly weary. The only sounds were the hum of computers and the incomprehensible murmurings of the young man.

'Yes, sir.' A voice, suddenly loud, woke James from a doze. The man was staring at him, alert and slightly aggressive.

'I've been sent by the student accommodation office.' The man looked at him blankly. 'At the university.'

'Yes?'

'You have a house on your books that I'm interested in.'

'A house to rent?'

'Not exactly,' said James. 'It's an unusual arrangement.

Apparently it needs renovating, and the owner is –'

'Oh, *that* house.' The man stared, with an expression of utter misery, at the papers on his desk.

'Has it gone?'

A ghost of a laugh. 'Gone? No . . . no, it's not gone.'

'So what's the matter?'

The man ran his hands through his hair. 'You're right, it is an unusual arrangement – and it sounds like a very attractive deal in theory. But, quite frankly, we're beginning to wonder if the whole thing isn't a ruse.'

'What do you mean?'

'So far, we've forwarded at least a dozen perfectly good applications to the owner, and he's said no to them all. He's refused to even meet them. It's all very odd – almost like he's looking for someone in particular.'

This last sentence was spoken quietly, as if the man were talking to himself. He seemed surprised when James said, brightly, 'Perhaps *I'm* that someone?'

The man shrugged and reached behind him to the filing cabinet. 'Fill in an application form. You should learn either way within a week or two.'

'A week or two?'

'Yes . . . the owner is not the easiest man to get hold of. On top of all the other difficulties.'

'Have you met him?'

'I've never even spoken to him on the phone.'

'I heard he was famous. An artist or a singer . . .'

The man gave a hostile stare. 'I have no idea, sir. The client requested absolute confidentiality, so naturally that's what Harrison is providing.'

'Of course,' James said. 'What's the address, by the way?'

'That is also confidential.'

James filled in the form, leaving a single blank space: daytime telephone number. 'I haven't got a phone,' he explained.

'Then you too are going to be rather hard to get hold of.'

'Maybe I could buy a mobile?'

'As you wish, sir.' The desk telephone rang and the man answered. 'Harrison Lettings, how may I help you?'

James crept, unregarded, out of the office.

He got the cheapest mobile phone deal he could find – incoming calls only – then went back to Harrison Lettings and wrote the number on the application form. The form was where he had left it on the man's desk. The man was still on the phone. Again, he did not acknowledge James. The smell of sweat was, if anything, even worse.

James cycled out of the old town and back along Haight Road. On a whim, he stopped off at The Polar Bear. It was nearly midday. He locked the bike by the side of the building and entered the lounge. Remarkably, after all this time, it looked almost exactly as he remembered it: the same maroon-and-gold flock wallpaper, the same sticky brown carpet, the same fake-leather wall-benches in the corner.

It was a sunny day, but the lounge had only one source of natural light – a small, square, grimy window, located high up the back wall – so the electric lights were on, giving the room a sad, wintry feel. It was cold, too: the fireplace was empty and there was a strong smell of damp.

James ordered a pint of bitter. He watched, in silence, as the barman pulled the draught pump. Behind him the room grew suddenly dim. The barman looked up. 'It'll come back on in a minute.'

'Does it do that often?'

The barman nodded wearily. 'Needs rewiring.'

James sat down and drank his beer in the gloom. After a while the lights flickered, then came back on. The pub, he thought, was actually a little different to how he remembered it: harsher, drabber. In James's memories of The Polar Bear, it was always warm and glowing. This could be a question of lighting and heating, or of general wear-and-tear, but James suspected it had more to do with the fact that he was sober.

He took out his wallet and counted his money. He had

enough to last a week, perhaps two if he slept in the van, but either way he would soon need more cash. And, as alluring as the offer of the mystery house was, he had to consider the possibility that his application would be rejected. When he'd finished the pint, James went up to the bar again and wrote his name and mobile number on a piece of paper. 'I'm an electrician,' he explained to the barman. 'I could rewire this place if you wanted. Reasonable rates.' The barman looked surprised, but said he would pass the message on to the landlord.

On the way back to campus, James stopped off at the little supermarket on the corner of Green Avenue and Hayes Street to buy some food. The name had been changed since James had moved away – from Ablett's to the Happy Shoppa – and inside it was almost unrecognisably clean and bright. An Elton John ballad played tinnily from hidden speakers.

He rode back to the van, plastic bags hanging from the handlebars, and ate lunch alone in the empty car park. It was half-past two and the day was turning hot and overcast: the atmosphere heavy, the clouds nicotine yellow. James felt suddenly exhausted. He drank some water, then lay down on the futon mattress in the back of the van and fell asleep.

When he woke, it was night-time. He put on a jacket and went for a walk. He wandered all over campus: to the Union Bar, the gymnasium, the cafeteria, the library . . . Outside each of these buildings, he felt his heart speed up, his legs weaken. He was remembering, or his body was. The problem was that his mind would not supply the missing pictures. His memories, like these buildings, were locked and unlit: mere outlines, absences; ominous bulks in the darkness.

He had nothing to do, and needed to save money, but the thought of going back to the van alone was unbearable, so he headed towards the city centre. He bought a bag of chips on Lethe Avenue and ate them as he walked, ending up at a dark and familiar-looking pub called The Anchor.

Inside it was quiet and half-empty: a normal Tuesday evening. James sat at a table in the corner, ordered a pint of bitter, and attempted to read another story by Borges. This one was called 'Funes El Memorioso' and was about a man who could remember *everything*. Halfway down the first page, James became aware that someone was staring at him.

He looked up. The man at the next table, who was also alone, stood up and said, 'Mind if I join you?' He was a tall, stoop-shouldered man with dark, thinning hair and thick-framed spectacles, and his face was oddly familiar, though it took James a while to place the memory. James would have preferred to read his book in peace but he didn't want to seem rude, so he said, 'Of course not.' The man sat down. He smelled of tobacco, though he wasn't smoking, and wore an old-fashioned suit – brownish, with a sort of check pattern – that made James feel depressed.

The man was quite drunk, but his voice was accentless and educated. James had no memory of what the man said to begin with – something about the government? – because he was busy racking his brain trying to work out where he had seen that sombre face before. Finally it came to him and he blurted out, 'Has anyone ever told you that you look like Philip Larkin?'

To James's surprise, the man scowled and said, 'That wanker.'

'Did you know him?' James asked.

'Know him? That cunting bastard. I *am* him.'

'Philip Larkin is dead,' said James, though as soon as the words left his mouth he became unsure as to whether this was actually true. He was fairly certain it must be, but the horrific possibility that he had just told a living man that he was dead made him question the accuracy of his assertion.

For a moment the man looked as though he was going to get angry, then he said, 'Of course he is. He died in 1985.'

'Yes,' James said, relieved. 'That's what I thought.'

There was a pause while the librarian sipped his beer. Then, staring into space, he announced, 'First he went to hospital where they cut out his oesophagus. The surgeon said they'd found a great deal of unpleasant stagnant material; Larkin thought that sounded like a good description of his life. The surgeon also told him he would be a new man after the operation, but he wasn't. He was still the same old miserable git he'd been before. Still 62, still going to die. Through the window he could see some trees, blue sky, sunlight on the leaves and grass – it was summer – but it seemed so far away, so alive, so alien, that it was almost like a tableau: The World You Are Going to Leave Behind. Or, worse, The Whole Point of Life (And You Missed It, Pal).'

'Pardon?' said James.

'He knew time was running out, had known it since he was a young man, but still he wished it wouldn't drag by so slowly. It was a private hospital so he was allowed to drink; that made the evenings easier. But then he got rat-arsed one night on whisky and swallowed his own vomit. Went into a coma. Not that he remembers all this: only waking up in a different hospital, grimmer, National Health, where booze was banned and he was surrounded by other people.' The man's face was sour. 'He hated that.'

'You seem to know a lot about Philip Larkin,' James remarked.

'I took over from him when he went.'

'What do you mean?'

'I'm the university librarian.'

'Oh. You mean you took over his job.'

'And the rest. Came with the post, they said.'

'The rest?'

'His old manuscript books. His diaries. His photographs. His memory.'

James was nodding blithely when suddenly he realised what the librarian had said. 'His *memory*?'

'To preserve his thoughts and his life for posterity.'

'Er . . . how did that happen?'

'I can't remember.'

'Right.'

There was a long pause. James drank some beer, and looked down at the book he wanted to read. Still the librarian was silent, staring into space somewhere to James's left. James was about to reopen his book when the librarian said, in a weary voice, 'It's not like you'd imagine. I can't remember every detail of his life. Only odd flashes. They often come to me when I'm falling asleep or waking up. Sometimes I have dreams that I know can't be mine. Sometimes I just see unfamiliar places, or feel strange emotions, or find myself thinking of jazz records that I've never heard before.'

'Jazz records?'

'Yeah. I don't even like jazz, but it's in my head all the time now. Jazz and porn. Jazz music and jazz mags. Duke Ellington and spanked schoolgirls. And death, of course. I never thought about dying before I got Larkin's memory. Now I can't even look at my bedroom wall without feeling this horrible rush of panic in my chest. Oh, and hate. Plenty of hate. Every time I look at someone younger than me, or a woman, or a black person, or a left-winger, I feel it. When I noticed you earlier, for example, I was immediately filled with hatred towards you. Anyway, that's pretty much all his memories consist of: hate, fear, jazz, porn and death.' He paused for a moment, apparently in thought. 'Yes, that's about it.'

James was feeling uncomfortable now – what *was* this man's problem? – but he was wary of upsetting the librarian, who was clearly deranged, by walking away or ignoring him, so he said, in a cheerful voice, 'No poetry?'

'I come across it occasionally. Usually on trains. By accident one spring day I got the train journey described in "The Whitsun Weddings", and some of the memories that came to him as he looked out of the window. But it's all so vague and banal. Reading the poem is a much truer, more profound experience.'

'That's interesting,' James said.

'After that, I went in search of certain other poems. Visited churches, thinking I might get memories of how he wrote "Church Going". Deliberately took a northbound train that stopped at Coventry, in the hope that it might inspire some memories of his childhood. You know, from the poem, "I Remember, I Remember"?'

'I remember,' James smiled. 'The place where his childhood was unspent.'

'That's it. Didn't work, though. I mean, I got the memory of having the memories, but not the originals. That's the trouble with people who spend all their time thinking. They never actually bloody notice anything.'

James stifled a yawn, then went to the bar and ordered two

pints. When he came back, the librarian was smiling at him in a strange way. Realising that he was expected to make conversation, James said, 'Do you have any other memories related to Larkin's poetry?'

'Only one. The time when he wrote "Aubade",' the librarian said in a grave, slurry voice. 'The one about death.'

James nodded. 'A great poem.'

'He didn't think so. His fear was great, but he thought the poem was the palest reflection of that fear. As if, by putting it into words, even good words, he demeaned it. And it didn't help with his fear of death. No reason why it should, of course, but I have the feeling Larkin thought it might make a difference; that in writing about the fear, he might also reduce it. But . . . no such luck: the fear got bigger in his later years, not smaller. He was still going to die, after all. In the end it was just another poem. Another drawing scratched on the wall of the mineshaft before the supports collapse and the black earth comes down.'

'Good metaphor,' James said automatically.

The librarian shrugged, modestly. 'I get them sometimes. I suppose they must have been ideas he had but rejected. The leftovers. That's what I get. The crumbs. I'd hoped his memory might make me a poet, but . . .'

'It hasn't?'

'I write all the time, but it's no good. Doggerel, really. Just crap.'

'I'd like to hear some.'

The librarian stared at James balefully, mistrustingly, for a few moments, as though he thought this youngster was taking the piss. Then he recited,

> Life is shit.
> What's the point of it?

The two men looked at each other for a moment. 'Concise,' James offered.

After that, the silences grew longer, the speeches sourer. Just before closing time, his story over, the librarian became melancholy and stared silently into his half-empty glass. James went to the toilet – as he stood up he realised from the whirling of the room how drunk he was – and when he got back, he found to his relief that the librarian had disappeared.

Back in the van, he undressed and got in the sleeping-bag. He was on the verge of falling asleep when the mobile phone started ringing. James pressed the green button, wondering who it could be at this time of night. 'Hello?' he said, but there was only a kind of hissing sound, as though the caller were somewhere remote, out of range.

'Hello!' said James. 'Who's there?'

The line went dead.

James woke early the next morning, before it was fully light. For some time he lay inside the sleeping-bag, staring at the grey ceiling of the van. He wanted to go back to sleep, but whenever he closed his eyes he saw the face of the librarian in the pub and felt a sudden panic. *What* had he been saying?

Finally James rubbed his eyes and got up. He plugged in the electric kettle. While the water heated, he stretched his aching muscles. Outside the sky was turning light and everything looked clearer, more solid. Already his memory of the previous night was fading, fragmenting. He thought about writing it down in his diary, but decided against it. I really ought to concentrate on the tasks ahead, he told himself, rather than worrying about some drunken conversation with a stranger.

It was cold and James desperately needed a bath and a shave. He resolved to go back to the student accommodation office that morning and ask again about renting a room for a few weeks. The office would not be open for another two hours, though, so when he'd drunk a mug of tea and eaten an apple, he got on the bicycle and set off to explore the residential streets near campus.

The houses with dark blue doors belonged to the university, and many of the numbers and street names seemed familiar – 52 Elm Road, 139 Cranbrook Avenue, 27 Mowlam Street. The hairs on James's arms stood up as he passed these addresses. He was sure he must have been to parties there, perhaps stayed overnight with friends, but the blank painted doorways gave no clues, and he felt guilty, loitering outside, staring at the curtained windows. He feared somebody might call the police.

He rode up Green Avenue to the Happy Shoppa, where he bought a loaf of thick-sliced white bread. An Eric Clapton ballad was playing on the in-store radio. James walked his bicycle across the road and chained it to the fence, then went into the park to feed the ducks. This, he knew, was a waste of money, but he felt compelled to do it all the same.

James was the only person in the park. Half-formed memories swarmed around him as he stood by the large pond and tore off pieces of bread. He saw no faces, relived no events, but a feeling settled on him as he watched those white fragments arc over the dark water. A bittersweet, hollow feeling. It reminded him of the final weeks at Ingrid's apartment, after she'd gone. The end of something; the beginning of something else.

When he had used up all the bread, James walked back across the road and entered Cathedral Street. He had lived here, his final year, in a single, second-floor bedroom at number 95, but looking at the building's façade did not inspire any particular feelings. A vague emptiness, perhaps; nothing more. He cut through an alley, running his fingertips along the ridged planking of the fence; he had done this before, his fingertips remembered. On Hayes Street he turned right, walked back down to the supermarket, turned left on Green Avenue, and found himself at the top of Lough Street.

He stared down its length. Like all these streets, it was wide and rather grand-looking, lined on either side with parked cars and chestnut trees. The houses were Victorian, redbrick, three storeys tall. The majority were semi-detached. In front of each house was a small garden protected by a low wall, a hedgerow and an iron gate. The early-morning clouds had dispersed by now: sunlight flashed golden from the distant windows; it glowed green through the chestnut leaves; it sparkled in the constantly moving water of a distant fountain. This fountain, which doubled as a kind of ornamental roundabout, was the last object on the horizon. But beyond that, James knew, one looked into a perfect study of perspective, the two rows of houses seeming almost to merge as Lough Street narrowed to vanishing point.

Lough Street . . . James remembered how, when he first came to the city, he had pronounced it wrongly – to rhyme with 'bough'. No, no, he was told, it rhymes with 'rough', 'tough', 'enough'. Lough Street, Lough Street . . . he sniffed the air (a distant bonfire?) and kicked absentmindedly through the few yellow leaves that had already fallen to the pavement. They made a crisp, cheerful sound under his feet. His heart was quickening now, his chest tightening. His breath steamed before his face, even though James was sure that the air was not cold enough for this to happen. Imperceptibly, his coat seemed to have grown heavier, his ears and nose colder, the sun lower in the sky. For no apparent reason, a wind of euphoria blew through him, swelling out his chest, tickling the ends of his fingers, and little tears of exhilaration started behind his eyes. Life, the world, was before him, at his feet. He felt younger, taller . . . he felt *glorious*.

What was it? What was his body remembering? He had lived in this street, his first year, in a ground-floor bedroom at number 33; the room with the sloping floor. Yet it was not the houses that were sparking the sense of remembrance, he realised, but the fallen leaves. His euphoria faded and his legs grew heavy. James stood still and stared at the ground: yellow leaves, brown shoes, grey concrete . . . gravel, puddles, treeroots, grass. Everything magnified. The sound of a bird in an otherwise immense silence. The song came to his mind again: those few, haunting chords.

> Part of my heart
> Will always beat . . .

In the tantalising silence that followed these low-sung words, James felt time slow down and a sense of foreboding grow inside him. He tried to move forwards, but found that he couldn't. He looked to his left, for dark blue doorways, but there were none. They were all, he remembered now, on the far side of the road. The odd-numbered side. He saw the first one and counted them off. Nine, thirteen, seventeen . . . Suddenly he stumbled, as if drunk, and the street scene lost its perspective: narrowing road, sun-reflecting cars, looming redbrick houses, all swirled together, close to his face. His body was lead, his head perilously light.

When he came to, James was sitting on a grass verge, leaning against a tree. The sun was in his eyes, so he closed them again. His neck and back and face were covered in cold sweat. His skin felt numb and fuzzy all over, as though he had somehow slept on all of his limbs at the same time, cutting off the circulation of blood. He reopened his eyes and tried to think.

What had happened to him? Slowly it dawned on him that he must have blacked out. He recalled the strange emotions that had filled him as he walked along Lough Street: the euphoria, and the way his breath had begun to steam, his coat grow heavier. You must have been imagining it, James told himself. No, you must have been *remembering*. For a moment, he felt a surge of hope at this realisation, but it was quickly replaced by another emotion as he recalled how the euphoria had faded and his body grown weak. What was it he had been feeling as time had slowed down, just before he lost consciousness? James didn't want to think about it.

Gingerly he stood up, holding on to the tree trunk. His head was clearer now; his vision normal; the blood was flowing through his veins again, returning sensation to his fingers and toes. His muscles felt bruised, but that might just have been the night in the van. Careful not to look at any doorways, James walked down the road to where he had chained his bicycle and rode back to campus.

Mrs Quigley found him waiting outside her door when she turned up for work, a few minutes late. 'Oh hello,' she said, perhaps a little less thrilled to see him than she had been the day before. 'You're back quickly. How did it go, with the house I told you about?'

James explained about the application form, and the delay. 'I was wondering if you could find a room for me.'

'Oh yes, I'm sure we can manage that,' she said, unlocking the door. 'I racked my brains last night, you know, trying to think of that man's name. I even asked my friend who'd told me about it, but she couldn't remember either. I'm sure it begins with M . . .'

'It doesn't matter,' James said. 'You don't happen to know the address, though?'

'Yes, that I do remember. It was Lough Street.'

Without even thinking, James added, 'Number twenty-one.'

Mrs Quigley smiled at him, amazed. 'That's right! You have been doing your homework.'

'I used to live near there.'

'Oh, did you? Good memories, I hope.'

I hope so too, thought James.

'Now, there's something else, you know,' she said pensively. 'Didn't something happen in that house?' She had put her bag down and was seating herself, slowly, as though she had a sore back, behind her desk. Her eyes were half-closed. 'Some tragedy or . . .'

'I don't remember,' James said quickly.

'Well, it's not important now, is it? What's past is past. There's no such thing as a haunted house. Not in real life, I mean. It sounds like a good deal to me. I'll keep my fingers crossed for you. In the meantime, Mr Purdew, let's find you somewhere to sleep.'

The house that Mrs Quigley found for him was on Newland Road, at the other side of the park, a mile or so from the municipal swimming pool. It was small for a student house – only four bedrooms – and he shared it with just one other person: a mature student called Graham, who lived there in term-time and clearly regarded James's presence as an intrusion. Graham was a shy, bearded man with a strong Mancunian accent who seemed either to glare at James with hostility and suspicion, or to go out of his way to avoid him. In the four weeks James was there, the two of them exchanged no more than a dozen words.

It was a soulless house, and an awkward arrangement, but James liked being able to have baths in the evenings, and it was convenient living so close to the swimming pool. He would cycle there each morning and do twenty lengths. Afterwards he would buy bread and milk from the cornershop and eat breakfast in the empty common room, looking out at the chain-link fence and the neighbours' garden. At ten to ten he would set off for The Polar Bear, where he would spend the day working on the wiring.

The landlord had called him on James's third day in H. He was a tight-fisted, unpleasant man, but James needed the money – and the job itself was not difficult. The lounge was closed to the public while James worked there, so he was alone with the gloom and the smell of damp. Occasionally he would hear music and the sound of laughter coming from the other side of the pub, but it had a distant, dreamlike quality. Though James knew that he had been in this lounge many times before – though the room itself was deeply familiar – he did not remember anything new while he worked there. Somehow the cold, lonely present seemed to paint over the warm, peopled past. At odd moments, looking up from a fusebox at the empty lounge, he caught glimpses of what he thought must be memories: faces wreathed in smoke, tabletops crowded with glasses. But these mirages never lasted; they were gone in the blink of an eye.

He stopped at twelve for lunch, which he ate in the public bar. He rarely spoke to anyone. The bar staff weren't friendly, and most of the other customers sat in groups or couples. There was one man, bald and bearded, who came in on his own and sat at a table near the window, but he was always busy reading, so James didn't want to disturb him. He looked vaguely familiar, this man, but James couldn't remember where he might have seen him before.

Unlike me, however, James does not remember much of this. What he remembers most clearly from that period – not in his mind but in the tensed muscles of his body – is the *waiting*. The torture of the unringing telephone. How its unringingness prolonged each second. Over and over again, James imagined pressing the green button on the mobile and hearing the voice of that charmless young man from Harrison Lettings, his tone altered now from contempt to respect. 'Mr Purdew, I have the pleasure to inform you that our client has accepted your application.' Sometimes he varied the fantasy: he would be a fly on the wall of the Harrison Lettings office, watching the man receive a phone call from the client ('Of course, of course, I'll get on to it right away, sir') or he would be a private detective, secretly pursuing the client down dark, zig-zagging streets as he approached the office building, then following him up the stairs and through the door, and watching as the young man's face showed surprise and fear ('But . . . I'm sorry, sir, I didn't realise it was so urgent!'). The effect of these daydreams was narcotic. Each time he had them, James felt a slowly spreading happiness that got him through the next few hours of boredom. But as the days passed, he found he needed them more and more often, so that by the end of the second week he was living almost constantly in this happy, conditional future.

Outside of the daydreams, he could hear nothing but the phone's tormenting silence. He carried the mobile with him everywhere in the daytime; it was always switched on. Each night he plugged it in to recharge the battery. And when it did ring (cold-call salesmen, wrong numbers), the hope that flooded his chest was, if anything, worse than the silent waiting. James had so little then – no friends, no home, no lover, no clues – that his hope expanded to fill the vacuum. But hope, I can tell you, is an exhausting emotion; perhaps, along with fear, the most exhausting of all. It is like juggling eggs: the hope is the shell, and inside is despair. A single crack and the despair might spill everywhere, stain everything.

And then one day, a fortnight after he came to the city, James discovered a new opening in the labyrinth. It was a Sunday; he had already been for a swim and eaten breakfast in the common room. He was doing the washing-up when he noticed a newspaper on the windowsill of the kitchen. Graham must have left it there. James dried his hands and picked it up. It was the same tabloid he had seen that first day in the café on University Road. Curious, he opened it to the page with the stars. This is what he read:

CANCER 21 June–22 July. Things are looking up, so why are you feeling down? Saturn, the planet of work, is dominating your chart. But don't worry, that is about to change. The news you are waiting for will come when you least expect it. Now is the time to forget your hopes and confront your fears. Beware of the letter M and the number 21.

James felt a sense of relief as he read this. Relief, but also anger at himself. Ever since his last blackout, he had been trying not to think about the dread that had risen in his chest that

day as he walked up Lough Street; about the numb recognition he had felt when Mrs Quigley mentioned 'some tragedy
or . . .'. He had cycled past Lough Street twice each day, yet
never even glanced in its direction; it was as if the street had
been erased from his mental map of the city. Yet in suppressing his fears – and daydreaming instead about a phone call
that might never come – James had, he realised, been wasting
time, and ignoring the biggest clue he had yet found. Whether
it was pure chance or some mystical insight that had led the
astrologer to write this was beside the point, James thought.
The advice was good: now *was* the time to confront his fears.

James put on a jacket and left the house. It was a dry, windy
day. He walked through the park and crossed Green Avenue.
Staring straight ahead, avoiding the sight of the dark blue
doors on the other side, he walked quickly up Lough Street.
They should rename it Memory Lane, he thought, and laughed
nervously under his breath. By an effort of will he kept the
music out of his head; by taking deep, regular breaths, he kept
the dread out of his chest.

Suddenly he stopped and turned to face the houses on the
other side. And there it was: 21 Lough Street. It was a large,
detached, redbrick house with an old slate roof. Downstairs
there were two bay windows, blank and lightless, one with a
cracked pane. The two upstairs windows were boarded-up.
The place was derelict, and must have been drastically changed
from the last time he had seen it, but even so James felt absolutely sure. *This was the place*. Part of his past lay behind that
door.

He stood there on the curb for some time, gazing and thinking, in a deep trance. His thoughts came slowly. The house
looked like a face, he decided: the face of a dead man. Eyelids
closed; mouth stuffed or bound.

Or perhaps he wasn't dead after all, thought James. Perhaps
he was only unconscious?

A few cars passed in either direction. It started to rain, lightly. An old woman walked past, pulling a shopping trolley on

wheels. The shopping trolley squeaked as it rolled by. The streetlamps came on, and the rain began to fall more heavily. For a long time nothing else happened, and James was on the verge of leaving when he noticed a small movement.

He squinted through the rain. The front door of the house opened slightly. James held his breath. He continued to stare, and seconds later the door closed again.

It had been the tiniest imaginable movement – most people probably wouldn't have noticed it at all – but James knew it was significant. The house had opened its mouth, as if it were trying to speak. As if it were trying to tell him something.

The rewiring of The Polar Bear's lounge was completed on a Thursday afternoon. The landlord, having paid James a small daily rate before this, inspected the work, declared himself satisfied, and handed over the balance of the fee. That was how James came to have £500 under his mattress.

Ever since he had seen the house on Lough Street, James had been unable to remove its image from his mind. Awake and asleep, he saw it all the time, like a vast brick and wood face: the eyes nailed shut, the cheeks bruised, but the mouth opening, ever so slightly, as if the house were trying to whisper its secret. And, of course, James was aware that the doors of houses did not open by themselves. Someone had been inside that house. Someone who had seen James, who knew him. Someone, James guessed, from his past.

He remembered his first thought on arriving in the city. I am a private detective, he had told himself. Now, he decided, it was time to begin his investigation.

On Friday morning he woke early and crept out of the house. It was not yet dawn and the air was cold. Pausing in the empty street before he got in the van, James watched his breath steam and felt suddenly very alive. He was the only person in this street who was not asleep. Everyone else was in their own dreamworld and he, alone, occupied the real world. He felt like a little boy, on the edge of some great discovery. The day is a blank page, he thought, and I can write on it whatever I wish.

James drove randomly through a maze of sidestreets and alleys before entering Lough Street. He looked in the rear-view mirror every few seconds and couldn't see anyone following, but it seemed wiser not to take any chances. It was 5.19 when he parked the van. Luckily there was a space on the even-numbered side of the road, directly opposite number 21. James had a perfect view of his quarry, but was far enough away to be undetectable.

He made himself comfortable, and began his watch. In the cabin of the van he had a flask filled with black coffee, a small rucksack filled with food, a pair of binoculars, and a new green notebook, in which he would write his detective's observations. All around, the houses seemed asleep, their eyes dark and curtained. He ate some dried figs. He scratched his stubble. He drank coffee. He stared at the house. At 5.55 a milkfloat passed; a vision of electric yellow, softly clinking. James wrote this down in the notebook, thinking it might prove significant. He began to wish he was a smoker, so he would have something to occupy his hands. He ate some cashew nuts and drank more coffee. At 6.27 he had to get out of the van to relieve himself. He did this against the roots of a chestnut tree, on a grass verge. The air was still cold, but above him the stars were fading, and over the park he could see the first stains of pink in the sky. His bladder must have been fuller than he had realised. After a while, as the steam rose from the treeroots and the yellow liquid ran in a sinuous line on to the pavement, James began to worry that it would never end; that he would be stuck here as the sun came up and the front doors opened and the pavement filled with angry residents, watching a stranger turn their street into a river of piss.

Back in the van James took out the binoculars and trained them on the downstairs windows of the house. He thought he could make out a faint rectangle of light, and the silhouette of some round shape; perhaps the edge of a sofa or a lampshade. He wrote this observation in the notebook and then settled back, his raincoat folded behind him as a pillow, to watch events unfold.

When he woke the sun was shining directly into his eyes. He could hear a persistent tapping noise. James blinked and saw two laughing schoolchildren through the side window of the van. He shouted at them and they ran away. In panic he looked at his watch. It was 8.34. He must have fallen asleep. The cab was warm now, the roof of his mouth dry and sticky. He looked across the street at number 21: apart from the daylight on the walls and windows, the house appeared unchanged. James might have missed him, of course – he could have slipped away while James was asleep – but for some reason James felt certain that he was still in there. Who? The quarry. The client. The famous writer or singer or whatever. The man whose name probably began with the letter M. The person from his past. Him. Whoever *he* was. James drank deeply from a bottle of water and put the binoculars to his eyes.

At 9.15 the postman went to the door of number 21 and slid something through the letterbox. At 9.24 James noticed a movement through the right-hand downstairs window. At 9.42 the old lady with the squeaky shopping trolley walked down the pavement. At 10.05 the front door opened wide and there was a movement in the doorway. A man – dark-haired, dark-coated – left the house and walked quickly, though with a slight limp, along the pavement on the far side of the road. James couldn't see his face, of course, but he knew who it must be.

He put the binoculars into the small rucksack and wrote in the green notebook, '*10.08: M leaves #21 – 10.09: I follow.*' He watched as the man turned the corner into Green Avenue. When he was out of sight, James jumped from the van, locked it, and jogged to the bottom of Lough Street. At the corner he peered around and saw the man, twenty or thirty metres ahead, then began to follow.

M walked all the way down Green Avenue until he reached the T-junction. Here he took a left, crossed the road at the next pelican crossing, and continued down Sand Street. Watching him, James noted that it was M's right leg which dragged a little, though this did not seem to slow him down. Opposite a large pub called The Riversticks, he turned left again on to University Road. When James reached that junction he saw M crossing at a traffic light. He was headed towards campus.

On campus there were more people around than there had been a few weeks before, although term still hadn't started. James had to keep closer to M in order to avoid losing him in the crowd. Still he walked rapidly and decisively, never hesitating or glancing behind. James had the impression that this was a route M walked regularly. He was moving towards the library; James followed.

At the turnstile the guard nodded respectfully to M and let him in without checking his bag. James watched as M walked through the lobby and then opened a door on the right marked 'COMPUTER ROOM'. He closed the door behind him.

For some reason the guard insisted on removing every object from James's rucksack. He held up the binoculars and asked James why he needed them in a library. James told him he had just been birdwatching. The guard regarded him suspiciously, but finally let him through.

The computer room smelled of new carpet tiles and looked like a dentist's waiting room, only larger. Four rows of wooden cubicles were lined diagonally across it. James walked through the aisles between the rows of cubicles, looking carefully at the backs of people's heads. He counted eleven other people in the room, all sitting at computer terminals, but none of them were the man he had been following. There were no other visible exits. 'Damn it,' he hissed. He couldn't believe his prey had got away. A woman in a blue blazer and skirt came over to James and asked primly if she could help.

'No,' he said, and then he had an idea. 'Actually yes. Could I use one of these computers?'

'That is the general idea of a computer room,' she replied sarcastically.

Sitting down at the nearest cubicle, he went online and typed the words '21 lough street' into a search engine. This produced nothing of interest: a website on ancestry; an episode resumé for a 1980s American TV show called 21 *Jump Street*; a map of bus routes in Belfast; the minutes of a council meeting for the City of Imperial Beach, California.

Remembering Mrs Quigley's cryptic words, James added the name of the city and the word 'tragedy'. Then he pressed enter. The first item on the list was a news story dated Thursday 3 June, 1993. It was from the archives of the local weekly tabloid newspaper, and the headline was 'STUDENT SUICIDE'.

A first-year Psychology student died yesterday when he fell from the attic window of a house in Lough Street. The tragedy occurred about 2.30 p.m., police said, and is being treated as a probable suicide. There were several witnesses to the death. They are being counselled by university health employees. The student was taken to the city hospital, where he was pronounced dead on arrival. The student's name was not immediately released, pending the notification of his family.

James read this report twice, but it meant nothing to him. He scrolled down the list of items until he came across a longer report from the same newspaper. This was dated Wednesday 15 September, 1993. The headline was, 'TRAGIC TRUTH BEHIND PICNIC HORROR'.

A nineteen-year-old student who killed himself in June was a 'gifted but sensitive' person, an inquiry has heard.

Ian Dayton, a first-year Psychology student, committed suicide about 2.30 p.m. on Wednesday 2 June by jumping from his attic bedroom at 21 Lough Street. His death was witnessed by most of the house's other residents, who were in the garden eating a picnic. All have since been treated for shock.

Recording a verdict of suicide, Coroner John Morton

said there was no way the tragedy could have been fore-seen. Although no note was found, police added that there was nothing suspicious about the circumstances of the death.

The coroner read a series of statements about Dayton from his professors and friends. The head of the Psychology department, Dr Lanark, described him as a 'very bright student' who had 'seemed increasingly distracted' during his final term. Lisa Silverton, 20, a friend of Dayton's who lived in the room across from his, said he was 'intelligent and lovely, but very very sensitive'. Former room-mate, Graham Oliver, 19, said Dayton had seemed 'moody and isolated' in his last weeks. Anna Valere, described by several people as Dayton's girlfriend, did not attend the inquiry.

One friend, who wished to remain anonymous, said he thought that Dayton had been feeling guilty about something. 'He told me once he had a secret he could never tell anyone,' said the friend. 'I don't know if that has anything to do with what happened.'

Dayton's sister Catherine made a statement on behalf of the family. 'Ian was an emotional, imaginative person for whom the real world could never quite live up to expectations,' she said. 'We will miss him more than words can say.'

The university chancellor described the event as a 'tragedy' and said his thoughts were with the student's family and friends.

Ian Dayton. *Ee-yun day-tun*. James made the sounds of the name silently in his mouth, but they did not provoke any physical reactions. There was no photograph accompanying the article. James had no idea if this was someone he had known. He studied the other names mentioned in the article: John Morton; Dr Lanark; Lisa Silverton; Anna Valere; Graham Oliver. They were just names. Anna, of course, was the name of the girl with whom Ingrid had wanted him to 'sort things out', but there might be hundreds of Annas in a city this size. Perhaps the story has nothing to do with me, James thought. And yet it had taken place in the garden of that house, during the period of time of which he had no memory. At the very least, it was worth investigating. He printed both stories and put them in his rucksack.

Each of the next three days was spent in the cab of the van, eating and drinking and staring through binoculars at the house. In order to keep himself awake and alert during the day, James drank strong black coffee and trained himself to observe the minutest details of his surroundings. He took notes about changes in the weather; about the fragments of human speech and birdsong he overheard; about the clothes and shoes of every passerby, the expression on every face seen in every window. He plotted the positions of lampposts and postboxes and telegraph poles. He drew pictures of each chestnut tree and the pattern of their fallen leaves. He counted the number of aeroplanes that unzipped the pale sky and the number of stars that sequinned its night-time blackness.

It might appear that his efforts were wasted, but James did learn some valuable information from his days in the van. It was during this time, for example, that he worked out the identities of two neighbours, both of whom would have a part to play in the story that follows: the tiny, sallow-skinned man who lived at number 19, and who always emerged from his doorway blinking, as if unpleasantly surprised by the daylight; and the middle-aged businessman at number 12 who walked to the bus stop at the bottom of the road every morning and stood there filling in the *Times* crossword until the 7.45 bus arrived. James thought of asking these people about M. He thought of questioning them to discover if they knew what had happened in that house ten years before. But to do that he would have had to break his vigil, and he was afraid that even a moment's inattention would be fatal. Besides, they seemed so preoccupied, so deep inside their own worlds, that James guessed they were not even aware of each other's existence. He began to suspect that *he* was the only human being on this street who saw the subtle connections of neighbourhood: the spidersilk threads of coincidence and proximity that bound together these houses and the people who lived inside them, and whose patterns he sketched in the pages of the green notebook.

Re-reading those notes now, they seem to me a much more accurate and complete record of the days in which they were written than any of James's diary entries. His visual memories of those September days are surprisingly vivid and correspond almost exactly with what is written in the green notebook. This is, I suppose, because he managed to eliminate *himself* from the picture. Most of the time we do not really see the world when we look at it; what we see is a ghostly mirror image of ourselves; as when we look out through the window of a lit room at night. By cutting his thoughts and emotions off at the source – by switching off the light in the room – James was left with an objective viewpoint. He was an observer, and thus he saw what others did not see.

His mistake was to think that, by seeing objectively, he was seeing the street in its entirety. What he didn't see – what he completely missed – was the strangest and most remarkable sight in the whole of Lough Street: an unshaven, wild-eyed man sitting in a parked van, staring at an empty house through binoculars and furiously taking notes.

On the evening of the fourth day of the vigil, James decided to treat himself to a few drinks at The Polar Bear. It had been a grey and miserable day, and he felt he deserved a break. He was on his way to the pub when he realised that his wallet was almost empty. So he went back to Newland Road and up to his bedroom.

Glancing out of the window, he saw a man in a dark coat walking towards the park. It looked like M, and for a moment James thought of following. Then he got a grip. You're working too hard, he told himself, you're becoming obsessed. A man in a dark coat: it could be anyone. Just get the money, then go and have a few drinks.

He slid his hand beneath the mattress. There was nothing. James grasped blindly for several seconds, then lifted up the mattress and stared at the bare wooden slats of the bedstead. The money was gone. He searched under the bed. He pulled up the carpet. He ripped off lengths of wallpaper. He hurled his shirts and trousers from the wardrobe and emptied every drawer in the chest. The money was gone. Eight hundred pounds. Two weeks' work. Gone.

James lay on the mattress and stared at the ceiling. Something dark twisted itself into knots inside his gut. Without money, he could not pursue the truth. The need for money was just another locked door in the labyrinth, preventing him from going where he wished.

Suddenly an image appeared in James's mind. It was a picture of money. In the picture, however, money did not wear its usual disguise, of paper or metal or plastic; rather, it appeared as itself, naked. What did money look like? In James's mind it resembled a leech; an ugly black leech stuck to his skin. The bigger it grew, the more blood it needed; the smaller it shrank, the harder it sucked. It would never stop sucking and it could never be removed.

James covered his face with his hands and moaned softly. He felt like screaming or weeping or banging his head against the wall, but it seemed pointless when there was no one to hear or see. He thought of all the money he had earned and spent in his life, all the hours he had given to its joyless pursuit, all the precious thoughts wasted on how much of it he had and how much he needed. And all for what? Money didn't even exist. It was a conspiracy of belief and remembering. If only we could all just *forget* it, James thought. Watching him, I couldn't help laughing. He may as well have wished the earth flat. People forget most of their lives, but they never forget how much money they have, nor how much other people have.

In the end, he walked to the pub, determined to spend his last ten pounds on beer. He sat alone in the empty lounge and began to read the Borges story, 'Funes El Memorioso', about the man who could remember *everything*. He had started this story on his first night in the city, but that time he had been interrupted by the librarian. This time, he promised himself, nothing would disturb him. And nothing did, in fact, except the tides and eddies of his own memories, suspicions, fears, regrets.

After an hour spent trying to make sense of the first paragraph, James gave up. His mind kept returning to the moment, earlier that evening, when he had entered the bedroom, just before he discovered that the money was gone. He had looked out of the window and seen a man in a dark coat. It could have been anybody, of course, but what if . . . James put the beer glass down suddenly. Now he thought about it, the man he had seen had been limping slightly. What if it *was* him? James thought. What if M had stolen the money? But why? His mind raced through all the detective stories he had ever read, until it reached a plausible motivation. Because he is trying to scare me off. Why would he want to do that? He must have some guilty secret that he needs to protect. James recalled the story about the dead student. What if it *hadn't* been suicide? What if Ian Dayton had been *murdered*?

James remembered the choking shame and anger he had felt when he looked at the black box that he couldn't open. Three years of his life . . . gone. Now he felt sure that they had been stolen; that *he* had stolen them. James must have witnessed something; he must have known too much. If M is trying to get rid of me, James thought, he has failed spectacularly. I will get my revenge. I will expose his secret. This investigation is not over; it is only just beginning.

And then James remembered that he had no money. He looked up from his empty glass and saw the walls of the labyrinth all around him, smooth and black and unclimbably high. James wondered briefly if he was hallucinating, but if anything it felt like the opposite was true: that his everyday life was a hallucination, and this scene of utter horror the truth that lay behind it. In that moment his despair was so pure, so perfect, that he thought of imitating Ian Dayton, of escaping through the labyrinth's only exit. Instead, he decided to go through to the public bar. There at least he would be surrounded by people, voices, lights. There at least the labyrinth would be invisible.

James sat at the bar and ordered a pint. The man at the stool next to his moved away soon after he arrived, which made him feel paranoid, but then he noticed that the man had left his newspaper. The local tabloid. Instinctively, James turned to the page with the stars.

CANCER 21 June–22 July. Feels like it's been raining for a long time, doesn't it? And when it doesn't rain, it pours. And always, only ever, on you. Well, get over it, sunshine. Everyone's suffering, not just you. Why don't you stop feeling sorry for yourself and actually start using your brain for a change? One thing's for sure – you won't find the answer until you remember what the question was.

In the pub's warm air, James could feel his face burn. He stared at the words on the page, unable to believe what he had just read. The sound of laughter rose suddenly, as though someone had turned up the volume of the room by remote control. What *was* this? James wondered. This wasn't a horoscope; this was personal. He downed his pint and ordered another, then looked at the photograph of the astrologer again: Adam Golightly. That little squarish bald head, that neat beard, those staring eyes. I recognise you, thought James. Not from the newspaper, but from real life. At first he couldn't remember where he'd seen the man before, but then it came to him. It was here, in The Polar Bear. The man who used to sit on his own while James ate his lunch. The one he'd wanted to talk to, but hadn't because he was always reading. It had to be him.

James sipped his second pint. The despair he had felt earlier was fading now, but the anger was still there. The difference now was that his anger had an object. If only he could find that little man. He would give that astrologer a piece of his mind.

The next time James looked up, he saw him. Sitting at his usual table in the corner of the bar. He had a little book and a laptop computer. James watched him for several minutes, hardly daring to believe his eyes. The man would read something in the book, frown for a few seconds, and then type something into his laptop, as if he were translating. Finally James went over and said accusingly, 'You're an astrologer, aren't you?'

The man looked up, surprised, and replied, 'Yes, that's right. Can I help you with something?' His voice was calm and gracious. His eyes were friendly. James handed him the newspaper and pointed to his sign. 'Look what you've written about me.'

The astrologer glanced at it and said, 'Hmm. Seems about right. A little vague, of course, but that's the nature of the beast with these twelve-sign newspaper columns. Would you like me to do a more detailed analysis?'

Something in his manner undid James's anger. He sat down next to the man and said, 'OK.'

The astrologer asked for the date and time of James's birth. James told him. He nodded and typed it into his laptop. There was a pause while he looked at something on the screen. He began muttering about Moon in Aries conjunction in mid-heaven, and then said, in a louder voice, 'Let me put it in layman's terms. You are obsessed with the idea of fame, of standing out from the crowd. As a young man you wanted to be an actor, or a musician, or an artist. Something along those lines.'

James shook his head, relieved. It took an effort of will to stop himself laughing.

More muttering – 'Sun ascendant, Mercury in Cancer,' – and then, louder: 'You are a man of many moods. You present a tough and solid face to the world but inside you are slippery and incoherent.' He looked at James and said, 'Does that sound about right?'

James shrugged. He could have been talking about almost anyone.

'Saturn in Gemini,' whispered the astrologer. 'Transit Saturn now approaching sun . . .' He nodded and then said to James: 'Everything's gone crazy in the past couple of months, I suppose? You gave up your old life and now you're trying to find something important. You're not sure what it is you're looking for. A key of some kind.'

James gasped.

'You believe that you've lost it but you are wrong.' The astrologer's voice seemed immense now; it seemed to fill the entire room. 'What you think is lost is only misplaced. If you look for it in the right place, you will find it.'

James stared at him.

The astrologer smiled and said, 'Was that all right or would you prefer a second opinion?'

'A second opinion?'

'Bill?'

A grizzled old man at the next table turned around and said,

'Your analysis is fine, Adam.' He looked at James and added, in a stern voice: 'Do not abandon what you have started, young man. You must not be afraid to go back. And if you are afraid, you must overcome your fear. It is the only way. It is your destiny.'

A giggle escaped James's mouth. This man sounded like a character from *Star Wars*.

'What's funny?'

'You said it was my destiny.'

'Uh-huh?'

'Oh come on. You don't really believe that?'

The old man looked confused. 'What other term would you prefer?'

'Chance?' suggested James, and heard a few titters at the next table. 'Free will?' At this, there was open laughter.

'Ah, right,' said the old man, suppressing a grin. 'And I suppose you believe in *mortality* too. And, er, *evolution*. Not to mention the power of . . . *reason*.' At each stressed word his companions grew more hysterical, and so did the people around them until it seemed that everyone in the bar was laughing at James. Astonished, he stared out at them: the edges of his vision were blurred by alcohol, but it seemed to him that these people looked like the normal Polar Bear crowd. At least they weren't wearing purple cloaks or pointed hats.

'I don't know what you're laughing about,' James said, controlling his emotions. 'There's nothing funny or odd about any of those concepts. Chance and free will. Mortality and evolution. They're completely orthodox . . .' His voice was being drowned out by squealing, grunting, crying laughter now, so he had to shout. 'At least I don't believe in the influence of the fucking stars!'

The laughter died; was replaced by headshakes and tuts of disapproval. James was shot some dirty looks. He heard somebody say, 'Bloody cranks.' A woman shouted from the back of the room: 'I suppose you only believe what your physical senses tell you, do you, Mr Weirdo?'

He was about to stand up and shout back that yes, as it

happened, he did rely on his physical senses to perceive the world, just as any other sane person would, but the bald astrologer put a hand on his and said, 'Calm yourself.' James noticed that his own hand was shaking. Then to the other people in the room the astrologer added: 'There's no need to be cruel. Everyone is entitled to believe what they believe. If our friend here chooses to put his faith in ideas like "logic" and "facts", then that is . . .' – he waited for the laughter to die down again – 'that is, manifestly, his destiny.'

At this last word the people in the bar grew respectfully quiet. James tried to laugh, but found that he couldn't. The astrologer said, 'Allow me to buy you a drink.' James nodded. For some reason, he felt embarrassed by what he had said, and grateful towards the astrologer for having intervened on his behalf.

The two of them chatted for a while. The astrologer showed James the book of symbols he had been looking at earlier. James asked what the symbols meant and the astrologer stared at him strangely. 'Surely you've seen this before?' he said. James confessed that he hadn't, and the astrologer seemed shocked. He put a hand on James's shoulder – 'You poor boy' – and bought him another drink.

The astrologer told James the story of his life. In a whisper, he confided: 'As a matter of fact, I used to share some of your beliefs.' Then he laughed. 'Did you hear what I just said? "As a matter of fact". Ha! You see, even now I haven't completely forgotten the terminology.'

James asked how he had come to lose those beliefs. 'The workings of destiny,' the astrologer replied, as though this were obvious. 'When I was a young man, my girlfriend passed over to the next world.'

'She died, you mean?'

A condescending smile. 'You may think of it like that if you prefer. I loved her very much. I was twenty years old. She was on a train which crashed.'

'I'm sorry . . . that's terrible.'

'No, that's destiny. But at the time I felt as you did. I

"grieved" for her; is that the right word? Many times I considered "suicide". I lived in the attic room of a tall house, and each morning and evening I would open the window and look down at the garden and visualise my body falling to what I imagined would be my "death". The only thing that held me back was the thought of how my parents would feel. I stayed alive for their sake. Then they passed through to the next world too, within a couple of weeks of each other. My father of testicular cancer, and my mother of heartbreak.'

'People don't actually die of heartbreak,' James said.

The astrologer waved away the objection. 'Call it what you like. The point is they both passed through. After incinerating my mother's discarded physical shell I went up to the attic room, opened the window and sat on the sill with my hands holding the windowframe and my legs dangling over the roof. It was a steep roof. All I had to do was stand up, let go of the frame, and I would pass through to the next world, to join my parents and my girlfriend. For a long time I hesitated. Then, just at the moment when I had said my goodbyes to the physical world – it was a beautiful summer's evening – I heard a voice in the room behind me. I turned around and saw my girlfriend, in a pool of blue light. She told me it was not my time. That was when the first crack appeared in the husk of my physical senses; when the light began to pour through and liberate me from . . . those bizarre beliefs that I held before.' He looked at James hurriedly. 'Sorry, I didn't mean to offend you.'

'I'm not offended,' James said. 'Just confused.'

'Yes,' said the astrologer. 'You're confused. Quite right. You see the world as chaos because you do not see the world. You do not find the answer because you cannot remember the question.'

'What is the question?'

'The question is the key.'

'But the key is what I'm looking for.'

'But you're not, are you? You stopped looking. You must resume your search. As Bill told you: do not be afraid to go back.'

After that, they played darts and had a few more drinks. James doesn't remember saying goodbye to the astrologer or leaving the pub or coming home. But he remembers going to bed and seeing the ceiling spin above him.

He woke very late the next day; the sky was already dark, and James had a hangover. He went downstairs and made toast and black coffee, then took them back to his bedroom. The house was empty. There was no post on the mat. James sat on his bed, eating the toast and drinking the coffee.

Realising that he smelled of sweat, he took a shower; afterwards he felt slightly better. But when James went back into his room, the smell of sweat was just as strong as before. He sniffed in each corner of the room and realised that the smell was coming from his bedclothes. He hadn't washed them since he moved here, three weeks before.

Hastily he stripped the duvet cover, the fitted sheet and the pillowcase. As he shook out the last of these, something fell to the floor. James put the pillowcase down and looked at what was there. It was money. Joyfully, disbelievingly, he counted it. Eight hundred pounds in £20 notes. How it had got inside the pillowcase he didn't know; he must have misremembered the place where he had hidden it.

The astrologer's words came back to him. *What you think is lost is only misplaced. If you look for it in the right place, you will find it.* James was filled with renewed energy and purpose. If the astrologer had been right about the money not being lost, perhaps he was right about the other thing too. The key. The question. James's memory. What was it the other man had said? *Do not abandon what you have started. You must not be afraid to go back. And if you are afraid, you must overcome your fear.*

Immediately James understood the meaning of these words. He went to the desk, opened the drawer, took out the white notebook and began to write.

Memoirs of an Amnesiac

CHAPTER 4

I remember a room like this one: sterile and rented, with vague wallpaper and a desk by the window, overlooking a nondescript garden. There is no particular weather in the memory – I can see the garden in any season I choose: the trees bare or green, the sky grey or brilliant blue – but let us say it is autumn and it is raining. Perhaps mid-afternoon, the greyness beginning to darken, the hot water pipes clanking into life. A stale and sorrowful odour. The vestiges of a hangover . . . my possessions in boxes . . . and a sense of being in limbo, between chapters. A day much like this one, in other words.

I know the facts that came from that room; I know the choice I made while sitting at that desk. I can even pin a rough date upon it: October 1994, a time whose records are locked inside the black box. A few months before, I must have graduated from university and turned twenty-one, but this is as far back as I can go. Beyond is fog, and I am afraid to venture there. I do not mean that I am afraid of what I will remember, but of what I will fail to remember. I am afraid of the void that lies in wait where my life should be: the black hole that I glimpsed before, and the sense of shame and horror that engulfed me when I discovered it. So let us turn our backs on the fog, for now, and look forward, into the dazzling chaos. This room is where Chapter 4 begins.

So it was an ordinary English Sunday: overcast, spitting with rain; hardly begun and already almost wasted. To kill off what remained of it, I was leafing through the different sections of the newspaper and I came across a review of a reissued Hitchcock film, *Marnie*, which I had, by chance, seen the night before. I disagreed with the review and, an hour later, I had written a counter-review. I sent this to the editor of the newspaper. I did so without hope or ambition; it was just something to do. A whim. Two weeks later, having forgotten about my article, I received a brief rejection slip from the newspaper's arts editor. It was the usual two lines, printed on a white postcard. In blue biro, above this, were the words, 'nice tho'. I pinned the note to my bedroom wall.

Days passed, each as long and complex and intermittently dull as the others. I went to other places, talked to other people, thought of other things. And, somewhere in the midst of all this otherness, I wrote a second review, this time of a Springsteen concert, and sent it to the same arts editor. I don't know why, exactly; I had no desire to be a journalist. I think it was just curiosity about that 'nice tho'. I saw it every day, above my desk, and it became a kind of itch. I found myself speculating about what it meant, if anything. The second review was designed to settle the question, that was all. I knew that the editor couldn't simply write the same thing again. Either he would write something longer and more specific, or he would not reply at all. I regarded the second possibility as by far the more likely.

In fact he telephoned me. This was early November, I think, and I was living with my parents at the time. The arts editor's name was Sam Caine. He told me he liked my prose style and asked me what else I would like to write about. I had no idea, and said so. I also told him I would be leaving the country in the new year, to explore the world and write a novel. He asked when I would be back. I said I didn't know; possibly never. Caine said something sharp and regretful then; he seemed irritated that I had wasted his time.

When I told my parents about the telephone call, they were furious. My mother mentioned gift-horses. My father used the word 'irresponsible'. Both demanded to know what it was I wanted to do with my life. I told them I was planning to work my way around the world: grape-picking, barwork, cruise ships, that kind of thing. I kept silent about my desire to write; I feared they would start using words like 'unrealistic' and 'pipedream'. I didn't have an itinerary, I explained, but that was because I didn't want one; what I wanted was Adventure. Uncertainty. Freedom. What I wanted was a blank page.

But there were long weeks to pass before I could leave. To save money for the trip, I was working six days a week in a warehouse, and in the local pub most evenings. Both jobs were numbingly repetitive. In the warehouse, I was one of a thousand or so workers. I can't remember exactly what I was doing there: I have an image in my mind of cardboard boxes and clothes wrapped in cellophane, and another image of long gloomy rooms filled with racks of coathangers. I remember looking at my watch more often than I should have done and being appalled by how slowly time was passing. I remember occasionally glancing up from my work at the walls and ceiling and getting the kind of recurrent claustrophobic panic that prisoners must get: the feeling that I would *never get out of here*. But what comes back to me most clearly is the soundtrack: Radio One was broadcast all day, from loudspeakers in the ceiling, and I soon realised that the station was playing the same eight or ten hit singles constantly, over and over again. And the DJs were even worse, like *soma*-drunk Deltas from *Brave New World*, all capacity for sorrow, fear and compassion permanently removed. It was like being brainwashed in the literal sense: being persuaded to think about absolutely nothing at all.

The bar job was marginally more varied, but if anything I hated it even more. At least in the warehouse I was anonymous, invisible. Behind the bar I felt exposed, constantly on display, and as a consequence I could never forget that my mind was located in the attic room of a clumsy, vulnerable tower of human flesh: the thing people called my body. Another reason I hated it was that everyone else in the pub appeared so happy and relaxed; I alone was there to work, while the landlord and his customers drank and talked and laughed. This strikes me now as a pretty good definition of hell: to be alone without the consolations of solitude; to be surrounded by other people without the consolations of company. It didn't help that the wages were shit, of course. In both jobs it was forbidden to sit down, and the soles of my feet ached constantly. When I lay in bed at night they sang with pain.

After a few tearful rows, my parents backed off. They confined themselves to gentle remarks over dinner, about rates of pay on newspapers and so on. One article would be the equivalent of a week's work at the warehouse and the pub, my mum pointed out. Even if you still want to go abroad, she said, it makes sense to try and earn a bit more cash before new year. I said I didn't have any ideas for articles. My parents suggested some. I shot their ideas down. Then, almost against my will, I came up with some of my own.

I phoned the editor and apologised for the other day. He seemed almost to have forgotten who I was. I suggested one of my ideas to him. He rejected it. I suggested another, and he said yes, all right, do it. Eight hundred words, to be filed by next Tuesday. As we said goodbye he asked me if I was still planning to leave the country and abandon my nascent career. I said I hadn't decided; I was thinking about it. Don't think too long, he said, the train will soon be pulling out of the station.

That was all it took. Although I continued to tell myself and others that I was undecided, the image of the departing train haunted my dreams. I wrote the article and faxed it to the newspaper. The next day, at the warehouse, I was summoned to the supervisor's office to take a telephone call. It was from a sub-editor at the newspaper, querying the spelling of a name. When the call was over, I thanked the supervisor and started to leave his office. He said, 'Looks like you're going up in the world, eh?' I shrugged and said I hoped so. 'I never would have guessed you had it in you,' he said. 'Remember us when you're famous, won't you?'

The following week the arts editor asked me to come down to London because he wanted to meet me in person. I wore my only suit and it rained. By the time I made it to the newspaper office, I was soaked. I spent ten minutes in the toilet, attempting to dry my clothes, skin and hair in the meagre jet of hot air exhaled by the automatic hand-dryer. Sam Caine, to my surprise, wore a pair of faded jeans and a jumper with holes in it. He was in his early forties, with greying hair and an assured but kindly manner. I was so nervous that my answers to his questions came out in stammering spurts, loud as a barking dog. We ate poached salmon in the staff cafeteria and I slowly relaxed. He asked me where I saw myself in five years' time. I looked at him blankly. 'Doing your job?' I joked, unable to think of any other response. He didn't laugh. He made a cathedral of his hands. 'James, you may need to lower your expectations. Journalism is a tough profession. You'll need a lot of patience and a thick skin if you want to succeed.'

———

I didn't believe Caine when he told me that, but he was right. The beginning of 1995 was a grim, frustrating time. Because I couldn't afford rent, I was still living with my parents; our house was in a suburban estate in the Midlands. Three or four times a week, I would drive to Leicester or Nottingham or Derby to stand on my own in dark crowded rooms, sip pints of bitter shandy and try to think of something to write about the four men playing music on the stage before me. This was an isolating experience: not only my absence of friends marked me out, but the notebook into which I scribbled. People stared at me appraisingly, amusedly, contemptuously. In the darkness it was bearable – I could lean against the wall and not be seen – but when the lights came on between bands I wished I could evaporate.

I had escaped hell, only to find myself in purgatory. What made it worse was that I wasn't even being paid for these lonely evenings. Though the arts editor was still commissioning me to write for the newspaper, opportunities were few and irregular, and he had already told me that he would soon be leaving the paper to go freelance. For that reason, I was trying to get work on a weekly music paper. This involved writing an indefinite number of 'dummy reviews' in the hope that one of them would, eventually, be printed. The objective of this initiation was mostly to humiliate new recruits, I think, but at the time I convinced myself it was a matter of perfecting my voice. The paper had a kind of unwritten house style, which consisted of diction (coded and matey) and attitude (either snottily cynical or rabidly awe-filled, depending on whether the artist in question was 'out' or 'in'), and I spent all my waking hours trying to learn and mimic this style.

I had lost touch with most of my friends by now, but I wasn't completely alone. During the course of the year, I had two girl-friends. The first was a friend of a friend of a friend; the second I met through the 'lonely hearts' pages of the weekly music paper. I don't remember much about either girl. Their faces, vaguely. Their names. Their voices. Moments in bed together. Awkward silences in restaurants or parks. Goodbyes at train stations, identical but for the place-names on the signs. The pleasantly tense beginnings and the unpleasantly tense endings. The feeling that we were merely going through the motions. In each case it felt like I was dating a ghost, though in truth, I suppose, it was *me*, rather than the girl, who was not really there.

My career path took the shape of a labyrinth. I soon became accustomed to its twists and forks and dead ends: the unreturned phone calls; the sudden and unexplained changes of mind; the constant air of bored panic on the other end of the line. Unconsciously I adopted my editors' manners; I became cold and short-tempered, especially with my parents. The angrier I got, the more they worried about me; and the more they worried about me, the angrier I got. Sometimes my dad would blow his top in return, which wasn't so bad, but my mum just kept asking, in a pleading voice, 'Are you all right, James?' I spent most of each day in my bedroom, sitting at the desk: writing, reading, making (and waiting for) telephone calls. My mother would come in three or four times a day, on tiptoe so as not to disturb me, carrying a tray of tea and biscuits, or a light lunch, or a glass of orange juice and sandwiches. I kept telling her to stop treating me like an invalid, but she took no notice. 'James's Work' became the sole subject of conversation at the dinner table. It was like a baby which quickly grew into a kind of ogre. It ruled the whole house, my work, and I was no less its slave than my parents were.

If I read my 1995 diary now, I am returned immediately to the present reality of that past: the feeling that I was walking through darkness, or thick fog, my eyes focused permanently on the next step; my head full of money earned and spent, ideas for articles, files of information on bands and record companies . . . the soul-less minutiae of today and tomorrow. Day after day of work and hope and work and fear and work and disappointment and work. Yet this is not the version of that time which exists in my memory. Memory turns the truth into a story: chance and choice solidify into fate; endless nights become little black dots on a map. And there is a reason for this. I cannot write the truth because it would take me almost as long as it took me to live it. And because it would be unreadable, unbearable. So let's forget the truth, for now. I will write the story instead.

————

On 14 September 1995, I came to a decision. I was eating a cheese-burger at the time, in an almost empty fast-food restaurant, watching rain dribble down the windows. I made the decision and became so excited that I had to write it down. I scrawled on the back of a tray-liner, 'I'm going down to London to make my fortune!' The note is sellotaped into my diary, with a soft-focus photograph of hash browns and bacon-and-egg McMuffins on the back.

Five days later I was living in a rented room in Wembley, near the old football stadium. The room was just a room, but it was cheap and close to the train station. It had a view of a car park and some trees, and at night I could hear traffic on the Harrow Road. The man who owned the flat was rarely around; he gave me a key and let me use his coffee machine.

The first few months were lean, and I reached a low point when I was fired by the music paper. I had known it was coming

– I always felt like an outsider there: the gauche intruder who says the wrong thing; the frowning idiot who never understood the office jokes – but it still came as a shock. I remember, pitifully, arguing with my editor, pleading for another chance. In the end he hung up on me. For a week or so I was in a panic, but the letters I sent out to other publications soon brought results. I got work with a music monthly and a London daily newspaper, and my confidence grew.

Soon after that the amount of work I was doing began to snowball. I charted my financial progress on a graph, and its curve was gratifyingly steep. Although Sam Caine was no longer the arts editor, I was doing more work for the Sunday newspaper, and other editors began to call and ask me to write for them: a young woman from a glossy fashion monthly; the music editor of a 'lad' magazine; the reviews editor of a serious film periodical. By the spring of 1996 I had so much work that I could barely keep up with it. I remember charging around London from office to hotel room to cinema to gig venue, listening to music or taped interviews on headphones and taking notes. The speed of my life was such that I never had time to think about what it was I was rushing so hard to achieve. Perhaps the speed was an end in itself? Perhaps I wasn't running towards anything at all but *away* from something that lay behind me?

In a matter of weeks I had, as in the cliché, become my job. Ruthlessly I eliminated every part of my daily and inner life which did not contribute towards the next, immediate goal. I developed tunnel vision. I kept my eyes on the prize. Everything else turned to a blank, a blur: friends, books, doubts, small pleasures and idle moments . . . all were ballast to be thrown from the basket of the hot-air balloon as I rose and rose. I was driven – that much is obvious – but what drove me? At the time I felt sure the rapid pulsing of my blood was born of exhilaration; only later did I realise it might have been another emotion altogether.

I remember a dream I had around this time. I was in an athletics stadium with my parents and some friends from school. It was a sunny day. It was a normal athletics stadium, with a running track and tiered seating around three sides. On the fourth side, however, was a sort of transparent slope. I don't know whether it was made of glass or ice or plastic; perhaps it was some dream mixture of all three. Anyhow, I decided to climb this slope. The people around me expressed their fear on my behalf; they warned me not to do it. I laughed at their anxiety and said I would climb it easily. And, indeed, it was easy to begin with – I was running – but the higher I went, the steeper the slope became, until soon I could no longer run but had to crawl on all fours. Still I went on. I felt as if everyone in the stadium were watching me now, their breath held. As I climbed higher, I began to realise the awful situation I had put myself in: the slope was now almost vertical and I could barely hold on to it at all. Suddenly, the desire to keep climbing was gone; all that remained was the terror of falling. It was at this point that I woke up: paralysed by fear, my fingertips beginning to slip, regretting the rash decision I had made. I remember the dream vividly now, perhaps because it has the air of a premonition, but I didn't give it much thought at the time; it was only a dream, after all, and I was busy.

Because the rent on my room was so low, and because I didn't pay much attention to what I ate or wore, I soon accumulated a large amount of money. It slept in my bank account, lazy and pointless. It existed solely as a means of gauging my success. Every time I went to a cash machine I would press the button marked 'CHECK BALANCE' and stare proudly at the newly grown figure on the screen. I invested my soul in those numbers. That's me, I would think; that is how much I'm worth. Every zero was like another closed door on the nondescript room in which this chapter began.

Yet, to my horror and incomprehension, I found myself in a kind of surrealist loop: each time I closed the door on that room, I entered another one that looked exactly identical.

One night a friend, whom I hadn't spoken to for more than a year, telephoned me; she told me about her new boyfriend, her job, her friends, her parents, her hopes and worries, then she asked how my life was. I told her about the magazines I wrote for, the money I earned, and then, staring around me, unable to think of anything else to say, I invented a looming deadline and hung up. I began to see for the first time how truly empty my life was.

It seemed to me that there were two ways of filling this void: with people, or with things. The trouble with people was that you had to spend time on them, whereas all you had to spend on things was money; and I had more of the latter than the former. So I went to the closest electrics store I could find and bought a TV, satellite dish, video recorder, stereo and laptop computer. Then I took a train to central London and went clothes shopping in Covent Garden. It was a source of immense and astonishing gratification to me, how quickly and easily I could spend so much money – and on so little. A thousand pounds on a suit! Two hundred and fifty on a pair of shoes! Fifty for a tie that I would never wear! When I had more paper bags than I could carry on the tube, I hailed a cab and got driven back to my cheap, lonely room.

The next day I looked in the 'property to rent' section of the London daily. I found a small, modern, white-painted and very expensive studio flat on the fourth floor of an office block near Liverpool Street station. I imagined this would put me in the centre of the city; and geographically, it did. But the area where I lived was mostly non-residential: at weekends it was deserted; even on weekdays, the pubs all closed at 8 p.m., and the only sounds at night were of groups of tourists being led on 'Jack the Ripper' tours through the maze of narrow streets below my window.

I was now spending as much as I earned, and my bank balance was down to three figures, but still the feeling of emptiness remained. I decided what I needed next was a new girlfriend. Most of the PRs I dealt with were women and several had asked me out to lunch or dinner; before, I had always said I was too busy, but now I began accepting. One night, one of these women, a pretty, ambitious, young blonde called Katie, said she had some cocaine in her flat; she invited me back to help her consume it. We took the coke and had sex, and at 3 a.m. I left her flat, still wide awake and with the feeling that I had just discovered a secret city, a dark and forbidden city, hidden inside the city of daylight and work which I knew so well. This was June 1996, the beginning of the summer of my first disintegration.

There was nothing unique or original about my fall. Indeed, its lineaments conform so neatly to the falls of other young men that you could almost call it generic. In short, the balance tilted. I began to spend more than I could earn; to consume more than I could produce. I sought relief from the pressures of work, and from the emptiness within me, in parties and drugs and sex with Katie and others, and in doing so damaged my ability to do the work that paid for all these things. In the daytimes I would feel wretched and regretful, but in the evenings I would start again on the alcohol and cocaine. In private clubs I would enter a room and dozens of knowing eyes would turn my way. I swore I could hear them whispering my name. At first I felt flattered, but at some point my confidence must have evaporated because bad things started to happen. Paranoia and rage would pour from my mouth, faces would sneer, glasses would break, doormen would throw me on to the pavement.

This can't have happened more than three or four times, over a period of three months, but it was enough. By October the telephone had stopped ringing. My name was crossed off lists. Unable to afford the rent but too cowardly and stubborn to admit the fact, I began paying for everything with credit. Now when I looked at the numbers on my statements, their largeness spelled not my worth but my doom. At the age of twenty-three, my career was in pieces, and those pieces were caught in a vortex, being slowly sucked around and around, each revolution taking them closer to the dark hole below.

———

A bit melodramatic perhaps; and the truth is that my fall was more complicated, more drawn-out, less absolute than I have described it. But stories must obey certain rhythms, or they would drag on interminably and end bathetically, like life. So let's just say I was in the vortex; my life was spinning out of control, and I was ready to surrender myself to the inevitable. Perhaps I even welcomed it – the thought of oblivion, the obliteration of all hope. Perhaps it would have come as a relief after so much stress and unhappiness? I will never know, because just at the moment when I was preparing to let go of the ledge to which I clung (if I may be permitted to change metaphors for a moment), I was rescued.

One morning in October 1996 – two years after he first altered the direction of my life – Sam Caine, my former arts editor, rang unexpectedly. He had been offered a job as editor of an upmarket listings magazine, he told me, and he was looking for a young, intelligent journalist who could be trained as a sub-editor. He knew I had no experience of subbing, but he had noticed that my copy was always 'clean' – no misspelt words, no grammatical errors – and he wanted to give me a chance. The hours were not too long, and the pay was good. It would give you a dependable income, he said, and leave you with enough time to write your novel. I had completely forgotten about the novel by then, and had no desire to even think about it, but financially I was desperate and so of course I accepted the offer. Caine did not mention my recent troubles, though he must surely have heard about them. In retrospect it seems obvious that he took pity on me – that the job offer was an act of mercy – but I don't remember seeing it that way at the time.

For eighteen months, my life settled down. I moved out of the expensive flat in Liverpool Street, and found a cheaper, roomier, more pleasant place in Bow, round the corner from the tube station. The job was repetitive, undemanding and anonymous, and for those very reasons it was perfect. Each weekday I took the tube to the office – an uneventful, half-hour journey – and began work at 10 a.m. The office was colourless and, but for the hum of the computers, eerily silent: people communicated with each other by email, even when they were sitting side by side. In my lunch hour I went swimming, then ate a sandwich at my desk. I finished work at 6 p.m. and took the tube back home.

As for what I did in the office . . . well, a sub-editor is essentially a kind of filter; it was my job to simplify and clarify other people's writing. I removed unnecessary sentences, corrected mistakes, reworked jumbled paragraphs. Where there was messiness, I brought order; where there was prolixity, brevity; where there was ambiguity, certainty. I was a policeman of words. I made each article fit neatly in its assigned box and sometimes gave it a headline too.

The headlines were the sole source of amusement in the job: whereas in all my other tasks, I was expected to be sober, straightforward, machinelike, with the headlines I was free to have some fun. Mostly this consisted of subtle plays on words, sly references to famous films or books or popular expressions. I don't remember now any of those headlines, but I remember the modest pleasure they gave me. The strongest memory I have of that time is of taking the tube home and sitting on a rhythmically shaking seat, arms folded, eyes closed, thinking of a witty pun I had just invented, and smiling. That was the high point of my working day.

Slowly but surely I repaid my debts. Virtuousness became my only vice; I was celibate, sober and thrifty. I was utterly alone. In the evenings I went to the cinema or cooked myself a simple, balanced meal which I ate in front of the television. (I remember passing pubs and fast-food restaurants during this period and thinking almost gleefully about the clogged-up arteries and dying brain cells of all those other people; how much longer I would live than them; how much cleaner and healthier my insides were than theirs.) In the mornings I read the newspaper. At weekends I slept late and went running in Victoria Park. On Saturday evenings I did yoga, and on Sunday evenings I went to a Spanish class. It was a tranquil, rather dull existence. I might even have felt happy had it not been for what happened to me nearly every night.

'I could be bounded in a nut-shell, and count myself the king of infinite space, were it not that I have bad dreams.' That line from *Hamlet* sums up my whole life during this time. In the day everything seemed containable, explicable, under control: the trees I saw through my sitting-room window, the swarm of expressionless faces on the tube, the striplights and recycled air in the office, the rows of letters and dots and spaces on the computer screen . . . none of these realities threatened me in any way; they did not change form or lurch suddenly from the background in which they belonged. They were fine. I was fine. All was normal. But when I closed my eyes and fell asleep I entered a universe in which these reassuring surface details were stripped away to reveal the noisy, brutal chaos underneath. The past. Other people. Hell.

I did my best to forget these dreams, to blink them away every morning, to tell myself they were only a kind of flickering debris: the unwanted parts of memory and imagination being jettisoned by my brain. But if that was so, how come they never ended? What was the point of my mind producing this limitless supply of horror? And why should such a quiet, blameless life breed such nightmares in the first place?

I don't remember those dreams now. I'm not sure I even remembered them at the time, at least not in terms of images or storylines. But I remembered how they made me feel: the sweats, the nausea, the vertigo, the guilt, the fear.

I suppose things must have begun to change in early 1998. I had paid off my debts by then – my goal had been achieved – but I felt no sense of satisfaction at the thought. Rather, what I felt was an absence. What was the purpose of this pleasure-denying life, now that I was in the black? I began to toy with the idea of quitting my job and writing a novel, or travelling the world. I began drinking again. I used a call girl for the first and only time in my life. My dreams began to seep into the fabric of daily life. I can see now that this was the beginning of another slippery slope. The slope did not have time to steepen because circumstances intervened, but I feel compelled to mention it all the same. Of course I cannot know for certain, but my guess is that, had what happened not happened, I would soon have sought self-destruction in any case. Out of boredom; out of perversity; out of self-loathing; for no good reason at all.

Anyway, this is what happened. On 25 May 1998, the company that owned the magazine announced a wave of redundancies. It was Sam Caine who gave me the news. I had been chosen by management as one of the 'necessary sacrifices'. It was no reflection on my work, Caine said, which was excellent; it was simply an unavoidable response to a serious advertising downturn across the whole group. How did I feel when he told me that? Embarrassed, mostly. Embarrassed for him that he had to use such dessicated, meaningless words; embarrassed for myself that I was now an object of pity.

I don't remember the details of that evening, but I know that I went to a bar in Soho on my own and got drunk. Oddly, what I do remember, quite vividly, is a phrase from *The Communist Manifesto* (read nine years earlier, lying on my bed, with the breathless excitement usually accorded a thriller) repeating in my mind as I sat there and drank. It is the most famous and poetic of all political slogans and, from the perspective of this new century, the most prophetic: '*All that is solid melts into air.*' That phrase echoed sadly through the night air around me as I walked back to the office after closing time, my body swaying but my mind suddenly sober and clear, and told the man on the lobby desk that I had to pick up some belongings I'd forgotten. He looked at me suspiciously and told me to wait a minute, but just then the lift door opened. I heard him shout as I entered and pressed the button for the top floor. After that, the memories grow vague and broken: I see desks falling over, a chair flying through a window . . . the light-sequinned void of London, its streets swimming invitingly six floors below . . . I hear frightened or angry voices, feel iron hands pulling me backwards . . . I see a neon striplight buzzing on the office ceiling. And then, mercifully, unconsciousness.

———

The next couple of months were spent at my parents' house. I really was an invalid now. I have only the vaguest memory of this, but apparently my allergy flared up and I went to see various doctors, one of whom gave me a new batch of pills: the round, sky-blue capsules that I still take now, occasionally. I spent my days in bed, reading, or on the sofa, watching television, or in a deckchair in the garden, sunbathing. Most of the time it was an easy, pleasant existence, but it did get rather boring. And so, in the absence of anything else to occupy my mind, I became quietly obsessed with football.

I had liked football since I was a child, but never fanatically. Now, however, the prospect of that summer's World Cup loomed as a major event in my life. I spent countless hours 'working' on various different line-ups of the England team, experimenting with formations, searching for the perfect balance. I collected fixture wallcharts from the newspapers and predicted the scores of all the group matches, even guessing the identities of the scorers and the minutes in which I thought they would score. I spent so long fantasising about all of this in advance that now, when I try to remember the games from that World Cup, often what comes to mind is not what actually happened, but what I had imagined was going to happen.

Perhaps inevitably, the tournament itself was a letdown. All the same, when England beat Colombia 2–0 to qualify for the second round, I became desperately excited about the possibility of 'us' winning the World Cup. I find it hard to explain the intensity of my feelings in this regard. The general obsession with football is easily comprehensible, I think, but the fervour of my desire for an England victory, though shared by hundreds of thousands of other people, strikes me now as bizarre. I am anything but patriotic. I do not think of myself as, in any meaningful way, English. Any pride I might feel in sharing a birthplace with Shakespeare, Blake and The Beatles, of living on the same island as Stonehenge, the Lakes and Cornwall, is naturally offset by a vague shame and repulsion regarding most other aspects of the country's history and present reality. Yet I suppose my life was so empty then that any chance of glory, however vicarious and momentary, seemed to offer redemption. If only 'we' could beat Argentina in the next round, then love might conquer death, and hope win out over fear.

The Argentina match took place on the evening of Tuesday 30 June. I watched it not at my parents' house, but at a pub in S., a small holiday town on the south coast of England. My parents had rented a chalet for the week, and had invited me along. For the first two days of the holiday I thought about nothing but the coming match. It turned out to be an enthralling game, but England finally lost on penalties and, while other people raged at Beckham and the referee, I exited the pub in a daze. Outside, the air was humid and blue. I felt drunk and depressed and ashamed of my now useless patriotism. I was like a child holding the string of a burst balloon. For a while I wandered aimlessly along the beachfront, then I spotted the lights of a funfair in the distance so I headed towards that.

I found myself in a place that I recognised: a children's adventure land called The Dream Park. I had been there once or twice as a young child, and as I walked around I felt increasingly nostalgic and melancholy. I began to think about my life, and what had happened to me. I was bothered by the suspicion that I must, somewhere along the way, have taken a wrong turn; that I was not the person I ought to be.

I don't remember much about that night, but I remember seeing a red-and-white striped tent with a sign saying Madame Something, Psychic and Fortune-Teller, and hesitating outside the entrance. I did not believe in fortune-telling, of course, but I was drunk and desperate. I needed some reassurance, some guidance about the years to come, which to me at that moment had a dark, cold and arid look, like a desert at night.

The first thing the fortune-teller told me was that I had never found true love. I kept a poker-face. But you will, she said, and soon. You will fall in love with a foreign girl. I might have raised my eyebrows at that. She said some other things, which I soon forgot, but the last thing she said, after peering deep into her crystal ball, was this: 'On or near your thirtieth birthday, something will happen that will change your life forever.'

Outside the tent I laughed, a little self-consciously, then began the long walk back to my parents' chalet. There was rain in the air, and a cold wind was whipping over the sea. I was wearing only a T-shirt and jeans, and I remember shivering as I walked. It was the preciseness of her words that struck me; usually, mystics were so vague. Still, thirty seemed a long way off, and I was fairly sure it was all nonsense. I didn't give the prediction much thought after that – until, three months later, I met Ingrid. And fell in love.

———

So now I sit at the desk in this anonymous room and wonder if any of this means anything. What is the point of mentioning the fortune-teller's prophecy? Am I seriously suggesting it is more than mere coincidence? I don't know if I am or not. 'Rationally', I want to begin, and then I hear the astrologers' mocking laughter. Perhaps all prophecies are self-fulfilling? But then, can we even say that the fortune-teller was right? I am thirty years old, but has my life really changed forever? Has it changed at all?

It is late and I am trying to escape the terrible suspicion that I have simply come full circle. I have been through so many doors since I left the room in which I began this chapter, and yet, here I am still: stuck in the same loop, with the same nagging emptiness inside me. Older, but no wiser. Closer to death but as far away as ever from the truth.

Is this really my life? Are these words really me? I hardly recognise myself at all. The single-minded workaholic; the self-destructive party animal; the boring, self-righteous sub-editor; the depressed England supporter . . . I don't even *like* the people in this chapter. I feel no sympathy for them at all. It is easy and comforting to think of these characters not as me, but as masks I have worn and discarded. And yet they were more than that. I remember thinking those thoughts; I remember feeling those emotions.

The sub-editor in me wants to eliminate these ghosts, to erase them and construct a simpler, clearer storyline, with a single character in whom the reader can believe; with whom the reader can identify. But that sub-editor is wrong. I cannot erase these ghosts, because I am the sum of their parts. I must not simplify and clarify, because I am trying to discover the truth. And this parade of masks – this trail of ex-me's – these are the only clues I have to follow. Besides, what if I were to rip off those masks and throw them away, only to discover that behind them lay . . . nothing at all?

It is hard to avoid the conclusion that the person who began this chapter was an impostor in the first place; that 'I' am not to be found here anywhere, but in the foggy void that lies behind . . . in the unwritten pages of Chapter 3.

Midnight, and I stare through the window. But outside is dark and all I can see is the bright-lit outline of my head: the face a blank, the edges blurred. One question reflects back at me in the glare of the desk lamp. One mystery, still unsolved.

Who am I?

As he opened the curtains, James felt like he had reached the end. Outside the sky was low and dark. Today was the last day of the rental period on the room in Newland Road. Tomorrow, James would be expected to move out. He could, of course, go back to the student accommodation office and try to find another room, but he had no money to spare, and besides . . . a whole month had passed. He had heard nothing from Harrison Lettings. He had discovered no new clues. He had not seen the man in the dark coat since that day at the library. All he had done was remember part of his past, and not, he thought, the part that mattered. His secret, it seemed, was doomed to remain a secret; it was hidden behind a locked door, and James had no idea where the key could be.

He sat up in bed and began to consider his options. There were not many. He could stay here, continue to scrape a living, and hope that something happened. He could travel south to other, more prosperous parts of England. He could go to a new country, like Greece or Chile. Or he could catch the ferry, and drive to Waterland, and ask Ingrid to take him back.

James did think about this. He told himself he would have a good job, a nice house, a pretty girlfriend, but it would, he sensed, be a defeat. From that moment on his life would be marked out for him. Some inner light would be extinguished. No matter what he did afterwards, he would always be a disappointment; not to his parents or to Ingrid or to his future children, perhaps, but to someone more important than all of them.

After several hours of thought, James decided to give himself one last day. If nothing turned up, he would pack his bags tomorrow and drive to London. He would sleep on a friend's floor, find some building work, save money, sell the van, and take a one-way flight to somewhere hot and crowdless. He had a vision of himself living in a beach hut, catching fish from the sea . . .

In such circumstances, he imagined, his lost years would cease to matter. Here, in the rain, in this land of money and things, their emptiness weighed down on him; but there, in the sun, he had the feeling that they would simply evaporate, that without the tug of them he would become another person. Perhaps he would even burn his diaries, jettison all that he had, all that he had been. As he thought this, James had a vision of himself as a child, at a village fair on a sunny day, holding a helium balloon by a string; he saw himself let go of the string and watch, his young eyes filled with awe and sadness and exhilaration, as the balloon floated up, up, up, into the blue, and finally disappeared, to who knew where.

As soon as this decision was made, James felt relieved. He had breakfast in a café and, with nothing to lose now, walked through the park to Lough Street. At number 21, he opened the gate, crossed the short driveway, climbed the three concrete steps, and knocked, hard and impatiently, on the door.

There was no answer, of course. Just to make sure, James rang the bell – one, two, three times, leaning on it the last time for perhaps half a minute. Deep inside the house, he could hear the muffled buzz. He imagined the neighbours must be staring by now, but he no longer cared. He would be gone from this city soon anyway; what difference did it make? He knelt down on the doorstep and shouted mockingly through the letterbox: 'Hello! Anybody home?'

It was then that James noticed the envelope. It had evidently been pushed through the letterbox, but something had jammed its progress. It lay in the door's mouth like a white paper tongue. James could see words on the envelope, handwritten in black ink, but he couldn't read them from that angle, so he pulled the edge of the envelope towards him. It felt light, as though it contained only one sheet of paper, and it had no return address. With a loud metal snap the envelope came free from the letterbox and James read what was written there:

Malcolm Trewvey Esq.
21 *Lough Street*

At first the name struck him as merely strange. It had an old-fashioned ring to it, James thought, like something from Chaucer. But this letter, surely, was proof of a connection between the name and the house, and the more he repeated it in his head, the more familiar it came to seem, until after a minute or so he was nodding and muttering, his breath quickening, as he felt himself on the verge of uncovering some buried memory. Malcolm Trewvey. *Malcolm Trewvey.* James knew that name, he felt sure.

Before leaving, he knocked on the door once again and looked through the letterbox. At first all he saw was the dim, grey hallway, and the bottom of the stairwell. But then he heard a noise – feet smacking rapidly on wooden boards – and saw a figure descend the stairs.

Suddenly frightened, James pulled his face away. His heart was pounding. Without thinking, he shoved the letter in the pocket of his coat and ran down the steps, up the driveway, through the gate, and across the road, where he hid behind a tree. A few moments later, he heard a door bang shut. The man was walking quickly along the pavement on the other side of the street. As before, James followed him.

This time, the man turned right up Green Avenue. He walked past the park and, at the top of the road, went left towards the city centre. Past The Polar Bear, past bookmakers and off-licences and minicab firms. As James followed him, he gripped the envelope tightly in his right hand. The man reached the end of Haight Road and turned into the busy shopping street, walking at a furious pace despite his limp. James ran to catch him up. There was a danger he would be lost to the crowd if he was allowed to get too far away.

Over the pedestrian crossing, past rows of growling cars; through an indoor shopping centre, past potted palm trees and coloured fountains; through the narrowing streets of the old town, past faux-medieval pub signs and darkened doorways . . . for an hour or more, James followed the man. Finally they walked under an archway and into a sunless alley. The buildings were high and close together here, showing their sooty backs: windowless on the ground floor, and the higher windows either blacked-out or draped with net curtains. James began to fear that he was being lured into a trap. The cobbled street was damp with moss from the near-permanent shade, and the air smelled stale and rotten. James could hear his footsteps echo. He began to walk more slowly. Ahead of him, the man disappeared under another archway. Slowly, reluctantly, James followed.

When he emerged through the second archway, he found himself in a dark courtyard. As far as James could see, there was no other exit. The courtyard was as narrow and long as a bus. James and the man were the only ones there. The man was standing outside a shop window at the far end of the court-yard. James didn't need to read the neon sign to know that it was a sex shop: the windows were mirrored with small dark eyeholes just below head-height, so the creeps who assembled there would have to stoop to view the corruption inside. The man was doing exactly this. James allowed himself a cold smile. This, he thought, must be the guilty secret.

James stood like this for some time, watching the man, who was motionless. Eventually James became bored and drew nearer. He moved slightly to the side, in order to catch a glimpse of the man's face, but the man was shading his eyes with his hands, so all James could make out was his ear and cheek and chin. Then James did something reckless. Without any idea how the man might react, he said aloud the name he had been whispering to himself.

'Malcolm Trewvey.'

Not quite immediately, but almost, the man stood up straight. He did not turn around. James held his breath. He watched the man's back, waiting for some violent movement, but none came. James exhaled and looked at the mirrored window. And there he saw the man's face. And he saw that the man was staring at him.

James has a vivid memory of that long, awful second. Neither man looked at the other directly; both stared at the other's inverted double. It was a strange moment, but James did not reflect on this. He was too shocked by the man's face to think of anything else.

The man did not speak or smile or scowl – there was hardly any expression on his face at all – but in his eyes James thought he saw swift judgment, a hint of cold amusement, and then, with a blink and a turn of the head, dismissal. James felt sure the man recognised him; that he knew who James was, and what he wanted. What most disturbed James was the idea, the instinctive certainty, that this man knew his past; that he knew more about James than James himself.

He stood still and silent, not breathing, as the man opened the door of the shop and went inside. The door closed behind him and James exhaled. He was left staring at a lost and frightened-looking figure in the bright mirrored glass who quickly turned away.

In a dark pub in the old town, James sipped a pint of bitter. For a long time he thought nothing. Halfway through his second pint, the shock dissolved and he began to form words in his head. He took the green notebook from his rucksack and wrote the words down.

How old is he, this man, whose name I can only assume is Malcolm Trewvey? My age, perhaps, though something in his eyes seems older, more clued-up. If I had to guess, I would say thirty to thirty-five.

Similar height and build to me. Less athletic maybe, but better-looking: his skin more tanned, his hair more stylishly cut, his clothes more expensive. A kind of innate superiority. The power that comes from knowledge.

In that moment, when our eyes met, it was as though I had shrunk, regressed, to the shy eighteen-year-old I had been when I first came to this city. Something in his glare stripped away the years, the layers of self-confidence. Why?

What is the name of this feeling he gives me? Hatred is only part of it; it's more like envy, but that word seems inadequate. Did I know Malcolm Trewvey when I was a student? If so, then I must have wished myself him.

Even now, I guess, deep down . . . even now I still wish it. I despise myself for thinking this, but it's true. I wish I was Malcolm Trewvey.

James couldn't even bear to read through what he had written. His handwriting was shaky. Feeling nauseous, he closed the notebook and looked at his watch. It was quarter to two. He ordered another pint. The minutes ticked slowly by. He would not be going south, he knew. He could not jettison his past. The plan he had formulated that morning seemed ludicrous and contemptible now he re-examined it. 'Considering his options' was a futile exercise; James had no options. It was his destiny to stay here. And to hope. And to wait.

When he emerged from the pub, it was nearly four o'clock and the sky was the colour of used bathwater. He walked to the docks and stared out at the rough sea, the dark horizon. He thought about the life he had left behind. It seemed unreal. He could not truly believe that Ingrid, their old apartment, her new house, her parents and brother, his former workmates, that all these people and places still existed, endured, went on changing, even now, separated from him only by miles of air and sea. 'Don't do it, mate . . . don't jump!' someone called. James looked around: it was a teenage boy, joking to impress his friends. They were all laughing.

From the corner of his eye, James caught a glimpse of the black walls towering over him, the endless pathways leading him nowhere. The labyrinth. He followed its twists and turns, mesmerised, until, after a while, the walls melted away and he found himself in a street he recognised. He had been in this street a thousand times in daydreams, but not once in reality since that first day. He went to the doorway: HARRISON LETTINGS. What the hell, James thought hopelessly, it can't do any harm. He rang the buzzer and the door clicked open.

The office was busier than the last time he had been here. Again, no one met his eye, so he sat down in a chair by the wall and watched them. The man who had served James was at the same desk; he was talking on the phone, head in hands. A woman in her thirties sat at the middle desk: dyed blonde hair, too much make-up, bustily confident; she was talking to a client. At the far desk, a heavy-set, middle-aged man in a suit was leaning over a younger man, whispering to him and pointing at a computer screen. James sniffed the air: the smell of nervous sweat was still there, but masked by a sweet, feminine perfume. He began to feel sleepy . . .

'Mr Purdew!'

James opened his eyes, shocked by the loudness with which his name had been shouted. The man at the first desk was staring at him, a mixture of anger and relief on his face.

'Yes?'

'Where have you been? We've been trying to get hold of you for weeks!'

The man was standing now, walking around his desk towards James.

'But . . . I gave you my mobile number. Why didn't you call?'

'You wrote it down wrongly. It was one digit short. Mr Harrison, this is the elusive client I was telling you about.'

The middle-aged man looked up and smiled. 'So glad you've finally made it, Mr Purdew. Shall we step into my office?' His voice was smooth and northern-accented, like a bingo-caller's.

Harrison went through a door at the end of the room and held it open for James and the other man. The office was small but plushly furnished. Daylight leaked dimly through a high window. Again James had the disorienting impression that he'd been here before. For some reason there was a picture in his mind of a shelf laden with jars of pills. He sat down in a leather armchair and the two other men smiled at one another.

'Would you like a drink, Mr Purdew?'

'No, thanks, I'm fine. Could you tell me–'

'Your application was accepted by our client within a few days of us sending it, Mr Purdew,' Harrison explained. He had a large, powerful face. 'To the great relief of us all. Unfortunately, we were unable to contact you, so the office has been a hive of anxiety for the past few weeks. Mr Crabtree here has been particularly fraught, waiting for you to call or walk in. And, finally, you have. Cigar?'

James shook his head. He couldn't quite believe what he was hearing. His first reaction was not excitement or relief, but irritation and a kind of lurking guilt. All those wasted hours, those pointless nightmares. And all of it his own fault. 'Are you sure I wrote my number down wrongly?'

Harrison held up a placatory palm. 'It is of no consequence now, Mr Purdew. What's past is past. You are here; that is all that matters. Mr Crabtree, would you telephone our client to let him know that we have located his chosen applicant?' The younger man nodded and slipped out of the office. 'So, Mr Purdew, I believe you know the basic outline of the deal that my client is offering?'

'I think so.'

'Allow me to fill in the details. You will, if you accept his offer, be entitled to a year's free accommodation in the house, plus the payment of all reasonable living and working expenses, to be listed weekly with receipts and presented to Mr Crabtree, who will reimburse you in cash, immediately. If the work you agree to is completed to my client's satisfaction within the allowed time, you will be entitled to 50 per cent of the profit from the sale of the house on the open market. You will also receive an unconditional gift of £1,000 in cash, payable upon signature of the contract, in order that you can make yourself comfortable in the house, which is, I should warn you, in need of considerable work.'

All through this monologue, Harrison had been staring at something on the desk. At this point, he paused, and looked up. James thought he saw something tender, almost fatherly in Harrison's eyes. As soon as he started speaking again, however, they regained their steely glare.

'Which brings me to your part of the bargain. In signing the contract, you will promise to carry out all necessary repair work, rewiring and repainting in accordance with our client's clear and detailed instructions, which you will find attached to the contract. You will also promise to carry out all of the work *alone*, and not to reveal any information about our client or the work you are doing to *anyone*. There are various other rules and regulations, but you can find out about those by reading the contract. Any questions?'

'Am I allowed to know the client's name now?'

A sly smile spread across Harrison's face. 'Mr Purdew, even *I* do not know the client's real name. If he chooses to reveal any such personal information to you, that is a matter for him, but it is beyond the bounds of the contract. As far as Harrison Lettings is concerned, the client will continue to be referred to as, simply, "the client". Does that answer your question?'

'Er, yes.'

'Is there anything else you would like to know?'

There must be something, James thought, but no questions came to mind. The only thing in his head at that moment was the image of the house, its mouth and eyes wide open, the secrets of his past life waiting to be discovered.

'Where do I sign?'

On his way back, James went to The Polar Bear and ordered a bottle of champagne. He sat in the corner and drank it, glass by glass. He had an urge to shout his good news to the drinkers in the public bar, but the memory of that strange night with the astrologers put him off, and anyway the terms of the contract forbade it. He drank some more champagne. Happiness was slow in coming, but he was determined to wait until it did.

Then James remembered his mobile phone; he took it out and switched it off and listened to the new silence. No longer tense, but blissful. Silence: who would have thought it could sound so different? You've done it, James told himself. You've found the key. He put his hand in his trouser pocket, just to make sure. There it was, solid and cold and small. In the other pocket was a wad of £50 notes. James swore to himself that he would not lose either.

Sighing, he held the champagne glass to his eye and gazed through it at the empty lounge. It looked like another world: warm, vast, glamorous, dancing with golden light. In the end James drank so much champagne that he mistook his inebriation for happiness, and left the pub singing and swaying.

Outside it was night-time and he could see more stars than he had ever seen in his life. He walked down Green Avenue and stopped at the Happy Shoppa. From the speakers in the ceiling, Phil Collins was singing something dour and ominous. Fuck you Phil, thought James as he bought wine and chocolate and oranges. The smell of the oranges drove him mad with desire; he couldn't stop sniffing their fragrant skins.

Lough Street looked magical in the sodium lamplight. At number 21, James stood with his hands on the gate and his eyes caressed the house's battered face. Soon those wooden eyelids will open, he thought; soon that mouth will speak. He could have crossed the threshold then, but it was dark and the electrics didn't work. And anyway . . . something held him back. He thought of the man he had followed that morning. Him. Malcolm Trewvey. James shivered at the thought of those all-knowing, all-seeing eyes.

He walked back to Newland Road in the gloom, hurrying a little as he thought he could hear footsteps behind him, and went straight up to his bedroom. He drank some wine and ate an orange, but soon his drunkenness was blurring into fatigue. Too tired to brush his teeth or take an anti-allergy pill, he put on his pyjamas, got in bed and switched off the light. I stayed there for a while, watching his face lose its daytime expressions of hope and fear, suspicion and regret, watching the eyes, mouth, forehead and cheeks as they were wiped clean by the miracle of sleep, and feeling the oddest kind of tenderness. He irritated me, this James Purdew, but I couldn't help sympathising with him, all the same. I took no pleasure from the thought of all the pain he was going to suffer.

As my eyes adjusted to the darkness, I lifted up the duvet and stared at the familiar contours of his body, the young muscles still enviably taut, curled into the unfamiliar shape of a question mark. I had never seen him sleep before. It was a strange experience. I could see the outline of his penis and balls inside the pyjamas, and laughed silently as the penis grew hard and he moaned. I knew what he was dreaming about. I knew *who* he was dreaming about. And he, even now, didn't have a clue.

III
THE WRITING IN THE WALL

The next morning, having packed all his possessions into the van, James drove to Lough Street. He parked at the edge of the road, under a chestnut tree, and sat there for some time staring at the house through the side window.

He remembered the long, lonely hours he had spent in the cab of this van, staring, just as he was now, at the familiar, damaged face of that house. Now, all was identical, and all was changed beyond recognition. It was a strange feeling, suddenly to have what he had so desperately, and for so long, desired. James felt nervous, apprehensive. Perhaps he had been wrong to want this? Might not the idea, so inviting, of the house – and the past it contained – be some kind of trap? For a moment he considered the possibility of taking the £1,000 and escaping. It was not too late. The airport beckoned, and beyond it a life of sunshine and freedom. Yet the very fact that the contract allowed this – the gift was 'unconditional', it said – made him more reluctant to do it.

When, eventually, he forced himself to move, James felt as if he had walked on to a stage; as though a thousand eyes were secretly watching him. On the doorstep he turned around, but the street was empty and he saw no faces in the windows of other houses. He listened: distant traffic sounds; leaves rustling in the wind; a telephone ringing somewhere. He put the key in the lock and turned.

The door opened without being pushed. Daylight made a

path through the dark, cold hallway. James took a step forward and unthinkingly called out 'Hello?' He listened: no sound but that telephone, still stubbornly ringing. He wondered which house it was coming from. One of his next-door neighbours, he guessed; it sounded quite close.

He removed the key from the lock but left the front door open. The hallway smelled of dust and damp. The first thing he needed to do was unboard the windows, to let in some light and air, but for some reason that was not what he did. As though hypnotised, he touched the powdery wallpaper with his fingertips and walked, dream-slow, through the gloom. When he reached the end of the hallway, he pushed open the door of the sitting room and stared in shocked silence at the sofa, the coffee table, the armchair, the television. Instinctively he stroked the warm leather back of the armchair and began to hum a familiar tune, and then he stopped. It was all *exactly* as he remembered it, even though, until that moment, he'd had absolutely no memory of it at all. The same furniture, the same wallpaper; nothing moved or altered. In its shadowed corners the room looked sepia, like an old photograph, but through the partially boarded rear window came a shaft of sun, so that closer to where he stood the light was golden, illuminating vast old spiderwebs that hung from the ceiling like veils. James had the sensation that he had stepped into the past; as though, in this room, time had been preserved in aspic. Memories came to him as he stood there – vivid images, almost physical in their intensity – but they were too brief and fragmentary to tell him anything other than what he already knew: that he had been here before; that the house was a clue.

It was then that he noticed something peculiar: the telephone was still ringing. It was not a modern ringtone, but an old-fashioned, bell-like drone; a melancholy sound that made James think of empty corridors in government buildings, closed hotels in winter, lost Sundays in the 1970s . . . the unanswerable call of the past. But why didn't it stop? Didn't his neighbours have answer machines?

Puzzled, he walked back down the hallway and looked at the place where his memory told him that the telephone used to be: on the wall, a couple of metres from the front door. What he saw was a padlocked wooden box, the size of a child's coffin. This was new. James touched the wood: it was roughly made, unvarnished but solid. He put his ear to the join and quickly pulled it away. It was *this* phone that was ringing. He looked around for a key that would fit the padlock, but could find nothing.

The ringing made him anxious. Why couldn't whoever was calling understand that there was nobody home? Why didn't they just hang up? *Unless*, he thought . . . unless it was someone who knew he was here. He went out to the doorstep again and looked closely at the other houses. No curtains twitched. There was a phone box twenty metres down the road. James ran towards it, but it was empty. He walked back to the house, staring wildly around. By the time he got back, the phone had stopped ringing.

It took James most of the morning to pull the boards from the ground-floor windows and move his things into the house. Now that he looked more closely, he could see that there *had* been changes, after all. The sofa's stuffing was all over the floor and there were patches of mould on the walls. James couldn't imagine what Malcolm Trewvey had been doing in the house, but he certainly hadn't been cleaning it.

He had already decided to attack the house one floor at a time. It was a large place, and he didn't want to daunt himself by exposing all the work that needed doing before he'd even started. And for some reason, the thought of going upstairs gave him vertigo. Besides, a quick investigation of the ground floor revealed that there was everything here that he would need to live.

There were two bedrooms, each with a window looking out on the street, and the large sitting room, with a window looking out on the back garden. There was a small cupboard under the stairs: James found a little door inside this cupboard, and when he opened it he saw blackness, smelled damp and cold ashes. The cellar, he thought, closing the little door. Adjoining the sitting room was a small windowless bathroom with a sloped ceiling, and the long kitchen, which was a single-floor extension to the house, running alongside part of the back garden. The kitchen had a clear plastic roof – yellowed and dirty now, of course – which made it both the lightest and coldest room in the house.

The outside door of the kitchen gave on to the garden, which was almost as big as James remembered it. In contrast to the inside of the house, the garden had been carefully maintained: the grass was no more than a few centimetres high, and the lawn's sole occupant – an old apple tree – was in good health. Golden-green, nearly ripe apples weighed down its branches. The garden was bordered on three sides by tall wooden fences; at the far end was a shed, in which he found a lawnmower and an axe, and next to the shed was a gate which opened into an alley lined with lock-up garages, from where, James knew, you could cut through to the surrounding streets.

He was surprised by how well he knew the house, how perfectly it fitted the hole in his memory. It was almost as if he had lived here. But could that be true? He closed his eyes and tried to think back, but there was a blank, a hole, that made him reel when he got too close. With relief, James gave up trying to remember. And then, as if to prove that it was still functioning, his memory flashed up a fragment of information that he had once heard or read somewhere: that the metaphor Freud had used to describe memories was *objects placed in the rooms of a house*.

James looked around again at the sofa, the coffee table, the armchair, the television. Don't worry, he told himself, your past is somewhere in this house. Now that you're here, it will all come back.

James worked hard that day. First he drove the van out to an industrial estate on the edge of the city, where, Harrison had informed him, there was a ParaDIYse store. James bought a generator, an industrial vacuum cleaner, a hurricane lamp, overalls, a facemask, gloves, workboots, rat poison, disinfectant, buckets, sponges, and an oil heater. Then he went to Harrison Lettings, filled in an expenses form, handed over his receipts, and watched as Mr Crabtree unsmilingly counted out the £50 notes. Back at the house he started up the generator and vacuumed the bedroom, the sitting room and the entrance hall. When he'd finished he was covered with sweat and dust. There was no hot water in the house, so James cycled to the municipal swimming pool and used the showers there.

Refreshed, he bought a takeaway pizza and some refrigerated beer. It was a bright evening. He ate the pizza in the garden, sitting with his back to the apple tree. When he'd finished, he drank a bottle of beer and watched the clouds on the western horizon turn a delicate, unearthly shade of pink. Above him the half-moon was clearly visible in the pale blue sky. It was so peaceful, James began to wonder if he was living in a ghost road, but when he listened closely he could hear children laughing, music playing. Again he felt that strange mixture of hope and fear: what was he doing here, alone in a derelict house, in a city where he knew no one? He didn't have a clue where his life was leading. And yet, at that moment, he felt fine. The beer was cold, the sky clear, the air fresh and warm. It was comfortable, leaning against the apple tree.

It was such a beautiful moment that James wished he could stop time, pin it down, fix it immutably in his memory. He worried that if he did not record the moment, it would quickly vanish into the depths of his mind, like a floating pollen seed drowned in a river. And yet, if he went now to fetch his black notebook and wrote a description of the cloud patterns in the sky, the tree shadows on the grass, the warm air, the sweet calm he felt, the moment itself would escape him, he knew, and he would be left with nothing but a few scribbled, inadequate words.

Paralysed by uncertainty, James sat there, in the shade of the

apple tree, wondering what he should do. Perhaps if he memo-
rised the scene now, he would be able to write it down later,
before it fogged over in his mind. He looked up at the sky. The
cloud resembled an elephant, he thought, or perhaps a domed
building. Yet even now it was changing, mutating, thin wisps of
translucent steam peeling off and creating a sort of long tail,
the edges of which seemed to vanish before James's eyes. He
was mesmerised for a moment by these little disappearings –
where did the cloud-edges *go*? – and when he looked again, the
elephant-cloud no longer existed. It had altered, vanished,
entered the past. Fucking hell, thought James, time is so relent-
less! It's always now, and yet . . . what is now? In French the
word was *maintenant* – literally, 'hand-holding'. In other
words, the present was the time that you held in your hand:
here, solid, graspable. But this was a lie, James thought: you
could no more hold the present than you could grasp the moving water in a river. Give the present the briefest thought or
reflection and it eludes you. The only way to live in the present
is to forget trying to grasp it, to float in its current, not to think
at all . . .

James frowned. Without his noticing, and contrary to the
normal laws of time, the air seemed to have grown warmer, the
sky bluer. He looked at the back wall of the house and saw that
the bricks were glowing, the window panes a dazzle of silverish
gold. The skin of his legs and arms was now bare and warm in
the sunlight, and there were voices around him, laughing, whispering. A blanket on the grass before him; the shape of his own
black shadow. He leaned back, smiled, and then . . . a silence,
another shadow. He looked up and the hairs on his forearm
stood erect, his heart plunged. What was happening to him?
What was it he was feeling? The grass and the tree and the sun
and the sky and the bricks of the house all blurred and merged
together, close to his face, the green, brown, yellow, blue and
red mixing until they were black.

James opened his eyes and shivered with cold. His mouth
was dry and his hands clammy. I must have fallen asleep, he

thought. I must have been dreaming. He looked around, at the darkening garden, and felt a familiar despair. The sun had set. The beautiful moment had passed. It had slipped through his fingers just as he knew it would.

Sighing, he finished his beer and walked back to the house. On the way, he felt something hard underfoot. He looked down and saw a flat rectangular stone. There were lines carved into it: a symbol of some kind, or a word. James couldn't make it out in the darkness, so he traced the letters with his fingertips, reading blindly. It said, ID.

He thought of Freud's unconscious: if memories were objects placed in the rooms of a house, he wondered, then where was the id located – down in the cellar? He thought of the word 'identity' and its strange double meaning: the quality of one thing being uniquely one thing; the quality of two or more things being the same as each other. Only after thinking all this did James remember the story he had read in the newspaper: of the student who had fallen to his death in this garden. And the student's name: Ian Dayton.

In the bedroom he lay in his sleeping-bag, on the futon mattress, and read through the client's instructions again. The most unusual demand concerned the colour of the house: the client had specified that everything – floorboards, walls, windowframes, doors, ceilings – was to be painted white. James didn't care about the aesthetics, but he objected on practical grounds: he knew from experience that it was almost impossible to keep white things white. Still, he thought, the client is always right.

He yawned and scanned the small print. It was then that he noticed something which had slipped his attention the first time. The 'telephone box', as it was called, was to be left intact (and painted white, of course). It was not to be opened or damaged in any way. *Under no circumstances is the telephone to be answered.* This struck James as rather a strange rule – why not simply disconnect the line? – but he knew there was no point

141

complaining. He had signed the contract; he would have to live with the consequences.

Before going to sleep, James took the hurricane lamp to the bathroom. He tried the tap. Water came out in violent spurts. It was yellowish and lukewarm, but it didn't taste too bad, and James was able to brush his teeth, wash his face and swallow his anti-allergy pill. He was meant to take these pills once a week, but James couldn't remember the last time he had taken one; perhaps in Amsterdam? The thought that he had missed his medication made James feel guilty, but it was, he reasoned, a long time since he had suffered an allergic reaction. In fact, he couldn't even remember what it was he was supposed to be allergic to. In any case the bottle of pills was nearly empty, and he had lost the address to which he was meant to write in order to renew his supply. Never mind, James told himself; if you get ill you can always go and see a doctor.

Back in the bedroom, he turned off the lamp. A feeling of loneliness engulfed him. Outside the wind was moaning. He stood at the window and gazed out into the street. He could see his van, at the other side of the road, and he wondered if, those days when he had sat in the van, watching the house, the man in the dark coat – the man he called Malcolm Trewvey – had stood here in the bedroom and watched *him*. If only there were someone in the van watching me now, he thought, I wouldn't feel so alone. Somewhere upstairs a loose windowframe banged in the wind. James tried not to think of the gravestone he had found in the garden.

He got in his sleeping-bag. The bedroom had no curtains so the walls were stained orange by the sodium lamps outside. He thought of Ingrid and wished she were here, if only for tonight. He imagined her inside the sleeping-bag, her skin warm against his, and masturbated. Just before he came, the hallway phone started ringing, and then, after five minutes or so, it stopped.

For the first time since moving to the house, he was not woken by daylight. As he opened his eyes, James saw the white curtains he had hung the day before and sighed with relief. His body ached, but he had given himself the weekend off; he had worked hard for the past five days and he deserved it.

What had woken him was a strange noise in the hallway. He got up to see what it was. On the doormat lay a pile of post: the first James had received at this address. He picked it up and took it to the kitchen. As he walked through the hallway and the sitting room, he paused to admire the cleanness of the walls, floors and ceilings. He breathed in: no dust, no damp, no rot. And if the smell of the disinfectant was still a little strong . . . well, that would fade.

He lit the gas under the kettle and looked at the letters. There was one addressed to him, from his parents; one addressed to 'The Resident', which he opened and which turned out to be a telephone bill; and one addressed to Malcolm Trewvey Esq. It was identical to the envelope that James had removed from the letterbox – and which was now pinned to the kitchen wall – but this time the word URGENT was scrawled across the top. James had decided to open the first letter today, as it was still unclaimed, but when he saw this second letter, he changed his mind. He felt guilty for not having made greater efforts to pass on the first letter to its intended recipient. What had he been thinking?

He made a pot of tea and some toast, and unpinned the first letter from the wall. He would take both letters to Harrison Lettings today. Crabtree could send them on to Malcolm Trewvey. Relieved at having made this decision, James sat down to eat his breakfast and studied the phone bill: no calls made in the past three months; only the line rental to pay. He would take this bill to Harrison Lettings too. He didn't see why he should pay for a service he was not allowed to use.

He finished the toast and read the letter from his parents. It was, as usual, full of their 'news', but it didn't really say anything. The true purpose of the letter, James knew, was to express their concern for him. Why had he split up with that nice Dutch girl? Where was his life going? Was he in some kind of trouble? How could they help? None of this was explicit, but he could sense it in the tortured politeness of the phrasing, the things that were not mentioned.

Reading the letter, James felt bad. He was sorry to be such a source of anxiety for his parents, who loved him and whom he loved. But there was really nothing he could do except write back and tell them he was fine. That was what he did. It was a short letter, though, and James worried that it would not set his parents' minds at rest. So he added a postscript: 'What are you doing for Christmas? I was thinking of coming down . . . let me know.' He guessed and hoped that they would be busy – they always planned these events long in advance – but at least they would be happy to know that he wanted to see them.

After breakfast, he posted the letter to his parents and drove to the city centre. At the Harrison Lettings office he gave the envelopes marked 'Malcolm Trewvey Esq.' to Crabtree, who sighed wearily. 'It's nothing to do with us, Mr Purdew.'

'But it says urgent.'

'The client was perfectly clear about our duties. Anything not covered by the terms of the contract is beyond the bounds of our responsibility.'

'So what am I supposed to do with them?' James demanded. 'Throw them in the bin?'

'Calm down, Mr Purdew. What makes you think they are meant for the client, anyway? As far as I'm aware, his name is unknown to you.'

James didn't know what to say. 'I just feel sure they are.'

Crabtree looked at him sceptically. 'Well, why don't you put them in a drawer and wait for the client to collect them?'

Because they're driving me mad with curiosity, James wanted to say. But he didn't. He handed the phone bill and his expenses form to Crabtree and watched as he counted out the money.

Harrison saw James and walked over to shake his hand. 'How goes it, Mr Purdew?'

James guessed he was talking about the house. 'Well, it's cleaner than it was. And I've got the gas and hot water working.'

'The client told me he was satisfied with your progress thus far.'

James, startled, said: 'He's seen it?'

Harrison hesitated. 'I have no idea, Mr Purdew. He merely said he was satisfied with your progress.'

James thought: he's been spying on me. The thought made him fearful and angry. At the same time, he felt strangely flattered by the attention. Malcolm Trewvey was spying on him. Malcolm Trewvey was satisfied with his progress. James remembered the face of the man he had seen reflected in the sex shop window. He had looked so sure of himself, James thought; so sure of *me*. How sweet my revenge if I could uncover his guilty secret.

He put the letters side by side on the kitchen table and stared at them while he waited for the kettle to boil. His heart was speeding. Calm down, he told himself, you're only making a cup of tea. He went outside in the garden and looked around. The sky was low and grey. A sparrow chattered from high up in the apple tree. The smell of cooking came from one of the neighbouring houses. From the corner of his eye, James noticed a movement in an upstairs window. He span around quickly and stared up at the attic: the window was half open, but as far as he could see the room beyond was empty. I really ought to go upstairs and shut the window, he thought. Otherwise the rain will get in.

Back in the kitchen, the kettle was boiling furiously. James switched off the gas and stared at the letters again. He made himself a cup of tea and stirred in some milk. He picked up the letters and weighed them in his hands. He span around quickly and stared out into the garden.

Nobody.

I'm getting paranoid, he thought.

Feeling like a real detective, he held the first envelope above the kettle's spout until it was slightly damp, then slid a butter knife under the flap. It came away easily. He sat down at the kitchen table and shook out the contents. It was not, as he had thought, a single piece of paper, but several small squares. On each square was printed a letter of the alphabet. A letter full of letters, thought James. He put them all the right way up and, without thinking about the order in which he was arranging the letters, placed them side by side. This is what they said:

V S M E L A G T O

James had no idea what this could mean, but he had read enough detective novels to realise it must be a clue. Could Malcolm Trewvey have sent him the two letters, in order to test whether he would open them? Might these nine letters, then, be nothing but a red herring? It was possible. But it was also possible that the letters really had been intended for Malcolm Trewvey, and that these letters inside represented some kind of information . . . some kind of code. The wheels in James's mind were whirring now. One word, or several words? He experimented by moving the letters around and writing down the results in his green notebook. This is what he wrote:

GLAT MOVES

146

STEAM GLOV
LOVE STAG M
SLAVE TOM G
SAVE TO GLM
LOAVES GMT

There were a finite number of possible combinations, yet James could find nothing that seemed to make sense. Not enough vowels, he thought. He wondered for a moment if there were an 'I' missing, but the envelope was empty. This was all there was. The message had to be here. He worked for another hour, getting nowhere, and was beginning to think the message itself must be in code, when he noticed something odd. He had, without meaning to, put the letters in four groups. This is what they said:

MT
LS
AV
EGO

It was EGO that he noticed first; more Freud, he thought. He looked the word up in the dictionary and discovered that its definition was 'the part of the mind that reacts to reality and has a sense of individuality'. That was interesting, but if it was a clue, then James wasn't sure what the clue could be telling him. However, as he looked at the letters on the table and thought about this, something about those first three pairs of letters snagged on his memory. He had the feeling that he had seen them somewhere before, but he couldn't remember where.

Tired of thinking, he went out in the garden. For a while, he walked around aimlessly, breathing the cool, humid air and looking at the trees and houses visible above the top of the surrounding fence. He recognised these views – each slotted into place in the jigsaw in his mind – and yet they did not bring the rush of memories for which he had been hoping when he first saw the house from the outside.

It was odd: he had imagined that simply re-entering this place would unlock the black box of the past. And in a sense it had. But the first black box had opened to reveal another, also locked, inside it. James's next task, he knew, was to find the key to the second black box. But he couldn't escape the suspicion that all he would discover inside it was another, and another, and another . . . a Russian doll of locked black boxes. Russian dolls were not infinite, however; there was always a last one, the tiniest and most important of all. Inside that one, James thought, I will discover the secrets of my past.

He stood under the apple tree and looked up into its branches. The apples appeared to be ripe. He reached his hand up to the nearest one and pulled; it came away with the stalk intact. It was the size of a cricket ball, quite heavy and perfectly firm. James didn't know what kind of apple it was, but it certainly looked good: golden-green with hints of red, its skin not too rough, not too glossy. It had a strong, sharp scent that made his mouth water. Instinctively he glanced around – might the garden's fruit be forbidden? – but there was nobody, and besides he could not remember any mention of apples in the contract.

He bit into it: crunchy and bittersweet. And, beyond the simple pleasure of the apple's taste in his mouth, James felt something else. A great and foreign emotion was rising inside him; an emotion he had experienced before but had, until now, forgotten. He had no name for this emotion, but it was a bit like the happy sadness he felt when he listened to The Go-Betweens, only much more profound and overpowering; as though what he felt when he listened to The Go-Betweens was but a faint echo – the glimpse of a reflected shadow – of the original emotion.

Where had it come from, this wave of feeling? James sensed that it was connected to the taste of the apple, but that it went far beyond it, could not be of the same nature. What did it mean? How could he grasp it? He looked at the apple and saw, in the perfectly white bitemark he had left, a little pink stain . . . a trace of blood. He closed his eyes and the garden whirled

148

around him in a multitude of weathers and was, for an eye-blink, populated with figures at once strange and familiar, evening sunlight, distant music, some sweet and heavy perfume, a dark-haired girl with her lips near his, all of which instantly dissolved again into blackness. James opened his eyes in astonishment. What had been happening to him? What had he been doing? He had been *remembering*.

Or had he? When he tried to resummon the image that had flashed up in his mind, he began to question the authenticity of what he had seen. Was this a real memory or was it merely the kind of thing he *expected* to remember? A thin, dark-haired girl with her lips near his. This might be nothing more than wish-fulfilment. And yet he had certainly felt something. The emotion that had invaded him had been unbidden, unexpected. Whatever tricks of imagination had embellished it, there was surely a core of truth there. James felt a surge of hope and was about to bite into the apple again, when he realised he couldn't move. He was remembering something else: the odd thing that had happened to time when he was sitting in the garden on his first afternoon in the house; the way the sun had seemed to grow briefly warmer, the sounds of other voices he had heard, and then that sudden silence and a glimpsed shadow on the grass. Yet, while the vision of the dark-haired girl filled James with hope, the silence and the shadow gave rise to a different emotion. He wondered what it could be. And then his memory supplied the name. It was fear.

Hope and fear. James thought about these emotions. He had always considered them to be opposites: one white, the other black; one good, the other bad. But he sensed now that they were more like reflections, each an inverted copy of the other. Or two sides of the same object. What is fear, after all, but hope in the dark? What is hope but fear bathed in light? Implicit in all hope is the fear that the hope will not be realised; implicit in all fear is the hope that the fear will not be realised. Hope/fear must be like the moon, then, thought James: we can see it half, full or eclipsed, bright or occluded, blood-red or golden . . . but always, behind this, is the same grey sphere.

But where had all this come from? He blinked. What had made him start thinking about hope and fear? What was it he was remembering, when he bit into the apple? James frowned for a moment, racking his brains, but it had gone. It had slipped his mind.

He ate the rest of the apple, then realised he was still hungry, so he stood up and walked towards the kitchen, thinking of the lunch he would make. Bacon and eggs, maybe, or spaghetti bolognaise . . . Not looking where he was going, James again stepped on the flat stone. As he did so, he felt a chill run through him. He looked down and those two letters looked back up at him: ID.

The chill faded and James had an idea.

He sat at the kitchen table and stared at the letters written on the squares of paper. MT, LS, AV. He felt sure he was right now: these must be initials; the initial letters of people's names. But which people? And where had he seen those combinations of letters before? His mind was blank so he began to make lunch. He chopped an onion, which made him cry. He boiled water for the spaghetti, fried the onion with butter and minced beef, and warmed up a tin of tomato sauce. It began to rain. The drops of water sounded heavy as stones through the plastic roof of the kitchen. James opened a bottle of red wine and poured himself a glass.

And then, for no apparent reason, it came to him.

He ran to the bedroom and picked up the cardboard box in which he kept all documents pertaining to the investigation. In black capital letters on the lid, he had written the word 'CLUES'. He took the box to the kitchen and looked through its contents. He found what he was looking for without difficulty: the print-out of the story from the newspaper, 'TRAGIC TRUTH BEHIND PICNIC HORROR'. And there, in the fourth paragraph, were the names: Lisa Silverton and Anna

Valere. LS and AV. James's pulse quickened when he read the name 'Anna' and thought of the dark-haired girl he had seen in his vision. Could it be more than coincidence?

Focus, he told himself. There's one more name to find. He looked at the two letters again – MT – and then his eyes slid to the envelope from which the letters had come. *Malcolm Trewvey*. James laughed, and banged the table with his fist. Of course! It was so obvious. How could he not have seen it before?

Malcolm Trewvey, Lisa Silverton, Anna Valere. The names of three of the people living in the house when Ian Dayton fell to his death. He read through the newspaper report again. There was no mention of Malcolm Trewvey in there, but there was a quote from a friend 'who wished to remain anonymous'. James smiled. How typical. The desire for anonymity spelled out his identity more clearly than any name.

All through lunch, James couldn't stop grinning. It was true that he still didn't understand how these names linked with the word 'EGO'. It was true that he still didn't know his enemy's dark secret. But these were only details; they could wait. The important thing was that he was getting closer. Closer to the truth. Closer to the centre of the maze.

That evening, James had a bath, shaved, brushed his teeth and put on some clean clothes, then walked to the union bar; he wanted to celebrate the breakthrough he had made with the letter of letters. He walked unhesitatingly, unerringly, even in the dark, and as he grew closer he felt a tight fluttering in his chest, as though a small bird was trapped in there, trying to escape. I must have come this way many times before when I was younger, he thought.

Campus felt like a different place at night: the cold air rich with scents and laughter, and the buildings looming vast and mysterious, more like holes than objects. When he reached the top of the steps that led to the union bar, James flashed his old student ID card at the doorman and, to his surprise, was allowed to enter. He pushed open the double doors and the sound of dance music throbbed from the large dark room.

The air smelled damp and faintly acidic, and the floor was sticky with some kind of black grease. In the queue for the bar, a girl in stilettos stood on his foot and a man spilled beer down his shirtfront. James ordered two pints and drank them quickly by the side of the dancefloor, watching the mass of bodies writhing under strobe lights. Everybody here was so strange, he noticed: their skin too smooth, their eyes too wild, their voices too loud, their bodies too alive. Young people. It was strange to think that he too had once looked and sounded like that.

He had a couple more pints, but continued to feel bored and

out of place. He was about to go home when he noticed another man standing alone against a wall, looking like James imagined he himself must look: older and less happy than the people around him. James approached the man, and was surprised to discover that he knew him. It was Graham, from the house on Newland Road.

'Hello Graham,' said James. 'Remember me?'

Graham glanced at James, then looked away. 'What do you want?'

James was taken aback by his rudeness. 'I just wanted to talk to you.'

'About what?' His voice was sullen and expressionless.

'There's no need to be like that. Let me buy you a drink.'

Graham didn't respond, but James bought him one anyway, and placed it on the bar. Graham took his pint without a word and began to sip it.

'So . . . what are you doing here? Doesn't seem like your scene.'

'I'm a senior resident. I have to look after the first-years.'

It was then that James noticed his name badge. 'Graham Oliver – Senior Resident – 14 Newland Rd', it said. To begin with, James didn't click. He went on making small talk for a bit longer, while Graham continued to ignore him. After a while, though, the muddled, beer-blurred synapses in his brain forged the connection: *Graham Oliver*. It was his name James had seen in the report on the suicide. He had been Ian Dayton's roommate. Without thinking the matter through any further, James blurted out: 'Didn't you use to live in Lough Street?'

Graham stared at him. 'So?'

'Number twenty-one.'

'What do you want?'

For some reason, Graham's defensiveness, his blatant rudeness, made James feel bolder. He felt himself becoming a private detective again, seeing the clues all around. Graham had been there at the time of the tragedy, a witness. As hostile as he seemed, he might well be able to help James discover the true nature of Malcolm Trewvey's guilty secret. 'I wanted to ask you about what happened there. Ten years ago, wasn't it?'

James watched Graham's face when he said this, but he could see no evidence of surprise. All he noticed was a slight cringe, as though he'd touched Graham in a sensitive place.

'Why are you doing this?'

'I'm a private detective,' James said. 'So, shall we go and talk somewhere quiet or do you want to have this conversation in front of your first-years?'

The next thing James remembers, he and Graham were locked in a toilet cubicle together. Graham was silent, his arms folded, his back to the door, staring angrily at James, who was thinking of what questions to ask. James stumbled, almost falling over the toilet, and laughed as he regained his balance. He was more drunk than he'd realised, and this made him feel slightly alarmed, but he knew there was no going back now. He had to pursue this line of inquiry. He had to keep probing.

Graham was wearing a white shirt with sweat stains under the arms and crease-covered brown trousers. In an attempt to lighten the atmosphere, James made a joke. Something about people imagining the two of them were taking drugs.

'Just ask your fucking questions,' Graham hissed.

James saw suddenly what a bad position he had put myself in: locked in a toilet with a very large man who seemed to harbour an intense and unreasonable dislike for him. He decided to play it cool.

'All right,' he said. 'What is your full name?'

'What?'

'Your full name. Is it just Graham Oliver or . . .?'

'Yes.'

'It's not Edward Graham Oliver, by any chance?' Graham Oliver stared at him blankly. 'Or Everett Graham Oliver?'

'Are you pissed?' Graham snorted. 'I don't have the faintest fucking clue what you're on about.'

James had been thinking, almost unconsciously, of the letters, EGO, but now, realising his mistake, he changed the subject. 'How did you like living in 21 Lough Street, Graham? I'm there now, you know. It's a nice house. Beautiful garden.'

'What the fuck do you want?'

'The truth,' James replied. 'Tell me about Ian Dayton. How did you find him, as a roommate?'

'You've got a tape-recorder! You're a journalist!'

James was beginning to think that Graham was a bit of a psycho. The way he kept getting angry about nothing . . . or perhaps it wasn't nothing. Perhaps he was not mad, but guilty? Perhaps he actually had something to hide? Something larger than James had yet imagined.

'No tape-recorder.' He opened his jacket to prove it. 'And I'm not a journalist – I'm a private detective.'

Graham looked unconvinced. 'If I answer your questions, you've got to promise you'll never bother me again.'

'All right, I promise. I'll never bother you again. So answer the question. How did you get on with Ian Dayton?'

There was a long pause. Graham had turned his back on James now. He was staring at the door of the cubicle. James could see the thick dark hairs on the back of his neck and smell his acrid body odour. 'I didn't have a problem with Ian Dayton.'

'Why did he commit suicide, do you think?'

A short, bitter-sounding laugh. 'I have no idea.'

'All right. How would you describe his relationship with Anna Valere?'

'Jesus.'

'Answer the questions and you'll never see me again. I promise.'

'He liked her, I suppose.'

'And what about you? Did you like her?'

A long silence. 'I don't see what this has got to do with . . .'

'All right. So tell me about the other people in the house. Was there anyone you *didn't* like?'

'Fucking hell,' Graham said. His shoulders were shaking; James couldn't tell if he was trying not to laugh or not to cry.

James wondered whether he should mention Malcolm Trewvey's name, but he decided against it. It was best to stay vague, he thought, to let Graham reveal the details. 'Was there someone in that house you blame for Ian Dayton's death?'

Silence. Heavy breathing.

'Yes or no?'

'Yes.'

For some reason Graham was enunciating all his words in the most heavily sarcastic voice imaginable. Yet James had the feeling he was telling the truth, all the same.

'That person, Graham, the person you blame . . . do you know where he is now?'

Graham turned on James then, his eyes furious, unstable. 'What do you think?'

'I don't know,' James replied, as calmly as he could. 'That's why I'm asking you.'

Graham turned away again, with a hollow laugh. 'Yes.'

James felt his throat grow thick. He was close to the truth now. 'Does he live in this city?'

'You know he does.'

James was so shocked, he couldn't speak. How did Graham know that he had seen Malcolm Trewvey? Suddenly he felt his ignorance, his amnesia, as a curse. This glowering stranger knew more about him than he knew about himself. There was a long silence. Graham turned to face him and said contemptuously, 'Is that it?'

James looked at his face – the little red mouth like a tiny wound in the forest of black beard, the large nose, the vulnerable eyes – and felt a tremor of recognition. Had he known Graham, before? The question came out of his mouth before he could think about it.

'Why do you hate me?'

Graham's eyes turned red then. It sounds unlikely, but that is what James remembers: a kind of smoky demonic glow emanating from the irises and staining the whites. The skin of his face swelled purple; his lips were white and trembling. He

looked like something from a horror film. This can't have lasted more than a second or two, but it remained seared on
James's memory for several weeks afterwards.

The next thing he recalls is a black shadow across his eyes
and the sensation of falling. He remembers the cold shock of
the porcelain banging his lips and teeth and the taste of blood
in his mouth. After that there was a blank, and then James was
looking at his face, distorted and ugly, like the face of someone
else, in a mirror, and walking home through darkness, coat
pulled tight around his shivering body.

Back at the house, James gently washed his mouth and went
to bed. He was exhausted but he couldn't sleep. His speeding
heart kept him awake, and so did that unanswered question:
Why does Graham Oliver hate me? He turned the question
over in his mind as he lay there, trying to recall if he could have
done anything to offend Graham during his time at the house
in Newland Road. Yet he had been so preoccupied then, he
couldn't really bring anything to mind. He found it difficult
even to remember having had a conversation with him. Perhaps Graham had felt he was being snubbed? Yet James was
sure that Graham was the one who, from the beginning, had
been morose and unfriendly. So what was his problem? Was he
paranoid or was he hiding something?

After several hours of dark thoughts, James finally got up
and took a painkiller. He made himself a cup of tea and drank
it. It was all too weird, too disturbing. The best thing, he decided, would be to forget all of this – these clues, these memories
– and concentrate instead on his work in the house. As soon as
he had made that decision, James felt relieved. He went back to
bed and fell asleep almost immediately.

For the next week he didn't leave the house. The world seemed a dark and threatening place now, and anyway it was raining. He worked each day until his skin was ghostly with plasterdust and his tongue felt like sand.

On Sunday evening, lying in the bath, James admitted to himself that he would have to venture outside again tomorrow. The thought made him nervous, but he needed fresh food; he needed a steamer and a sander. He had also been thinking of buying a bed: his futon was uncomfortable, and the only way he could relax his bruised muscles was to lie in deep water, as he was now, replenishing it from the hot tap every ten minutes or so.

He had been in the bath for half an hour, and his fingers were wrinkled. There was no sound except for the hum of the generator and the echoing gurgles of the bathwater. He finished his beer and dropped the empty bottle over the side, then closed his eyes and sank below the water line. At peaceful moments such as this James sometimes found himself wondering about the clues he had discovered: the initials in the envelope addressed to Malcolm Trewvey, and what they might mean. But these thoughts were inseparable in his mind from the vicious beating he had received, the inexplicable hatred of Graham Oliver, and all his private investigations ended in darkness, confusion, fear. It was better to leave the past in the past, James told himself, to think only of the present.

But the present, for James, was a hard, dull place: an unvarying landscape of pallet knives and wallpaper and dust. And so, with the past off limits, he found himself daydreaming again about various possible branchings of the future. He imagined the house complete, a vision in white, and the money he would receive from its sale. He imagined different amounts of money, and how he might spend them. He imagined again a hot, unpeopled island, with his hut on the beach and his fishing lines, and he gave himself a Girl Friday too. Sometimes she looked like Ingrid and other times she was thin and dark-haired, her face a blur and her lips near his.

When James had dried himself, he walked quickly through to the bedroom and put on his pyjamas. With the curtains closed and the hurricane lamp on, he would try to read. He was still on the third page of Borges's story, 'Funes El Memorioso', which he had begun reading six weeks before. For some reason James seemed able to read, and understand, no more than one sentence of this story each day. The odd thing was that, rather than getting lost and having to retrace what he had read before, he remembered it all with absolute clarity. The very slowness of his reading, the vast effort required to stay awake long enough to negotiate the labyrinths of Borges's winding Spanish clauses and sub-clauses, the powers of imagination needed to form pictures of the things described and named ('a huge slate-coloured storm'; the 'Villa Los Laureles') . . . all these seemed to burn the words of the story into James's normally weak memory. When I finally finish reading this story, James thought, it will not be merely something I have read, it will be part of me; the memories of Funes and of the story's narrator will be *my* memories too. That night, he read the sentence, 'This new event, told by my cousin Bernardo, struck me as very much like a dream confected out of elements of the past.' When he had fully comprehended and absorbed this sentence, James closed his eyes and sighed. 'A dream confected out of elements of the past,' he thought . . . isn't that the perfect definition of a memory?

*

The next day, James drove to the industrial estate and bought a sander, a steamer, a stereo, some CDs and a bed. He also went to the supermarket and stocked up on food and drink. Then he took the receipts to Mr Crabtree, who counted out another pile of banknotes. It occurred to James while this was happening that his feelings towards money had changed. He no longer imagined it as a leech on his skin, sucking his lifeblood. Now he saw these rectangles of paper as thin slices of freedom. They were so light, they seemed almost to be weightless. In fact, James thought, it was as if they weighed *less* than nothing: the more he carried around in his pockets, the lighter he felt.

In the weeks that followed, he stripped the wallpaper in the bedrooms and the sitting room. It came away easily with the aid of the steamer, but the glue, softened by the warmth and humidity, stuck to his skin and gave him a rash on his hands and wrists. He worried vaguely about the allergy pills he had missed, and took two at once, to try to catch up on his dosage.

The next day his rash was worse so he went to see the doctor. The doctor nodded impatiently as James told him about the missed allergy pills. He asked for the name of the drug. James said he didn't know, but he had brought the bottle. When he saw the round blue pills inside, the doctor's expression changed. He told James he would like to run a lab analysis.

'Don't you know what they are?' James asked.

'No,' said the doctor, 'but I'm pretty sure they're not what you think they are.'

The doctor gave James a prescription for allergy suppressants, and asked him to book an appointment with his secretary for the following week. James was irritated by the doctor's mysterious tone, but he did what he was told.

It was five days later, while stripping the wallpaper in his bedroom, that James discovered the manuscript. He had noticed the bulge in the wallpaper before, but had presumed it must be a patch of damp. Only when a few pages floated loose did James begin to suspect the truth.

In all there were seventeen pages, typed and numbered. The title of the story was handwritten over dried whitener. As soon as James saw the title, he felt a bubble of apprehension and excitement in his stomach. He knew this was more than just a story. It was a clue. The title was . . .

Confessions of a Killer

CHAPTER 1

From the window at which I stand the world has an aspect at once beautiful and terrifying. It is, I think, often thus; men do not mark the wonder of creation until they notice the bottomless pit which gapes at their feet, separating them from the indifferent glory and eternity of nature. Perhaps even Adam never saw Paradise as such until the day he was without it. It is loss, or the premonition of loss, which makes us grateful for all we have. The blueness of the sky, the greenness of the lawn and leaves: how sad and yet so thrilling it would be to die on such a perfect summer's day . . . But I forsake my duties as narrator: I speak of the story's end before its beginning. First I must retrace my steps; I must tell the dark tale of *how it came to this.*

My name is Martin Thwaite and, but three short years ago, my life was a simple and blameless one. I was nineteen years old and had, for the previous six months, been working as a general assistant to the famous detective Dr Lanark. My duties were sober and unglamorous: I answered Dr Lanark's mail; I organised his schedule of appointments; I wrote up reports on the cases he investigated and filed them neatly away. But I was an eager young man. The romance of detection was in my blood, and as earnestly as Dr Lanark urged me to be always logical and pragmatic, to learn the theory of my trade before I hazarded an attempt at its practical side, he knew that I yearned to escape the desk at which I laboured and, like his other employees, to discover clues, to solve mysteries, to pursue dangerous villains through the city's labyrinth of backstreets.

❧❧❧

It was around three o'clock on a gloomy afternoon in November and I was in the process of finishing my paperwork for the week. Dr Lanark was with a client in his inner bureau; I had been busy with a report when the client entered the office and had not looked up, so all I knew about him was his name: Mr Gerard Ogilvy. It was perhaps half an hour later, when he emerged from Dr Lanark's office, that I first caught sight of his face. I can still see him now, that poor gentleman: a tall, impressive, full-bodied man, and yet in such an obvious state of distress that I could only presume he had been cruelly reduced by some tragic circumstance. Soon afterwards, Dr Lanark came into the part of the office where I worked, and I heard him sigh. I asked him about the dreadful expression I had witnessed on the face of the young man, and he told me the story that lay behind it.

Mr Ogilvy, he explained, was a gentleman of some distinction – the eldest son of Lord Ogilvy – and also a brilliant young man in his own right. Although only seven years older than myself, he was expected to stand for Parliament the following year, after first marrying his beautiful and distinguished fiancée, Angelina Vierge. All of this was admirable, I agreed, but failed to explain the look of desolation I had seen on Mr Ogilvy's face. Dr Lanark nodded. 'You are right,' he said, 'though in fact, his troubles are due in some respect to both his future career and to his future wife.' He went on to explain that Mr Ogilvy had been receiving anonymous letters, insinuating that his fiancée was an evil woman, a seductress, a harlot. 'Nothing could be farther from the truth,' Dr Lanark avowed. 'I have met the young lady myself and she is in every respect a paragon of feminine virtue. Indeed a more delightful and innocent young lady could scarcely be imagined.'

As Mr Ogilvy was intending to stand for Parliament, I suggested that the letters were perhaps an attempt at blackmail.

'That is how I, too, interpreted them,' my employer replied.

'Then Mr Ogilvy wishes us to discover the scoundrel who is sending him these letters?'

'I wish that were the case, Thwaite, but no.'

'Then what, Dr Lanark?'

'I am afraid that Gerard Ogilvy came here today to ask me to investigate his fiancée. By some horrible twist of jealousy in his mind, to which the most honourable of men are, unhappily, susceptible, he has come to, if not exactly believe these accusations, at least not to be able to dismiss them out of hand in the manner which would be desirable. He is, in short, tortured by uncertainty. It is to this grave anxiety that the dark lines on his face can be ascribed. Mr Ogilvy has resolved to go away for one month, ostensibly to visit his dying aunt in South Africa. In his absence, he wishes us to have Miss Vierge watched, day and night, so that he may, upon his return, know for certain one way or the other.'

'I see.'

There was a pause while Dr Lanark relit his pipe. He breathed in and the office grew smoky with the familiar and agreeable fumes of his tobacco. I looked at my employer's face; he appeared to be deep in thought, so I turned my attention back to the report on my desk. It was perhaps a few minutes later that he spoke again. When he did so, his voice had lost its vague and melancholy tone. He was his more customary self: calm, assured, dynamic. 'Thwaite,' he said, 'I have decided that you shall take charge of this case. It is a delicate matter, and calls for someone of the greatest sensitivity. My other detectives, hardened by their experiences on the streets, might lack the necessary subtlety. I believe you will do a good job. You will report daily to me, of course, but I have the utmost faith in your abilities.'

'Thank you, Dr Lanark,' I said proudly, endeavouring to maintain a calm visage. 'I won't let you down.'

⌒⌒⌒

I began my new assignment early the next morning. At five o'clock, long before first light, I left my room in Kings Cross and walked through silent streets to the address in Mayfair where Miss Vierge kept her apartment. I arrived ten minutes early and relieved the night detective, whom I discovered smoking a cigarette in the doorway of an abandoned house on the other side of the road. He was the first of Lanark's detectives that I had met, though I had occasionally seen some using the back stairs to the office. Given my ambitions at this time, and the excitement I felt at being inducted into the profession, it is perhaps not surprising that this meeting should have formed such a strong impression in my mind. Yet it was not entirely due to the circumstances; and indeed this young man was to play a much greater part in the story of my life than I could possibly have foreseen at the time.

Ivan Dawes – for that was the detective's name – was not at all the kind of man I had been expecting. In place of the slinking, silent, dark-faced chameleon of my imagination, here was a boy – barely older than me – who wore dandyish clothes, had fair hair that poured in loose curls down to his shoulders, a thin, almost girlish face with red, lascivious lips, and eyes so lively that I immediately suspected him of what would have been a serious character flaw for a man in his line of work: a lack of discretion. I confess that Ivan made me feel awkward, shy, provincial in those few brief moments when we spoke to each other in the alleyway. I don't remember precisely what he said that morning, but I remember the tone (jocular, lightly demeaning) in which he referred to 'the target', and I remember the disapproval this roused in me. I also remember not trusting his apparent friendliness; I feared that, behind his open smile, he was laughing at my gaucheness.

I had the day shift: from six in the morning till seven in the evening. Though two hours longer than the night shift, this was generally considered the easier option because the nights tended to be either achingly dull and cold, or extremely dangerous. Naturally I dreamed of taking over the night shift, though perhaps not with this particular target; Ivan informed me that 'her ladyship' had extinguished her bedroom light at midnight and that nothing at all had occurred since then. Such cases were referred to either as 'sleepers' or 'deaduns', depending on whether the target's behaviour changed at a later time; thus, an apparent deadun could sometimes turn out to be a sleeper. 'I'm afraid she's a deadun,' Ivan sighed, 'though it must be said that she makes a very pretty corpse. I wouldn't have minded keeping a watch on her from in between the bedsheets.'

I tried not to think of what Ivan had said, after he left me in the doorway, but my mind defiantly conjured images of her ladyship's beauty while I waited for some movement in the doorway of number 21 Luff Street. I was desperately naïve for a man of my age, still a virgin, and with almost no amorous experience at all. I was also – and this is not unrelated to my bizarre and unnatural innocence – dangerously romantic. Even so, no age of rosy imaginings could have prepared me for the radiant reality of Angelina Vierge.

I have often, in the months that followed, gone over this moment in my mind again, trying to recall at what precise angle and time of day I first laid eyes on her; but it is useless; my memories of that first day are too confused for any single image to stand out from the bright tumult. What I do know is that she was dressed in white, quite simply, as was her style, and that from the moment she appeared in my vision, I was lost. The earth beneath my feet fell away and I felt that swirling, tumbling, churning sensation that I still feel, even now, at the remembrance of her face or her voice or her name.

For the whole of that long day I followed her around London, from boutique to restaurant to a female friend's apartment. She travelled by private cab, and I hailed hansoms as and when I required them. I had processed enough expenses forms to know the protocol. I was dressed inconspicuously in a dark and fairly worn suit, black overcoat and top hat; I carried a notebook, a pen-knife and a pencil in one coat pocket, a small revolver in the other, but was otherwise unburdened. I thought I did a good job of keeping myself concealed, though in truth, when the target is utterly innocent of the possibility that she is being followed, this is not in itself a difficult task. In my new-boy's fear of letting her give me the slip, however, I was somewhat over-vigilant. For instance, the sensible thing would have been to eat lunch when Miss Vierge herself did – with two female companions in an excellent French restaurant called Le Rendez-vous – but I was so nervous that I simply stood on the opposite street corner and watched the door of the restaurant, with the consequence that, by three o'clock, I was almost fainting with thirst and hunger.

The other unforeseen aspect of detective work with which I had to contend – more perilous in its way than a loaded pistol – was boredom. The reality of the job is that, for hours at a time, you are literally doing nothing at all; only standing and waiting and trying not to lose your concentration. To keep my mind active during these periods of inertia, I took copious notes. For the most part these notes consisted of geographical and temporal facts (the names of the streets upon which we travelled; the precise hour of our arrival at and departure from every destination) and irrelevant details such as the weather, the appearances of passers-by, and the tales of murder and disaster shouted out by newspaper vendors. Occasionally, however, my youthful fancy overtook me and I added speculative sentences about the nature of Miss Vierge's character and prudishly admiring comments on her appearance. I can be quite precise about all of this because I still have the notebook in question. It is, for those who know how to read between its banal lines (in other words, only myself), the first and longest love letter I ever wrote.

When the time came for me to be relieved by Ivan – in the same doorway where we had, thirteen hours earlier, first met – I was utterly exhausted. I was afraid he would make some joky remark about my shattered appearance, and thus reveal the folly behind my hunger, but – perhaps because he was about to begin his shift, perhaps because he guessed the truth and did not want to hurt me – he was less flippant than he had been that morning. He asked me if anything had happened during the daytime; I gave him a brief report. 'What did I tell you?' he said, 'She's a deadun.'

A week later, I was put on the night shift. Ivan, I think, had a couple of days' rest and was replaced by someone else; the details are unimportant. The point is that the nights were even duller and colder than the days. I remember wrapping myself up in blankets like a tramp and sitting in that doorway, staring at the glowing rectangle of her bedroom window with its hints of her shape – now bending, now upright – silhouetted behind the muslin drapes. I remember having to walk around sometimes to stop myself from falling asleep and my legs from going numb. I also remember how I felt, at eleven or twelve each night, when the light was put out: the intensified solitude mixed with a feeling that my mind was now free to dream what it wished. In general, during the nightshift, I wrote less and dreamed more; strong winds were blowing from the north that week, and the wild, irregular light cast by the streetlamps made it almost impossible to keep one's eyes on a page of text without feeling like a seasick sailor. The eerie quiet and loneliness of my vigil encouraged the dreams too; they were like the flames of a fire by which my heart was warmed. And it was only natural, I suppose – one might almost say crushingly inevitable – that my dreams were fixated upon the sole human being whose form my eyes had regarded during the previous seven days, through rain and fog, through sunlight and twilight, from behind and in profile, from a distance and sometimes, thrillingly, from up close – close enough to smell the scent she wore, to touch (though I never did) the glossy black locks of her hair, the tender white skin of her throat, the delicate bones of her wrist that I glimpsed once between the lace cuff of her sleeve and the doeskin hem of her glove; this heavenly woman whose habits, whose smile, whose daily life, though I was to her a total stranger, were as familiar to me now as my own, yet who, despite my unceasing watchfulness, remained to me a perfect mystery. Of course my dreams were dangerous, but I could never have understood that at the time. It was in absolute innocence that I descended – that I fell – into the depths of unrequited love.

What it is to fall in love with someone into whose eyes you have never once gazed . . . to whom, by force of circumstance, you are invisible, anonymous, an unnoticed blur in the horizon of a crowd. It was madness, it was torture, and yet in some ways it was also ideal. In that way, nothing could ever be spoiled. I could not say the wrong thing. She could not look at me, then carelessly away. I could not hurt or offend her. She could not grow weary of my presence. In the popular romances it is not like this, of course – the man is a physical presence in the relationship, as solid and real and desired as she – but life is not books, and in truth I cannot imagine a more intense way of loving someone than this: because not once in those weeks of slow uncatching pursuit did I think of myself before her; not once was she out of my sight or my mind. I was the opposite of her fiancé, absent in another continent. I was always there, while she was awake; and when she slept, I slept too. It was different when I began the night shift, but it would be wrong to say that I felt less close to her. True, I could not actually see her, but all the same I knew she was there, behind the dark wall; and what is more, I was privileged to protect her while she slept. No one is ever more vulnerable, more innocently and utterly themselves than while sleeping, and I alone in the whole city, the whole world, was awake, in her presence, while she voyaged into the darknesses within herself, and her body, unclothed, lay still and warm and breathing, under blankets and sheets, less than a stone's throw from my own.

∽∾∽

It was on the last night of my nocturnal shift that the deadun revealed herself to be a sleeper. The next day I was due to begin a five-day holiday; indeed Dr Lanark, though well pleased with my efforts, was thinking of taking me off the case altogether. I looked worn out, he said (and I suspect the vehemence of my denials only increased his certainty that it would be healthier for me to stop following Miss Vierge), and anyway it was clear – 'happily, Thwaite' – that he had been right about the lady's innocence, and that what remained of the month's watch would be no more than a routine case. I was, despite my very real exhaustion, in despair at this turn of events, but I had already resolved that I would not disobey my employer. The thought had crossed my mind, I admit – it was the kind of thing one read in detective novels, after all: the rebellious ex-policeman continuing to investigate the case even after he has been told to stop and rest, driven on by the power of his obsession – but I was still, at this point, sufficiently sane and ambitious not to take such a step.

My notebook tells me this was a Thursday, and the absence of concrete facts amid the half page of lachrymose entries for that night tells me that it began as another quiet and lonely vigil, and that I had no expectation of it being anything else. According to the notebook, it was 'another night of wind and fog, the one constantly battling the other so that one moment I am looking clear ahead of me at the black shape of the house, its face ghoulishly illuminated by gaslight, and the next I can see nothing but a solid wall of luminous mist, so thick that if I hold my arms out in front of me I can barely make out the shape of my own hand'. The notebook also informs, in a hasty scribble, that at 12.39 a.m. a female figure left the apartment building, alone and on foot, and that I set off in pursuit. There is nothing more in the notebook until 4.50 a.m., so the intervening hours I will have to recount based solely on my memory of them: a memory that is as vivid as any in my mind, and yet which seems at the same time to be barely believable; as wild and lurid as some penny-dreadful fiction.

She was dressed in a black cape and hood, and indeed were it not for my familiarity with her shape and gait, and the certainty that I had seen her emerge from the door of that particular house, I would have been clueless to the figure's identity. From thirty yards behind, I had to strain my eyes merely to keep the black shape in vision, wreathed as the night was with those clouds of fog – forever drifting, breaking up, remassing – so that I could not have sworn at that moment if it was even a woman that I followed. I would have liked to stay closer, but in Mayfair there was almost nobody afoot at that hour and I was afraid she would hear my step behind her on the pavement and take fright. Between looming mansions in the mist she walked, and I, like a lost fragment of her memory, a discarded piece of her past, followed, invisibly, inescapably. The only sounds to reach my ears, apart from the occasional clatter of a cab in an adjacent street, were my own footsteps and breathing, and the ghostly moan of the wind as it disturbed the bare treetops. I remember feeling that there was an air of unreality to the situation: these broad streets, the ever-shifting fog, the flickering lamplight, the sense of quiet endlessness; all of this had the quality of a dream. As for the shadow that I followed, its progress was slow but unhesitating, like a sleepwalker's. Not until she reached Piccadilly and suddenly ran across it into the Green Park did I wonder at the strangeness and dangerousness of her behaviour.

I will not deny that there was in my chest up to that moment a certain euphoria, a sense of triumph and excitement. After all, this was how I had dreamed the job would be: mysterious, daring, uncertain; a world away from the desk and its papers in Baker Street. When she disappeared into the park, however, my heart misgave me. I feared that she knew she was being followed – that she ran because she was afraid for her life – and I half wished to cry out for her to stop, to reassure her that I was here to protect her from whatever unseen dangers lay ahead. But of course I didn't. I merely ran, as hard as I could, in front of a cab on Piccadilly, the driver yelling something at me, and into the black expanse of the park.

For another hour, it seemed, we continued like this: the hunter and the hunted; the ship and the siren. Through the park, to Constitution Hill; down the Mall and into Covent Garden; past Charing Cross and to the embankment; and then, my heart pounding at the thought of her jumping or falling into the river, my mind dreaming of how I would rescue her from its black depths, across Waterloo Bridge and into the rat's nest of backstreets behind the train station. This was a part of London I didn't know, or rather knew only by reputation, but it seemed incredible to me that it could be known to this beautiful, innocent young gentlewoman. Watching her drift, with that serene grace, through narrowing and increasingly ill-lit passages, never once halting or turning back on herself, quite oblivious, it seemed, of the whole menacing, odious city that surrounded her – the drunks and panders, the thieves and whores, the whispering mouths, the molesting hands, the foul sulphurous air – I felt as though I were seeing an angel navigate its way through hell. It was uncanny, astonishing, and deeply disquieting. What weird truth could lie at the root of it?

The deeper we descended into that spectral, fog-blinded labyrinth, the more uneasy I felt. I walked more and more closely behind her, gripped the handle of the revolver ever more tightly inside my coat pocket. I was afraid for her and I was, I confess, afraid for myself. The quality of dream had long ago given way to that of nightmare, and a premonition of doom enveloped me as we walked. Finally, in a dark, crabbed street whose name I never knew (I was by now hopelessly lost), she stopped in front of a low black door and knocked three times. I was close enough to hear her breathe. I watched in wonder as she waited, her face, in profile, seeming utterly expressionless. Then, in a sudden gleam, the door was opened and she disappeared inside, without a word. It shut behind her.

I was sick at heart and no longer knew what to think. Could those vile accusations possibly be true? From inside the tall building I could hear the sound of women's laughter and strange, lewd music. The street where I stood stank of vomit and urine. This was, I knew, a den of vice; at best a tavern and at worst . . . but it was too incredible. I wouldn't allow myself to think any further.

For what was probably no more than fifteen or twenty minutes, but felt like much longer, I waited outside, in a welter of despair and panic. According to the rules of my engagement, this was the limit of my duties. I was tortured, torn between my instinctive obedience to the rules and my fear that something awful must be happening to the woman I loved. In the end my emotions conquered my reason. I knocked three times on the black door. It was opened by a woman holding a lamp, and at her silent beckoning I walked through the hallway into a subfusc firelit parlour. Behind me I heard the door close.

❦

The room's air was heavy with perfume: a sweet, cheap variety of which one often catches hints in the less salubrious parts of London. I stood in the entrance to the parlour for a moment, pondering my next move, and slowly became aware of the two other men sitting in armchairs in its sepulchral corners: one young, one middle-aged, both with an air, it seemed to me, of quiet malice and depravity. The young man drank gin and met my gaze insouciantly; the older man studied the pages of a magazine as if transfixed. At length a tall, blank-faced woman – the same who had silently opened the door to me – entered the parlour, took my hat and coat, and gestured to an empty armchair. The chair's stuffing was old and it sank beneath my weight, so that I felt I was being swallowed whole by some velvet-skinned, toothless monster. The woman offered me a drink and, to calm my nerves, I assented. When she had fetched me a glass of lukewarm gin, she nodded to the young man, who followed her through a curtained doorway.

Time passed. I waited. From upstairs I could hear various noises: gasps and grunts and bursts of laughter. Despite my naivety, I guessed what those noises must mean – I knew the business of the place in which I waited – and my heart sank, even as its beating grew louder and faster. I drank the gin and tried to gather my thoughts: in vain because I was too agitated, too warm. Unable to think of any particular plan of action, I loosened my tie, removed my jacket, smoothed back my hair. It was a cold winter night and the fire in the hearth was small, but to me that room felt infernal. The middle-aged man belched and I smelled stale beer and pickled onions on his breath. Eventually, to my relief, he too was called through the curtained doorway and I was left alone.

It is an embarrassment to me, how long I waited in that parlour, docile and silent. I knew I ought to have raised a stink – that I ought to have pulled aside the dark curtain and run through the doorway, calling out Miss Vierge's name, threatening the law on any who barred my way – but somehow the oppressive warmth and dimness and sour-sweet smell of that room unmanned me. And I must also confess to the odd, betraying, impure thought. At any rate, by the time the tall woman reappeared and nodded in my direction, I was more zombie than man. I levered myself out of the chair, picked up my jacket and stiffly walked towards the archway where the curtain had been held back for me.

I passed into a corridor much darker and colder than the parlour. A large man held out a hand; without the need for speech, I handed him my purse. He withdrew a sum of money and returned the purse to me. He moved aside and I saw that the tall woman was now ahead of me in the corridor, and that she was beginning to ascend a flight of stairs which I could just make out in the gloom. I took it that I was meant to follow her. At the top of the first flight she turned down another dark corridor, though this one had pools of candlelight coming from below two or three doors, and lively sounds, including that throbbing, repetitive, disquieting music which I had heard earlier from the street. The tall woman stopped outside one of these doors and knocked. A voice came from within – a coarse, unladylike voice. Finally, at this moment, I mustered enough courage to speak. I don't remember my precise words, but I made it plain through my stutterings that there was only one woman in this establishment whose company I desired, and that was she I had seen enter some quarter-hour before myself; and I proceeded to describe her. Troublingly, there was no hesitation or perplexity in the woman's face; she merely nodded and held out her hand. I gave her my purse and she withdrew some more money. I knew what this had to mean, and yet all my reason and instinct rebelled against it. I felt sick with anticipation as the woman returned my purse and pointed me up a second flight of stairs.

How well, and how strangely, I remember that staircase. For some reason its dozen or so steps seemed to me an ascent as strenuous and fear-filled as the near-vertical summit of a mountain. I began to feel dizzy, as it were with vertigo. I took, I suppose, a couple of steps and then suddenly the close dark walls were rearing up either side of me, the vista of slightly curving wood slipping in and out of focus. For the briefest of moments my mind was a blank. I had, as it seemed, no idea who I was or where I stood or what I was in the process of doing. It was the weirdest sensation. I could smell warm flesh and dried blood and excrement, I could hear someone coughing from behind a closed door; and yet these facts, these present realities, gave me no clue to my whereabouts. At that moment, one might say, I was not even I. And then . . . how to explain the rush of doom that entered my chest? It was as though I suffered a premonition of my own fate. It was as though a future ghost of myself passed through me. I realise that must sound fanciful, but I swear I do not know any other way to describe the feeling. It was like déjà vu in reverse: I glimpsed the future and it looked back at me, its eyes horror-filled and pitying. Long seconds passed. Sweat poured from my forehead, and ran into my eye. It stang and I blinked, and suddenly the fog of confusion cleared. My memory returned and a vision of Miss Vierge, alone and vulnerable, flashed inside my mind. I began climbing the stairs two at a time, ignoring the vast dark bubble of fear that now filled my chest. Presently I came to another door. I knocked twice and entered. The door fell shut behind me.

To my surprise, the room appeared to be empty. It was a small, bare space with grey walls, lit by a few large candles. The air was smoky and sweet, though I noticed it was a different sweetness to that which had pervaded the parlour. In the wall to my left was a tiny window which looked out on to the sidestreet where I had stood before. In the wall facing there was a small hearth with a fire burning, and a bucket of coals. To one side of this was a vanity cabinet, on which the candles stood, and a cheval-glass, and to the other a linen screen. And, in the centre of the room, unveiled, unornamented, brutally clear in its purpose, was a bed. It was a bed without pillows or blankets; and, though the sheet was clean and pressed, various dark stains could be discerned on the mattress beneath. I stared at this bed for quite some time, as if paralysed; I could hardly believe it was there, and that it was as it was. And yet, as I said, the room appeared to be empty, which puzzled me. I was badly startled, therefore, when I heard the creak of a floorboard beside me. I turned to see the figure of a woman emerge from behind the screen.

Even in that dim and flickering light I knew it was she, and my heart rose to my throat as I beheld her. She was dressed in black lace and her skin was pale and smooth as alabaster. Her body was . . . oh God, it breaks my heart to describe her in such mean, inadequate words. The word made flesh, that was a miracle; but her flesh made word . . . She was perfection. Her figure exquisitely slim, yet womanly. Her beauty of a kind that can be nothing but pure, yet which, to my lasting shock, breathed a carnality so overpowering as to seem almost obscene, attached as it was to that angelic face. She had let her hair down and brushed it out – or someone had – and it flowed down over her shoulders and some strands of it veiled part of her face, but I could see her lips, as I had seen them before, only painted now in the most provocative scarlet gloss, and, though half closed, her eyes, which were grey and fathomless and looking at me.

Or should I say, through me? I honestly don't know. I had the impression she was looking at me, that she knew I was there, a solid object, a corporeal being, in the same room as her, and yet there was no expression on her face, no recognition . . . though, of course, there wouldn't have been; to her, I was not I, but merely a stranger. But, though her gaze was anonymous, it was also unmistakably sensual. Her lips were slightly parted with what looked, to my admittedly untrained eyes, like desire, or its facsimile. With aching slowness she moved towards me, her feet bare on the cold wooden floor.

I did not move. I could not move. I recognised in myself the symptoms of sexual love, which had, until that moment, been for me only uncomprehended words on a page, those of Sappho in Catullus' translation. 'Whenever I see you, sound fails, my tongue falters, thin fire steals through my limbs, an inner roar, and darkness shrouds my ears and eyes.' Oh, it was all true, it was all true! I was half blind, half deaf and utterly immobile, yet with a rawness of feeling that was both agonising and ecstatic, like a statue composed only of nerve-endings.

Closer she came and still I did not move, did not speak. I could smell her now – not some expensive bottled scent, but her flesh; *her* – and I could feel the lowest part of me, the beast I could not control, straining to reach her through three layers of cotton. She moved closer, closer, so close I could feel her breath on my neck and her hair brush my lips. And then she moved her hand to the swollen beast and I said her name.

'Miss Vierge.'

Why did I do that? The truth is, I don't really know. I could claim it was moral righteousness that moved me to break that wondrous spell, repulsion at the thought of taking advantage of an innocent gentlewoman. And part of it was this, I suppose. But a greater part, I suspect, was fear. Fear of the consequences of my actions in the world beyond the door of this room, and also a more primal fear, a fear of my own desire, and hers, and that bed, and the other, unknown world into which she might – must – have led me.

~~~

Up to this point, my memory is vivid, but with the breaking of the spell something seems to have ruptured in my remembrance. All is hazy, fragmented, cold. Yes . . . what I remember more than anything is feeling suddenly cold. Of being aware of the sweat drying between my shirt and my skin, and seeing her shiver, disgust and incomprehension in her eyes, and run back behind the screen. And shame. As though it were *I* who had brought her here; as though it were *I* who had hypnotised and seduced her.

I remember struggling to put my jacket on: an action complicated by the desire for haste and the shaking of my limbs. I remember hearing the door bang, feeling the chill draught of air from the corridor. I remember running through corridors and down stairs, following her once more. I remember seeing the blank face of the mute woman as I passed her in the parlour, and of being suddenly breathless as I stood in the street, the steam rising from my open mouth, and staring wildly about me, trying to discern her vanishing form in the mist. I remember a maze of sidestreets and the panic in my chest as I ran. I remember discovering her body on the ground and thinking oh God what if she is dead. I remember my relief at the feel of her warm breath on my fingertips, at the rapid pulse I detected in her wrist. I remember lifting her – how heavy she seemed for one so petite – and my shame and lust and tenderness at the sight of those red lips parted again, so close to mine. I remember the single soft kiss I stole as she lay unconscious in my arms, and I remember waving down a cab somewhere near Waterloo station. I remember holding her around the shoulders to keep her warm and to prevent her slipping down the seat and banging her head. I remember using the last of my money to pay the cab driver, and his suspicious look as I lifted her body up the steps to her door. I remember discovering, with relief, the key to the front door in the pocket of her cloak. After that I remember nothing until she was asleep, in her nightdress, in her bed, the covers tucked chastely to her throat, breathing comfortably, and I was sitting in a straight-backed wooden chair near the curtained window, a single candle burning on a table beside me, and writing in my notebook. What I wrote, unfortunately, was not an account of the night's strange adventure, but a description of my feelings at that present moment; a three-page eulogy that I will spare you, o reader, as you can probably well imagine its contents, and as time is short.

I began writing, as I have said, at ten to five in the morning, and I would guess that I wrote for at least half an hour. I cannot have slept, then, for more than a few minutes, as it was not yet light when I left her house, but however short a time I was asleep it was enough for my world to change utterly. From being her saviour, proud and enraptured, when I fell asleep, I woke to discover myself a strange and frightening intruder, sitting *for no reason whatsoever* in a chair at the end of her bed. She was too scared to make much noise; her scream came out as a whisper, as when one is asleep and dreaming, and cannot swim free of the lower world (which is as of water) to breathe and speak and move in the higher (which is as of air). For that reason only was I not discovered by one of the servants and delivered into the hands of the police.

The time between my waking and my escaping was infinitesimally brief. As soon as I saw the look in her eyes, I knew without a shadow of a doubt that she had no memory at all of the night before; that what she remembered was falling asleep in her bed, alone in her room, and waking in her bed, with a man in her room; a man she had never seen before: a stranger.

And so . . . I ran from her room, from her slowly gathering screams, down the broad curved stairway, out of the door, and into the dark, lamplit street, where in the split second before I turned and fled in the direction of Kings Cross, I saw, secreted in that familiar doorway across the road, the silhouette of a man, barely detectable were it not for the single red circle of a lit cigarette, and knew that the game was up; that Ivan Dawes had seen me, had recognised me, had recorded in his notebook the strange fact of my appearance and disappearance, and that everything for which I had wished and dreamed had, in a single night, been stolen from me, and that the rest of my days would be lived in the shadow of this regret.

MT, Summer '93

James looked out through the window of The Green Man. It was evening, and the streetlamps were lit: modern streetlamps, their glow orange and bland. The Green Man was a cosy pub, with wood panelling and a real fire. He liked it a lot, though he rarely came here. Why had he come tonight? Because it had a fireplace and no trivia machines, James thought. Because, if you were to remove the crisps packets and the stereo system and the electrically pumped Australian lagers, it might almost pass for something from the nineteenth century. Oh, he knew it was ridiculous, but James couldn't help it: how he envied Martin Thwaite and his drifting banks of fog! How he envied him his revolver and his pipe-smoking detective boss! How he wished that were *him* following the mysterious gentlewoman through gaslit London streets! The past as a foreign country. It was all so romantic, so unreachable . . .

And it was not only the milieu, but the characters and the story. Why can't *I* be like Martin Thwaite, James wondered, my life connected to those of the people around me? All the other people I know seem so remote. Are they actual human beings, or merely figures to fill a background? Why can't *I* have moral choices, and consequences stemming from my actions, and the feeling that I am heading towards some sort of climax? Even a horror story or a tragedy must be better than this aimless drifting. I seem always to be forgetting why I'm here, what it is I'm searching for. The days erode my purpose. I mean, what is the point of me living in that house if nothing changes, nothing happens, nothing comes back to me at all?

And yet, the more James considered this, the more holes he began to see in his own logic. After all, it was not so long ago that things *had* been happening to him. He had been spied upon. He had discovered some clues. Someone had beaten him up. It was he himself who had shied away from these openings, preferring to concentrate on simple actions such as stripping wallpaper. And even then, he hadn't been able to escape the clues: it had been beneath the wallpaper that he had discovered the manuscript.

Confessions of a Killer, Chapter 1. James looked at it again, the title and the opening lines. It was a clue! Of course it was. He had allowed himself to be swept away by its veneer of romance when what he needed to do was remain calm, detached, analytical. James ordered another pint and read the manuscript again, taking notes as he went along. This is what he wrote:

Martin Thwaite	MT	*Malcolm Trewvey*
Ivan Dawes	ID	*Ian Dayton*
Angelina Vierge	AV	*Anna Valere*
Gerard Ogilvy	GO	*Graham Oliver*
Dr Lanark	DL	*???*
21 Luff Street		*21 Lough Street*

'MT, Summer '93': Martin Thwaite, 1893 . . . or Malcolm Trewvey, 1993?

It all seemed to fit – the address, the signature, the four double-initials he had found in the letter of letters – but somehow the characterisation struck James as being wrong: Martin Thwaite, whose initials suggested he was the fictional representation of Malcolm Trewvey, was likeable and innocent, while Ian Dayton, described by those who knew him as being sensitive and delicate, was here portrayed as the cynical, knowing Ivan Dawes. Yet if the initials did not correspond, then the whole basis of his investigation fell to pieces. If Martin Thwaite was not Malcolm Trewvey, then there was no real reason to presume that Angelina Vierge was Anna Valere, or that Gerard Ogilvy was Graham Oliver.

James stared into space. Perhaps, he thought darkly, I am no closer to solving this mystery than I was two months ago? For a moment he could see the high black walls again, rearing up all around him, leading him into new dead ends, wrong turnings, folding back in on themselves endlessly. The labyrinth. The murmur of gentle laughter and conversation reached his ears as if from a great distance. He closed his eyes, picked up his pint glass and savoured the earthy, complicated, almost sweet flavour of the beer. When he opened his eyes, the black walls had faded and the pub's interior swirled pleasantly once again in a mix of browns and reds and yellows. James sighed with relief.

After all, he reasoned, this *is* only chapter one. There is still time for the emphasis of the narrative to change: for Ivan Dawes to come into focus, for Martin Thwaite to be revealed as a psychopath. He wondered how many other chapters there might be, and where in the house he might find them. He thought about the coincidence of the word 'story' and the word 'storey': would he discover the second story somewhere on the second storey? And what about the third story? Would he find that up in the attic, or down in the cellar? James felt his head spin as he imagined these secret places, and the shadow of a memory moved over him. Again he felt that hybrid emotion: equal parts hope and fear. Soon after that, he stopped thinking about the mystery. He bought a third pint and began to plan his activities for the following day. He would sand the floorboards in the second bedroom, he decided, and after lunch he would go to the launderette. Oh, and at three o'clock he had a doctor's appointment.

At closing time, half-drunk, he walked home. That night he dreamed that Malcolm Trewvey was hanging batlike from the ceiling over his bed, staring at him. When he woke up the next morning he could see nothing on the ceiling but a damp stain.

From outside, he heard the sound of footsteps and whistling. He put on his dressing-gown and opened the front door to find the postman searching through his bag.

'Morning,' said the postman. 'Morning,' James replied. 'I'm sure I had one for you somewhere,' said the postman. He and James stared at the envelopes as his fingers flicked through them. 'Ah, here we are. Number 21.' James looked, but his attention was caught by the name on the letter behind his. He stared at it in shock.

'Thank you,' said James, as the postman gave him his letter. They said goodbye. James closed the door, and read the letter in the hallway. It was from his parents. They sounded happier this time, he noted, and then he discovered why: they had not made any plans for Christmas and would be thrilled to have James stay with them. James's heart raced as he read the letter; not at the thought of seeing his parents, but because of the addressee on the envelope he had spied in the postman's bag: *Dr Lanark, 19 Lough St.*

James sat in the cab of his van and stared at the façade of the house next door. It was a semi-detached house, the two door-ways either side of a fence that divided the small front garden. It was twilight now, and the windows in number 17 were brightly lit, but at number 19 all was lifeless. James might almost have imagined the house to be uninhabited were it not for the letter he had seen in the postman's bag and the man he had observed leaving that door on several occasions when he had been spying on number 21. James closed his eyes and remembered the man's appearance: he had been small, almost hunchbacked, with oddly squinting eyes that suggested both a suspicion of the world outside and an intolerance of daylight. He had not been at all like James had imagined the detective in the story. Could this really be the same Dr Lanark?

James thought of the doctor he had just been to see. What had *his* name been? Dr Norton, that was it. The first time he met him, James had found him abrupt, but this time his manner had changed. There had been something concerned, almost tender, in his voice, even as he refused to give James his allergy pills back.

'Why?' James had asked.

'Because they are not allergy pills,' Dr Norton had replied.

'No? What are they, then?'

'That is precisely what I would like to ask you, James. Who gave you those pills?'

James had tried to think, but it all seemed so foggy, so long ago. 'I can't remember.'

The doctor had nodded when James said this. 'I see.' For a while there had been silence as the doctor scribbled something on a piece of paper, and then he had said: 'James, there's someone I'd like you to go and see. Dr Lewis. She's a specialist, a very good doctor, and I think she'll be able to help you.' He had put the piece of paper in an envelope and sealed it. Then he had phoned Dr Lewis's secretary and booked James an appointment for the following day.

James looked at the envelope the doctor had given him. On the front was written: *Dr Lewis, T.R.A., 3rd floor, The Health Centre, Lethe Park*. James wondered what kind of specialist she was; he had wanted to ask Dr Norton, but had been worried that this might seem a stupid question.

He yawned. It was dark outside now. He lay back against the window of the van and began to imagine what Dr Lewis would look like. In his imagination, she was dark-haired, in her late thirties. She took off her glasses to examine him more closely. Beneath her white coat he caught a glimpse of black lace . . .

James was thinking of going back to his house to continue this fantasy when he noticed the small figure scurrying up Lough Street. Under one, two, three streetlamps he passed, a bent-sinister silhouette. James got out of the van as the man turned into the driveway of number 19. 'Excuse me!' James shouted. The man looked up for a moment, then hurried up the driveway. There was something ratlike about him, James thought, something shifty. The man was opening his front door when James reached his driveway. 'Dr Lanark? I'd like a word with you if I . . .'

Without a word, the man opened the door, entered the house and banged the door shut in James's face. James rang the doorbell, but there was no response. Before this moment, James had been following the clue more out of duty than expectation. It had seemed unlikely that the man next door might really be involved in the mystery; James had merely wanted to eliminate him from the investigation so he could get back to painting his walls white with a peaceful conscience. But the man's reaction to James's polite inquiry had ruined everything.

He stood in the doorway and tried the bell again. Please answer, he thought; please tell me you don't know me, that this is all a harmless coincidence. In the silence that followed, James felt the world grow once more murky and menacing. It was time for him to become a detective again.

The first thing he did was to open the box marked 'CLUES'. James had been bothered every since he read the story by the feeling that he had seen Dr Lanark's name before, in some other context, and now he was determined to find out where. One by one he sorted through the clues he had collected. The printouts of the newspaper reports on the death of Ian Dayton. The nine little squares with letters on them in the envelope addressed to Malcolm Trewvey. The second envelope addressed to Malcolm Trewvey, marked URGENT and still unopened. The manuscript of the story, *Confessions of a Killer*, Chapter 1. He placed these pieces of paper on the floor of his bedroom and stared at them. He imagined that they should, somehow, spell out the solution to the mystery, or that they should fit together to reveal some hidden pattern. But no matter how long he stared at them, he saw nothing but bits of paper.

Sighing, he skim-read the story one more time, and did the same to the newspaper reports. Halfway through the second report, he gasped. There it was, in black and white.

The coroner read a series of statements about Dayton from his professors and friends. The head of the Psychology department, Dr Lanark, described him as a 'very bright student' who had 'seemed increasingly distracted' during his final term.

So that was where he had seen the name before. He put the story back in the box, and took the newspaper reports and the second envelope with him to the kitchen. He put the kettle on and read through the longer newspaper report more carefully. He copied each name into his green notebook. This is what he wrote:

Ian Dayton (dead student)
John Morton (coroner)
Dr Lanark (head of psychology dept)
Lisa Silverton (ID's friend, room opposite)
Anna Valere (reputed to be ID's girlfriend)
Graham Oliver (ID's room-mate)
anonymous friend (Malcolm Trewvey?)
Catherine Dayton (ID's sister)

The first time he had read this report, in the computer room at the university library, the names had meant nothing to him. Now, of the eight names, five had associations in his mind: not meanings, exactly, but they were no longer merely combinations of letters. 'Ian Dayton' was a dead person, commemorated by a stone carved with his initials in the garden of the house where James lived; he was the sum of all the words with which other people had described him after his death; he was also, by a peculiar extension of James's imagination, a young, blond detective in nineteenth-century London. 'Anna Valere' was a thin, dark-haired girl who haunted his dreams, and she was also a young Victorian gentlewoman dressed in black underwear who haunted his dreams. 'Graham Oliver' was a fat, bearded man with whom James had shared a house for four weeks, and who had, quite recently, beaten James up in a toilet cubicle for no apparent reason. 'Malcolm Trewvey' was, thought James, the anonymous client and the pseudonymous writer; his enemy, and the man he wished himself to be; he was the enigma at the centre of this mystery, and James strongly suspected he was guilty of murder. As for 'Dr Lanark' . . . well, it appeared that he lived next door to James and had something to hide.

James wrote all of this in his notebook and then, seeing that there was steam pouring from the spout of the kettle, he turned off the gas. He took a deep breath and picked up the second envelope. As he held it over the kettle, the glue softened and he was able, as before, to open the envelope without damaging the paper. He shook the contents of the envelope on to the kitchen table. Nine little squares of paper. First he counted them and then he turned them over so he could see each letter. Randomly he arranged them on the wooden surface. They said:

STEVMAGOL

After staring at them suspiciously for a while, James consulted his notebook and discovered that these were the exact same letters that he had found in the first envelope. At first he was disappointed. What was the point of sending two letters containing exactly the same thing? And then he noticed the word URGENT on the envelope. Of course! They had been sent again because Malcolm Trewvey had not responded to them, or acknowledged them, or acted upon them. The sender was not merely passing on information; he was expecting some kind of consequence. This led James to wonder who the sender could be. And, in the same moment, his mind supplied the answer.

He made a cup of tea and told himself to calm down. There was, after all, no logical reason to suppose he was right. It was only a hunch. But hunches, he knew, were what detectives had; and when they had them, they always followed them; and, more often than not, the hunch turned out to be correct. James's hunch was this: the sender of the letters of letters must be . . . Dr Lanark.

An hour later, James was sitting in the computer room of the university library, typing names into a search engine. It was night-time – the library would close in less than an hour – and, with the exception of a bored security guard who wandered in now and again, James was alone. As before, the room smelled of new carpet tiles. The only noises were the buzzing of the neon lamps on the ceiling, the hum of the computer, and the tap-tap-tap of James's fingers on the keyboard.

He worked his way methodically through the list of names. The results were somewhat mixed. 'Ian Dayton' yielded no other results than the newspaper reports on his death. 'Lisa Silverton' he discovered through a schools website: according to her entry, which was written in an ebullient, oddly condescending tone, she was a partner in a London accountancy firm and was engaged to someone called Piers. 'Graham Oliver' was also listed on this website, but there were no details next to his name, and 'Anna Valere' and 'Malcolm Trewvey' were not to be found anywhere on the web. There were several 'Catherine Dayton's, but only one with the right age and nationality: she was working for an IT company in Geneva. As for 'Dr Lanark', it appeared that he had changed jobs. He was no longer listed on the university's staff page, but his name occurred several times at the head of scientific papers sponsored by a company called Tomas Ryal Associates, which had offices in three cities in the UK: Belfast, Edinburgh and H. The company's website declared it was 'at the frontline of memory research'.

At five to ten the security guard came in and told him it was time to leave. James collected the printouts he had made, put them all in his rucksack, and walked outside. It was a bitterly cold night. He decided to go to the union bar, where he bought a pint of bitter and sat alone in a corner. The bar was crowded and noisy. He had not been here since the night he was attacked, and the memory of that incident made him nervous. James stared at the faces around him: laughing faces, earnest faces, drunken faces. Hundreds of people, and he didn't know any of them. Here I am, he thought, surrounded by nameless faces, in pursuit of a few faceless names. For a moment he wondered whether this was ironic or merely sad. Then, sighing, he finished his pint and walked home.

At five o'clock the next morning, James was in the cab of his van. It had been an effort to leave his warm bed after so little sleep. Now he was wrapped in a blanket, remembering those September days when he had sat in the cab of this van and stared at the façade of number 21, waiting for Malcolm Trewvey to emerge. James's heart ached as he thought of that time. There had, he thought, been something pure about it . . . something innocent . . . something he had lost and would never find again.

Undoubtedly his nostalgia was influenced by the weather. Back then it had been cold but bright, the leaves on the trees just starting to yellow. Now dark clouds hung low in the sky and the branches were mostly bare, the pavements slippery with brownish leaves. The effect was almost unbearably bleak. And, if he was honest with himself, James was less than thrilled by the identity of his new quarry. Dr Lanark, though it was easy to believe him capable of evil, did not inspire the same level of emotion as Malcolm Trewvey; or, as he had been then, the nameless man in the dark coat.

He found himself wondering what had become of that man. Where was Malcolm Trewvey now? James cast his mind back. He had no memory of having seen him since the day when the two of them had stood outside the sex shop and their eyes had met in the mirrored glass. How long ago that seemed! Of course James had heard of Trewvey since then: he had dreamed about him; he had opened two letters addressed to him; and Harrison had told him that 'the client' was pleased with his progress in the house. But that was all. No sight nor sound since the day he got the keys to the house. Either Malcolm Trewvey is a very good spy, James thought, or he has lost interest in me. The latter possibility struck him as more likely. Well, if that were true, then there was only one way to regain his attention: by uncovering his guilty secret.

James looked through the windscreen again at the street scene which was beginning to emerge from the dark. It was a scene he knew well. Like the back of his hand – that was the cliché – but James knew this street *better* than the back of his hand. In fact, now he thought about it, he wasn't sure he knew the back of his hand at all well. He looked at it: the tendons, veins, hairs and knuckles; the squarish shape; the irregular gaps between fingers; the bulging egg-shaped muscle below the knuckle of his index finger and above the knuckle of his thumb. Had he been asked to draw this hand from memory, he doubted he would have accurately replicated any of these details.

Lough Street, however, that was different. Naturally there were vague and missing elements in his recollection, but if he closed his eyes he felt confident that he could remember almost all of it, from the view of it narrowing before him, framed by the van's windscreen, to individual weeds that grew near particular trees and the look of the brickwork on certain walls in the golden moment before sunset. It felt much more *his* than did the back of his hand.

And why was this? Not merely because he had learned it by heart during the days of spying. No, he had known it – loved it – felt himself a part of it and it of him – long, long before that. His memories of Lough Street went back much further than six weeks. Something had happened to him in this street: something that had burned it into his memory; something that, even after it had somehow been forgotten, had flashed the memory into his consciousness over and over again, in daydreams and in night-dreams, during the years that had followed his leaving of it. And as he thought all of this, the song came back to him, those sad chords and words – 'Part of my heart / Will always beat . . .' – and the image that always accompanied this fragment of music: the image of a long street of terraced houses, seen from above, and a couple walking, hand in hand, along the pavement, everything stained blue. As James replayed the image in his mind – her head on his shoulder, the policemen under a streetlamp; the tenderness and ephemerality of it all – it suddenly occurred to him that the long street in the image was *this* street.

Of course it was. The moment he realised this, all the vaguenesses in the image were replaced by details, just as the street now, before his eyes, was being revealed by daylight. And, as the memory of the street coalesced with the current reality, the missing chords and words came suddenly to James's mind.

> Part of my heart
> Will always beat . . .
> In 21 Love Street

James froze, as the sad, triumphant chorus echoed in his head. Was it Love Street . . . or was it Lough Street? Had the song been written about this place? If so, who could have written it? Whose voice was it that he could hear singing in his head? He recalled Mrs Quigley's words when he first came to H. and she told him about the man who owned the house: 'An artist or a writer or a singer' . . . Malcolm Trewvey?

For one glorious moment, James seemed to be floating above the labyrinth, to see the whole mystery, and its solution, clear on the ground below him, the walls of the labyrinth spelling out a word or the lineaments of a face . . . and then exhaustion clouded the image, like breath on glass, and he was back down on the ground, back inside the maze, lost in its blind alleys and twisting corridors, clueless and alone. After all, he still didn't know the identity of the couple in his vision, nor what connected them to the song, nor what all this had to do with himself.

A light came on in the front room of number 19 and he put the binoculars to his eyes. The curtains were drawn so he could not make out any details, but there was no doubt that someone was there: the curtains, which were beige, glowed dully and a silhouetted figure moved behind them. James looked at his watch: it was 6.36. He wrote this down in the green notebook and resumed his vigil.

At 6.54 the front door opened and the short, pale-skinned man came out, carrying a briefcase. As before, he squinted – even this murky twilight was too bright for his sensitive eyes – and then walked quickly away. After counting to twenty, James opened the door of the van and followed him. The man, whom James thought of as Dr Lanark, was dressed in a grey overcoat and scarf and walked at quite a furious pace, considering the shortness of his legs. He crossed Green Avenue and cut through to Newland Road. James felt nervous as he passed number 14, remembering Graham's fists, but the street was empty, the house unlit. Dr Lanark turned left up Pool Drive and waited at a bus stop. James hid in a doorway, two houses behind. A number 63 bus arrived; Dr Lanark got on and so did James.

James watched Dr Lanark step from the bus and walk into what looked like a park. It was a grey morning and the park had a quietly desolate air. James got off and paused by the bus stop for a while, trying to work out where he was. Somewhere on the northern outskirts, he guessed. He had nodded off during the bus journey, so the precise location was unknown. The sign said 'Lethe Park', and James felt a flash of recognition as he read these words, though he couldn't think why. When his quarry was far enough away that his whole body would have fitted into the palm of James's hand, James began to follow. It was a wide, flat, open park and there was no one else about. There was no danger of Dr Lanark disappearing.

They walked briskly across the grass until a large white building came into view. Dr Lanark was heading towards it. There were no signs anywhere, and only one door, which looked like a fire exit; James guessed this must be the rear of the building. He was about twenty metres behind Dr Lanark when the latter went through the door. But when James reached the same place and pushed, nothing happened. The door did not open. Angrily James banged on the wire-strengthened glass. He slammed his shoulder against the door. After a while he noticed a metal grille with a button on the wall beside the door. He pushed the button and a robotic voice spoke from the grille. 'Authorisation please.' 'I'm here to see Dr Lanark,' James said. There was silence, and then the robotic voice repeated, 'Authorisation please.' Defeated, James began the long walk around the perimeter of the building.

It was larger than he imagined, however, and by the time he found a sign saying 'RECEPTION', he had lost all desire to speak to Dr Lanark. The glass double doors parted silently as he approached them and James entered a spacious but functional-looking lobby. He went to the desk, intending to ask the woman who sat behind it where he was and how he might get back to the city centre, but before he could speak, she said in an emotionless voice, 'Name please?'

'Erm . . .'

'Could you spell that please?'

'No, sorry, what I mean . . .'

'Name please?'

'James Purdew. But . . .'

'Ten o'clock appointment with Dr Lewis? Go through now please, Mr Purdew.'

Dr Lewis. At the mention of her name, James thought: Of course, I am here for my appointment. This is the Lethe Park health centre and I am here to see Dr Lewis. He felt inside his coat pocket and there was the letter that Dr Norton had given him. Reassured, and pleased with himself for having remembered the appointment, he walked in the direction that the woman behind the desk had indicated.

'Please take a seat,' said the doctor. She spoke in a clipped Australian accent, wore glasses, had greying hair tied in a bun, and a thin, hard face; upon seeing her, James quickly repented all his dreams of black underwear. He handed her the letter from Dr Norton and, as she read it, he looked around her office. It was just a normal doctor's office: computer, desk lamp, framed photographs of husband and children, posters of brains and body parts. It was impossible to tell from the décor what kind of specialist she was. When she had finished reading the letter, James asked, in a voice he wanted to sound unconcerned, 'Is this about my allergy?'

'Your allergy?' Dr Lewis seemed surprised. 'What is it you're allergic to, James?'

'I don't know. I thought you were going to tell me that.'

She looked at him curiously. 'Those pills that you gave Dr Norton, were they for your allergy?'

James nodded.

'Do you remember the name of the doctor who gave them to you?'

James shook his head.

'I see. Could you tell me your date of birth, James?'

'Eight, seven, seventy-three.'

She wrote this down. 'Your parents' names?'

'George and Penelope.'

'Uh-huh. Do you remember where you were when you heard that Princess Diana was dead?'

James was somewhat nonplussed by this question, but he knew the answer and felt an instinctive desire to appear confident and unworried in front of the doctor. 'Yes. I woke up and went to the kitchen to make breakfast. It was about 8 a.m. I switched on the radio and they were doing a report on her life. I thought that was a bit strange. Then it went back to the news studio and the announcer said she'd been killed. I felt quite shocked. I'd seen her so often, in newspapers and on television, that I felt like I knew her. I'd even dreamed about her a few times.'

'Very good,' said Dr Lewis. 'And do you happen to recall what you ate for dinner yesterday evening?'

'Yesterday evening? Yes, of course. Chilli con carne with rice, and half a bottle of white wine.'

'Fine. Now, I'm going to say a few words and for each one I'd like you to tell me the first memory that comes to mind. It doesn't matter whether it's recent or from a long time ago, just whatever comes to your mind first. Is that all right?'

James nodded.

'Rain.'

'Staring out of my bedroom window when I was young and watching the raindrops turn to silver worms on the glass. In my memory, the air beyond is always blue-grey and I feel miserable. I must have spent half my childhood staring at rain. Like everyone in England, I suppose.'

She wrote something down in her notebook. 'Pain.'

'I broke my ankle in the summer. I was running upstairs and I felt it crack. It really hurt. I was in a plastercast for six weeks afterwards, in the middle of the heatwave.'

'Stain.'

After a second or two of panic, he said, 'Oh, when I was young, my mum gave me a new shirt. It was white and I wore it to school. She didn't want to let me because it was new and I might ruin it, but I promised I would be careful. Then, when I was in the playground, I forgot all about it and started messing around with the other boys. One of them had a nosebleed and I got red stains on my shirt. I must have been about seven or eight. My mum was sad when she saw the shirt. I felt really guilty.'

In fact, James felt guilty now. This was not a real memory: he had made it up because he was embarrassed at not being able to remember anything associated with the word 'stain'. Or rather, all the 'stain' memories he had were to do with semen or menstrual blood, and James had felt uncomfortable talking about such matters with a severe-looking older woman he had never met before. All the same, he regretted lying; he wondered if it would nullify the effects of whatever treatment Dr Lewis ended up prescribing. Nervously he watched her face, but she did not seem to have guessed that the memory was invented. Without looking up from the notebook in which she was writing, she said, 'Train.'

Suddenly James was no longer in the office, but standing on a platform at a busy train station. He was feeling the most intense anguish and sadness he had ever felt. A train pulled slowly away and he saw a hand waving from an open window. As the train grew smaller, James felt a great wrenching hollowness inside him; as if his heart had been tied to the train, and was being slowly pulled out of his chest. He stared at his hands and when he looked up the bland details of the office had reassembled around him. He didn't know what to say. Was that a memory he had just experienced? If so, it was not one that he recognised or could place in the narrative of his life. To be precise, it felt like *someone else's* memory. And yet it had been so intense, so real . . .

'Train,' the doctor repeated, tonelessly.

'Um, I don't know,' said James, his voice shaky. 'Catching the train when I was young. We were going somewhere. I can't remember where. On holiday. Maybe to the beach, or . . .'

He looked up. Dr Lewis was not writing down what he said; she was looking at him. Her eyes were filled with pity and concern. 'What happened? Can you remember?'

'No,' he said, and suddenly tears sprang to his eyes. James was angry with himself. He didn't want to cry in front of a doctor. 'No!' he shouted.

The doctor came out from behind the desk and moved towards him. The light in the room was growing dim. 'Calm down, James, it's going to be all right. It's Cathy, don't you remember?' The softness of her voice was intolerable. He was shouting at himself to stop crying and she was coming closer and the room was losing its colours and straight lines. 'Hold still, James. This will make you feel better.'

He felt a sharp pain in his arm.

He opened his eyes and stared at the ceiling. At first he had no idea where he was, but slowly he came to understand that he was lying on a hospital trolley in a white corridor. Dr Lewis must have left me here to recover, thought James. He sat up, feeling a little groggy, and looked around. The corridor was empty, and at either end, equidistant from where he sat, were double doors with circular windows. Through each set of windows he saw nothing but more empty corridor, stretching away to more double doors. James realised he must be somewhere in the heart of the large white building, and that he had no idea how to find his way out.

He got off the trolley and began walking. There were doors leading off the corridor on either side, but he tried them and they were all locked. He called out, but no one answered. He tried looking at his watch but it wasn't there. That was when James realised he was not wearing his clothes: he was dressed in a white hospital gown, and beneath that he was naked. He started to feel afraid. What had happened to him?

He walked along the corridor, through double door after double door. The corridor tiles were cold on his bare feet and a draught blew unpleasantly up between his legs; he could feel his penis and scrotum shrinking. Finally he came to a lift. He pressed the call button and the doors opened. There was no button marked 'o' or 'LOBBY' or 'RECEPTION', so James pressed the lowest button and waited as the lift descended. It seemed to take a long time. Only later did it occur to him that the building, though large, was not particularly tall: no more than four or five storeys. Yet there had been at least ten buttons in the lift.

The doors opened and James got out. Another empty corridor, but he could hear voices further along. He walked in the direction of the voices and came to a half-open door. He could hear a kind of low hum and some high-pitched tweeting noises and the sound of a man sniggering and muttering. He knocked softly on the door and said 'Hello?' There was silence. James put his head round the door and saw Dr Lanark, in a white coat, staring back at him, a fluffy yellow chick in one of his hands. James was afraid he would be recognised, but the doctor's expression was blank.

'Who are you?' he said.

'Sorry . . . I'm lost. I'm looking for the exit.'

'The exit?' Dr Lanark looked thoughtful. 'Are you a patient?'

'I was, yes. I came in to see Dr Lewis, but the next thing I knew I was lying on a trolley and there was no one around. I don't know what's happened to my clothes.'

A strange expression flashed across Dr Lanark's face. James couldn't tell what it was exactly. He looked excited, greedy, sly, jealous. In the next moment his face was back to normal and he was speaking in a soft voice, as though to a child. 'Have you lost your memory?'

Without thinking, James answered truthfully. 'Part of it.'

'Really? Have you any idea how much time has gone missing?'

'About three years.'

'Three years? That's . . . that's very interesting.' The doctor stood up and put the chick into a glass cage, ushering James forward like an obsequious courtier. 'Come in, come in. Would you like a cup of tea? It's the best treatment for shock, you know.'

James was pleasantly surprised at being treated so kindly by Dr Lanark. 'Well . . . all right. Thank you.'

'Milk? Sugar?'

'Milk no sugar please.'

'Milk no sugar,' Dr Lanark repeated, and then scuttled through a door. While he was gone, James looked around the room. It was a sort of laboratory, he guessed, very neat and pale, no windows, lit by long fluorescent ceiling lamps. There were lots of glass cages with chicks inside and others with eggs. On the desk at which Dr Lanark had been sitting was a notebook with lists of numbers followed by ticks or crosses, a large pair of scissors, and what looked like a small fridge. There was a large bin next to his chair; James peered in and saw lots of yellow and red. At that moment, the doctor returned, a mug of tea in his hand. 'Here you go,' he said, smiling. He had the smile of someone who is not used to smiling, thought James. 'Please, take a seat.' James looked behind him, but couldn't see any other seats. 'Have mine,' said Dr Lanark. James sat on his chair and the doctor perched uncomfortably on his desk. He seemed to be waiting for something.

'I didn't mean to interrupt you,' James said.

'No, no, that's fine. Please . . . drink your tea. It'll do you good. It sounds like you've had a rough time of it. You must be feeling . . . traumatised.'

'Well . . . I suppose it was a bit worrying, waking up in an empty corridor like that.'

'Of course, of course. That's it, drink it all down. You'll feel better after that.'

'Thank you.' James took a gulp of tea: it tasted funny, but he didn't want to appear ungrateful so he decided not to mention it. 'You don't happen to know where my clothes might be, do you?'

'Your clothes? Don't worry, I'm sure we can find them. I'll call someone in a minute to go and look for them. But . . . I'm so rude. I haven't even introduced myself. My name is Dr Lanark.' James almost said 'I know', but managed not to. 'And what is your name?' he asked.

'James Purdew.'

'Now, tell me about those missing years, James. I'm very interested. Memory is my job, you see. I'm a neuroscientist. And I have a particular fascination with cases of amnesia. It's a very rich field.' He was rubbing his hands. 'When did you first become aware of your memory loss?'

James thought about this, and as he did so, he began to feel more and more worried. 'I don't know,' he said finally. 'I remember thinking about it a few months ago and being shocked by it. But at the same time I'm pretty sure I must have known about it before and just . . . forgotten.'

'You don't mind if I tape-record your answers, do you, James? It's so interesting. Please go on. So . . . you'd forgotten that you'd forgotten?'

'It sounds funny when you say it like that, but . . . yes.'

'Do you forget many things, James? In everyday life, I mean?'

'I don't know. I suppose so.'

'What kind of things do you forget? Appointments? Where you've left things?'

'Not really. It's more just . . . time seems to slip away from me. It seems to dissolve. I write things down to try and keep myself from losing it all, but . . .'

'But what?'

'Those three years . . . I kept a diary, but I can't get to it. It's locked away. I don't know where the key is.'

'James, this is fascinating. But please tell me, have you had any serious head injuries?'

'No.'

'No major accidents?'

'I broke my ankle in the summer, but . . .'

'Brain disease? Tumors? Epilepsy?'

'No.'

'James, a lot of scientists would have difficulties believing your story. You see, there is an orthodoxy among people in this industry that retrograde amnesia is a myth.'

'Retrograde?'

'I mean the inability to remember incidents in the past, before whatever it was that caused the amnesia occurred. As opposed to anterograde amnesia, which is the inability to remember ongoing, day-to-day experiences. Anterograde amnesia is by far the more common of the two, but because its effects are less dramatic, less simple to imagine, it's rarely used as a plot device in novels or films. Retrograde amnesia, however, is used all the time, in spite of its rarity. That's why many scientists suspect people who claim to have retrograde amnesia of faking it – unless there is evidence of some kind of brain trauma.'

'Why would I fake it?' James asked.

'Well, precisely. You're not a criminal, are you? I believe your story, James, don't worry about that. Honestly, some of these scientists are so unimaginative. Scepticism is a kind of religion to them, and they cling to it against all evidence. In fact, there are lots of documented cases of all kinds of bizarre amnesias, and in some cases the causes are still unknown. But scientists – the orthodox ones – detest mysteries. They see a hole and they want to account for it, and if they can't their instinct is to fill it in, to deny its existence.' As he spoke, he was becoming more heated, his face redder and angrier. He was standing now, pacing around, and his smile had gone. James had the impression the doctor was delivering this speech to an imaginary conference hall. 'I was born in the wrong century, you know. A hundred years ago, scientists were free – free to experiment alone, to follow their instincts and desires; their hunches. They were like Sherlock Holmes, whereas now they are like the police force. Do you know what my job is here, James? Do you know what I was doing when you walked in on me? Don't worry, I'm only locking the door so we won't be interrupted, it's perfectly safe. I was decapitating chicks, James, that's what I was doing. Look in that bin. Yes, that's right. Every day I take a score of day-old chicks and I put a bead in their cage – sometimes the beads taste nasty, sometimes they're dry, sometimes they have a drop of water on them. And . . . God but it's boring, isn't it

James? You're bored already, I can see it in your eyes. Or are you just sleepy? No? Well, don't worry, I don't blame you in the slightest. Even *I* find it boring, and it's my job. So . . . I give them this bead and I write down their response – do they peck it or not? – and then I cut their head off and take out their brain and I slice it up and put the slices on glass slides and freeze them. That's what I do. Years of postgraduate research, all my natural brilliance, and this is my reward. And what do we learn, James? Perhaps in five or ten years we might have discovered some tiny, very specific structural facts about how the brain works. The *chick's* brain. And do you want to know something, James? I don't give a flying fuck about chicks' brains. That's not what I'm interested in at all. I'm interested in memory. Human memory. Do chicks remember? Do they feel nostalgic? Do they close their tiny chick eyes and try to wish themselves back into a blue-remembered past of some paradisiacal battery farm, following their mother's feet around in the dirt and wondering at the sadness and beauty of those lost moments, and all the time passed in between? Do they? Do they? Do they fuck, James! They're stupid, stupid, stupid animals. And . . . are you feeling sleepy now, James? Your eyelids are drooping. Don't feel ashamed, it's quite normal, after all you've been through. Would you like to lie down? Yes, of course, there's a couch just through here. That's right, make yourself comfortable. Your clothes? Absolutely. I'll go and see to that myself in just a moment. There we go, now isn't that better? Yes, I'm just going to tighten this belt around your chest, James, so you can't fall from the couch in your sleep. Not too tight, is it? That's right, your ankles and wrists too, we can't be too careful . . . so yes, as I was saying, the real problem with this century of ours is that it is almost impossible, outside of certain enlightened dictatorships, to experiment on human beings. Oh yes, I'm perfectly serious! You see, I've been waiting a long time for someone like you, James. At last I have the opportunity to follow in the footsteps of William Beecher Scoville – what do you mean you've never heard of him? The man is a giant, a legend – but why? Because he experimented on a human being. It wasn't even that long ago. Nineteen fifty-three, can you believe it? The year I was born, Dr Scoville operated on a twenty-seven-year-old epileptic called Henry. You know what he did, to relieve his epilepsy? He bored two holes in the bone above his eyes – his eyes were open by the way, did I mention that? Henry was awake during the operation. There are no nerves in the brain, you see – all one need do is pump a little shot of lidocaine, like this, *voila*, into the skin of the scalp, and after that you won't feel a thing. So . . . Dr Beecher, he drilled two holes in Henry's skull, and then he took a spatula and used it to lever open the skull and to look upon the beauty – the oh so fragile beauty – of the human brain. Oh James, it's *so* breathtaking. What a shame you won't be able to see it for yourself. Anyway, there was one particular part of the brain in which Dr Scoville had a special interest. You see, he had performed this operation before – he had removed the hippocampus of epilepsy patients, and without fail they had all ceased to exhibit the symptoms of epilepsy after the operation. Remarkable, wouldn't you agree? The only catch was that all Scoville's previous patients had been psychotics, so, frankly, it was rather hard to tell whether there might be any side-effects to this bold experiment. But Scoville had Henry's permission to perform the operation. He had Henry's parents' permission. It was all quite above-board. So . . . yes, please do try to stay awake, James, I'm saying all this for your benefit . . . so Dr Scoville inserted a thin silver straw into Henry's brain and, using a suction device, he – whoosh! – sucked out the hippocampus. He took a few other bits with it, of course – neurosurgeons weren't terribly precise in those days. But anyway, James, do you know what happened? Something quite amazing. Henry's epilepsy was cured, just as advertised, and in many respects he remained the same young man he had been before. With only one small difference. He couldn't remember. Oh, he remembered his childhood, and the broad outline of the decade leading up to the operation. But the two years just prior to it . . . whoosh, it was gone. And ever since the operation, he has never remembered anything that's happened to him. Nothing. Oh yes, Henry is still alive, an old man now of course, a famous man too, at least in the world of scientific literature. We call him HM. We do love initials, us scientists. In Henry's mind, Truman is still president. Henry's mother died in the 1960s. Every time Henry hears this news, he cries: he thinks it is the first time he has heard it; the grief is always new, always raw. Can you imagine, James? Not only that, but Henry is aware of his condition. He says he feels like he is constantly waking up from a dream. Oh James, it's *such* a rich field of inquiry, I can't tell you how thrilled I am that you have agreed to let me investigate the mysteries of your brain. Now, I'm just going to have a drink of water and then we'll begin. There, that's better. Don't worry about the drill, James, I know it must look large and frightening, but I can promise you won't feel a . . .'

At that moment, very suddenly, Dr Lanark stopped talking. He appeared to have been frozen, paralysed; his mouth open as if in the middle of a word, his hands suspended in the act of holding the drill above James's skull. And then James saw another figure move beside Dr Lanark. He squinted: the other figure was Dr Lanark as well.

There were two Dr Lanarks, side by side: one motionless, the other normal. The new one looked identical to the other in every respect and yet, at the same time, he was quite obviously not the same person. He spoke differently too, even though his voice was unchanged. 'I'm terribly sorry about that, Mr Purdew. I realise you must have been rather frightened, but let me reassure you that you were never in any danger. I was watching the whole time. Yes, I could have intervened sooner, but, you see, I learned so much in those final moments; that was precisely when his readings jumped off the scale.'

By now the belts had been unstrapped so James was able to sit up. He was still groggy, and his vision was blurred, but he could feel strength returning to his muscles. Now he looked more closely he could see electrodes attached to the head of the first Dr Lanark, and behind him a desk on which sat a laptop computer and a printer. The printer was spewing out graph paper. The second Dr Lanark studied it. 'Remarkable,' he muttered. 'Unprecedented, in fact. Anyway, we can leave that to the boys in IT to interpret. In the meantime I suggest you come with me. You must be feeling a little shocked by the night's events.'

James nodded.

'Completely understandable,' said Dr Lanark. 'Come with me and I'll give you a drink. How about a glass of brandy?'

James followed him silently through the laboratory full of trilling chicks and into a small, cosy room with a log fire and two leather chairs. 'Welcome to my parlour,' the doctor said proudly. 'Do sit down, Mr Purdew. Make yourself comfortable.'

'Um . . . my clothes?'

'Are on their way, don't you worry. I've already sent a security guard to fetch them. They should be with us quite soon. While we wait for them, though, I wondered whether we might have a chat?'

James nodded as the doctor handed him a large glass of armagnac. He sniffed it suspiciously, but it smelled fine. Dr Lanark sat in the chair facing James and sipped the amber liquid from his own large glass. 'Ah, this is more like it, don't you think. Cigar?' James shook his head. 'Mind if I . . .?' Again, James shook his head. 'Well, then, let me say first of all, Mr Purdew, that I was fascinated by what you told my colleague. Don't worry, I have no desire to drug your drink, lever open your skull and suck out part of your brain. Really, neurosurgeons can be so crude at times. I myself, though I am well acquainted with the science of the brain, have a background in psychology and philosophy. These fields of enquiry require more than mere intelligence and training. They require sympathy, imagination, humanity . . . qualities in which my colleague, as you saw, is sadly lacking. However, it would be wrong to single him out in this respect; the truth is, I am afraid, that the vast majority of scientists have similar failings. You see, the myth remains that scientists are disinterested and pure in motive, but in truth they are as pettily ambitious and as morally blinkered as everyone else. They are rats in a maze, frantically searching for the key to the next door or level, never sitting still and wondering what the purpose of the maze is; never imagining, even once, the possibility that they are being 'tested' by some other, unknown, infinitely greater power – chance, fate, God, whatever you wish to call it – in ways that may be random or meaningful, but whose meaning, if it exists, will always elude us. The highest form of human wisdom I have ever come across is that line from the Upanishads, have you read it? "To know is not to know; not to know is to know." So simple, so profound; the very antithesis of modern science. But anyway, Mr Purdew, that is my own personal bugbear and I apologise for burdening you with it. More brandy?'

James held out his empty glass. He had another sip and sighed appreciatively. The leather chair was tremendously comfortable, and the fire was warm and mesmerising. In truth, he hadn't been paying much attention to this first part of the speech, despite Dr Lanark's evident passion, but what he said next made James sit up and take more notice.

'But let us turn our attention to *your* condition, Mr Purdew. Do tell me, is it actually the case that you remember nothing about those three years? Nothing at all?'

'Well, not quite.'

The doctor sat back, looking pleased with himself. 'Ah . . . I thought as much.'

'I know where I was during those years, for instance, and I can remember certain places, certain emotions . . .'

'Sorry to interrupt, Mr Purdew, but would you mind telling me: where *were* you?'

'Here.'

'Here?'

'In this city, I mean.'

'I see. So you've returned, in a sense, to the source of your amnesia. You have come, as Proust put it, *à la recherche du temps perdu . . .*'

'Yes,' James agreed quickly. He was worried that Dr Lanark was about to launch into another long speech. 'That's right.'

'And has anything come back to you?'

James considered telling the doctor about the brief vision of the dark-haired girl he had seen when he bit into the apple, and the image of the train that had affected him so strongly in Dr Lewis's office, but they seemed too odd, too vague to describe. So in the end, he just said, 'No.'

The doctor nodded thoughtfully. 'Tell me, Mr Purdew, do you ever have what you might think of as daydreams or hallucinations?'

'What do you mean?'

'Well, they can take many different forms, but amnesiacs often experience what seem to be strange, unknown images, or inexplicable emotional reactions, or blackouts, or recurring dreams, or instances of déjà vu. Sometimes, it is as though one's body can remember what one's mind cannot. Have you ever had anything along those lines?'

'I'm not sure,' James said cautiously.

'Or have you ever had memories of day-to-day events that seem – how can I put this – unrealistic? In other words, they are as vivid and clear as normal memories, but when you consider them rationally, they seem so outlandish that you conclude it must have been something you dreamed or imagined.'

James's heart was beating fast now, as he recalled the librarian with Larkin's memory, the pub full of astrologers . . . 'I might have done,' he said warily. 'What are they? What do they mean?'

The doctor stared at him for a few seconds, as though trying to read his face. 'The first phenomenon that I described – the strange images and emotional reactions – are a classic symptom of retrograde amnesia. They go under various names – Pierre Janet called them "hallucinations", Freud and Breuer "hysterical reminiscences". They are what we might call "leaks" from the past. Hence the apparent strangeness.'

Again James thought of the blood-stained bitemark in the apple and the vision of the dark-haired girl; he thought of the train he had seen, pulling out of the station, and how wretched it had made him feel. He also remembered the bittersweet, hollow feeling that had come over him when he was feeding the ducks in Pullen Park, and the unaccountable euphoria he had felt, walking along Lough Street, with the dry leaves crunching beneath his feet. Finally, the vaguest memory returned to him – of having seen and felt something in the back garden of the house, the day he moved in. Some clouds, a sudden silence, a shadow on the grass, a surge of dread . . . He exhaled and looked around him at the warm parlour, the flickering firelight, Dr Lanark's thought-lined face; the reassuring solidity of the present. Could these have been 'leaks', he wondered ? Could he, during each of those moments, have been living in the past? He nodded mutely, and the doctor continued.

'The second set of phenomena is . . . well, that is a particular theory of mine. I have observed such unsettling confabulations, such mergings of dream and reality, many times among my patients, and have even had them myself once or twice. I call them "dreamemories", Mr Purdew. An elegant conflation, don't you agree? They are often associated with the influence of intoxicants, but not exclusively so. They may also be brought on by some kind of trauma, or a general feeling of stress or confusion or fatigue. Indeed, the more I investigate the matter, the more I wonder if they are not, to some degree, an everyday part of life.'

'You mean . . . it's normal?'

'To *some* degree. You see, memories are not as most people imagine them to be. The modern analogy with computer memory is deeply misleading: human memory has more in common with an ocean than a microchip. This is not only my opinion, by the way. Most neurosurgeons and molecular biologists and psychologists would agree with the basic principle: that memories are fragile, constantly mutating, easily distorted. Memory is eight parts forgetting to two parts daydreaming, as Tomas Ryal put it. Have you ever heard of the term "dissociation", Mr Purdew?'

James shook his head.

'Perhaps the easiest way to imagine this is to visualise a river with another river following its course underground. In this underground river are all the monsters too dark and disturbing to be allowed in the first river. You know the monsters must exist somewhere, but you can't find them no matter how long you spend fishing in the first river.'

'But then, how do I catch the monsters? How can I fish in the underground river?'

'Bravo, Mr Purdew! That is, if I may say so, a highly perceptive and intelligent question.'

James blushed. 'Thank you.'

'To which the answer is: one must fish more deeply.'

'I don't understand.'

The doctor smiled, as though he had just hooked a fish himself. 'Hypnosis. Would you allow me to . . .' The next thing James knew there was a silver watch on a chain swinging gently before his eyes. Soon after that, the watch was still and the parlour was spinning. 'Close your eyes,' said a voice and, in the darkness that followed, it echoed somnolently: 'We are going back in time, James Purdew . . .'

James opened his eyes and saw Dr Lanark sitting across from him, only now there was a desk between them, and the room they sat in was not the warm, luxurious parlour, but a beige-painted office with a single high window through which daylight leaked in a desultory way. The room smelled faintly of body odour and Dr Lanark looked suddenly thinner. He was writing something on a piece of paper while James watched. 'I knew you before,' James said. 'You were my . . .'

'James!'

He was surrounded by darkness and a voice was calling. James thought at first it was his mother's voice; that he was asleep and she was waking him. It must be time to go to school, he thought. 'Just a bit longer, mum . . .'

'James!'

It was not his mother. The voice was harsher than hers and the room in which he lay was warmer than his bedroom.

'James!'

He opened his eyes and he was back in the parlour. It felt as though he had been gone a long time, but around him the scene was unchanged: the leather armchairs, the gently licking flames in the hearth, the half-smoked cigar in the ashtray, the empty armagnac glasses on the low table; the only thing that had changed was Dr Lanark. He was now a woman.

James blinked. It was Dr Lewis. Her voice and expression were as they had been before, in her office, but now she was leaning back in the armchair, her legs crossed and suddenly visible without the intervening desk. She wore black stockings and, where her white lab coat ended, halfway up her thighs, he could see her lace stocking tops and the beginnings of suspenders, some snow-white flesh and a triangle of shadow. James looked down and saw a large tent in his hospital gown. Dr Lewis was talking, but he had missed most of what she had said so far. Something about the two Dr Lanarks being clones, each mentally altered by the use of experimental medicines and conditioning. James heard himself say, 'like Dr Jekyll and Mr Hyde', and saw Dr Lewis smile – she was wearing red lipstick – and say, 'Quite so.'

After that, his memory is vague and fragmentary. He remembers her red lips around the head of his penis. He remembers following her through empty white corridors. He remembers feeling cold and sad and angry and helpless. He remembers getting dressed in a men's toilet and seeing a man who looked like Dr Lanark pissing in a urinal. He remembers discovering the exit and running through the park. He remembers lying on the ground and not being able to see. He remembers being lifted by someone else, a man in a dark coat. He remembers dozing in the back of a taxi cab with the silent man holding him round the shoulders. He remembers sitting in the back of a taxi cab and holding a thin, dark-haired girl around her shoulders. He remembers a train pulling out of a station.

James did his best to forget about this distressing experience, and because he had suffered no physical damage, this proved easier than it had after he'd been beaten up by Graham Oliver. He told himself it was just a bad dream. Dr Lewis left several messages on his mobile, but James erased them straight away and eventually she stopped calling.

Throughout the dark weeks that followed, his mental life was as smooth, blank and featureless as the surfaces he plastered and painted. Memories, like electrical wiring, were neatly covered up and hidden away. He knew they must be there, somewhere beneath the surface, but he had no desire to expose them again. What purpose would it serve?

Instead he threw himself into work, as if work were an ocean, and the days came and went like waves. He was carried by them and deposited by them. Often he thought of himself as a shipwrecked mariner, clinging to a piece of driftwood, alone in that grey and unanimous expanse of water, with nothing to see in any direction but the endless, circling horizon. The driftwood was his diary; and, just as a sailor might orient himself by the sun and stars, James took his bearings from the names of the days. Routine was his compass.

On Monday mornings he took his expenses form to Harrison Lettings. On Tuesday and Friday mornings he went to the Happy Shoppa to buy groceries. On Thursday and Sunday mornings he went running, unless it rained, in which case he did press-ups and sit-ups. On Saturday mornings he rode his bicycle to the municipal pool and swam twenty lengths. On Sunday afternoons he went to The Polar Bear to eat lunch and watch the football on television. On Wednesday, Friday and Saturday evenings he went to The Green Man. These events were his markers. All the rest of his life was white and black: the white of the paint he applied to the walls and the black of sleep.

Unconsciously he avoided his old haunts. Campus, with its youthful, happy, coupled masses, was a place to be visited only in emergencies, and he rarely went to the park or through the back alleys behind the house. It was too cold, for the most part, to sit out in the garden. And when he went to The Polar Bear he sat in the public bar, not – as he always used to – in the lounge. That still left a few places which had resonance but were unavoidable, such as the house itself and Lough Street, but he had been back in the city for months now, and the longer he stayed here, the more the new memories covered up the old. When he walked past the fountain and up to The Green Man and smelled hops in the air or was passed by a teenager on a bicycle, he was reminded of other occasions when the same confluence of events had occurred, but these occasions were more likely to have been ten weeks ago than ten years ago. The simile didn't occur to James, but to me it seemed obvious that the city was being renovated in his mind, just as the house was being renovated at his hands. In both cases, the present was conquering the past: the old being erased to make way for the new.

Occasionally the telephone in the hallway rang, usually in the evenings. Its sound was melancholy and oddly familiar, but muffled by the wooden box, and by now James was more or less immune to it. Something in the drone of its ring made him feel the caller had no hope anyway – that whoever was at the other end knew the phone would never be answered – and this eased the guilt he felt at not answering. Even had the box not existed, he probably wouldn't have picked up the receiver. He would hardly have known what to say, the sound of his own voice had grown so strange to his ears.

Yet still he clung to the driftwood; still he kept his diary. Nothing happened – there was nothing to write – but he wrote it anyway. His words, true to life, were stale and dull, but he could not bring himself to stop their flow. The black notebook was part of his life, and he was reluctant to abandon it. Even so, as the days grew ever shorter, the entries in his diary grew shorter too, and, after a while, less frequent. He missed the odd day, and then two or three at a time.

One day, bored and curious, he borrowed Philip Larkin's *Collected Poems* from the university library. He flicked through it and, attracted by the title, read a poem called 'Forget What Did'. This is what it said:

> Stopping the diary
> Was a stun to memory,
> Was a blank starting,
>
> One no longer cicatrised
> By such words, such actions
> As bleakened waking.
>
> I wanted them over,
> Hurried to burial
> And looked back on
>
> Like the wars and winters
> Missing behind the windows
> Of an opaque childhood.
>
> And the empty pages?
> Should they ever be filled
> Let it be with observed
>
> Celestial recurrences,
> The day the flowers come,
> And when the birds go.

James took this poem as a sign. He read it and he read it again. Then, even before he read it for a third time, he decided to stop writing his diary. He let go of the driftwood.

The effect was disorienting. It was like being drunk for the first time: there was a sense in which he felt giddy, liberated, rebellious; but some other part of him remained disturbed by the loss of control . . . by the idea of falling through time, of it slipping past him with no record, however small or pointless, of its ever having been.

These diaryless days made little impression on James's memory. When he thought about them afterwards, what he saw was the slow but steady progress of the walls, floors and ceilings; the rooms turning white, one by one: the kind of scene that, in a movie, is always shown in montage, scored by light, hopeful music.

So fade the music and let us fast-forward to the moment, one dark cold evening, when James finished retiling the bathroom. He washed his hands in the sink and stepped back to look at the room. It was utterly, dazzlingly white: every surface reflected the fluorescent shaving light. He dried his hands on the white towel and walked into the sitting room. That, too, was perfectly white and finished. White sofa, white chairs, white coffee table – all as specified by the client. The white ceiling mirrored the white floor and the white walls mirrored one another. He opened the white door and went through to the kitchen. The white floor tiles, put down the previous week, gleamed stainlessly up at him. From the white vinyl work surface shone the white toaster, the white microwave and the white breadbin. James opened the white door of the refrigerator and stared at its contents, neatly arrayed on the white wire shelves: cream cheese, milk, eggs, natural yoghurt, mushrooms, white chocolate. He was hungry, so he broke off four squares of chocolate and greedily ate them. Then he walked to the hallway.

This, too, was white and perfectly finished; as were the two bedrooms that adjoined it. James exhaled with relief. He had done it. The ground floor was finished. He stood there in the hallway, waiting for a feeling of triumph to well up, but instead there was only silence – no one to whom he could tell his good news, no one to congratulate him – and a horrible emptiness deep inside him. Darkly he thought of the man who had commissioned this work: Malcolm Trewvey. He might ring to say thank you, James thought. He might send a brief note of encouragement. But James knew he would do no such thing. Malcolm Trewvey had forgotten all about him.

He was alone. He had devoted the last three months of his life to renovating this house – and for no one but himself. He sighed again, and looked warily, wearily up the dark flight of stairs. Of course, he thought, my work is not finished. The rest of the house is still up there, lightless and cold and mired in the past. There is a long, long way to go. And yet the thought of starting the first floor today was unbearable to James. He had worked so hard, so intensely, and he deserved some kind of rest. He deserved some kind of celebration.

James decided to go out. He put on his coat and opened the front door. Outside, it was snowing. He looked up at the immense black-blue void, at the tiny, white crystals falling slowly towards him, and felt a sudden shiver of consciousness. He was alive and the world was beautiful. He was thirty years old and time was slipping away. He stood on the threshold for a moment, inhaling the cold, fresh-smelling air and watching his breath steam and vanish in the darkness, and then, in the distance, he heard music. It was a familiar song, and it made him feel happy and sad at the same time. No, not *that* song. This was a carol, sung by children. In an instant its melody carried him back to his childhood, to the suburban estate in which he had grown up. He thought of his parents, his grandmother, and with a flicker of panic he checked the date function on his watch. He knew it was a Wednesday, but what was the date? 24-12, his watch replied. Christmas Eve, thought James. He went back into the house, packed his rucksack, and within an hour was in the white van, driving south.

In my own van – which is black, not white – I followed, a discreet distance behind.

IV
THE TIME MACHINE

He stood with his elbows on the windowsill and watched the rain pour blue down the glass. Across the street was a row of identical houses, their eyes curtained and lightless; the shapes of chimneys and satellite dishes and floating raindrops were discernible in the sodium haze of the streetlamps. It was nearly midnight and the cul-de-sac was empty.

The room in which he stood had once been his bedroom, but these days his mother called it the guest room and his father the study. It held various layers of history. Many of the objects it contained (the books on the shelves, the board games in the drawers, the brass and glass ornaments on the desk) were relics of James's earliest childhood. The furniture, in contrast, was new, and incongruously sleek and businesslike. As for the room itself . . . well, this was not James's childhood home – his parents had moved house when he was eighteen – but its yellow wallpaper and beige carpet provoked memories of three distinct periods of his life: the summer of the World Cup, when he had been unwell; the winter and spring when he'd been working in the pub and the warehouse, and then as a freelance journalist; and the summer before he went to university in H.

In his mind, these memories flared, and for a few moments it was as if he were travelling through time. He turned around and saw his dream brothers in typical poses: the twenty-one-year-old hunched tensely over the computer; the twenty-five-year-old reading a newspaper in bed; the eighteen-year-old standing next to him at the window, staring out into suburban gloom. After a few moments the ghosts dissolved, and he was alone once again in this blank present, dimly aware that he too would soon be past . . . just another vague flickering sensation in the mind of some future James.

From the room next door, he could hear his parents arguing in loud whispers. Wearily, uneasily, James thought back to the moment of his arrival, three hours earlier.

His mother had answered the door. As soon as she saw him, she had seemed embarrassed. They had thought he wasn't coming; that he must be too busy. Of course she was pleased to see him, but . . . couldn't he have called to warn them? She had run upstairs to make up the sofa-bed while his father had put the kettle on and made him a sandwich. Then they had fetched his grandmother and the four of them had sat in the living room together and had a slow, distracted conversation. The five of them, I should say: James, his mum, his dad, his gran, and the television.

'So,' said James's dad over the blare of sirens, 'how's it going with that house you're doing up?'

'Not bad,' James replied. 'I've finished the ground floor.'

'Good. It's progressing, then?'

'Yes. It's progressing.'

'There's one thing I don't understand,' said the television. 'The window was closed, wasn't it?'

'It's a lot of work, I imagine.'

'It is, yeah. A lot of work.'

'It must have been somebody she knew. She must have *invited* the killer into her home.'

'But it's going OK?' his gran persisted. 'You're enjoying it?'

'Yeah, it's going fine.'

'Good. That's the main thing.'

'Mmm.'

They followed the murder mystery for a while. 'It's the stepfather,' his dad said. 'It's obvious.'

'He's got an alibi,' said his mum.

'It'll be false. It's always the same, this show.'

'Shhh, you made me miss a bit.'

'Sarge, did you see this?' asked the television. 'Could be a clue . . .'

'So how's work, dad?'

'Same as always,' came the toneless reply. 'Work is work.' Suddenly his father grew excited and shouted, 'Look, I told you! What did I say? It's the stepfather!'

'It can't be. It's too early. There's another fifteen minutes to go yet. This is a red whatsit.'

'Herring,' said his gran.

'Exactly.'

Later, when the murderer had been apprehended – it was the brother-in-law – James's mum asked him about Ingrid. Did he want to talk about it, or . . .?

'There's nothing to say, really.'

'OK. That's fine. I understand perfectly.'

He could see the pain and anxiety in her eyes.

'She was a lovely girl, that one,' said his dad. 'I think you're mad, letting her go.'

'Brian, you don't know anything about it,' his mum scolded.

'I know she was a nice girl.'

'But you don't know the . . . *situation*.'

'We got a lovely card from her last week, didn't we?' added his gran.

'What?' said James.

'Yes,' said his mum. 'She remembered us for Christmas. That was thoughtful. What's the matter?'

'Nothing.'

James had not received a single letter from Ingrid since the day she left.

'You know,' said his mum in a soft voice, 'sometimes you think something is over and it turns out later that it isn't. It's never too late, if . . .'

'I don't really want to talk about it, mum.'

'Of course,' she blushed. 'Sorry.'

'I think I might turn in now, if that's all right. I'm tired from the journey.'

She kissed him on the cheek. 'Good night, son.'

His grandmother hugged him tight and whispered, 'Sleep well, love.'

His dad, eyes fixed on the screen, said, 'Yeah, see you in the morning.'

'Here are some handy hints if you're thinking of brightening up your dull patio,' added the television.

He lay in bed, unable to sleep. The mattress was hard and narrow, and the pillow too thin. The radiator made loud clanking noises at irregular intervals. The light in the hallway had been left on, just as it always was when he was a child, and it spilled through the glass rectangle above his door, illuminating part of the ceiling and the far wall. Too tired to think, James found himself staring at this lit-up corner. His eyes kept crossing so the corner slipped in and out of focus. He closed his eyes.

Hours passed, or seemed to, and still sleep did not come. He half-opened his eyes again and squinted at the corner. The lines were black and the surfaces milky white, but the longer he stared, the less sure he became of the divide between the two; they appeared to melt into one another. After a while, his head began to feel strangely light, and he had the sensation that the corner was alive. It grew and shrank, in time with the filling and emptying of his lungs. Sometimes it was tiny and faraway, like a star; in the next breath it would invert itself and bulge towards the bed, looming over him like an angry ghost. He tried to sit up, but he couldn't move. He knew now that the corner was slowly expanding, that the space was closing down on him; that, if the corner kept pulsing and growing in this way, soon it would fill the room and he would be suffocated silently beneath his bedclothes. 'Mummy,' he tried to call, but his voice made no sound. Terror gripped him. He was five years old and he was having an asthma attack.

He was thirty years old and he couldn't sleep.

With a sigh of irritation, James got out of bed and put on his clothes. I may as well go for a walk, he thought. Downstairs he grabbed his coat, took the spare key from the porch, and walked out into the cul-de-sac. The rain had stopped now, and the pavements glistened. The evening snow, with its promise of whiteness, had not lasted more than a few minutes. Without thinking where he was going, James exited the cul-de-sac and crossed the main road.

After a few minutes, he came to a place he recognised. He was standing in the centre circle of a football pitch, the goal-posts shining like vague symbols at either side. Ahead he saw the low wide bulk of the junior school. This was where he had spent half his life between the ages of four and ten. As he traversed the muddy ground, images came to his mind of small boys running, games of marbles and conkers, grey hours spent in detention during playtimes, a black, green and white anorak he used to wear, a frightening teacher with bad breath called Mr Murray, an ugly girl called Lydia Knight showing him her ginny for 20 p in the red-curtained reading corner. All of this was a reassurance: his memory worked. He was not a nobody, an amnesiac. This place was a part of his life and, now he was here, the past would reassemble itself before his eyes; he would remember.

And yet . . . how small everything looked. Could this tiny building really be the repository for such fathoms of wonder and fear? Of course, James told himself, it looks small because you've grown. Once upon a time you sat in little plastic chairs like those, you stared longingly out of the window at this minuscule football pitch and thought how grand and green and magical it seemed. But could that really have been *me*? he wondered. Somehow the disparity in scale made him question what he had always taken for granted. Could *he* truly once have been a *child*?

James wandered across the playground and came to a classroom window. He looked through the glass at the shadowed desks, the blackboard on the wall, the Santas made of toilet rolls, cotton wool and tinsel hanging from the ceiling like executed prisoners. Without knowing why, he felt guilty. Something to do with the determined happiness of the decorations and the way the darkness seemed to mock them. Something to do with a grown man spying on children's innocent secrets. Once he had belonged here, but now he was an intruder and he looked for a way out. He passed the dining room and saw chairs stacked on tables. He passed the gymnasium and saw hula hoops lined neatly against a wall. Finally James found a pathway that led him to the main road. As he looked back briefly at the school and its grounds, his heart filled with an ache he couldn't name.

He followed the road up to the crest of the hill. It was the middle of the night and the estate was asleep. There must be thousands of people here, James thought, and I am the only one awake. Are they dreaming me or am I dreaming them? Exhaustion made him feel floaty, unsolid. He read the names on the street signs – Denbury Road, Oakfield Close, Chapel Lane – and his head was flooded with pictures. In one of those houses he had undressed an older girl called Sharon; in the pub at the end of this road he had been sick on someone's shoes; in the woods behind that garden he had built a den with friends.

He began taking paths at random, following the endless trail of streetlamps and staring at the illuminated pavement as he walked. Cocooned in memories, he drifted aimlessly, sightlessly, and when next he looked up he realised he had no idea where he was. He looked around: anonymous suburban houses, their windows dark; a long straight road, grass verges and young trees, circles of orange light; and, somewhere in the distance, a silhouette under a streetlamp. It was silent, but he could hear music: a well-known song whose chorus never seemed to arrive, as though the record had stuck. On James walked, his pace slowing, and imperceptibly the street seemed to change: the houses grew taller, narrower, older; the road broadened slightly and parked cars appeared along one side; front gardens shrank and iron gates appeared. And, at his side, there was someone else . . . a girl. He could feel her shoulder leaning against him, and instinctively he put an arm behind her back. He was wearing a long, heavy coat with a silk lining and he could smell the girl's perfume, sweet and familiar, and as they continued walking, ever more slowly, as though reluctant to reach their destination, her head touched his shoulder and he felt her hair on his face, and now he could remember her name in his mouth, his jaw lowering, lips widening, the tip of his tongue touching the hard strip of flesh above his front teeth to make the beloved sound. Ahead of him the silhouette moved forward and he saw that it was a policeman. The policeman stared at them for a moment, then said 'Good evening', and James nodded in reply. The girl murmured something, her breath warm on his neck as she spoke. And then, just as he was feeling utterly blissful and content, something odd happened; something irreconcilable. He was no longer walking with the girl along the street; he was watching the two of them (her and himself?) from above. The air was warmer now, he could smell honeysuckle, and the bliss he felt before had turned sour, haunted, anguished. He said her name again, inside his mouth, and then everything was black and James didn't know where he was.

He stared at the surrounding darkness in confusion. The ground was sloping upward as he walked. He breathed in and could smell rain, tarmac, planked wood, cat piss. And then it came to him: he was not on Lough Street, not in H. at all, but inside an alleyway in the suburban estate where he had grown up. James sighed and kept walking. It had not been real, after all; just another hallucination of the past. And yet still the mingled emotions lingered: bliss and anguish; one memory with two faces. And the song repeating in his mind . . .

He wished it away and forced himself to concentrate on the here and now. An alleyway. The estate was veined with such paths, he recalled: narrow, ever-dark, steeply sloping. This one, like all the others, was protected on either side by tall wooden fences, and crossed above by overhanging tree branches. It seemed to go on forever. His calves were aching now, and he had to stop for a second. In the sudden silence he thought he could hear footsteps behind him, but when he turned around there was only darkness. He listened closely: no sound but the quiet internal roaring of his own lungs and blood. Another hallucination, James told himself, and began walking again.

Halfway up the alley, he noticed a light in a window and stood still, staring at it. The drawn curtains were red and seemed to glow, like the inside of his eyelid when he closed it against the sun. With a shock, James realised where he was. This had been Jane Lipscombe's house. Her bedroom window. His breaths grew slower, felt darker. In his mind, a decade was compressed into a second: he saw her in the window as the large-eyed six-year-old who used to follow him around the playground and, simultaneously, as the tall sixteen-year-old in the blue skirt, sitting at the desk in front, secreting pheromones that drifted over his maths test, blurring the equations, eating up the air in the room. Sighing, James moved on.

As he entered more deeply into the alleyway, he found himself thinking of lost friends. Jane Lipscombe, Philip Bates, Clare Budd . . . He thought of all the people he had known here but with whom he was no longer in touch, their faces moving past in a floating identity parade. And then he tried to *imagine* what he had always taken for granted: that these people were alive, somewhere in the world, at this instant. That, if they looked up now, as he was doing, they would see that same moon, those same clouds and stars. (Or perhaps they wouldn't. Perhaps they were on the other side of the world, where it was daytime and summer.) He thought about the idea that these people were alive, not only now, when he was thinking about them, but all the time. At every instant. Doing something, thinking something, seeing, feeling, experiencing a life utterly estranged from his. He tried to imagine how *he* seemed to these other people. Did he ever cross their minds the way they were crossing his now? Was he anything more to them than a momentarily recalled image, an unidentifiable twinge

somewhere in the stomach or the chest . . . He thought of ringing them up or writing to them, if only to ensure that he could,
for that instant, exist again in their self-contained universe,
pass across the sky of their mind.

This is my life, thought James, looking around at the alleyway and the dark suburb beyond. This is where I entered the
maze. This is where I come from.

And yet, a cold voice reminded him, these events, these
images lived only in his memory; the suburb knew nothing of
them. The suburb existed only in the present. The people in his
mind were surely long gone by now, living elsewhere, pursuing
careers, perhaps even married, their ties to childhood as
stretched and fragile as his own. For all his memories, James
was a stranger here. He was alone.

Emerging from the alleyway, he followed a path through a
small wood and into a long, brightly lit street. For a moment he
merely frowned – where was he? – and then recognition hit
him. Of course . . . this was Commercial Drive. He turned right
and walked past sloping driveways and front gardens, their
details familiar but rendered strange by the lamplight. His
heart was beating faster. Number 36, number 38, number 40
. . . he was nearly there now, he knew. Finally he came to number 46, and stood in the driveway, staring up at it. There it was:
the house where his parents used to live; the house in which his
childhood had been spent. Home.

Yet as James looked at the house's façade, he found himself
bemused and then irritated. *This* was not the house in his memory. It had changed, and not only in small, incremental ways,
like a person's face. The building's front had been completely
renovated: the walls pebbledashed, the wooden windowframes
replaced with plastic double-glazing, the roof retiled, the door
repainted. And now here it stood, a shameless impostor.

James walked up the driveway to the gate at the side of the
double garage. He tried the handle, and it opened. The path,
which had been paved with flagstones before, was now
smoothly concreted. He followed it into the back garden. A

cloud moved in the sky above, and moonlight drenched the scene. For a moment he hesitated, thinking he must somehow have come to the wrong place, and then he began to notice small elements of the garden that had not been altered beyond recognition. That magnolia tree, for example, and the branches of the neighbours' weeping willow, still leaning disconsolately over the wooden fence. But so much had changed that his memories were disturbed. The shed was gone, and the carport; the patio and the slide; all of these places and objects, which had seemed so solid, so permanent, in his mind, had simply ceased to exist. Now James stood on a sort of raised concrete terrace, looking out at this strange landscape, and felt a wave of sorrow move through him. His childhood. Gone.

A sound woke him from his reverie and made him look around again. He noticed a movement on the rockery: a flitting shadow that caused the branches of the young fruit trees to shiver. Probably a cat, he had time to think, and then the moon was covered again by cloud and the whole garden disappeared. James heard a series of noises: a rustling, a small crack, footsteps. Suddenly he felt afraid. Had someone followed him? An image of Malcolm Trewvey's half-remembered face came to him in the darkness. He turned around and, groping with his hands, found his way back through the side-alley to the safety of the lamplit pavement.

James lit a cigar and lay back on the sofa. It was two o'clock in the morning. A picture appeared in his mind of the last time he had smoked a cigar: on the balcony of Ingrid's flat, with the plastercast poking between two railings, blowing smoke into the sky. The memory was vivid, and yet it seemed so unlikely. To James, the summer was another world. He tried to recall the heat, the dizzying colours, the putrid smells, but in the middle of winter it was unimaginable. I can't even prove that any of it existed, he thought. The canal and Harry's Bar. The view from the apartment. Ingrid's body. Had they been real? And the plastercast. There, at least, he found a link between past and present: at night, in the cold, his ankle bone hurt so precisely that he could put his finger on the line where the fracture had healed.

His vision was spinning, so he stubbed out the cigar and got up to look at all the Christmas cards his parents had received, hanging by string garlands from walls and ceiling. James had not sent or received any cards this year; when she discovered this, his mother had started worrying about him becoming 'disconnected'. But do any of these people really care about you, mum? he wondered. And do you really care about them? He stood up and began reading the names and greetings inside them. 'Best wishes for the festive season from Geoff and Sandra.' 'Wishing you a merry Xmas . . . lots of love, Miriam, Keith and all the Joneses xxx.' Who *were* these people? What

232

connection did they have with his parents? He kept going until he came to a name that didn't make him smile ironically. 'I hope you have a happy Xmas and all my good wishes for the new year. Love, Ingrid x.'

James took the card down and stared at the familiar handwriting, with its curly dots above the i's, its neat round lettering. His heart was beating fast. On the front of the card was a child-like drawing of a green tree against a white background; inside were the printed words, '*Vrolijk kerstfeest en een gelukkig nieuwjaar*'. Ingrid. He closed his eyes and tried to remember her face, but already it was fading. He knew what she looked like, of course – if he saw her now, he would recognise her instantly – but still, when he tried to picture her all at once, he found there were parts missing, blurred, frosted over. For a few seconds of panic, he couldn't even remember the colour of her eyes, but then it came to him – they were blue – and slowly the other details returned. Yes, if he tried, he could probably recollect every centimetre of her skin, from the soles of her feet to the crown of her head . . . but then, what would be the point? She was gone from his life. She no longer existed. She was nothing to him now but an awkward silence during dinner, a name on a card sent to someone else. And to her, he guessed, I am just the same. A handful of dust, let go in the wind.

To distract himself he began to scan the bookcase. The top shelf contained various detective novels belonging to his mother. In his mid-twenties, James had gone through a phase of reading nothing but detective stories. Each time, he remembered, he had become obsessed with the mystery, thrilled by its complexity; and each time, when he discovered the solution and finished the book, he was left feeling hollow and let down. Detective stories, he thought, should be read backwards: that way the reader could get the disenchantment out of the way at the beginning and end up in a beautifully perplexing world, like his own but subtly different; a perfect maze, in which each word was a cipher suggesting an infinite number of hidden clues, meanings, possibilities.

The next shelf contained works of serious literature belonging to James himself: novels and plays by Kafka, Melville, Camus, Beckett and Shakespeare that he had bought or been given when he was younger. It would be an exaggeration, however, to say that James had read all of these; certainly he had *begun* them all, but in each case he had become irritated and impatient with the protagonist's indecisiveness, lack of common sense, apparent insanity, or sourceless melancholy. As far as James was concerned, these so-called antiheroes deserved everything they got. Surely it was obvious that the land surveyor, K, should just have forgotten about trying to reach the castle and gone home? Similarly, Ahab should have given up on trying to catch the white whale and gone home; Meursault should have lied; Vladimir and Estragon should have left Godot a note and gone to the pub; and Hamlet should just have made up his mind.

On the bottom shelf were works of philosophy belonging to his father. Mr Purdew was a philosophy lecturer, but it was his opinion, based on years of studying and teaching these books, that philosophy was a waste of time. James had never read any of them. Curious, he scanned the titles and pulled out a *Dictionary of Philosophy*. He began by reading it alphabetically, but quickly realised that this was impractical as almost every entry ended with a list of cross-references which took him to other parts of the book. Soon he became pleasurably lost in this labyrinth of clues and associations. James was amazed. The way his father talked about philosophy, he had always imagined it to be dry and boring, but it was not like that at all. Indeed, though its language was at times as foreign-seeming as German or Japanese, James felt more excited than he had since his early days as a detective. He was on the trail of a mystery once again, though quite what the mystery *was*, he couldn't be sure. Reading philosophy, he thought, was like reading the beginnings to an infinite number of detective stories, without ever having to read their bathetic endings. And yet, because it was all interconnected, it was also like reading one, multilayered, never-ending detective story: a mystery in which the solution, if there were such a thing, was not the identity of a murderer but the meaning of life itself.

At quarter to four, his eyelids growing heavy as he read the two-page biography of Socrates, his eye was caught by another entry heading: 'Solipsism'. James had never realised solipsism was a philosophy. He had thought it was only an insult. According to his father, solipsism was a modern disease. But as soon as he read its basic principles, James knew he had found what he was looking for: an explanation for why he felt the way he felt; why the world seemed the way it seemed.

The name, he learned, came from the Latin: *solus* – alone; *ipse* – self. The philosophy could be traced back to Descartes's supposition, in his *Discourse on the Method*, that the search for truth required the thinker to 'reject as if absolutely false everything in which one could imagine the least doubt, in order to see if one was left believing anything entirely indubitable'. In his First Meditation, Descartes used this method to question such seemingly straightforward observations as 'I am sitting here by the fire', as there was no guarantee that this apparent experience was not a dream. By the end of the First Meditation the philosopher had accepted that everything in the universe (and the universe itself) might be illusion – with the single exception of himself. *Cogito ergo sum*: I think therefore I am. In later Meditations, Descartes regained his belief in the existence of outward reality, but only through the fallacious argument that God must exist.

Solipsism, therefore, began with Descartes' single irrefutable truth – there is no external, verifiable evidence that anything exists beyond one's own mind – and followed this through to its logical conclusion: i.e. nothing exists but me. James tried to imagine what this would mean in practical terms. Everything and everyone around me, he thought – this house, my parents, the neighbours, the television, the pubs, the school, the sky, the earth, the sun and stars and the entire universe – these would be merely the projections of my mind. Was it possible?

Yes, he whispered. *Of course*. That was why he always felt so alone. That was why communication was impossible. That was why his memories seemed so unreal. Why he often had the feeling that the people around him were mere actors, there to fill out the background of a scene. Why none of his actions provoked any real consequences. He was alone, and the whole world, his whole life, was nothing but a dream.

He was about to close the non-existent book and go to his non-existent bed when he noticed the cross-references at the foot of the entry: 'See also: Descartes, René; egocentric predicament; Nagel, Thomas; philosophy of mind; private language argument; problem of other minds; Ryal, Tomas . . .' The last name snagged on something in his mind. Where had he seen it before? He was sleepily brushing his teeth in the bathroom when the memory came back to him. *Tomas Ryal Associates*. That was the name of the company for which Dr Lanark worked.

James switched on the computer in the spare room. It hummed and flickered into life. He went online and typed 'tomas ryal' into a search engine. There were no exact matches. James frowned and checked the spelling of the name in the *Dictionary of Philosophy*. It was correct. He tried a different search engine; again, nothing.

He went downstairs to pour himself a large glass of water. He brought it back up, changed into his pyjamas, and was about to switch off the computer when he noticed that the top entry on the list of sites containing the words 'tomas' and 'ryal' *was* an exact match, after all. 'The Life and Works of Tomas Ryal (1900–197?),' it said. Beneath that was the address: encyclopaedia-labyrinthus.com. James felt sure that this entry hadn't appeared earlier, but he knew that made no sense, so he decided to forget about it and clicked on the web address.

Seconds later he was looking at a list of names. And there, in the centre of the screen, between 'Ruysdael, Jacob Van (Dutch painter)' and 'Ryan, Lacy (English actor)', was 'Ryal, Tomas (Czech philosopher)'. James clicked on this and a new screen appeared. This is what he read:

The Life and Works of Tomas Ryal
(1900–197?)

Tomas Gregor Ryal, known variously during his lifetime as a playwright, pornographer, poet, novelist, drunkard, womaniser, war hero and recluse, but chiefly remembered now as the philosopher who controversially denied the existence of memory, was born in the town of H., near Prague, on Christmas Eve, 1900.

Tomas was an only child. His father, Gregor, was a tutor and philosopher, and his mother, Patryshka, worked for many years as her husband's assistant and book-keeper. Little is known about Tomas's relationship with his parents, but one famously ironic line in his posthumously published (and unfinished) novel, *The Labyrinth*[1] – which, according to his diaries, he began as an attempt at an autobiography – suggests that it was largely harmonious and uncomplicated.

After attending the German-language Gymnasium in Prague (the same school Franz Kafka had attended one generation before) the eighteen-year-old Ryal moved to Berlin, where he read Philosophy. His four years at university were incalculably important for Ryal, introducing him in a short space of time to love, alcohol,

---

1. 'M was permanently and deeply scarred by his upbringing. On many occasions he was heard bemoaning the fact that his parents had bequeathed to him the worst of all possible fates: they had, by behaving at all times reasonably and lovingly, made certain that they could not be blamed in any way for the nightmarish mess that was M's adult life. They had deprived him of the one thing all true artists need in order to write out their demons: a scapegoat.' *The Labyrinth*, tr. H. Mann (New York: 1974), p. 24.

philosophy, fame and guilt – five elements which would come to dominate his life in various ways.

It was while in Berlin that Ryal met Kirstya Elberg, a fellow Philosophy student two years his senior with whom he fell deeply in love. Few details are known about their relationship, as only three letters survive, but it seems they had a brief, illicit affair,[2] which was ended by the guilt-stricken Elberg. Thereafter, they remained close friends for the next two or three years, but – if we are to judge from descriptions of M's student girlfriend Karina in *The Labyrinth* – Ryal never lost his passion for Elberg, and relations became increasingly volatile until what was apparently a sudden severance of communication in 1923. It is not known if Ryal ever learned of the fate of his first love,[3] but he continued to allude to her in letters, diaries and poems until he stopped writing altogether in August 1970.

It must be said at this point that a large part of the 'volatility' in Ryal's lovelife stemmed from his drunkenness. His diaries from this period, which are themselves disordered and strangely incomplete, record many episodes of amnesia, all of which seem to have been induced by overintoxication. Half a dozen times in his first year, Ryal writes that he woke up in a strange place with no memory of how he had arrived there or what he had done. There are hints in the diaries that our hero's beverage of choice was absinthe, which would certainly explain the frequency and length of his blackouts,[4] and would also suggest a root cause to the gradual blindness which affected him towards the end of his life. Some critics maintain that these experiences also explain Ryal's notorious claim that 'we are all of us amnesiacs, and memory nothing but a lie we tell ourselves every day';[5] in other words, that

2. Elberg was engaged at the time to a French aristocrat called Laurent de Silva, though this engagement was broken soon after.
3. According to several (unsubstantiated) reports, she died in a train crash in 1930.
4. On one occasion Ryal 'woke up' while walking the streets of a strange city (Amsterdam) in broad daylight with no recollection of his actions or whereabouts during the previous *five days*.
5. Tomas Ryal, *On the Impossibility of Remembering*, tr. H. Mann (New York: 1970), p. 3.

this was not an expression of a universal human condition, but an obscure cry for help from a deeply sick individual. But the same criticism could potentially be applied to many great writers, including Poe and Kafka.

In any case, the final three years of his university career remain a mystery. His diaries do not cover this period, and there is an unmistakable alteration in tone between the writings before and after this blank time. There appears also to be a very deep sense of guilt and regret. Its source is unknown, though there has been no lack of speculation as to its possible causes, among them the improbable suggestion that Ryal witnessed, or even committed, the murder of a fellow student, Idrizaj Deisler.[6]

At the time, however, there was no suggestion of any impropriety or scandal, and it would seem that, after toying with the idea of travel and writing, Ryal chose a more expedient route and accepted a job on Berlin newspaper *Die Zeit* as a general arts correspondent. He kept this post for five years, during which time his drinking apparently grew more and more uncontrollable, until finally he was fired in 1927.

All we know of Ryal's life in the years that followed is that he spent two years travelling around Europe and the United States before finally settling in England. He rented a small cottage in Devon and endeavoured to live self-sufficiently – growing his own vegetables, rearing sheep, chickens and a cow, and spending the money from his modest inheritance[7] on nothing more extravagant than pints of ale in the local pub, to which he would row every Saturday evening in a wooden dinghy. Ryal lived this way for a total of five years, and he wrote to his mother that it was 'a hard life, but a good one. Nothing makes you feel so alive, mother, as having *only just enough* to eat.' The English weather disagreed with him, but he added that 'rain is good for writing, if less good for living',[8]

6. See G.L. Wise, 'Tomas Ryal: His Life, Parts One and Two', *Literaria Magazine*, May 1986, and M. Trewvey, 'The Philosophy of Murder: Did Tomas Ryal Kill a Fellow Student?', *Bizarreland Quarterly*, June 1993.
7. Gregor Ryal died in 1925.
8. *Collected Letters*, tr. A. Lee-Yun (London, 1980) pp. 95–6.

and certainly his time in Devon was extraordinarily productive in literary terms, considering that he must have spent seven or eight hours a day working on the farm, and that, according to his diaries, he generally fell asleep from exhaustion long before midnight.

It was during this period that Ryal wrote and published his first book of poems, *The Sky as a Mirror of the Land* (1930), his first philosophical work, *On the Impossibility of Knowing* (1931), and most importantly, the 400-page 'meditation', *Solitude* (1934). This book is divided into two parts of equal length and symmetrical structure (a formula that evidently appealed to Ryal, as he would attempt to repeat it in two of his later, major works):[9] part one, 'Oh Why Do I Feel So Alone?', and part two, 'The Benefits of Solitude'. In part one, he posited the solipsistic theory that nothing existed beyond the confines of his own mind,[10] in nine chapters of increasingly passionate, intricate and absurd argument, culminating in the much-(mis)quoted aphorism, 'Thus, if God exists, then I, perforce, am He'. In part two he argues eloquently that solitude is 'the necessary prelude to all true communication – because the right words, the words that come closest to expressing our truths, our human essence, are buried so deep within us. Only through meditation – only, one might say, through obsession, desperation, loneliness, darkness, madness and loss – can we reach and uncover them and bring them up, out, into the air.'

'The Benefits of Solitude' is, with its long mesmerising sentences and aura of utter stillness, a beautiful and inspiring proof of its own thesis, but unfortunately it was part one that stole the critics' attention. Ryal was ridiculed and reviled by several prominent philosophers, and his name, for a while, became a byword for selfishness, inertia, apathy, for every supposedly ignoble emotion of the age.[11]

Ryal, stung by this reaction, later threw himself heroically into

9. *The Labyrinth* and *Heaven and Hell*, both of which were written in the 1960s and published posthumously.
10. A theory he 'disproved' on several later occasions, but somehow never entirely convincingly, at least not to himself, as he seemed haunted by the idea in his final years.
11. It is notable that nothing Ryal wrote in 'Oh Why Do I Feel So Alone?' would cause the slightest stir were it to be published now, in our self-regarding and

the resistance effort in first Czechoslovakia and then France, but that was after several years of illness and regret. He contracted pneumonia during his final winter in England, as did his then girl-friend, Irene, a young dairy maid on an adjacent farm. She died; he survived. Ryal apparently never spoke or wrote about this period, but there are (admittedly cryptic) suggestions in *The Labyrinth* and in some of his letters that Irene was pregnant when she died, and that the two of them were planning to bring up the child together.

Certainly, mortality was the dominant theme of his writings over the next few years, though whether this was due to Irene's death, his own ill health, the war, a mixture of all of these, or something else altogether, is impossible to say. What we do know is that, in 1937, Ryal, now living near Pau, published his second book of poems, *Intimations of Mortality*, and in 1938, his two-act play, *What Happens When We Die*, was staged, albeit briefly and unsuccessfully, in Paris. But, as powerful as they were, these two works were mere throat-clearings in comparison to the monumen-tally morbid *Darkness*, published in 1939. Part philosophical medi-tation, part political diatribe, part apocalyptic prose-poem, *Darkness* was – fittingly, perhaps, given its tone and subject matter – swallowed up into obscurity by the clouds of war, though it later enjoyed respect, if not success, when it was republished alongside Ryal's far more optimistic book, *The Light*, in 1968. Sartre is said to have referred to it admiringly as 'the bleakest, deepest well into which I have ever descended', and it is certainly Ryal's most diffi-cult and depressing work, though not without its small epiphanies.

By the end of the war[12] Tomas Ryal was a forgotten man. *Soli-tude* had been unfairly ridiculed, while *Darkness* simply went unread. For most of the 1950s, punctuated by financial worries and alcoholic misadventures, Ryal led an anonymous, peripatetic life, moving from town to town through France, Germany, Italy and Ireland, making enough money to live by translation work,

atomised present; his observations on the individualistic impulse in society have been made to seem brilliantly prescient by the passage of time.

12. For a full account of Ryal's heroic exploits in the Czech and French resis-tance, see *Tomas Ryal: A Life* by Hugh Mann (New York: 1988), pp. 171–205.

hack journalism and pornographic stories, all of which were published pseudonymously, and all the time writing the diaries and notes that would later resurface in his great final works, *On the Impossibility of Remembering*, *The Book as a Mirror of the World*, *The Light*, *The Labyrinth*, and *Heaven and Hell*.[13]

Had it not been for a young Austrian psychologist, Dr Felice Berger, Tomas Ryal's name might never have re-emerged from this obscurity, and these wonderful books never been published, perhaps never even written. But in 1958, while working on a thesis about the causes and effects of fear and hope, Berger came across a mimeographed copy of Ryal's 5,000-word essay, 'On Fear and Hope in the Novels of Kafka', which had been published in a small Vienna-based magazine called *Brainwaves* in 1928. Astonished by his insights, which she described as 'ahead not only of his own time, but of ours too', Berger set out to find the man who had written the article.

Her search took nearly two years[14] but Berger eventually tracked Ryal down to a seedy apartment in Helsinki, where he was working as a private detective and spending his earnings on vodka and whores. Upon being asked by Berger about his seminal essay on fear and hope in the novels of Kafka, Ryal claimed he had no memory of ever having written anything of the kind. Later, when Berger had gained his trust and helped wean him from his alcohol dependency, he recalled writing it 'in the course of two white nights one week while passing through Vienna. I'd bumped into the editor of the magazine at a bar and we'd had a conversation about Kafka. His books had only just come out at the time, and very few people knew about them. He was interested in what I had to say about *The Trial* and *The Castle* and he urged me to write it down. At first I refused, as I was planning to leave Vienna the following day, but he promised he would buy me a good meal, and I was very hungry at

13. Ryal is also supposed to have written a symbolical fantasy novel, title unknown, in the style of J. R. R. Tolkien or Mervyn Peake. There are references to this book in several diary entries from 1965 onwards, but no such manuscript was ever found.
14. For details of this quest, see the highly recommended *In Search of a Lost Genius*, by Felice Berger and John Graves (London: 1963).

the time, so that was why I wrote it. I ended up distilling a lot of my emotions from the previous few years into that essay, which is, I think, where its power comes from. On the surface it may appear quite scholarly and abstract, but in truth I was performing open-heart surgery on my own past. As for the idea that hope and fear are, at root, the same emotion, and that, of the two, hope is the more dangerous and unbearable variation . . . that was something I had believed for a long time – and I still believe it now.'[15]

On Berger's invitation, Ryal – by now a thin, white-bearded man of sixty – moved to a rural village 100 km from Vienna, where Berger's parents owned a large country house. In the grounds was a cottage, originally intended for the gardener, which had lain empty for years. Berger had this cottage renovated, and it was in this remote and beautiful place, close to a forest, that Ryal lived during the last and most prolific decade of his writing career. Each morning he chopped wood for the stove, made himself breakfast, and immediately set to work. He wrote all morning, ate lunch, and then set off for long walks in the afternoon, often disappearing into the forest for hours on end. In the evenings he would go to the main house to eat dinner with Berger's parents, who were slightly younger than him and in awe of his talent, and then go back to his cottage to read and drink wine and 'daydream before the fire'.

It was from this quiet, bucolic routine that Ryal's greatest

15. *In Search of a Lost Genius*, pp. 282–3. According to Ryal's essay, *The Trial* is 'a book of absolute fear' and *The Castle* 'a book of absolute hope' – and the second 'is by far the more terrible. Why? Because it has no end. The torturing hope is never resolved. In *The Trial*, death comes as a relief; in *The Castle*, the words run out, halfway through a sentence, with no sign that K's hope is dwindling in the slightest. Rather it seems to grow, his hope; it goes on and on, feeding on scraps of nothing, growing ever larger and more monstrous, eating him up from inside. Were it ever to be resolved, the disappointment would come as a relief, but the horror of hope is that it does not die. It lives as long as we do. And this is why, for me, *The Castle* is more terrible, and more true-to-life: because none of us has ever experienced death; none of us has ever felt that true, lasting relief. Our condition is K's condition: the grim, blind, teeth-grinding tension of someone who believes that they are *getting closer, ever closer, to finding the key to it all*.'

books emerged. The first to be published was *Longings* (1963), his third collection of poetry, which was quickly followed by *The Book as a Mirror of the World* (1965), a collection of literary essays including the now-famous one on Kafka and another, described by the *London Times* as 'strange and revelatory', on Jorge Luis Borges and Philip Larkin,[16] which would come to be even more famous.[17] It also contains a speculative physiognomical essay (illustrated with photographs) called 'The Good Eye and the Evil Eye' which has been anthologised more often than any other of Ryal's writings.[18] Yet by the time these books were

16. This Freud-inspired essay, 'The Double-Sided Mirror', posits the provocative theory that Larkin and Borges are literary representatives of the 'twin poles of existence'; that everyday life is always experienced as either Larkinesque (mundane, banal, futile, miserable; a work-oriented adult world of reductive and observable 'reality' ruled by the rational Superego) or Borgesian (dreamlike, imaginative, random, infinite; a playful, childish world of emotional and perceptual 'fantasy' ruled by the irrational Id), and that quite often we switch between the two 'from hour to hour or even second to second'. The example Ryal used was a bookshelf – 'on the one hand a simple object manufactured from wood and filled with books – simple objects manufactured from paper – and on the other hand, the memory of each book on the shelf read by the perceiver, the thoughts and fantasies released by the reading of the book and the memory of the book, the memories of the time when the book was read, the way the sight of the bookshelf and the wall behind it make you feel, depending on the light and the time of day and your mood, etc'.

17. This intuitive vision of human experience as a dualistic process of 'permanent dreaming with interruptions of reality' has, like several of Ryal's ideas about the mind, since been proven scientifically sound, at least in its broad outline. Rodolfo Llinas and his colleagues at New York University, comparing the electro-physiological properties of the brain in waking and dreaming, suggest a single basic mechanism for both – a ceaseless inner talking between the cerebral cortex and the thalamus, a non-stop interplay of image and feeling, irrespective of whether there is sensory input or not. When there is sensory input, it is integrated into the dreaming to generate waking consciousness. Thus waking is a kind of dreaming; a dreaming influenced (to varying degrees) by external reality. (Ryal, of course, was not the first philosopher to suggest such an idea. Variations on this concept can be traced back to Plato and even beyond, while in more modern times Schopenhauer came up with perhaps the most striking analogy, when he wrote that life and dreams were pages from the same book, and that to read them in their proper order was to live, but to leaf through them randomly was to dream.)

18. 'We think of our faces as whole and in harmony, everything neatly symmetrical, yet this is a lie. Study the face of the most beautiful person you know. Now

published, Ryal had already been working on his 'autobiographical novel' *The Labyrinth* for three and a half years. A year later, midway through the third draft, he finally abandoned this and, driven to despair by the vague uncertainties of his memory, wrote *On the Impossibility of Remembering*.

Published in 1966, this slim book, though condemned by certain critics as a work of 'pseudoscience', drew the approbation of several renowned scientists, who, inspired by its instinctual insights, changed the nature of their research in an attempt to 'prove' what Ryal believed. Put simply, his contention was that memory was a myth; that all our attempts at 'recalling' the past were in fact reconstructions, recreations, acts of fiction. To demonstrate the extremity of his theory – what he called its 'radical absoluteness' – Ryal came up with the concept of the Mneman:[19] a human being whose essential character, whose soul, ceases to exist every time he falls asleep, and is born anew each time he wakes – not as the same person, but as someone else, someone new.[20] 'And one could go further,' he writes at the end of this chapter. 'One could say that "I" become a Mneman not only every morning but in every waking moment, during every second; that "I" am in a constant state of flux, that what "I" call "myself" is describable only in the present. If "I" talk about how

---

cover half their face. Now cover the other half. One of those half-faces is hideous, confess it. Each of us has an evil eye; an eye half-closed by the world; an eye made ugly by the ugly things it has seen. That is not surprising. The miracle is the other eye: the good eye; the eye that sees the world, and is seen by the world, as it did when you were a child – with the same wide-open wonder and innocence . . .' As persuasive as these words are, it was the startling juxtaposition of two photographs that made the essay such a *succès d'estime*: a photograph of Ryal at nineteen and another, in exactly the same pose, of Ryal at fifty-nine. In the first his eyes are quite similar in shape and expression; in the second his left eye is a battered, malignant squint, and his right eye almost completely unchanged despite the passage of forty years.

19. To be pronounced 'new man'.

20. Fittingly, the epigraph to the chapter on the Mneman came from *Alice's Adventures in Wonderland*: 'I wonder if I've been changed in the night? . . . But if I'm not the same, the next question is, "Who in the world am I!" Ah, *that's* the great mystery.'

"I" was, at some point in the past, then "I" am lying, if only to "myself".'[21]

By this time, Ryal had already begun exhibiting signs of what Berger's alarmed parents called his 'manias'. Other observers confirmed that his working routines were now far more erratic and obsessive – he would sometimes shut himself up in the cottage for as long as seventy-two hours, his light burning continuously, and then sleep for a whole day and night – and that his moods swung wildly between an infantile serenity and a furious, wall-eyed despair.[22] The Bergers' spiritually intense Alsatian maid, Gabrielle Schwarz, whose job it was to deliver meals to Ryal during these last five years, and who consequently saw him more often than anybody else, remarked that 'he could appear very good or very evil, but most of the time he was neither. He was like a ghost: his soul had departed elsewhere, and left behind this living shell. I was not surprised at all when his body too disappeared.'[23]

Such observations fit well (perhaps suspiciously well?) with the near-ecstatic 'abandonment to nature' of The Light, published in 1967 as a slender single volume, and a year later alongside its lengthier and more earthbound companion piece, Darkness. Nominally a 'philosophical meditation', The Light is closer in tone to a prose poem or indeed a work of religious revelation. Though unequivocal in its denial of the existence of any kind of god or afterlife, it has a serenity and certainty which is gloriously at odds with the tortured dread of Darkness. Both books are essentially about death, and you could argue (as several critics have) that The Light is merely Darkness rewritten by someone in the grip of senile dementia. But such a conclusion ignores the indisputable fact that this same writer was, at the same time, working on the utterly clear-eyed Heaven and Hell. And, whatever you call the

21. *On the Impossibility of Remembering*, pp. 112–13.
22. The latter may well have been brought on by his slowly deteriorating eyesight. By the time of his disappearance in 1970, Ryal is said by Felice Berger to have been 'almost entirely blind'; a condition which must surely have contributed to the nagging fear that he was, as he phrased it in *Solitude*, 'all alone in the universe'.
23. *Tomas Ryal: A Life*, p. 402.

state into which Ryal transported himself (or was transported) during his composition of *The Light* – 'senile dementia' or 'mania' or 'all-seeing ecstasy'[24] (the latter being his own preferred term) – the book retains an otherworldly power which is, to many people, undeniable and inspiring. It is, by a long way, Ryal's most enduringly popular work.

The last book published by Ryal in his lifetime was *Dreams of Elsewhere*, his fourth (and most perfect) collection of poetry. Unlike his other collections, *Dreams of Elsewhere* is divided into three titled parts: 'Past', 'Present' and 'Future', each containing seven sonnets. The first section is characterised by a melancholy but transfixingly beautiful nostalgia. The second mixes the 'Larkinesque'– bald descriptions of the insides of his cottage, the view from his window, his sagging flesh and aching joints – with 'Borgesian' flights of fancy, dreams, memories and inner voices. The final part occupies a similar territory to *The Light*, though leavened with self-deprecating wit and disturbingly detailed and untroubled descriptions of worms feeding on dead flesh, fingernails growing and scratching the coffin's underside, skin and bones being incinerated into ash, ash being scattered by the wind. *Dreams of Elsewhere* was published in September 1969.

All the evidence suggests that Ryal kept writing until the end of his occupancy of the cottage. On the evening of 23 August 1970, Schwarz took Ryal's dinner to the cottage, as he had not appeared at the house, and was surprised to find the door ajar. She entered, and discovered the cottage empty. It was eight o'clock, and this was the first time he had ever been absent at this hour. Schwarz left the meal on Ryal's desk, next to a neatly stacked pile of black

24. Ryal's American biographer Hugh Mann speculates that Ryal was taking LSD during this period. While this is in many ways a plausible and attractive hypothesis – it would explain many aspects of the author's behaviour, as well as the uncanny visions described in his book – there is absolutely no evidence to support it. LSD was, at the time, still a relatively new drug, and its use was far from widespread. And let us not forget that Tomas Ryal was, by this point, a sixty-six-year-old man living miles from any city in a gardener's cottage in rural Austria. On the grounds of probability alone, the suggestion ought to be ruled out.

notebooks and a single white notebook, and returned to the main house to inform the Bergers. Alarmed by the old man's disappearance, the Bergers and their servants organised a search party, but by ten o'clock it was dark and they had discovered no sign of him. The police were called, but despite a full-scale, three-day operation involving dogs and helicopters, they found nothing. Newspaper stories were accompanied by obituaries, but Felice Berger denounced the publication of the latter, saying there was no evidence that her friend was dead.

During September and October, Berger took up residence in the cottage and devoted her time to reading the notebooks on the desk. This, she concluded, was Ryal's *Meisterwerk*, the book he had been talking about and working upon for the past six years, ever since his abandonment of *The Labyrinth*. The book, Berger announced, was entitled *Heaven and Hell*, and was intended to be two volumes of equal length. Yet, while *Hell* is now famous for its 530 pages of aphorisms, anecdotes and parables expressing Ryal's clear-eyed horror at the reality of existence,[25] all that has ever been found of *Heaven* is a few pages, in that single white notebook, of seemingly incoherent notes. It has been speculated that the MS of *Heaven* was lost or destroyed, but given the careful orderliness of the desk which Ryal left, the assumption has to be that it was never written. Some critics maintain that these notes (amounting to no more than 14 pages in all, and quickly dismissed by most readers as nonsensical ravings) are in fact a sort of code or key for re-reading *Hell* in a different way. But other critics point to phrases in *Hell* which suggest an alternative solution, notably the

25. Commenting on the two famous twentieth-century definitions of Hell – Sartre: '*L'enfer, c'est les autres*'; Eliot: 'Hell is oneself,/ Hell is alone, the other figures in it/ Merely projections' – Ryal drew the bleak conclusion that 'Hell is the inevitable, heartbreaking, self-evident truth that Eliot and Sartre are both right. Hell is oneself *and* Hell is other people. Hell is nothing more nor less than a perfect reflection of life, ourselves and the world – with no distortions or concealments – looked at unflinchingly and remembered, always, in every detail. In other words, although we live in Hell, all the time, it is only in rare, indescribable moments of insight that we recognise this. Our forgetfulness, our stupidity, our blindness are all that save us from the eternal abyss, the endless black-walled labyrinth.'

sentence 'Hell is a place with only two exits: the black door and the white door. The black door leads nowhere. The white door leads to Heaven.'[26]

Tomas Ryal's body was discovered on 8 July 1973, deep in the forest. By the time of its discovery, it had been picked clean to the bones,[27] so it was more or less impossible to calculate the timing of Ryal's death, other than to say it must have occurred at some point between autumn 1970 and spring 1973. What we will never know is what Ryal's life was like in those final days: what he was thinking, how he was feeling. But then, the past, as Ryal told us in *Hell*, 'is always inaccessible, forever lost'.

Hell was published in German the following year, in other languages the year after that, and the reviews were almost embarrassingly adulatory. Tomas Ryal, the man who claimed memory was a myth, ironically refuses to be forgotten.

26. Tomas Ryal, *Hell*, tr D. Hyde (London: 1975), p. 330. According to Hyde's commentary, the black door represents death, and the white door madness.
27. It was identified from Ryal's dental records.

James sat up in bed and tried to collect his thoughts. The thirteen printed pages of 'The Life and Works of Tomas Ryal' were spread out over the duvet. He regarded them in the stark light of the desk lamp, wondering what it was that made him feel so uneasy. The first time he had read the article, he had been fascinated, purely and simply: Ryal, it seemed, had lived a strange and eventful life, and the descriptions of his books had made James want to read them.

But when he'd gone online to order the books, he had been unable to find any references to them whatsoever. Puzzled, he had typed in the address of the Encyclopaedia Labyrinthus, but this had produced only a white screen with the words, 'The system cannot find the path specified.' He had tried again, with the same result. And that was when he had begun to suspect that the article was not what it purported to be.

His suspicions had deepened as he re-read it. There was nothing he could put his finger on, but the more closely he looked at this story, the more he seemed to detect another, different, vaguely familiar story, somewhere beneath it. This had made James fearful: he was, he realised, thinking like a detective again. And so, resolving not to jump to any illogical conclusions, he had spread the pages out on the duvet in order to examine each of them, objectively, one by one, taking notes as he went along.

As he read again the details of Ryal's life story, he was disturbed by several unwelcome images. For instance, the moment he came to footnote number 3, about the possible fate of Ryal's girlfriend, Kirstya Ellberg, he saw a picture in his mind of a departing train and felt a wrench of deep unhappiness. He was going to note this down, but in the end he decided it was a bad idea. After all, the image was nothing but a stray emotion, a vague feeling; if he began to take account of all such feelings, he would soon end up lost again in a labyrinth of hopes and fears. The important thing was to establish the *facts*.

He kept on, scrutinising every sentence, every word. And then he found something that made him gape in shock. In the seventh footnote, the name of the writer who accused Ryal of murdering his fellow student was M. Trewvey. This was, surely, too strange to be a coincidence. It was only one small anomaly, but it was troubling none the less, and James found that the more he thought about it, the less convinced he was by the rest of the article. The reference to Trewvey was a loose thread, and when he pulled at it, the entire garment began to unravel. Within a few minutes, he had lost all belief in the document. It seemed to him flimsy, absurd, quite clearly fabricated: Tomas Ryal had never existed, those books had never been written. Why anyone would have gone to the bother of perpetrating such a complex fraud was beyond him. Only the author could answer that . . . whoever he might be.

James remembered the footsteps he had heard behind him on his walk through the suburb earlier that night. Was he being followed? Was someone persecuting him, teasing him with meaningless clues? *Malcolm Trewvey*, he thought, looking wildly around, and I stiffened. Was it possible he could see me, standing here watching him, just beyond the pool of light cast by the desk lamp, just beyond the limits of his consciousness? For an uncomfortable moment, I wondered if the game was up, if he was on to me. But finally, thankfully, James sighed and switched off the light.

No, he told himself, you're just feeling tired and paranoid. The best thing to do is sleep on it; everything will seem different in the morning. He looked at the digital figures on his radio alarm clock: 05.50. As he closed his eyes and fell asleep, a last, fleeting thought crossed his mind: when I wake up it will be Christmas Day.

James had a hangover when he woke, and he felt foolish as he gathered the sheets of computer paper and put them in the dustbin. Solipsism . . . Tomas Ryal . . . what a load of nonsense! He really ought to stop drinking so much. His head ached and his mouth was dry, but for some reason, as he walked downstairs, he felt a small throb of excitement in his chest.

Melted butterlike daylight was staining the walls and carpet of the sitting room, the metal angels that hung from the branches of the tree reflecting it in bright and dreamy blinks. He could hear the ticking of the wall clock and, if he held his breath, the distant joyful twittering of birds. Through blurs of condensation on the French windows he could see the back garden, covered in sparkling frost. Under the tree were four small piles of objects; of course he guessed they were probably nothing special, but at that instant, wrapped in their gold and silver skins, they looked so perfect and mysterious that James felt like a child again. The world seemed magical, full of infinite possibilities.

He found his parents and grandmother in the kitchen, wearing dressing-gowns and making tea. Involuntarily he grinned at them. They all wished him happy Christmas and his grandmother hugged him. She had tears in her eyes, and as he felt the pressure of her limbs round his body, the warmth and wetness of her lips on his skin, James almost started to cry himself. It had been a long time since anyone had held him like that.

The rest of the day passed pleasantly enough. They opened the presents – the usual anticlimax – and ate lunch. Afterwards, bloated and serene, he listened to his gran as she described all the friends who had died or been hospitalised in the last year. She wasn't afraid of death, she insisted, but of losing her marbles. She made James's father promise he would have her 'put down' if the time ever came when she didn't know who he was. There was a long silence after that.

Some time later, James excused himself and went to the bathroom. It was pleasantly cool in comparison to the sitting room. He had only just unbelted his trousers and lowered himself on to the toilet seat when the doorbell rang. Carol singers, James guessed, but instead of a polite 'no, thank you' from his father, he was surprised to hear loud voices and clattering feet. Just at that moment, an enormous fart echoed in the bowl beneath him, and someone laughed. Despite the coolness, sweat trickled from his hairline.

The doorbell went again and James groaned with pain. More voices, laughter, the harsh tapping of stilletos on tiles. Who were all these people? he wondered. What were they doing here? His father's voice rang out, strangely loud and confident, silencing the others. James couldn't make out what his father was saying, but he could tell it was meant to be witty from the intonation and the bursts of laughter that punctuated each pause in his story. After a minute or so, there was a particularly loud, long guffawing, and then a new silence, as though his father had grown serious. James tried to listen more closely. What was he saying? '. . . our son James, who is, as I speak . . .'

He was so surprised to hear his name that his bowels relaxed and let out a machine-gun fart of extraordinary duration. There was a brief silence, during which James held his breath, then his father said something and suddenly there was a banging at the door, a strange man's mocking voice, and peals of laughter. The door handle moved up and down and James stared desperately at the slender bolt, praying it would not give way. Sweat poured down his face. The stink in the bathroom was unbearable now. Finally, to James's relief, the voices went quieter and a door closed, reducing them to a distant murmur.

When he was finished, James washed his hands and face and opened the bathroom door. He looked out warily into the hallway. It was empty. He was about to go upstairs and hide in his room, but curiosity overcame him. He hadn't even known his parents had friends; now, it seemed, they were at the centre of a lively social circle, and his father, normally so shy and gruff, had turned into some kind of raconteur. It was all too strange, and James felt compelled at least to see these people's faces.

Trying not to make any noise, he pressed down on the handle and opened the sitting-room door a few inches. He could smell cigar smoke and hear music and echoing conversations. But still he couldn't see anything more than a few inches of wallpaper, so he pushed the door again. It squeaked on its hinges and the room fell quiet. A hundred eyes were staring at James. He was about to mumble something and leave when a man's loud voice said, 'James! Come in, mate, we were just talking about you!'

Astonished, James looked at the man who had spoken: he was florid-cheeked, balding, obviously drunk, and dressed in a check suit and bow tie. More to the point, despite his familiar tone, James felt certain he had never seen the man before in his life.

'Sorry?' he said in a cold voice.

'Sorry?' The man cruelly imitated James's voice, and then laughed. 'Ooh, aren't we posh?' The room was filled with shrieking, braying laughter.

Without really knowing what he was doing, James moved towards the man. 'Who are you?'

'Who am I? Blimey! Didn't the doorman introduce me? Have him sacked, somebody – that's *outrageously* negligent!' Again the room erupted into laughter, and the man, clearly enjoying himself, pressed home his advantage. 'Or perhaps he did introduce me and you didn't hear because you were too busy *farting*?'

There was uproar at this – hoots, cackles and a whole range

of imitation trump noises. Furious, James scanned the faces for his parents and grandmother. He was sure they must be equally angry at this man's rudeness. He wanted his dad to grab the man by the arms and brusquely escort him outside. He wanted his mum to slap the man's face, his gran to knee him in the balls. But then James finally saw them, all three together, and realised that they were laughing too.

The man was staring insolently at James. When the laughter had died down, he said, 'Your parents and your gran were just telling us about when you were young, James. You were a strange one, weren't you? Writing poetry! Too shy to go out with girls! Always ill and daydreaming, playing with your imaginary friends . . . Such a *sensitive* boy, as that Portuguese doctor said when you had your first asthma attack.'

James gasped. He couldn't believe his parents would have revealed such personal details to a stranger.

'And how about that time you pissed yourself in someone else's house because you were playing Monopoly and you were afraid someone would cheat if you left the room? Ha! Or the day those older lads called you a bum boy and stole your trousers and hung them from the top of the tree in the school grounds and you had to run back home in your underpants, crying! That was a good one, eh?'

The people around the man were weeping with laughter. James wanted to punch his face, but the cruel words seemed to disable him. He was so shamed by these forgotten memories that it was as if he had become that small child again, weak and helpless in front of everybody.

'Oh yes,' said the man, when the laughter had died down again. 'Some of the things you did were quite funny. But then you got older, didn't you, James? You became a teenager. A sulky, stuck-up, smart-arsed teenager. You know what it was like living with you then? Do you? What was it like, Maggie?'

'Hell,' said his grandmother, in a venomous voice.

James stared at her, dumbfounded.

'How would you describe it, Brian?'

'A living nightmare,' said his father, without irony.

'What about you, Penny?'

James looked at his mum pleadingly. She bit her lip, looked away, and said, 'I don't want to talk about it.'

'I'm sorry,' said James.

'Sorry?' laughed the man. 'We've hardly begun. Better wait till we've finished before you start apologising, you little twat.'

James does not remember all the vile accusations the man made against him during the long, awful minutes that followed, all the personal embarrassments and petty misdemeanours he exposed to this group of drunken, laughing strangers. Some of the incidents seemed unfamiliar and James began to wonder if the man was making them up, but after a while he lost the power to distinguish fact from fiction. Even if they were invented, he told himself, that doesn't mean they're not true: deep down, you must deserve the hell this stranger is giving you, not for the minor crimes he has inventoried, but for a major one that he hasn't. Something large and dark and unspoken. Something only he, James, knew about, and which he had forgotten. *His own guilty secret.*

After that he must have said or done something because the next thing he knew, the whole room had been silenced, and all the laughing eyes had grown shocked and serious. People were shaking their heads, turning away in silence. Quickly and quietly the strangers said their goodbyes and filed out of the room, each of them pausing before James to stare contemptuously. And then he saw his mother crying, and his father and grandmother comforting her.

'Mum,' he said, but no one seemed to hear.

Alone, he left the room and climbed the stairs.

The next morning, when James woke up and the memories returned to him, he told himself they couldn't be true. His gran would never had said 'Hell' like that. His parents would not have let a stranger insult him. His memory must have merged, during the night, with his dreams, and now he could no longer tell where one ended and the other began.

Even so, he still had the uneasy sensation that these little lies were half-covering some bigger truth. Again he thought of the three missing years. What had happened to him? What had he done? It suddenly occurred to James that he should ask his parents. They hadn't been in H. with him, of course; they might not know the whole story. But surely they would have some inkling, some vague idea.

There was a soft knocking at the door. 'Come in,' James said, deciding that he would apologise to his mother for all he had ever done to upset her, tell her how much he loved her, and then ask her to help him with something. When he looked up, however, he saw that the person carrying the heavily loaded tray towards his bed was not his mother but his grandmother.

'Good morning,' she said cheerfully, her voice vibrating slightly with the effort of holding the tray.

'Gran, let me help you . . .'

'No, you're all right!' she shouted, lurching suddenly to one side. Some tea spilled on the floor and pain creased her face.

James got out of bed quickly and steadied the tray with his

hands. He could hear his grandmother breathing fast. On the tray was a pot of tea, a rack of toast and a full English breakfast. 'You shouldn't be carrying all that,' said James.

'*Why* shouldn't I?' Her face was red and she was swaying.

'Sit down, gran. Have a rest.'

'Well, maybe for a little while.'

She sat on the bed. When she had got her breath back, she urged him to eat his breakfast.

'Delicious,' he mumbled.

She explained that his parents had gone away for a few days, so she would be 'looking after' him instead. James felt a spasm of anxiety at the news – why and where had his parents gone? – but smiled so as not to alarm his gran. 'That's nice,' he said, 'although really I should be looking after you.'

'Don't talk rubbish,' his gran replied. 'Do you remember when I used to look after you when you were a little boy? You used to come to my house every other weekend.'

James frowned. There was a fuzzy picture in his mind. 'Was there a gas fire?'

'That's right. And we used to sit and eat toasted crumpets in front of it in the evening. Do you remember that?'

'I think so. So did I sleep at your house, then?'

'Many times. And when you did, I'd always make you a full English breakfast and bring it to you in bed. You remember that, don't you?'

'I'm not sure.'

'Oh, I thought you'd remember the breakfasts.' She looked crestfallen. 'What about our backgammon games? And when we made boats out of paper and floated them in the reservoir? And when I took you to see my boss Johnny at the bookmaker's and he'd spin you round on his chair . . .'

James shook his head. 'Sorry.'

His gran sucked her false teeth and he thought for a moment she was going to cry. But finally she said, in a low thoughtful voice, 'Never mind. It'll maybe come back to you when you're older.'

He looked at her, surprised. 'Do you think so?'

'Oh yes. I remember ever so much more now than I used to when I was your age. It's probably because I spend more time remembering now. The older I get, the more details I can make out, like with a telescope, little things far off in the distance. All the way back to when I was a ween.'

'Hang on, I thought a ween was a baby.'

'Aye. A toddler. A littlun. I remember being pushed in my pram and laughing at the big faces. I remember walking for the first time, and falling into my dad's arms . . .' James looked at her sceptically. Such memories were, he was fairly sure, impossible. Presumably his gran merely *imagined* she could remember such events. 'I remember the bedroom I used to sleep in with my brothers and sisters. There were five of each, you know; I was the youngest of eleven kids . . .'

James, impatient, interrupted her. 'Gran, do you remember what happened to me when I was at university?'

There was a long pause and his grandmother's face turned white. 'Well . . .' she said finally, her voice weak. 'Well, you were ill, weren't you, love?'

'Ill?'

'Yes. You were . . . not yourself.' She gave him a fearful look. 'I don't know any more than that, love. Just that you weren't well and now you're better. Some things are best forgotten, you know.' She stood up and began straightening the duvet, her hands shaking slightly. 'So anyway, I grew up with all these brothers and sisters, and I still remember when . . .'

James sighed. Evidently his grandmother wasn't going to tell him any more than she already had. She continued talking, but James had heard all this before and he soon stopped listening. He was thinking about what she had said earlier. She remembered more because she spent more time remembering. Could this be true? If so, it meant his cause was not hopeless after all. The few blurred fragments that he could recall from his childhood . . . perhaps if he spent more time thinking about them, they would sharpen into focus, other details would be revealed, forgotten events called back from the darkness. He thought of the previous attempts he had made to write his memoirs. He had been trying to follow the thread back through the maze, but these attempts had failed because the thread had been cut long before. The only way to retrieve those lost years was to enter the maze at the beginning. But the true beginning – his birth – was for ever lost. What he needed was some other entry point; a crack in the wall of time. Not a memory – they were too hazy, too prone to change – but something solid. Something immutable. Suddenly it came to him. 'Gran, do you have any photos?'

'Of course, love – I've got a big book full of 'em. Right from when I was a baby to when I got married . . .'

'No, I mean photos of *my* childhood.'

'Oh, right. I've got the lovely framed ones, but I think your dad put most of the old pictures in boxes. To protect them, like.'

'And where are the boxes?'

She pointed with her eyes to the ceiling.

There were three boxes, all made of thick grey cardboard, with neatly fitting lids. James brought them down from the attic, one by one, and wiped away the coating of dust. The boxes were heavy. On the first box, in black felt pen on a white label, it said, '72–76'; on the second, '77–84'; and on the third, '85–92'.

He opened the first box. Inside were eighteen packets of photographs, each marked with a season and year. He laid the packets out in chronological order on the floor of the spare room and began with the earliest: Summer 72. This was a year before James's birth. The photographs seemed to have been taken mostly on a foreign holiday: there were palm trees and mountains and dramatic sunsets in the background. It was strange to see his parents looking so young – younger than he himself was now. In the photographs, his father was always laughing; he had shoulder-length hair and a gingery beard, and wore shorts and T-shirts and little round sunglasses. Less extrovert, his mother tended to smile beatifically; she had long hair and her pert breasts were clearly visible beneath the blouses and summer dresses she wore. Both of them looked happy and in love. James could not believe these people had become his parents; or, rather, he could not believe that his parents had once been these people.

The second and third packets were more or less the same, but with different clothes and backgrounds. There were gloomy-looking interiors and crowds of other people: James recognised certain relatives and friends, but most were strangers to him. The fourth packet contained his parents' official wedding pictures, the fifth their honeymoon snapshots. James skipped these as he had seen them many times before. But the sixth packet – Winter 72/3 – was completely new to him. There were images of several houses, one of which he recognised as 46 Commercial Drive, the house in which he had grown up. The other houses, he guessed, must have been places his parents had visited with estate agents around the same time. He stared at these with fascination. Had they made a different choice, taken a different path, it might be *these* anonymous living rooms and staircases and brick façades that were making his heart swell.

He dwelled lovingly on the photographs with his old house and garden in the background. It was comforting to know that, even if the physical realities themselves had been erased, removed, destroyed, then at least these paper images of them remained, slowly fading perhaps, but not distorting or whispering lies as his memories did. And yet, as he examined the pictures' little details – the patterns on carpets and wallpaper and curtains, the fabric of sofas and shirts and coats – he couldn't help feeling slightly disappointed. Oh yes, he thought, that's how it was. Now he could see these things before his eyes, they seemed suddenly less wondrous than they had before, when they had been only memories, floating hazily in his mind. For the first time it occurred to James that memory might, after all, be his mind's way of making the past seem more beautiful and mysterious than it truly had been; that his memory, far from being an enemy, was perhaps his closest friend.

There was one strange photograph at the end of the sixth packet: it was taken in the kitchen and James could see the garden, dark with rain, in the background. In the centre of the frame his mother stood in profile, wearing striped pyjamas and lifting up the top so that her breasts were half-revealed. Yet there was nothing salacious about the picture. James couldn't figure out what it meant until he came across an almost identical image in the next packet; the only differences he could see were that the garden looked brighter and his mother's stomach slightly larger. And then he realised. His mother was not the subject of this photograph at all. *He* was.

I look like a gift, he thought: a small, mysterious shape covered in someone else's skin. In the eighth packet the gift was unwrapped – and there he lay, naked and screaming, swaddled and asleep. There were dozens of photographs of this small, helpless creature, but they meant nothing to James. Plainly there was no real connection between the newborn baby in the photographs and the thirty-year-old man who held and stared at them. They shared a name, a set of genes, but nothing else. They were not the same person. They were not even similar. James shook his head. He had imagined that looking at photographs of himself as a child would have helped him to understand how he had changed, but it seemed only to annihilate the possibility of any such understanding. It was inconceivable, and that was all. It could not be.

Through the next ten packets of photographs, James watched the impossible slowly occur. In poorly lit bedrooms and in dazzling gardens, the baby grew longer and thinner, sat up, began crawling, stood on two feet and took its first steps. There was no punctuation; there were no chapters to this story. James sat on his dad's shoulders (the beard had gone now, he noticed) and James played football. James stroked a cat and James climbed a tree. James made a sandcastle and James slept on the sofa. He put the packets back in the first box and, as before, he was overcome by the certainty that he would never be able to write *Memoirs of an Amnesiac*, Chapter 1. Whatever his grandmother might say, the truth was that his early childhood was irrecoverable. Those pages must remain blank.

When he opened the second box, however, things began to change. Some of these photographs had been taken when he was nine or ten years old, and he recognised many of the locations and other people. But each time he closed his eyes and tried to let the memory unfold, he was disappointed. His mind was unable to move beyond the frame of the photograph. The sole exception to this was a picture of a large cardboard box painted silver and blue. As soon as James saw this, he felt a mysterious flame inside him. What *was* it? He couldn't tell, but he knew that it had meant something to him, that there must be a story behind it: photographs of cardboard boxes did not normally make his heart beat faster. He examined the image more carefully: there were words and numbers written on the side of the box. What did they say? Unable to make them out, he took a magnifying glass from the drawer of the desk and looked again. '1995 – 2000 – 2005 . . .' James gasped as the memory came to life. He grabbed a biro and his white notebook and began to write. This is what he wrote:

I must have been eight or nine years old, and I was obsessed by the idea of time travel. I don't think I had read H. G. Wells by then, so my fantasies were probably inspired by the television series Dr Who. Even without that model, however, I suspect the idea of travelling through time is something I might have dreamed up on my own. I was fascinated by it. One rainy holiday I spent days, weeks, inventing and building my own time machine. It was made from paper and cardboard and painted beautiful colours and I kept it under the desk in my bedroom. Each morning I would crawl in there, strap myself in, close my eyes, and count backwards from 100. When I reached zero I would open my eyes and find myself in Ancient Rome or medieval England or the Wild West, or I would go and visit my grandparents, back when they were young, in the days when everything was black and white. But the journey that excited me most of all was when I visited the future.

The future! How that word used to thrill me. Later, when I was a teenager and had given up my time-travel fantasies, I would stand with my face pressed to the bedroom window, looking down at the suburban street and imagining that I would suffocate if the future did not, in the very next moment, swoop down and rescue me from the prison cell of the present. The future! How did I see it, when I was nine? Oddly perhaps, my visions were not of shining cities or high-speed spacecraft, but of myself, grown, changed, living in a world that was subtly different to the world in which I lived then. In the future, I believed, I would not exist within the confines of days and nights, waking and sleeping, working and eating, staring through windows, as I had always done before. No, in the future, I would truly live . . .

I remember being nervous at the idea of meeting the grown-up me; nervous that he would not recognise me, or would disapprove, or be embarrassed by my presence. It never occurred to me that I might be less than enraptured by him — by the person I had become. I talked to my dad about this, and he pointed out that, theoretically, there wouldn't be only one future version of myself, but literally thousands. The thought enchanted and disturbed me: all those future me's, those nearly identical versions of myself, like Tomas Ryal's Mnemen, one for each day of my life, existing somewhere, watching my progress through time . . . I remember wishing that I could befriend one of them: a me slightly older than I was then; a kind and caring me who could recall how confusing and frightening it felt to be eight or nine or ten; who could hold my hand and guide me through the labyrinth of childhood.

I don't remember if I ever 'met' any of my future, adult selves. The one image that remains with me from those childish yearnings is of a handsome, wide-shouldered, unshaven, sleepy-eyed young man in a leather jacket, standing in a sparsely furnished loft apartment, sunshine pouring in through the skylight, bending down to wake the drowsy naked girl beneath the sheets on the vast double bed: an image taken, I am fairly sure, from a TV commercial for a credit card or a car. Yet how ironic it seems to me now that, in the moment when my life began to come undone, I was living in a world that corresponded almost perfectly to my nine-year-old self's idyllic vision of the future.

James put down the pen and the notebook. That was the end of the memory. I watched him from the other side of the room, barely breathing, wondering if he might make the next mental leap and discover my identity. But, as usual, he was distracted by his emotions. What he was feeling now, spoiling his excitement about this discovered fragment of the forgotten past, was a mixture of sadness and regret. A picture of Ingrid flashed in his mind again, and he blinked it away. He made himself a cup of tea, ate some chocolate and talked to his grandmother for a while. Then he went back upstairs and opened the third box.

Hours passed and he was crawling over a carpet of photographs. It was like staring into a gigantic smashed mirror, his face reflected a thousandfold, and seeing only strangers. Finally, halfway through the final packet, James found a picture that made something move inside him.

It was a photograph of himself, standing on a train platform. He wore a faded denim jacket which looked too big for him – his wrists seemed tiny, emerging from the wide cuffs – and carried a large rucksack. His face, though tanned, was covered with spots. A stranger might have guessed that the boy in the picture was fifteen or sixteen, but James remembered the moment it was taken and he knew that he had in fact been eighteen, and on his way to Paris for the first time. He closed his eyes, now, in the present, and saw and heard the bustle of the station around him, felt sunlight on his face, wind in his hair, saw his parents standing in front of him, his mum looking anxious, his dad winking through the viewfinder of the camera. And he felt again the queasy melancholy he had felt then, and remembered its cause.

James sighed. He had found it at last: a crack in the wall of time . . . a tunnel into the past. He opened the white notebook and began to write.

Memoirs of an Amnesiac

CHAPTER 2

My parents waved as the train pulled away. I waved back, but I was facing the other way, so the farewell was a brief one. In a few seconds they were gone from my frame of vision and the horizon was rushing towards me. I felt excited, but with the faintest stain of some other emotion: some subtle commingling of sadness, regret and the desire to forget. What was it I wished had not happened? What was it I was trying not to remember? Her name was Jane Lipscombe, and I had known her since I was a little boy.

She sat next to me, our first day in junior school; I remember thinking how annoying it was that I had to sit next to a girl. She had shoulder-length, dark blonde hair and a somewhat solemn face with soft unfocused freckles that looked, from a distance, like smudges of dirt. She was tall for a girl, even then. She used to chew her lips. I didn't think much about her at the time, but she quickly became obsessed by me. All the other girls in the school would fall in love with someone new every week, but for a reason I could never fathom, Jane singled me out as the sole, enduring object of her affections. For most of the school year, this obsession would manifest itself as little more than a general mooniness: she was forever following me silently down corridors, sitting close to me at lunch and assembly, watching expressionlessly as I played football with my friends in the playground. Both of us were teased about this, of course; Jane seemed not to mind, but I did, and would sometimes say and do horrible things to her in order to show the others that our apparent closeness was nothing to do with me. She never took offence, though, even when I yelled at her to leave me alone or put a spider in her hair or called her 'Jane the Pain'. Only once did I hurt her. It was Valentine's Day and she had baked me a whole box of heart-shaped biscuits. She put it on my desk and kissed me on the cheek. Everybody jeered. Blushing, I began breaking the biscuits into pieces and sharing them out with the rest of the class. 'I baked them for *you*,' Jane told me afterwards in a serious voice. I felt so ashamed, I couldn't speak. We were ten years old.

When we moved up to secondary school, the atmosphere changed. The school was a large comprehensive in a mining village a few miles from the suburban estate where we lived. I didn't like most of the boys in my class: they were thick and aggressive and bigger than me. But I did like the girls. They were bigger than me too. I remember them, at that age, all being tall and thin, standing round me in a circle and telling me their dirty secrets. I don't know why they chose to confide in me – perhaps because I looked (and was) so innocent – but within a few weeks I knew exactly who had been fingerfucked by their boyfriend the night before, who was on the pill, whose nipples were constantly erect, who used to 'go all wet' at the sight of the lads in the sixth form playing football. This was the most intensive, useful education I ever received, and it was worth going to school for those lunch-break tutorials, if nothing else.

As for Jane the Pain, well . . . she disappears from my memory around this point. She was in a different registration class, and I suppose we saw each other less often. The next time we sat together was in German. This was in the second or third year, so Jane and I would have been twelve or thirteen. Our teacher was a middle-aged German woman whose name I don't remember, but who was obviously of a rather nervous disposition; such weakness is always picked up on by groups of schoolchildren, and Frau X was relentlessly teased and bullied. She responded by either running out of the room in tears or screaming and throwing things at us (blackboard rubbers, pencil sharpeners, crumpled homework assignments): both responses which delighted her pupils. As a result of her wild temperament, the classes were invariably anarchic and soon became an opportunity to do whatever we pleased. For Jane and I, this turned out to be a kind of erotic tickling. I have a vivid memory, possibly an amalgamation of several different times, of the two of us sitting at the back of the classroom, white daylight (snow?) shining through the windows behind us, blue-uniformed adolescents shouting and standing on desktops in front of us, and the two of us oblivious to it all, exploring each other's erogenous zones with thumbs, fingertips and palms. Sometimes this would get painful, but mostly it was pure pleasure. I used to get an erection just thinking about German.

Despite this weekly intercourse, I never thought of Jane in 'that' way. She was (kind of) a friend; she made me laugh, and she gave me a hard-on; but, perhaps because I had developed the reflex of pushing her away from me during those years in junior school, she never even entered my mind when I thought about possible girlfriends. (And I thought about possible girlfriends pretty much all the time back then.)

This situation changed one evening, at a school disco. It must have been summer because I remember the curtains in the assembly hall being closed to keep out the daylight. I also remember that the hall was lined with plastic chairs, on which the girls sat, while the boys hung around the drinks table, downing plastic cups of lemonade and cola in the same nonchalant but determined way they would later knock back pints of beer. I spent most of the evening in a state of inertia, hopelessly eyeing up my current favourites, but then – how and why I have no idea – I worked up the nerve to ask Tess Mallow to dance with me. Tess had long dark hair, a pretty face, a slim body, and was above all very quiet, sweet and mysterious-looking; the kind of girl with whom I would, I thought, stand no chance. It must have been the last song, a slow song ('True' by Spandau Ballet? 'The Power of Love' by Frankie Goes to Hollywood?), because we danced in each other's arms. As the music ended, Tess moved her face towards mine. I pursed my lips, and felt a soft tongue. She looked at me curiously, and then tried again. This time we kissed, awkwardly, messily, sexlessly, but I didn't care. It was my first kiss, and it was Tess Mallow. I couldn't believe my luck.

I didn't see Tess the next morning, but I spent the hours floating around school, dreaming of her. This was, I think, the last day of term. Certainly, it has that feel in my memory. I have a vague recollection of there being balloons on the ceiling, and of us having a lot of free time. Anyway, I can find no other explanation for the fact that Jane was able to ask me out while we sat in the school library. She did so very calmly and gently; she didn't seem nervous, although I suppose she must have been. I said no with equal gentleness and calmness. I am proud of myself in retrospect, even if the answer I gave was the wrong one. I explained that I liked her a lot and normally would have been happy to go out with her, but that I had kissed Tess Mallow at the school disco the night before and, even though I didn't know what would happen between us, I felt I had to give that relationship a chance to develop. (It seems strange, I admit, that at thirteen I should have been speaking like this – like an adult – but that is how I remember it.) Anyway, Jane didn't give up that easily. I remember her pleading with me – seductively, not whiningly – for what felt like half an hour or so, saying that I'd only had one little kiss with Tess, but that she and I had been touching one another for a whole year; that, in effect, she was real while Tess Mallow was only an illusion. 'We have fun, don't we?' she said. I agreed that we did. 'So think how much more fun we could have if we were going out together . . .' The strange thing to me now is that I don't even remember feeling tempted: I had given my heart to Tess Mallow, I said, and there was nothing I could do to change that.

How I came to regret that decision! Things never worked out with Tess; indeed, they never even got started, though that was entirely my fault, not hers. What happened, I think, was that I asked her out that afternoon, in her form room; she was surrounded by friends and must have felt embarrassed, so she just said, 'Maybe.' I nodded and walked away, and she called out, 'I'll phone you.' Two or three days into the summer holiday, my dad came to get me in my room. He said there was a call for me – 'from a girl'. He may have winked, or perhaps he only raised his eyebrows. The telephone was in the hallway, and he and my mum were in the kitchen; the door between the two rooms was ajar. I don't know if they were listening or not, but I was very aware that they were interested, and that knowledge made me desperate to end the call as quickly as possible; it also, to me, made it seem impossible that I could say yes. So when Tess asked if I would go to the cinema with her the following night – when the illusion turned suddenly real – I blurted out, 'Sorry, I can't, I'm busy,' and hung up. My parents looked at me as I entered the kitchen; I only shrugged and said, 'It was nothing.' Poor Tess. I don't remember ever speaking to her again.

That must, I think, have been the summer that Jane Lipscombe walked on to the squash court where I was playing with my friend Philip Bates, and began undressing. Yet I may not be right about this: it's all so mixed up. In my mind, the gap of time between her asking me out and her entering the squash court feels immense, more like two years than two months, but then time did move more slowly when I was young. And besides, I have no other way to account for all that lost time.

When I bring the memory to mind, my body reacts now as it did then: muscles tighten, lungs graze, legs weaken as though I am standing in a suddenly descending lift. I remember the knowing, half-glazed look in her eyes when she opened the door in the back wall of the sweltering squash court. 'Do you mind if I get changed in here, James?' That voice, deeper than before, suddenly full of secrets. I shook my head. I don't recall what clothes she was wearing, nor what clothes she changed into. But I remember watching her walk, with a strange, swaying assurance, towards the back corner of the court, out of sight of the viewing balcony above us, and slowly, casually strip down to her underwear. I remember Philip turning away from her, with an odd smirk on his face. I remember not being able to take my eyes off her. More than anything I remember the seeming vastness of her breasts, and my disbelief, akin almost to fear, at their growth. I remember the goosebumps on her thighs and the warm thickness of the air and the sound of the squash ball going thwack thwack thwack against the wall as Philip waited for her to leave the court.

Could she really have changed so much in the space of a few weeks? I honestly don't know. It may just have been that I wasn't really looking at her before this; that I was blind to the changes taking place in her. Either way, the effect was the same. The balance of the scales tipped. The world turned upside down. From the moment she stripped off in that humid white-walled room, our positions were reversed: the years of hopeless desire were transferred instantly from her to me, and I felt at once the unbearable burden of wanting and not being wanted. I fell in love with Jane Lipscombe just as she fell out of love with me.

———

I suppose, looking back, I was in love with Jane for the next five years – I was certainly in lust with her – but I should add that within that time there were various degrees of obsession. Were you to plot my feelings on a graph, you would see little hills and valleys, but only two major peaks. The first occurred during the late autumn and early winter following the squash court incident, when we were fourteen, and ended when Jane told me she had a boyfriend: a twenty-year-old car mechanic called Trev. The second peak rose more slowly during the upper sixth, when we were seventeen, and kept rising until the bitter end, a few days before I went to Paris.

But between these two major blooms of love, I was not as faithful in my yearnings as Jane had been. At that age I was forever daydreaming of sexual acts, leaving my shirt untucked to cover up the constantly painful bulge in my trousers, furtively rubbing my legs against those of strange girls and women who sat next to me on the bus. And I was forever falling in love. I remember the names of some of those girls now – Vicki Stead, Emma Morley, Claire Conn, Nikki Kewell, Katie Blair, Lisa Wyatt – and their sound is like a litany of beauty, ripeness, unattainability; like an atlas of far-off countries I would never get to visit.

Reading my diary from that time, I am struck above all by the repetitiveness of the pattern of my falling in love. From a distance there seems something almost rhythmical about it. The process, from beginning to end, would last between two and six weeks, and afterwards there would be a disgusted period of *désintoxication*, during which I would go back to the other interests and obsessions that sustained my adolescence: poetry, politics, football, music, dreams of travel and writing. This period would last perhaps a couple of months, but after that I would begin to feel empty, restless, unfulfilled, and the process would begin again. It's hard to say what was at the root of this peculiar persistence – the power of young hope? the unquenchability of young desire? Perhaps, but I suspect the truth is that I would simply *forget*. Forget the agony, the humiliation. Forget not to fall in love again.

Sometimes the feeling would sneak up on me over a number of days: friendliness, tenderness, slowly growing in the hothouse of my introspection, swelling into something more beautiful and dangerous: a kind of euphoric enchantment. Sadly, this state never lasted more than a couple of days. Because pretty soon, hope – that sly, insinuating monster – would creep into my heart. I would maybe smile at the girl in question and she would smile back, and I would speculate obsessively over the meaning of that smile. I would construct immense, elaborate fantasies of our future life together . . . and then I would see the girl the next day and she would blank me, or flirt with someone else. And thus would begin the third stage in the process: the fear.

Sometimes I would do inadvisable things during this stage of the process. One time, I remember, I began staring at the girl in question. Her name was Judith, I think. Or Judy, Julie . . . something like that. She was a chunky, black-haired girl, always in trouble with the teachers; alluring in a surly, rebellious way. Anyway, I used to stand a safe distance away from her at breaks and lunchtimes, in the queue for the chip shop or the bus, and stare. That was all: I wouldn't smile, I wouldn't speak. All I would do is stare. Normally the stage of fear lasted a week at most, before it gave way to disillusion, anger, despair, self-loathing, resignation, denial, and, eventually, amnesia. With this Judith girl, however, the fear went on for ages. Literally weeks, I think. In fact it had gone beyond fear by now; it had become something else. A kind of doomed, irrational defiance. Day after day I would stand twenty or thirty feet away from her and bore my eyes into her face or her blouse or the vertical seam at the back of her skirt. God knows what the expression on my face looked like – somewhere between melancholy and psychosis, I would guess – or what I imagined I might achieve by this; but nevertheless that was what I did. It came to a head one day, out in the playing fields around the school. These were grassy and hilly. I remember standing on one of those hills and staring at Judith. She was with a group of other girls, and as often happened she would become aware of my gaze and begin talking with her friends, each of whom would take turns to gawp at me, hostile or curious or amused. This time, however, she broke off from them and began walking towards me, a determined expression on her face. I felt strangely calm. As she walked up the hill, my eyes followed her: that vision of voluptuousness in tight pale blue blouse and short dark blue skirt and thick shiny black tights, her eyes on mine, her body moving ever closer. When she reached the summit of the hill she stood in front of me, looking suddenly pale and worried, and said, in a quiet voice, 'Well . . .' Before she could say anything more, my face assumed an expression of annoyance and boredom and I said, 'Why do you keep staring at me?'

So there were other girls . . . dozens, scores, of them. But the one unchanging thread in this pattern was my love and desire for Jane Lipscombe. In some ways I wonder if all the other girls were not half-conscious attempts to exorcise her ghost, to escape my deepest obsession. As I have said, between those two flowerings of love, at fourteen and seventeen, my desire for Jane remained under control. I fancied her, and she liked the fact that I fancied her. We flirted. Oh God . . . for years, we flirted, cuddled, played footsie. I do wonder now if Jane's teasing of me wasn't some kind of punishment: a long, drawn-out revenge for the years of indifference she had suffered at my hands when we were young. But on balance I don't think that's true. I never had the sense that she hated me or wanted to hurt me. It was more that school bored her – the juvenility of it, the dryness – and I was her one source of amusement during those long hours. I kept her distracted, kept her titillated, until she got home and Trev fucked her brains out.

I tried not to think about Trev, and for the most part I was successful. It wasn't too difficult, as I never saw him (I didn't even know what he looked like, although I thought I could probably guess) and Jane rarely mentioned him. It was only when we entered the sixth form that I began to realise that there was more to their relationship than I'd imagined; that it was not quite as perfect or permanent as it had always seemed.

One morning she came to school with a black eye. Other times I would notice peculiar little round bruises on her arms. And, now I think about it, it was quite rare to see Jane's skin at all. In the spring and summer, on fine days, those of us with free periods would take chairs to the flagstoned square outside the sixth-form block and sunbathe while drinking coffee and studying. Most of the girls would wear vest tops and short skirts on days like these, but Jane never did. She wore, almost always, a denim jacket over a T-shirt, and long, flowing, satiny skirts in mauve or orange or black. Looking back at this now, the pattern of clues seems obvious, the solution unavoidable, but for some reason I never put it together like that at the time. In my defence, I had several distractions, one of which was the fact that, though I never saw Jane's bare flesh, I certainly felt it often enough.

Our physical flirting had never really ceased and, now we were in the sixth form, it grew steadily more daring and intense. We sat together in English four times a week, and each class lasted an hour and fifteen minutes. So for five hours a week Jane and I were close enough to hear each other breathe, and our legs were closer still. What I remember most vividly are the moments *before* contact: the held breath; the uncertainty; the suspense. Steadily, however, inch by inch and week by week, we grew more and more deeply entwined. We must both have had to make some strange-looking contortions during these classes, and I have no idea how we managed to answer any questions about *The Merchant of Venice* or Hardy's poetry, but the fact remains that we were never discovered. Or, at least, not until I began using my hand.

It seemed a natural progression. I used my right hand to hold my biro, while my left slipped under the desk and on to the skirted thigh of Jane Lipscombe. Sometime later, stroking, caressing, it had moved beneath the satin and was touching the skin of her knee, her long inner thigh, feeling the warmth of the blood there. Further and further upward it crept, over tightened tendons and stray hairs, and my little finger had just touched the warm damp cotton of her underwear when she said suddenly in a loud, mock-innocent voice, 'James, what is your hand doing on my leg?' Embarrassed and angry, I removed it, and our legs separated under the table. Strangely, there was no big inquisition about this; the rest of the class seemed to ignore Jane's outburst and returned to their discussion. But I did not forgive her so easily. For the rest of the year, I sat next to Clare Budd instead. And pretty soon it was *her* legs that were touching mine under the table.

Naturally, I fell in love with her. Clare Budd. I don't remember too much about her now. Her face, which, though tanned and quite regular, was actually rather ugly. Her calves, which, presumably because of some special wax or cream she used, were astonishingly shiny and smooth. And, most vividly of all, her car – a metallic-green Mini which she would park outside the main entrance every day and the sight of which, when my desire for her was at its peak, would make my insides tingle with excitement.

But anyway, I mention Clare Budd only as an example of the kind of distraction that caused me to be blind to the signs of abuse in Jane's relationship with Trev. I was also wallowing in melancholy at the time, because all my friends seemed to have paired off (Clare, too, had an older boyfriend), and I was the last one alone: the final freak on the shelf. I remember going out drinking with that gang, and feeling stale, bored, lonely, yearning for a life with new friends in a new place. Often I dreamed of going abroad. I remember talking about this with Clare, and her saying that she too wanted to live in Spain or Greece. I was disappointed (but not surprised) when she turned up one day and announced that she'd got a job at the TSB. So much for hiking around the Pelopponese; she didn't even bother finishing her A-levels. She wasn't the only one either. It was a time of encroaching reality, and I was shocked by how easily most of my friends surrendered their hopes and ideals to such pragmatism; how happily they embraced dreary adulthood and rejected the poetry, politics and dreams of freedom which we had shared for the past few years. In that sense at least, I regarded my aloneness, my differentness, in a positive light. *I* was not going to sell out. *I* was not going to give in.

———

This determination was gloriously confirmed one day during the Easter holidays in the lower sixth. We were on a Geography field trip in Cornwall, a group of about twelve people. The teacher split us into twos that morning and gave each pair an O/S map marked with our final, common destination. We were then deposited at various equidistant points in the surrounding countryside. I was paired with a boy called Adam Draycott. I felt slightly nervous about this at first; of all the people in the group, he was the one I knew least well. He was also the only boy in the sixth form who didn't come from the middle-class estate in which I had grown up: his dad had been a miner and was now unemployed; his mum worked as a cleaner; he never came out drinking with us because he didn't have enough money. I had always tried to be kind and friendly towards him but, because of this gulf in our backgrounds, the kindness always came out as condescension, and Adam, I felt sure, was aware of this.

The two of us studied the map, then looked around. It was a beautiful spring morning, very early. The sky was yellowish pink over the horizon and a few last stars were still visible. Birds were singing in some trees nearby. The road on which we stood, a narrow country lane, wound vaguely north-south through fields of sheep and cattle. We decided, after a few minutes' discussion, to follow the road for a mile or so and then cut across the fields, due west. As we walked, I wondered what we could talk about. I had never had a proper conversation with Adam. I remembered, the first time I had met him, asking about his politics; what he thought of Thatcher and the miners' strike. I had imagined, with his dad having been made redundant, that he was bound to have strong opinions on the issue. But he had disconcerted me by shrugging his shoulders and saying he wasn't really interested in politics. Over the year that followed, I had formed the impression that Adam wasn't really interested in anything. He was that kind of boy: strangely inert and passionless. Physically he looked like a long-distance runner: tall, thin, wirily muscular. Though not blessed with good looks – his face was narrow and chinless, and already, at eighteen, his hairline was receding – he did at least look healthy. He was, I imagined, one of those hardy, stoical souls whom age would barely touch.

My memories of that morning are mostly still images. I had forgotten to take my camera, and Adam didn't own one, so I can be certain that the memories are not plagiarised from photographs, but they have that kind of feel about them all the same: as though I had mentally framed each scene – a cat drowsing on top of a stone wall in the morning sunshine; three full milk bottles standing in shade outside a front door; a pretty, dark-eyed schoolgirl at a bus stop watching us walk past – and released the shutter, freezing the image forever inside my mind. I also remember how I felt when I saw these pictures, these realities, for the first time: as though I had discovered a new world.

I don't remember what we spoke about as we walked up that country lane, but I do remember that the conversation came easily, and that he was as captivated by our surroundings as I was. It was the first time I had ever seen enthusiasm, never mind wonder, on Adam's face, and it moved me. Suddenly all the petty barriers between us seemed to melt away, and we talked as friends. I have a vague recollection that I told him about my dreams of travelling around Europe: how I wanted to get away from the big cities, the tourist centres, and hike an untrodden path through rural villages like this one, to sleep beneath the stars, to swim in rivers, to swap greetings with strangers over breakfast in lonely cafés . . . I think I even suggested he come with me, and that he grinned in response, though deep down we both knew he would never do such a thing.

Anyway, we followed the path, walking slowly and savouring the beauty of the land and the sky, then cut through a field to the right. But the field did not take us out where we thought it would, or the map was wrong . . . I don't know. Whatever, we were lost; the day was growing hot; we were sweating and hungry. There were no houses around, and no people in the fields. After standing helplessly in the road for a while, we noticed a small dog trotting towards us. It stopped and barked, and we began to talk to it.

'Have you come to show us the way, little dog?'

'Woof!'

'Is it this way or that way?'

'Woof woof!'

'That way? Are you sure?'

'Woof!'

'All right, then. Let's go. Do you want to come with us, little dog?'

'Woof!'

And off he went, ahead of us, in precisely the direction we had indicated. We were laughing, but twenty minutes later, following the dog across fields and up narrow, winding paths, we found the teacher's minibus parked ahead of us, outside a pub. This was our destination. Adam and I turned to each other with astonished grins. We went inside the pub, to tell the others what had happened, but we were told to buy the next round and order ourselves some food and, by the time we got to the table and waited for a gap in the conversation, a good ten minutes had passed. I told the story, Adam nodding as I did so, but somehow it sounded less amazing in the telling than it had felt to us both at the time. The others laughed sceptically. 'Let's see this dog, then,' said one of them. We took them outside, but the dog had disappeared. After that, the story was dropped and I never talked to anyone else about our strange and magical day. Even with Adam, the subject never came up again, but it was a comfort to know that we had experienced those moments together; that there was some-one else in the world who had witnessed the same wonders as I. And even though Adam and I were not close friends, even though we barely spoke to one another, I always felt that day was a kind of bond between us; something defining and unbreakable.

The Geography group went back to Cornwall the following year for another field trip, but by then Adam Draycott had got a job in an accountancy firm, and somehow it wasn't the same. We didn't go back to the place with the milk bottles and the dog, but even if we had, I felt sure the magic would have gone. It was a moment only that we had loved, not the place itself. And Adam had been part of that moment.

It came as a shock when I heard that he had died. A fast-spread-ing cancer, they said. One day he was perfectly fine; three weeks later he was dead. I didn't go to the funeral. I didn't cry either, and would have felt guilty if I had. After all, my sadness was almost entirely selfish: I mourned his death because it left me alone. With Adam gone, I was the only one who remembered that day in Corn-wall. My memories, in an instant, had become doubly precious – and doubly fragile. If I lost them, the world would lose them too. The miracle day would disappear into oblivion. It is a relief, now, to write this down; to remember. And to know that, as you read this, whoever you are, the day is being resurrected, if only imper-fectly and momentarily. After all, the past is dead – it does not exist – but through words or images or music, some tiny part of it may still live on, like a particle of dust dancing in a beam of sunlight.

———

According to my diary I found out about Adam's death in late April, but in my memory it feels like part of that final, momentous week in early June when we sat our A-levels and the temperature soared. It was too hot to concentrate on anything other than keep-ing cool, and I had long since given up trying to memorise facts and essays. A feeling of overpowering lassitude descended, strip-ping me of determination, ambition, even of nerves. I felt a rush of adrenalin only on the morning of the first exam; after that, I entered the exam room each day with the slow, resigned footsteps of a condemned prisoner. I don't have individual memories of any of the tests, only a vague compound memory of the room itself: a small, boxy place with windows on either side, through which I saw achingly bright fields and buildings; the creaky hum of the electric fan on the invigilator's desk, spraying warm air around the room, lifting the papers on each desk in turn, like a Mexican wave; and the silhouetted shape of Jane Lipscombe, sitting by the window. Each time I looked up at her, she was staring outside, apparently in a daydream. I never saw her write a word.

I was deeply in love with her again by this time. The feeling had been growing in me for months. I think part of it was a poignant sense that our time together was coming to an end; that a friendship, a desire, a closeness that had begun thirteen years before was approaching its final moments. I had, for a while, still held out the hope that Jane and I would go to the same university, that we would, after all, end up married. But when the heatwave began, I knew suddenly that this was impossible; a childish dream. I knew she would fail and I would pass, and that our paths would diverge and never recross. I became intensely nostalgic about the times we had shared – and the times we were sharing now. Nostalgia for the present, fired by the sad knowledge that it will soon be past: a strange emotion, but not, I think, an uncommon one. A new tenderness had entered our flirtations and our talks. We would stroke each other's cheeks, suck each other's fingertips, sometimes even hold hands. She never talked about Trev any more. I thought her silence was only to spare my feelings. I didn't notice that she no longer had those bruises. And I never asked.

I am sure that the depth of my feelings was partly, too, a reflection of a more general uncertainty. As long and as intently as I had yearned to escape these people, this place, the reality of leaving, as it drew nearer, also filled me with panic. I would be going to a place where I knew no one, and where no one knew me. In more honest moments, I acknowledged the truth that I was desperately young and naïve, hopeless at communicating with other people, that I had lived my childhood and adolescence inside the bubble of a daydream, and that I feared what would happen when that bubble finally burst. Jane, in some sense, was both bubble and daydream: the thing that protected and the thing I wished to protect. But my love for her was also linked, in a more obscure, barely articulable way, to Adam Draycott's death. He had gone, leaving me with fading memories, and now she was about to go too. I clung to her out of fear . . . fear that the past was disappearing before my eyes.

On the ninth day, we took our last exam – the English oral – and then we were free. It was one o'clock in the afternoon; another scorcher of a day. We gathered, all two dozen of us, in the sixth-form block. Some people burned their essays and exercise books, others stared moodily at the school they were about to leave. After half an hour or so, we set off for the pub – The Archer, across the road from the school entrance – where we ate sandwiches and crisps for lunch and then got steadily drunk.

I have no memory of what happened that day. I never had any memory of it. When I woke the next morning, hungover and fully clothed in my bed, those hours were already a blank. I began to put the pieces of the puzzle together that afternoon, when Philip Bates came round for a cup of tea. He, too, was hungover, but he was in a light-hearted mood.

'You were pretty smashed yesterday.'

'No worse than normal.'

'You're kidding. Don't you remember?'

'Er . . . not much.'

'Oh.'

'Why, what happened?'

'Well . . . I never knew you felt that way about Jane Lipscombe for a start.'

'Didn't you? I thought it was obvious.'

'No, I mean, I knew you fancied her, but . . .'

'But what?'

'You were all over her.'

'Oh come on, we're like that in English class . . .'

'I've never seen you crying in an English class.'

'Crying?'

'For hours. Fucking hell, do you really not remember?'

Eventually, after a tortuous hour of prompting, I was able to work out from Philip's hints a rough sequence of events. I had begun, as I dimly recalled, by stroking Jane's leg. Then I started kissing her hands, her cheeks, her neck, and telling her how much I loved her. She smiled through this, replying that I was just drunk. Then I began touching her breasts. She showed the first signs of embarrassment. I sat on her lap and attempted to kiss her on the mouth. After a while, she stood up to leave. I started crying. I pleaded with her not to go. I promised to be good. I asked her to marry me. At some point she mentioned that she had a boyfriend, and he probably wouldn't be very pleased if she married someone else. 'Oh bloody Trev,' I slurred, 'what a wanker.' 'He certainly is,' she replied coolly. 'I dumped him over a year ago.' And thus I discovered that, for nine months, Jane had been single; had in fact been waiting for me to ask her out. But I had been infatuated with Clare Budd at the time, and then, just at the moment when I began paying more attention to Jane again, she had met Mark, her new boyfriend. It was too late. I had blown my chance. Apparently I wept desperately at this news, and had to be escorted out of the pub because my behaviour was upsetting the regulars. Jane tried to comfort me, but I was too caught up in my own tears, and in the end she left without even saying goodbye. After that, the details are unimportant: a taxi home . . . vomiting in the sink . . . more crying. David said I talked to him for about an hour before falling asleep: a rambling, incoherent monologue about Adam Draycott and dark-eyed schoolgirls, the death of youth and the need for poetry. 'I tried to listen,' David said, 'but you were so pissed and confused, I just couldn't make head or tail of it.' I told him not to worry about it and thanked him for looking after me.

Two days later, I left for Paris.

———

I got there in the early evening and wandered around in a daze, searching for the youth hostel mentioned in the guidebook. By the time I found it, all the beds had been taken. A man explained how to find a cheap hotel nearby, but I soon got lost. I ended up sitting in the doorway of an office building, close to a pool of lamplight. It was not even midnight and I was terrified of being found and beaten, whether by criminals or police; I thought there was no chance I would actually fall asleep. The next thing I knew it was dawn.

I opened my eyes and the sun was rising behind the strange skyline, making the leaves on the plane trees shine green. Even the air seemed different there: warmer, velvety, rich with unnameable scents. I could hardly believe that I was in Paris, and that I had slept in a doorway. It was true that I was as alone as ever and that my back ached and I was shivering; true, as well, that I was too nervous to speak a word of French and too shy even to look anyone in the eye. In spite of all this, however, I couldn't stop myself feeling happy. I had done the thing I always used to dream about as a teenager, staring from my bedroom window ... I had, finally, entered the future.

After that I became slightly braver. I visited the Eiffel Tower and the Louvre, Notre Dame and the Pompidou. I slept three nights in a row at the hostel, and on the fourth night I caught a sleeper train to Nice. I have a vivid memory of waking up and seeing the rose-lit vineyards and olive trees move past, of opening the window and breathing in the already warm air. The beautiful south. How I loved it there! I shared a room with two Irish girls, one of whom spent the night in bed with me, much to the displeasure of her friend, who kept rolling around in bed and sighing heavily to let us know she was still awake. Later I travelled to Venice, Verona, Rome and Munich, where I lost my virginity in an enormous marquee tent to a very drunk Australian girl. At the end, when I came, she mumbled someone's name – Greg? Geoff? I don't remember, but it certainly wasn't mine. I wondered afterwards if the whole event had been a case of mistaken identity, but she was probably just remembering someone she had once been in love with. When I woke the next morning, she had gone. I have no memory at all of what she looked like.

It was in that marquee, eating breakfast on my own the next morning, that I first began to wonder about the meaning of my life – or, rather, its lack of meaning; its inconsequentiality. For years I had imagined the loss of my virginity as either the culmination of something or the beginning of something. In both these versions, the sex was an event that formed part of a narrative; it possessed, beyond the physical pleasure of the moment, a purpose, a significance. Had it happened with Jane Lipscombe, for instance, it would have made sense of a long series of flirtations, frustrations and misunderstandings. Those years would have been given shape and substance by their end result. Now, however, I was forced to contemplate the probability that I would never see Jane again, that all we had shared had led to nothing, that those thirteen years had been inconsequential. Similarly, what happened with the girl in the tent . . . that was neither culmination nor beginning; it was merely a random event. Her drunkenness, the fact that I never knew her name, her having gone by the time I awoke . . . all of this gave the experience an air of unreality. And if she was really drunk, I thought, then perhaps she doesn't even remember. Images of that golden day in Cornwall came to my mind – the milk bottles, the schoolgirl, the clever dog – and I realised that already they were fading. Again I was confronted with the brutal responsibility of being *the only one who remembers*; of the inevitable paling of my memory being equivalent to the slow death of those moments. As I packed my bag and walked to the train station that day, I made a resolution. The past is dead, I told myself. It has vanished, meaninglessly. Now you must find a future that does mean something, that cannot be forgotten. To me, at eighteen, my mind filled with romantic adolescent ideas, this meant only one thing. It meant Love.

A week later, back at home, I got my A-level results. A in everything. I phoned Philip Bates; he had the same. The two of us went out to celebrate, and he told me that Jane had failed, but she didn't care; that she was planning to marry Mark and have kids. I pretended not to have heard. In late August my grandad died. His funeral was in the south-coast town of S., where he and my grandmother had been spending the summer. We drove down there and buried him under the bluest sky imaginable. In September, I was ill. I had a chest infection, and lay in bed for a fortnight, coughing up phlegm, feeling nauseous and re-reading the complete works of F. Scott Fitzgerald. I cried at the end of *The Great Gatsby*. I remember all this because I kept a diary until the day before I left for university. For what happened next there is no record. The days are steeped in fog and I . . .

James stared blankly ahead of him, his mouth open. His eyes were pointing at the page on which he had been writing, but that was not what he saw. Something strange had happened. He had been about to write 'I don't remember' when suddenly he realised that he did. The fog was clearing.

And the strangest thing was that his memories, fragmented as they were, made him think insistently of the story he had found beneath the wallpaper of the house in H: *Confessions of a Killer*, Chapter 1. In the memories, he was following a girl down a long, misty street; he was standing in darkness and staring at the façade of 21 Lough Street; he was climbing a narrow staircase, filled with fear and desire.

But what sense did that make? How could Malcolm Trewvey have written a story based on James's own private memories? To do that, he would have to be able to read his mind, see inside his dreams . . . As James thought this, however, he remembered the look on Trewvey's face, that time he had seen him reflected in the sex shop window – how sure he had looked, as though he knew more of James's past than James himself – and he shivered. Was it possible?

I held my breath.

No, James told himself, after a long pause; what must have happened was that his memories of the time in H. had been contaminated by his memories of the story he had read, and . . .

His train of thought was interrupted by some odd noises

coming from below. Closing the notebook, he went downstairs to investigate and discovered that his parents had returned. They had been gone four days, during which time he had done nothing but sit at the desk in his room, remembering and writing. It was late afternoon now and the sky outside was dark. Eating dinner with his parents and grandmother, he thought about asking them what had happened to him in H. But when he recalled the shocked look on his gran's face a few days before, he couldn't bring himself to do it. He had hurt these people enough already. There was no need to dredge up even more painful memories.

After dinner he went back upstairs and looked at the words he had written. He had remembered. He could remember. And however contaminated his memories may be, they were still clues. A door that had been locked was now open. He knew he ought to re-enter the past now, to start writing again before the memories had a chance to fade, but for some reason he found he couldn't. He was too tired. Not frightened, he told himself, just unbelievably weary. Travelling through time was hard work, after all; it was perfectly normal that he should need a good night's rest. Fear had nothing to do with it.

Just before he went to bed, James plugged in his mobile phone to recharge the batteries and discovered that there was a message for him. The message was three days old. James pressed play and listened. This was what he heard: 'Hello, Mr Purdew, this is Mr Harrison, from Harrison Lettings. I trust you're well. I have a message for you from our client. He says: *it is time to start work on the next floor*. That's all. I'll be in the office all day tomorrow if you need to talk to me. Goodbye.'

James slept badly that night. The next morning, he woke early, packed, showered, dressed, and ate a quick breakfast. His parents and grandmother stood in the driveway in their dressing gowns to see him off. As James pulled into the street, he looked in the van's wing mirror and saw them waving woodenly like figures in a cuckoo clock. They got smaller and smaller and smaller until finally they vanished.

V
AT THE CENTRE OF THE LABYRINTH

It was with a feeling of relief that James steered the van into Lough Street and saw the empty parking space in front of number 21. He had been haunted during the journey by the fear that he was being followed: every time he looked in the wing-mirror or through the side window, he seemed to see a black van, otherwise identical to his own, just behind or just ahead of him. Crossing the bridge into the city, it had finally disappeared from sight, and he had been worried that he would find it here, taking his rightful place. He got out of the van and looked around: there was no sign of it. James sighed. He wasn't too late, after all.

Walking under the bare-branched chestnut tree, through the gate and up the driveway to the front door, James looked up at the house's closed eyes – the boarded first-floor windows – and said to himself, you have been as blind as this house. Now he saw the world as one whose blindness has been suddenly cured. He saw all his mistakes, his denials of the truth, as culs-de-sac leading from the central passageway of the maze. It had all been so easy, so clear. And yet, each time he had found a clue, he had been frightened by the darkness of the place into which it seemed to be leading him, and had found an excuse to turn away. What he had lacked was something all good detectives possessed: not intelligence, but courage.

He knew perfectly well where the trail of clues was leading him next. In some way he had known all along.

He took the ladder out to the front of the house and unboarded the two first-floor windows. They fell into the overgrown front garden with a crash like thunder. Then he went upstairs. With each step, the air grew colder. Dust and dimness gave the light an underwater quality. He felt like a diver exploring a shipwreck.

At the top of the stairs he stood still and took in the details of the scene that greeted him. It was a large, sombre landing with four closed doors. It smelled damp, faintly rotten. The first door he opened, to his near left, revealed a long, narrow bedroom. The second, to his near right, led to a large bathroom containing two toilet cubicles, two sinks with mirrors, and two shower cubicles with their plastic curtains drawn. The third door, on the right-hand side of the far wall, opened into another bedroom, smaller than the first but otherwise identical. None of these rooms provoked any physical reactions in James. They were not completely unknown to him, perhaps, but seeing them again did not feel significant. They were not part of the mystery.

That left only one door: the door behind which he had imagined he would find the next clue. It had only been a hunch, but now he felt sure about it. This was the room. James touched the metal handle and exhaled. Courage, he reminded himself. He pushed down and entered.

Like the other rooms, it was at first sight unremarkable: a bare, pale space, crudely furnished by two sheetless beds, two desks with chairs, and a large wardrobe. Weak sunlight came through the grime-covered window. He moved forward and the sunlight was lower, a deep orange, and it shone more strongly through the suddenly clean glass, illuminating thousands of dust flakes. They were whirling, he noticed, as though in a draft of air. He felt exhausted, ready to sleep, but as he took a step further into the room, he noticed something odd on the floor. There was a pile of clothes: several pairs of trousers, a jacket, some shirts. He turned to the wardrobe and saw its doors flung wide open, the hangers bare. Then he looked across at the bed and there she was: a thin, dark-haired girl, in jeans and a T-shirt, her cheeks red, her chest heaving, her eyes shining – with anger? jealousy? desire? – and her mouth opened to say something and he blinked. The wardrobe was closed, the floor bare, the light dim, the girl gone. James walked to the window and stood before it, breathing shallowly. Below him on the street a man was walking his dog. James thought he heard something behind him, and turned quickly. The bare, silent room stared back.

But it was the same room, undoubtedly. The room in the memory or the hallucination or whatever it was he had just suffered, and the room in which he stood now: they were identical. James had been here before, and so had she.

When he had calmed down, James began to search for clues. He did so methodically, looking under the beds, behind the radiators, in the drawers of the desks, around the back of the wardrobe. Nothing. Finally he swallowed drily and stood up in front of the wardrobe's closed doors. The key was in the lock: he turned it, and the doors fell open with a creak. And there, arranged neatly on hangers and shelves, were the remains of someone's life.

A man's clothes: jackets, trousers, shirts, socks, shoes. In the shelves he found some books, videos, records and CDs. A cardboard box full of notebooks and photographs. And, at the bottom of the cardboard box, some loose sheets of paper covered with typewritten words. The first page bore the title Chapter 2 and James realised immediately that it was the continuation of the story of Martin Thwaite: *Confessions of a Killer*. This must have been his room, James thought. Malcolm Trewvey's bedroom. And he, James, had been here too. Perhaps they had been roommates, James and Malcolm? Perhaps, in searching for Trewvey's guilty secret, James might also find the truth of his own life?

He read the first page in a fever of excitement – this is it, he thought, this is the next clue – but when he came to the second page he was confused to discover that it did not begin where the first ended. He puzzled over this for a while, then noticed that the pages were numbered: the first page was 20, the second 25. He flicked through the rest of the pages and found to his dismay that what he had in his hands was not Chapter 2, but mere fragments of the manuscript: twenty-three pages out of 100 or so. Shaking his head at this disappointment, James went back to the beginning. He would read what was here, he decided, as carefully as he could, and afterwards he would attempt to fill in the gaps.

CHAPTER 2

For two days and nights I did not leave my room. Indeed, I was barely awake during this time. The shock and exhaustion produced by the events of that strange night had taken their toll on my body and mind, which, seeking recuperation, plunged me into profound unconsciousness. When I finally awoke, it was late morning and I was frail with hunger and thirst. There was no food in my room so I went out to a tavern round the corner – The Green Man – and wolfed my way through a bowl of onion broth, a loaf of bread, two plates of mutton stew and two tankards of ale. Only after I had done this, and wiped my lips on the rough cloth napkin, and sat back in the wooden chair and thoughtlessly surveyed my surroundings for several minutes – only then did the memory of what had happened that night, and its sombre implications for my career, slowly dawn on me.

Curiously, my fear was not great. I fully expected to lose my employment, and thus I resigned myself quickly to this idea and, having done so, more or less dismissed it from my mind. The truth was I felt joyful. I was so utterly in love that all else seemed unreal, meaningless, laughable. My only fears, my only worries, my only sadnesses were at the thought of not seeing *her* again. And yet this, I knew, was impossible. I had to see her, and I would see her. Only death could have prevented me.

I wonder now if this was not perhaps the single happiest moment of my life. Sitting in that dim, dirty restaurant, my belly full of food and my body relaxed from the longest sleep I ever took, this side of the womb; the pale winter sunlight coming in through the window and warming my skin; the taste of ale and pewter still vivid on my tongue; all fears and hopes and uncertainties demolished; my whole life narrowed to a single path, every step upon which was an act of deepest devotion. If I did nothing else in my life, I swore, I would continue to watch over her, to keep her from harm, to guard her every night . . .

. . . it in a state of dishevelment and was amazed to see Dr Lanark standing there. As soon as he saw me, an expression of grave concern clouded his face. 'My dear Thwaite, I had been afraid when you failed to turn up for work this morning that you must be ill, and I see now that you are indeed so. What is it that ails you, my young friend? A fever? Have you seen a doctor? I will send for one at once.' All the time that he was speaking, he was ushering me, his arm around my waist, back to the bed from which I had just emerged. I seemed to swoon as he talked, and I realised, in the strangest possible way, that he was right; I truly *was* ill. I *did* have a fever. I was so grateful for his solicitude, having never expected to see him again, that I burst into tears and soon after fell into a slumber.

The doctor came that afternoon and assured my employer that I was suffering from nothing worse than a heavy cold and nervous exhaustion. He prescribed rest and regular meals, and Dr Lanark informed me that I was to take the next week off work and get myself well again. 'You are not to leave your bed, Thwaite, do you hear me? I will send my eldest daughter round to nurse you. She is a good girl and a fair cook and will, I am sure, take the most wonderful care of you. Now I must leave you, for I am dealing with a most interesting case which will, if I am not mistaken, reach its bloody climax this evening. Therefore, adieu Thwaite – and remember my instructions!'

And with that he swept out of my humble room, his cape making a dramatic swirl of black, into the twilit streets to confront this latest villain. For a while I lay quietly in the fading light and daydreamed of Dr Lanark. Then I must have fallen asleep because the dream mutated so that he was mortally wounded and I, his faithful assistant, had to take over. I tracked the villains down to a small, dark, terraced house in an evil-looking district of London and smashed open the door with my shoulder. Then I saw them – the mute woman and the large man, holding a knife to the throat of Miss Vierge. 'No!' I cried, but with a horrible slow motion the woman drew the blade across my darling's delicate white throat and the man, with appalling vigour, pulled her head clean off her . . .

. . . from Dr Lanark's daughter, whose name was Sarah. I use the past tense, but I believe (and fervently hope) that she is still alive and well; I pray that she has recovered from the wounds I thoughtlessly inflicted upon her, and that, if she can never forgive me, she can at least forget me. She deserves better than to be haunted by the selfish follies of one such as I. She was seventeen years old then, and looked perhaps even younger. She had a fair, pleasant face – not beautiful, but full of goodness – and the calmest, gentlest manner. She touched my forehead with a cool damp cloth and whispered, 'It's all right, you were only dreaming.' I surrendered myself to her care.

For the next week the pattern remained the same. During the days Sarah cooked me hot nutritious meals and prepared medicinal drinks; she washed me and read to me and soothed me when the nightmares came; she watched over me unceasingly and, at my request, told stories of her father and his adventures. It was clear she worshipped him. It ought also to have been clear that she was, in her innocence, falling in love with me. I blush to think that I failed to see this, but I was so preoccupied with my own obsession that I was totally blind to hers.

But anyway, as I say, the pattern did not vary: she nursed me in the daytime and, before taking her leave at sundown, pronounced me in much better health than I had been that morning, which was never anything less than the truth.

When she had gone, I got out of bed, dressed quickly, and walked to Mayfair as fast as my weak legs would carry me. And there I passed each night in that doorway, exposed to rain and sleet and icy winds, watching the blank façade of a sleeping house. Each morning when Sarah found me, she was shocked anew by the deterioration of my health. Surmising that I was suffering from insomnia, she procured me a sleeping draught. I did not swallow it, of course, but Sarah never guessed that, and consequently she became even more perturbed by the exhausted look in my eyes each morning. She even asked her father if she could remain with me at night to discover the cause of my affliction, but naturally Dr Lanark would never allow such a thing. Thus I was free to pursue my . . .

. . . past eleven when her light went out that night. I remember thinking that it was early for her; recently she had been reading (that, at least, is what I assumed she was doing – she might just as easily have been sewing or sketching) until long after midnight. Conscientiously I wrote this in my notebook. I had determined to take as many notes as I could in the event of a second abscondment; it had alarmed me, the realisation that the only proof I possessed of the previous sequence of events lay in my own memory and in the memories of two unknown criminals somewhere in south London – a type who would undoubtedly, instinctively have denied ever having seen me if asked by a policeman or a private detective.

At half-past one the front door opened and a figure in a cape and hood came out on to the street. This time, with the moonlight full upon her, I was in no doubt as to the figure's identity. It was Angelina Vierge. I wrote down the time of her appearance and, heart aflame, began to follow, at a distance of about twenty paces. I did not look behind me. Some part of me must have been aware that I, her shadow, had a shadow of my own, following at a similar distance, but I don't remember thinking or worrying about it.

As before, she walked through Mayfair to Piccadilly, crossed over to the Green Park, and cut through to Pall Mall. From there she traversed Charing Cross and Covent Garden and went down to the embankment. I tried to remain calm and open-minded as I followed, noting down the name of each street we took, but as the reader will surely imagine, it was hard to control the excited, horrified supposition that she was heading towards the same vile place as before. This in turn sparked off various contradictory emotions in me: fear of the mute woman and the large man (especially after the horrible events in my dream) and a shameful (and quickly suppressed) desire to find myself again in the small smoky room with her; to watch her, a glory in black lace, moving towards me; to feel her hair touch my skin, to see her soft-soled feet on the splintery floorboards, and this time *not* to say her name . . . Perhaps I was distracted by these erotic imaginings, perhaps she had stopped or slowed down without my noticing – I do not recall – but the next thing I knew I was almost upon her – close enough to smell the . . .

CHAPTER 3

I woke up in a strange place. Through a window I could see daylight and rooftops, but the room itself was crepuscular. A small fire, burning in a hearth to my right, was the sole interior source of light. I was lying on a narrow bed, one side of which was pushed against the wall. I sat up slowly. My muscles ached; my skin was tender all over; even my bones seemed bruised. Vague memories of the fist-fight came back to me, the sharpest of which was the terrible visage of that rough-looking fellow wielding an iron bar. All in all, it seemed incredible to me that I was still alive and in one piece.

'How are you feeling?' said a voice behind me. I turned and, in some astonishment, beheld the face of Ivan Dawes. He smiled and his blue eyes pierced me. He was sitting in an old, patched-up armchair, drawn close to the bed. His legs were outstretched and crossed, so that one large black leather boot lay at an obscure angle across the other.

'You!' I said. 'Where am I?'

He replied that I was in his apartment and had been for the past two days. While he talked me through the events that had led to me lying unconscious in his sitting room, I stared more often at his boots – the way the black shone in the light of the fire – than at his face. Something in those eyes of his seemed to undo me; some cool irony, some secret knowledge, that shone from them with the power to see through solid objects and lies and silences, as it is said the German scientists' 'X-rays' do, penetrating countless layers of skin and flesh to the skeleton that, like truth, underpins all.

He had been talking for perhaps three or four minutes when the full horror of remembrance suddenly gripped me, tightening the bones around my chest, and I blurted out, 'Where is she? Is she –?'

'She is alive,' he said . . .

. . . is reconstructed. As I did not take notes, I have no way of knowing whether these were the actual words spoken by myself and Ivan. I cannot even be sure whether we discussed all this in the same conversation; I was still groggy and in shock when I regained consciousness – it is possible that I learned the truth slowly, over a number of days and conversations. Indeed, the more I try to remember what has happened to me, the less sure I feel about the whole process of remembering. We see, it is said, through a glass, darkly. The past is an ever-fading vision; something glimpsed in a dream. I hardly dare trust myself with this burden of remembrance. Perhaps Angelina or Ivan would tell the story differently if they . . . But it is too late for what-ifs. I am the only one now in possession of the truth; and if at times it seems less an object, solid and graspable, than some kind of cascading liquid or wind-blown vapour, then that is all the more reason for me to strain my mind, searching for clues in the shadows. The past is all in here now, inside this skull, and the only way I can resummon it is through this nib, in the movements of this hand. Without doubt the story I tell will be a poor substitute for the truth, but the truth itself is already gone. It has vanished, reader, and all I can endeavour to do is draw its image from memory, however partial or warped or glass-darkened that image may be.

～∽～

I stayed in Ivan's flat for another several weeks. This was due not merely to my injuries, but to a range of symptoms – nausea, nightmares, cramps, fatigue– that the doctor said were all attributable to the events of that unfortunate night. Exactly what Ivan said to Dr Lanark – how he accounted for my presence as a detective on a night when I was meant to be at home asleep – I do not know. But clearly it was nothing to my detriment, because Dr Lanark arranged for me to be paid my full wages for as long as it took me to recover. Remarking this, my suspicions about Ivan's motives in keeping me in his flat began to evaporate. Either he was playing an extraordinarily subtle and long-term game, I thought, or he really was a good friend. Slowly, like a long-beaten dog with a new, kind master, I began to trust him . . .

. . . unpalatable as this story was to me, it did at least fit with my own experience of the lady in question. It made sense both of her apparent innocence and the smouldering carnality which her body had exuded that night in the brothel. What the story inspired in me, more than anything, however, was a profound pity. What a life she had led, poor Angelina; my own early years seemed banal and eventless next to hers. The ability to be bored by the ordinariness of the passing days was, I saw, a kind of privilege. And, though Ivan's descriptions of her abasements and her instability did not lessen the love that I felt for her, they did make me feel out of my depth. What possible use could I be to her? How could I ever protect her?

I repeat that I did not stop loving her. I did not stop thinking of her, dreaming of her, desiring her and fearing for her. And yet, while it is true that absence can in some senses increase the fondness one feels for someone, it also subtly reduces that someone. They become less real, more ghostly, more fictional. They become an *idea*. I was utterly in love with the idea of Angelina, completely devoted to it, as some widows are to the memory of their dead husbands. But at the same time I did not fight against the reality that she was gone from my life. I had no thought of pursuing her, of continuing to spy on her. True, she was now in Kent, not in London; but Kent was not so many miles away. The actuality of following her was not impossible; it merely seemed so to me.

~~~

Things became easier when I returned to work. Dr Lanark had been to see me every week during my convalescence, and he seemed to take a personal pride in my recovery. He greeted me joyfully whenever he saw me and asked how the job was going. And, after a few weeks of deaduns, I was finally assigned an interesting case – a respectable man who led a double life – and became immersed once again in the alluring mystery of detective work. To some extent, I suppose, I became the job; but I did not treat it as personally, as obsessively as I had before. I saw the folly of that now, and . . .

. . . huge fireplace. We would drink beer and laugh about our targets, the secretaries, the other detectives. Sometimes we would sit in silence, enjoying the taste of the beer and listening to the echoing conversations around us. Often he told me about his latest conquest – he got through girls like he smoked cigarettes – and I told him about Sarah.

I started seeing her regularly in early spring. We met by accident one afternoon at the office. As it was getting dark and we were both leaving, she asked whether I would walk her home. Of course I assented. When we reached her parents' house – a soot-darkened townhouse in Montagu Square – we fell into conversation about our plans for the weekend, and at length it was arranged that we should meet in Regent's Park and go walking. I don't remember who made the suggestion – it seemed to crop up naturally – but I am fairly sure that, prior to that afternoon, the thought of courting Sarah had never occurred to me.

Nevertheless, the walk in Regent's Park was pleasant, and we arranged to repeat it the following Saturday. Thereafter our excursions became a fixed, weekly affair. We were shy with each other initially, but it helped that we had interests in common – literature and detective work – and thus we spent a great deal of time talking about books and criminals. I remember us laughing at the ridiculous depiction of her father's (and my) profession in Conan Doyle's stories, and also a long conversation about Stevenson's novel *The Strange Case of Dr Jekyll and Mr Hyde*, which I admired greatly, but which Sarah had found so deeply disturbing that it had given her nightmares. However, I never felt quite as relaxed with Sarah as I did with Ivan. I always had the nagging impression that she was waiting for me to do or say something; that our meetings must have had some secret purpose which I had not yet fathomed. I mentioned this to Ivan and he cleared up the mystery in his usual blunt way. 'She wants you to kiss her, you dolt.'

That Saturday, eager to relieve the odd tension between us, I pressed my lips to hers quite suddenly while we hesitated before a fork in the path. She sighed and her body melted into mine. I knew then I had done something I would not be able . . .

... drinking, and dreaming wildly of escape. But I was like a beast in a trap: the more I struggled against my bonds, the more tightly they gripped me. Then, after one brief, thin-lipped conversation with Dr Lanark at the office, the last Friday before Christmas, I understood the situation all too clearly. Either I married his daughter and became a junior partner in the firm, or I forfeited everything: employment, reputation, his fatherly love and regard. I spent one dark weekend alone in my room, agonising over my choice. I suppose, when it came down to it, I felt I had too much to lose. And too little to gain. After all, what was freedom? You could not buy bread with it, or burn it on cold nights, or drink it to dull the pain of existence. Freedom, I told myself, was no friend of mine. I decided to turn my back on it; to put it from my mind as I had put *her* from my mind. To be reasonable. To move on. To forget.

I spent Christmas Eve with the Lanarks. It was a large gathering: the house was full with uncles and nieces, friends and neighbours, detectives and secretaries. I remember the vast, blazing fire, the magnificent fir tree decorated with shining baubles, the steamed-up window-panes, the perilous trays of glasses filled to the brim with champagne ... the nausea in my gut when I saw Sarah, arm in arm with her father, and the look of expectation on both their faces. Midway through the evening, sharing a joke with Ivan, I felt a hand on my elbow and looked around to see Dr Lanark. 'A word, my boy, if I may,' he whispered. Ivan raised his eyebrows. I followed my employer into the corridor. It was much colder there, and gloomier, and there was the scurry of servants all around us. He said, in a low voice, 'I take it your presence here indicates you have at least made a decision.' I nodded. 'Would you mind letting me know what you have decided?' Automatically, staring at the strange, swirling pattern on the carpet, I recited the fateful words. 'Sir, I would like to ask your permission for your daughter's hand in marriage.' When I looked up again, I saw a grin on Dr Lanark's face; of what nature that grin was, I cannot say for sure. Relief? Joy? Perhaps. But it seemed to me then that his expression was one of triumph. And mine – of defeat. Within seconds he had disappeared back into the living room and I heard his voice, strained loud above the babbling mass, declare ...

. . . was divided between work and wedding preparations. I still met up with Ivan at The Polar Bear, but we rarely managed more than one night a week now, and sometimes even that had to be sacrificed to the busy routine of our lives.

All of this changed – came to a sudden, thunderous halt – one sunny Saturday in June. I was walking through Regent's Park on my way to Dr Lanark's house. It was one of those perfect London afternoons: the air warm; the sky a rare, high blue; and the panorama aswirl with bright parasols and flowers and black-painted shadows. I could not help but feel optimistic on a day like that. I remember I was deep in my own thoughts as I passed the lake, and that the woman in white coming towards me was, at first, nothing more than a particularly vivid shape on the horizon. As she drew nearer, my eyes focused on her and I felt my chest constrict a little. A dog barked from somewhere and I looked away. When my eyes returned to their previous position, the woman was much closer. I looked at her face and . . . those eyes, those lips! She was wearing a hat and her hairstyle had changed, but the resemblance was so absolute that I couldn't breathe. I stopped dead and stared at her. I could hear nothing now but the roar of my own blood. And then, something amazing happened.

She saw me and stopped. She smiled. She spoke. A moment later the two of us were sitting at a table in a tea garden, like old friends. Around us the scene was as lovely as before, but I remember my eyes hardly moved from hers. Those pupils were like wells. That conversation . . . the details of what we said are irrecoverable now; my memory is simply of being adrift from the world, enclosed in some perfect island of air where time stood still and all barriers of communication melted away. I had never talked with anyone like that. Our words were like a river, so flowing and natural. Usually in the presence of ladies I would stammer and blush, would search haltingly for topics of interest, points of commonality, but with Angelina – she bade me call her that, one white-gloved hand on mine – it was as though I had entered some other world, where the usual laws did not apply; where differences of station and gender vanished and we floated serenely, as happy and astonished as if gravity itself had ceased to hold us fast to the earth . . .

Chapter 4

We honeymooned, at her father's expense, in the United States, travelling by cruise ship to New York and then by rail to the West. We had our photograph taken before that magnificent void named the Grand Canyon; we shopped and visited theatres in gay San Francisco; we admired the ancient Redwood trees in Sequoia. It would, under other circumstances, surely have been a marvellous trip, but our marriage, only days old, was already dead, and our honeymoon a mere sham.

It had been so from the moment I received her letter. It arrived three days after the wedding. Even before I opened it, I think, I had a kind of physical premonition – a hollow throb in my chest, some impossible sense of déjà vu – which was merely confirmed by the miraculous, devastating words I discovered therein. My memory of our conversation in that Regent's Park tea garden was not, as I had feared, an illusion, a sweet dream. It was real; it had meant something to her too. The letter was brief, but it said all it needed to say. And it was signed by her. In black ink; her own fair hand. *Angelina Vierge.* How strange that these ordinary letters, arranged in this and only this order, could inflame such ecstasy of pain and desire!

Those three weeks were Hell. Not only for me, of course; I am certain that poor Sarah suffered even more than I did; I, at least, understood the cause of our affliction. Though we went everywhere together, the two of us were desperately lonely. Each was the other's prisoner, and the other's torturer. Slowly our agony turned to mutual hatred. The silence in our bedroom at night was terrible and heavy. Perhaps I should have confessed – told her the truth, even shown her the letter – but in all honesty Sarah's emotional welfare was the last thing on my mind. I moved through those American days in a haze of longing, seeing Angelina's face in canyons and sunsets, leaves and bridges and oceans ...

. . . came during the final week in Portland, Oregon. It was a week-day morning in early August and yet that pretty town looked as bleak as any place on earth could, its squat buildings cowering under dark sheets of rain, the pavements turned to waterways. More terrible still was the bitter, blank expression in my wife's eyes. She lay propped up by pillows in the hotel bed and silently watched me dress for breakfast. When I asked her if she was not also going to rise, my voice almost breaking as I spoke, so unused was it to speech, she stared at me with a disgust so frank and so ugly that I could not help but be shocked. That I had reduced my poor, sweet, subservient Sarah to *this* . . . the shame I felt was more than I could bear. And so, of course, I pushed it away, ignored it. 'No appetite?' I inquired blandly, and then, without waiting for a response, left the room and went downstairs to eat.

I took advantage of Sarah's absence to compose another letter to Angelina. Like the others, its contents are lost to my memory; all I remember of those letters is the naïve absoluteness of the passion which inspired them. Angelina's letter to me, which I have even now at my elbow, is brief and tantalisingly ambiguous. It suggests deep reserves of passion without explicitly stating anything of the kind; probably she expected a similarly discreet reply from me. But what she received was something altogether rawer and more copi-ous. I do not believe there was a trace of irony in any of my missives.

When I had finished writing, I addressed and sealed the envelope and untastingly ate a croissant and drank some black coffee; then I went outside into the rain, the letter smuggled safely under my coat, and walked to the post office. On the way back I stopped at the town library and passed a few hours in contemplation of poetry. Keats, Wordsworth, perhaps Coleridge . . . I don't recall what I read; my abiding memory is of staring through those large, rain-streaked win-dows at the bruised sky and letting the minutes flow emptily by. If I thought of anything, it was certainly of Angelina, on the other side of the world, and not the hollow-eyed woman I had abandoned in the hotel. When I got back to our room, sometime in the early evening, Sarah was gone. She didn't leave a note. I suppose she must have caught the train to New York. I never saw her . . .

. . . found the side gate open and slipped through to the garden, which was large but surprisingly unadorned: a flat and well-tended lawn with a few bright flower beds and, at its centre, an old and beautiful apple tree. No sooner had I closed the gate behind me than the drone and clatter of the street was silenced. I felt I had surely entered Eden. The sun was high, the sky a dazzling blue: the Indian summer so glorious I could not but help remember that day in June, in the park. The memory came to me so strongly I gasped and had to stand still, one hand touching the brickwork of the house, as I waited for the dizziness to fade and for my equilibrium to reassert itself. It was in that moment of desire and disorientation that I noticed her, a dark shape behind the sun-bright glass of the kitchen window. I had the brief impression that she was watching me, though I could not possibly have made out her face, and then I saw her walk into the garden, wearing the simplest and most beautiful of summer dresses – thin white cotton, almost like a nightdress – with her legs and feet bare, and slightly brown. My heart was in my mouth, I could not speak or move, as she softly paced the lawn, her eyes fixed ahead on the apple tree, as though she had yet to mark my presence. At once, regathering my wits, I felt at a loss . . . embarrassed, guilty: here I was, a trespasser, stealing in on Miss Vierge's private property, unannounced and uninvited, now silently watching her in a state of undress. And yet still I said nothing.

She stood beneath the heavy branches and plucked a ripe fruit. Then, showing no surprise, she looked up at me and held the apple out in her hands; an offering. Dumbly I moved towards her, out of the shadow of the house and through the hot sunlight. For a moment I was blinded and then the tree's shadow covered me, covered the two of us, and Angelina stood close to me, her eyes speaking of things her mouth never could. 'Take a bite,' she whispered finally, and lifted the apple in one hand to my mouth. She held it as I bit. Afterwards in the fruit's perfect round skin there was a rough crater of exposed white flesh, and staining it a little blood from my gums. I wanted to apologise, to remove the stain myself, but before I could say or do anything of the kind, she placed it directly to her own mouth and slowly, gently, deliberately licked the blood with the tip of her . . .

309

. . . woke with the scent of the harlot's flesh on my skin and bed-clothes. It was late morning and brash sunlight came pouring through the gap between the curtains. My quarters were modest at best, of course, and the view from the window nothing short of dismal, but even so on that morning I felt a kind of pride and relief at the course my life had taken. Whatever else happened to me, at least I would not die a virgin. True, I had no prospects, no hope of happiness, but at least I could say I had *lived*.

I went to work and by the end of lunch felt dead on my feet. The customers were moaning and the chef was screaming, and my eupho-ria dimmed beneath the weight of fatigue. When my shift ended, however, I walked to The Polar Bear and had a drink with Ivan, who told me all the office gossip and toasted my manhood. Thus it was in a vainglorious and slightly drunken state that I entered my room.

The first thing I noticed was that a light was on; the second that the floor was covered with my clothes. I stared at them, jackets and trousers splayed violently across the room, like the raiment of invisible corpses on a battlefield. Stunned, I moved further into the room and stared at the weird disorder. The doors of the wardrobe were wide open and the coat hangers bare. I turned around, seeking some explanation, and it was then that I saw Angelina, sitting demurely on the bed.

'Your sheets stink of her,' she said.

I shrugged, feigning coolness. 'How did you know?'

'A little bird told me. There's no need to look so damned pleased with yourself.'

Suddenly I felt angry. 'Why do you care anyway? You're engaged. You told me so yourself.'

'That's why you did it, isn't it? To get revenge. Because you hate me.' I said nothing; it occurred to me that she was right. She stood up and came towards me. It was then that I noticed she too had been drinking. Her eyes were so lovely, loosened by wine. 'And you know perfectly well why I care.'

'Do I?'

The scent of her, sweet and carnal, was overwhelming. She swayed as she moved . . .

. . . with Ivan had, I felt, lost some of its old closeness. I suppose this was my fault; certainly I felt guilty about it at the time. After all, best friends are meant to tell each other everything, and I had, for the past month, been keeping him in complete ignorance of the most important and dramatic development ever to have occurred in my short life. He knew nothing of Angelina and I. Part of me wished I could tell him, wished to celebrate my great happiness, but I held back for two reasons: firstly, because Angelina had begged me not to breathe a word; and secondly, because I remembered all too clearly Ivan's warning to me about her – how vehemently he had declared that I ought never to see her again.

As I have said, I felt bad about this, but at the same time I had begun to wonder how open Ivan was being with me. Sometimes I had the feeling that he, too, was keeping something from me; his words, when I thought about them afterwards, seemed oddly ambiguous, full of potential secrets and double-meanings. In fact, as I learned later, he had been like this with me from the beginning. It was not his behaviour towards me that changed at this time; it was my perception of his behaviour. Call it liar's sense. Before, when I had been fully honest with him, I had innocently assumed he was acting the same way with me; now, because of my own duplicitousness, I suspected it in him. It is often thus, I fear: when we look at another person, what we see is not their otherness, but a mirror image of ourselves.

∽∾∽

Whatever guilt and worry I felt about Ivan, however, was easily put to the back of my mind. In truth, everything in my life at this point was an afterthought, a fast-fading whim, in comparison with my love for Angelina. That first month, and the month and a half that followed, were, for me, a golden age. Those were my miracle days.

It is almost impossible to be objective about such periods in our life – to see them afterwards as we saw them at the time. Hindsight alters everything. I can make intelligent guesses about my state of mind, the precise nature of my happiness, during the final months of 1891. I can infer that there must have been times, even then, when I was bored or frustrated; I can conclude that sometimes I might even have felt relieved to get away from her presence, to relax with a tankard of beer or to sleep alone all night. And yet those assumptions of mine, while doubtless correct, do not *feel true*. It is analogous to the fact that I can quantify the length of time this period lasted. My calendar tells me it began on 22 September and ended on 11 December; my calculations tell me that this means I was deliriously happy for exactly eighty days, which is approximately equal to eleven and a half weeks, or just over two and a half months, or a little less than a season; or, just as meaninglessly, to nearly two thousand hours, or seven million seconds. Yet these numbers – all of them, to me, monstrously small – are also a kind of lie. Because that autumn was (and is) in some sense *eternal*. What I mean is that the nature of my bliss was eternal; that, in loving Angelina, I existed in a sort of temporal vacuum; that my hours – our hours – were breathed not in the late nineteenth century nor in London, but in that timeless Paradise that all lovers inhabit.

And yet, while dates and times were immaterial to our bliss, *places* certainly were not. Indeed, often what comes to my mind when I remember that time is not an image of Angelina or myself, but of the living room in 21 Luff Street. In my memories, it is always six or seven o'clock in the morning in that room, the sun just rising, its silver rays ghosting through the window, illuminating the garden, with its dew-pearled grass stalks and its tree of knowledge, and spreading warm pools of gold over the flea-bitten lionskin on the parquet floor, the blood-red Chesterfield, and the tatty old armchair, once a favourite of Angelina's beloved grandfather, in which I always sat, those sweet mornings, staring into the fire and reflecting on my scarcely believable happiness. How I loved that room and its furniture! If, by some medical miracle, a Dr Jekyll were able to wipe all these memories from my brain and restore me as a blank page in a book whose story was yet untold, I still fear and hope – I still believe – that the briefest sight of that armchair would bring everything back to me in an instant: the love, the ecstasy, the horror . . . all!

It seems pointless to describe what we did during this time. We did what all lovers do. We kissed and talked. We undressed one another. We caressed one another. We made love. And we did so secretly, which was at once maddening and glorious.

I have so many memories of that time, yet it will suffice, I think, to recount one only. When I close my eyes at night and wish to dream of something sweet, this is the image that comes first to my mind. Perhaps when I die, I will summon it one last time, to soothe my dark and lonely fall into the void. The memory is this:

It is three or four o'clock in the morning and I am walking Angelina back to her house in Mayfair. We have spent the last few hours in my room, our bodies naked and our two hearts beating as one. Now, out on the street, we both wear cloaks, though the night is not too cold. The air is filled with tiny, floating raindrops, almost like a clear mist, and the streetlamps' outer haloes lend it a kind of soft blue hue. We do not speak as we walk, but we hold hands, and communicate through little squeezes and strokes of the other's palm, wrist, fingertips. Our footsteps echo, but otherwise there is no sound at all. The street is empty and it feels as though everyone, at that instant, is holding their breath to let us pass, as though time has stopped in our honour. Angelina sighs – with contentment, I think – and leans her head gently on my shoulder. I put my arm around her back and we continue to walk, more slowly now. In that moment I possess her and she possesses me. We are each the other's special secret. Ahead of us, under a distant streetlamp, I see a dark human form, vague in the mizzle. As we draw closer, I recognise it as the constable who patrols this area. He is young; not much older than me. He says 'Good evening' and nods, and we murmur the same as we pass.

An hour or so later, I walk back the way I came, the taste of Angelina's goodbye kiss in my mouth, her scent on my skin, my body and mind reeling pleasantly from fatigue, and notice that there are now two dark shapes under the lamppost. I reach the point where the policemen stand and the new one, obviously senior, moves towards me. He begins to speak, his voice stern, and I hesitate. And then – and this is the most sublime part of the memory – and then the constable, the one we passed earlier, puts a hand on his colleague's elbow and says, 'It's all right, sergeant, I know this gentleman. He's just walked his fiancée home.' And the sergeant nods, apologetically, respectfully, and I am allowed to go past. And the pride, the satisfaction, the perfect happiness I feel when the constable pronounces the word 'fiancée' in his official-sounding voice; that is what stays with me as I walk the last mile back to my room in Cathedral Street.

CHAPTER 5

Looking backward now, what happened when I saw Angelina again after Christmas has the cold, inevitable logic of an Aeschylean tragedy. Everything was foreshadowed. The signs were there, if only I had dared to see them. Angelina herself had told me on many occasions that this could not last, that it was wrong; she had sobbed with the pain and the guilt of it, and I had wiped her tears dry and kissed her better . . . and kissed her worse. I had closed my eyes to the warning signs; I had turned a deaf ear to her pleas and avowals. I had told myself it could not end because my life without it – without *her* – did not bear thinking about.

I do not regret my wilful ignorance. At least I tasted true, undiluted happiness, if only for a short time. Who, in all honesty, can claim more than that? It was something Angelina always talked about – the brevity of life, the certainty of death, the misery of the human condition, the cruelty of the world; and the miracle, the glory, of any happy moment one can snatch between the jaws of all these conspiring horrors. One time she said to me, 'It's good to know it will end soon, in a way. It makes the pleasure more intense.' I had thought she was talking about life and death. Perhaps, though, she was hinting to me that eighty days was the sum of my allotted stay in Paradise?

I saw her the day after she returned, and I knew as soon as she walked through the door that nothing would ever be the same again. The joy on my face was not reflected on hers. I asked her what was wrong and for a long time she could not speak at all; she only wept, silently, her face strangely expressionless. When finally I begged her to tell me what had happened, she said, in a voice almost blank with misery, 'It's over, Martin.' I demanded to know what she meant – why she would say such a thing – and she told me that she and Gerard Ogilvy had been married over Christmas. She showed me the diamond ring on her finger. To me it was like a dagger, thrust into my heart and . . .

. . . water torture used by the Chinese. That vicious circle of temptation, seduction and remorse which the two of us kept repeating, like a famished dog chasing its tail . . . well, there was certainly something purgatorial about it. What got to me in the end, though, was the pain in her eyes. By continuing to love her, I was turning my sweetheart into the most miserable wretch on earth, and for a few weeks after we finally stopped seeing each other, the thought that I had thereby ended her agony was enough of a consolation to keep the blackness at bay.

Soon, however, the sleepless nights, the unrelieved banality and futility of the days, the haunting knowledge that she was living her life, with another man, only two or three miles from where I stood, howling for the want of her, became too much. I saw that I had escaped purgatory only to find myself in Hell.

Finally, in early May, I decided to make a clean break. Those weeks of transition – the quitting of my job and room, the packing of my belongings, the muted farewells to the few people I could still call friends – are, in my recollection, characterised by a kind of numbness. The one person (other than Angelina) who loved me, I did not even call; the thought of contacting Ivan again, only to tell him that I was leaving the country, was too sad to contemplate. Of the sensations of spring undoubtedly blossoming around me, I recall nothing. In my memory, all is grey. I felt no emotion at all – no pain, no relief, no hope or fear – as I junked the remains of my life in London and booked passage on a ship to Australia. It was as though I had shed a skin, and a new creature – colder, less sensitive – had been born to take my place.

～～～

The voyage lasted nearly a month and consisted, for me, of little more than continual nausea. I shared a cabin with ten other male passengers, most of them the lowest dregs of humanity; the air in that small, windowless room was almost unbreathable. To pay for my passage, I was obliged to work as a waiter in the staff canteen. The ceaseless . . .

. . . so much so that, after four or five months I was able to get through whole hours without being flooded by memories of her face and voice. Slowly the physical ache I had felt since our last parting began to ease, and I found myself drawn to other women.

The good weather helped. It was October by then – a time that, in England, would have been filled with pathos and remembrance, walking down the same leaf-carpeted avenues I had walked with her, breathing the same misty, smoke-scented air. Living in the southern hemisphere, I was spared such painful reminders. In Melbourne, the trees were budding, early flowers blossoming. It was true I had paid for my flight south by suffering two winters in a row, but at least I had avoided autumn; and, nursed through the anniversary of my joy by the soft distractions of spring, I felt as though time had somehow been accelerated, the healing process miraculously quickened.

The first woman with whom I had an affaire on that side of the globe was a secretary at the post office. Her name was Catherine Lewis: she was older than me and, though no beauty, had a pleasantly voluptuous body and a freeingly modern attitude towards sex. I remember with fondness our sticky bouts in the store cupboard after hours, her skirts riding up those hot, fleshy thighs and the sigh of entry to that other world, where one glimpses eternity even though one cannot remain there more than a few seconds. In some ways, the essential sameness of that moment, with Catherine and with Angelina, was a comfort to me. It suggested to me that what I had fallen in love with was the act of love itself, and that I need not pine for ever in the shadow of one particular passion.

It did not take me long to realise that this was wishful thinking. For, though I told myself that I enjoyed Catherine's light-heartedness in regard to our lovemaking, there was also something in it that left me feeling empty and cheated. To hear her say briskly, in her flat, nasal accent, only a few seconds after orgasm, 'Well, that was very nice, Martin. Thank you – I enjoyed that', was disillusioning in the worst sense; I felt like the ladder to heaven had been pulled from beneath me, and that I must fall all the faster from those Olympian heights . . .

. . . trips with my new friends to the beach or the theatre, and many warm evenings passed in the bars of the old town, drinking the local beer among the wide-shouldered, red-faced natives. For the first time in more than a year, I felt happy; not happy in the same way I had felt with Angelina, of course, but at least not miserable, not aching with loneliness and regret. It was a shallow kind of existence, I freely admit, but at the time that was, I think, exactly what I needed. Perhaps, had I continued like that for another decade or so, I might eventually have been able to spend a night alone without being overwhelmed by sudden surges of panic and sadness. Perhaps I might, now, still be working in the sorting office, just a regular young suntanned Australian, winking at my colleagues and repeating the national mantra of 'No worries'. Alas, it was not to be.

It was early autumn in Australia – the fourth of April 1893 to be precise – when I first heard, through a prostitute I knew, that a young British aristocrat called Ogilvy was frequenting the place where she worked. She told me about him as a matter of curiosity, not because he was young or rich or handsome – a surprising number of her clients were thus – but because he had the unusual habit of sobbing at the moment of ejaculation. In spite of her natural hard-heartedness, she was moved by the sight of this and would often stay with him for half an hour or so afterwards, stroking his hair and whispering sweet consolatory nothings into his ear.

I explained that I would be greatly interested to meet this gentleman, and she divulged to me the date and time of his next rendezvous. Thus it was that two evenings later, I was sitting in the salon, smoking a pipe and caressing one of the girls, when a tall, well-dressed Englishman walked in. I recognised him instantly, despite his shockingly changed state. His skin had turned grey, his body obese, and he had grown a ragged beard which concealed the natural handsomeness of his face. Worst of all, however, were his eyes, which were hollow-looking and bloodshot. I did not engage him in conversation then: it was apparent, despite his politeness, that he had only one thing on his mind. But later, seeing him 'by chance' in the street, I invited him to take a drink with me in a . . .

... excitement and confusion into which this threw me can readily be imagined. The news that Angelina was no longer married – that she was *free* – was so unexpected and glorious that the surge of hope it produced inside me was almost unbearable. At the same time, however, I was naturally disturbed by Ogilvy's dark hints about her behaviour. His judgment was not unclouded, of course, and – given that she had rejected him – he had every reason to spread slander about her. But I had seen enough of poor Angelina's nocturnal adventures myself to be concerned on her behalf, and I hadn't entirely forgotten the story that Ivan Dawes had told me about her. Could it, after all, be true? I had, while in love with her, dismissed it as his invention, designed solely to keep me away from her – after all, she herself had told me the story of her past – but now the old doubts and fears came back to haunt me, and I no longer knew whom or what to believe.

One thing was certain: I had to return to England. Nothing could be resolved by my remaining in Melbourne. I had to find Angelina and talk to her. I had to discover the truth and – perhaps, *perhaps*, o suspenseful heart – reclaim the great love of my life.

He finished the story and put it down on the bed. He felt excited and afraid, though it was difficult to pinpoint the reason for either emotion. The story, for all its melodrama and artificiality, for all its missing pages, had stirred something inside him. The events and emotions it described, though patently fictional, were also disturbingly familiar.

When James tried to analyse the story, however, he became confused. Several of the images it contained corresponded almost exactly to certain memories, or hallucinations, that had come to him in recent days. The pink stain in the flesh of the apple; the jealous girl who had thrown all the clothes from the wardrobe; the night-time encounter with a policeman. He had remembered these events, and then he had read about them in this story. But how was that possible? Where did *he* fit into this mystery? James felt as if the solution to this puzzle was standing there, clear and unconcealed, directly before his eyes, but that, perhaps because it was so close, so obvious, he could not see it. He thought of a detective story he had read once, by Edgar Allan Poe, in which a letter, for which the police had spent weeks methodically searching the culprit's house, had been pinned to the wall, in plain sight, the whole time. James wondered if the solution to *his* mystery could be just as self-evident. What am I missing? he thought. What is it that I am failing to see?

I must admit I felt like laughing, watching the contortions

that disfigured James's face during these moments, feeling the thought-processes in his mind twist themselves into ever-more complex labyrinths. But I didn't. After all, I knew how he felt. I had experienced the same torture once myself.

He spent the rest of the day in the bedroom, sifting through the contents of the wardrobe. There were lecture notes, drafts of stories and poems. There was a vinyl copy of *16 Lovers Lane* by The Go-Betweens. There was a well-thumbed copy of the Borges book, *Labyrinths*, translated into English (it fell open at the story 'Funes the Memorious', which James read all the way through, shivering when he noticed the words 'MEMORY IS HELL' handwritten in the margin). And, most significantly of all, there were snapshots of Ian Dayton, Graham Oliver, Lisa Silverton, Anna Valere, taken in this house, the back garden, this very room; as soon as James saw their faces, he recalled their names; he remembered them. There were also several photographs of a plump, pale-faced girl who had, he knew instantly, been in love with him. As he studied each object, or tried on the clothes, memories swarmed around him. Dozens of them, hundreds of them; a dust storm of memories. But, to James's dismay, he found not one single mention of his name in any of the notebooks; not one photograph of his face. It's unbelievable, he thought: I remember all these faces, these names, these jackets and shirts – they fit me; they fit the holes in my memory – and yet *I* am not here anywhere. It was as though he had been erased from history.

But then another thought occurred to him. It was a simple idea, and yet it seemed to change everything. James had, until this moment, been working on the assumption that the clothes and photographs and notebooks belonged to Malcolm Trewvey. But, James thought, what if they are not his . . . what if they are *mine*? That would explain why James's face was in none of the photographs – because James would have taken them. That would explain why his name was not in any of the notebooks – because to him, he would not be James Purdew, but *me, myself, I*. That would explain the presence of *16*

Lovers Lane: it was *his* copy; the copy he had thought lost.

But if that was true, then what did Malcolm Trewvey have to do with all this? Who was *he*? James held his face in his hands. He was dizzy and exhausted, and the light in the bedroom was fading. Outside it was nearly dusk. He hadn't eaten since early morning, and he felt suddenly weak with hunger. Unseeingly he walked downstairs. The telephone in the hallway started ringing again. He wondered who it could be, the person at the other end, trying so desperately, so patiently, to get through.

James went to his bedroom and, about to draw the curtains, looked out of the window. What did he see? The branches of the chestnut tree, moving in the wind; the shadow of the parked van on the pavement; lit-up windows in the houses across the road; all of this stained dark blue; and, too close to see clearly, a face. At first he thought it was someone else's face – *his* face – but after a moment's shock he realised it was his own reflection. He took a step back and focused on this mirror image. Strange, he thought, I almost look like . . .

And then, suddenly, he understood. 'Of course,' he whispered, 'it all fits!' That was why he had received letters addressed to Malcolm Trewvey. That was why Graham Oliver hated him. That was why he sympathised so powerfully with Martin Thwaite in *Confessions of a Killer*. That was why he remembered the song, '21 Love Street'. He had written the story! He had written the song! He *was* Martin Thwaite! He *was* Malcolm Trewvey! Stunned, James remembered the only time he had ever seen Malcolm Trewvey's face: it had been outside the sex shop and . . . *their eyes had met in mirrored glass*. He had been looking at his own reflection.

For a few moments he was as though hypnotised; he saw and heard nothing. Then his ears picked up again on the vibration of the telephone's ringing. The sound sparked off another thought: If I am Malcolm Trewvey, then the person at the other end must be . . . Anna Valere. This, he told himself, was what he'd been waiting for. This was the meaning of it all: the purpose, the secret, the grail.

He took a hacksaw from the toolbox in his bedroom and began sawing the wooden telephone box, the back-and-forth moan of the metal teeth in time with the desultory ringing of the phone. But this was too slow, he realised: she might hang up before he had opened the box. Remembering the axe he had seen in the shed, he ran outside. The garden was dark and for a while he got lost. All the time he prayed to the person at the other end not to hang up. When, eventually, he found the shed, he picked up the axe and ran all the way back to the telephone. He stood in front of the white box, his vision swimming and his lungs wheezing. For a moment all he could hear was the sound of his strained breathing, and he thought the phone must have stopped ringing. Finally he managed to catch and hold his breath, and to listen.

Brrrnnnggg. Brrrnnnggg.

Triumphant, he swung the axe head over his shoulder and brought it down on the wooden box. It collapsed in a mess of splinters and nails and the receiver fell from the hook. It dangled there at the end of the coiled wire. He threw the axe to the floor and put the receiver to his ear. 'Hello?' he said. At first there was silence, and James's heart sank, but then a woman's voice said, 'Hello?'

James was about to say 'Anna?' when the woman announced, in a cold, mechanical voice, 'I am calling on behalf of Malcolm Trewvey. He wishes to speak to you.'

James was too confused to speak. Malcolm Trewvey?

'He would like to call round tomorrow morning,' the woman continued. 'Could you confirm that you will be on the premises at nine o'clock?'

'Yes,' James managed to gasp. The woman said, 'Good, Mr Trewvey will see you then,' and hung up.

James poured himself a glass of wine and tried to calm his flying thoughts. Malcolm Trewvey was coming to see him. The man whom he had followed and spied upon, whose guilty secret he had tried to discover, now wished to speak to James. What could it mean? With a chill, he remembered that strange footnote to the story about the life of Tomas Ryal: the man who had accused the philosopher of murdering his fellow student had been called M. Trewvey. James began to worry that he had misunderstood the situation all along. Perhaps it was not he who had been following Malcolm Trewvey, but vice versa? Perhaps it was not Malcolm Trewvey who possessed a guilty secret, but James Purdew?

He lay awake in bed for several minutes, listening to the noises. Buzz buzz. Bang bang. He had slept badly and his head hurt. Bang bang. Buzz buzz. He put on a dressing gown and walked to the hallway. Buzz buzz. Bang bang. There was someone at the door. James looked at his watch: it was 8.59. Barely able to breathe for the fear that filled his chest, he opened the door.

A middle-aged man stood there. He looked ordinary, insignificant. 'Hello,' said the man.

'Hello,' said James.

'My name is Malcolm Trewvey,' said the man.

'What?' said James.

'My name is Malcolm Trewvey,' repeated the man. 'My secretary telephoned you yesterday evening, I believe. I'm a member of the Scrabble Club of Great Britain.'

'What?' said James.

'The Scrabble Club of Great Britain,' repeated the man. 'I live at number 12 Lough Street. I was talking to the postman yesterday and he said he thought he'd delivered some letters addressed to me at number 21. And I said, "Oh really? How odd." And then it occurred to me that I hadn't received my letters recently.'

'What?' said James.

'My letters. The Scrabble Club of Great Britain sends participating members nine letters each month, chosen at random of course, by a computer, you know, and each member then has to ring up with their highest-scoring word. It's very exciting. You can win all sorts of prizes. They call it Red Letter Day, although the letters aren't actually red. But anyway, I haven't received mine recently. So I put two and two together, and I rang the Scrabble Club of Great Britain's headquarters in London, and I asked them to check the details they have for me: my name and address and so on. And guess what? They had me down as 21 Lough Street. Someone must have got their numbers muddled up. *Scrabbled*, so to speak!' The man laughed.

'What?' said James.

'So . . . I was wondering, have you received any letters for me? Addressed to Malcolm Trewvey?'

The man stood smiling, hopefully.

'No,' said James.

And he closed the door.

James sat in the white armchair all morning. He did not eat. He did not move. He did nothing but breathe and stare into space. Not for the first time, he felt like a detective in someone else's mystery; a detective who, instead of steadily tracking down the solution, finds himself further and further away from it with every chapter.

Someone should write a true-to-life detective story, James thought bleakly; an existential mystery in which the answer is not to be found, clear and logical, at the book's end, but only to be glimpsed, or half-grasped, at various moments during its narrative; to be sensed throughout, like a nagging tune that you cannot quite remember, but never defined, never seen whole; to shift its shape and position and meaning with each passing day; to be sometimes forgotten completely, other times obsessed over, but never truly understood; not to be something walked *towards* but endlessly *around*.

He tried to make sense of the mystery with which he had become obsessed. How could he have got it all so badly wrong? Malcolm Trewvey had nothing to do with his past at all: that much was clear now. He was merely a middle-aged scrabble fanatic who lived in a house on the other side of the road. His post had been mistakenly delivered to number 21 and James had woven an elaborate fantasy around a series of randomly chosen letters. It had been coincidence, nothing more.

He remembered the dream he'd had, in Amsterdam; of the

doctor peeling away the bandages on his leg to reveal . . . an absence, a nullity, a blank. Nothing meant anything, he realised. Everything meant nothing. All that he had believed in was illusion. All that was solid had melted into air. He had tried to discern a pattern in his life, but the only pattern was chaos. He had tried to find his way through the labyrinth, but now he had reached its centre and discovered . . . another labyrinth.

In the afternoon he went outside for some fresh air. He walked all the way to the old town, and then began taking streets at random, looking not where he was going but at the people around him. He listened to their earnest conversations, he gazed at their worried frowns. James began to smirk, to snort. Soon he was standing alone on a pedestrianised shopping street, laughing uncontrollably at the passers-by.

No one could see it, that was the funniest thing. The people all around him, hurrying from A to B . . . none of these people could see the labyrinth. None of them could see the huge dark fingers of chance idly building walls in their path, squashing them like ants, lifting them on to a pedestal, just briefly, for no reason at all, and then flicking them down into the maze again. No one could see the horror and hilarity of it all. They took it so seriously; they believed that it mattered, that it *meant something*. They went around asking each other, 'How are you?' 'How's it going?' 'How's life treating you?' And this was what they called sanity! Oh, it was just too funny. James couldn't stop laughing.

After some time, his laughter died away. He went to a pub nearby and drank a pint of bitter at a table on his own, watching with disgust and amusement as the others hugged and sang and laughed. It was New Year's Eve and everyone was optimistic; they all seemed to believe that the year to come would be better than the year just gone. The fools. After a few more pints, he left the pub and walked back to Lough Street. All around him rose the sheer black walls of the labyrinth, solid and visible and undeniable. For the first time in my life, James thought, I am seeing the world as it truly is.

As he drew close to the familiar face of 21 Lough Street, however, he felt a tiny kindling of faith inside him. True, he was lost in the labyrinth, like everyone else, and all that he did was futile, inconsequential . . . but perhaps his existence was not quite without meaning, without centre. He did, after all, have this house, and its walls, painted and as yet unpainted. He did have his work.

That evening James walked slowly around the ground floor of the house, through every room, inspecting the perfect whiteness of the walls, ceilings, floors. By the time he went to bed he had begun to feel grateful. Whatever he had lost had been unreal in the first place. This house, at least, was real; it was solid; it could not simply melt into air, like all the rest.

During the weeks that followed, James stuck relentlessly to his task. He did not pick up the telephone. He did not answer the front door. He read no newspapers, watched no television. He let the post pile up unopened on the doormat. Sometimes he had bad dreams and occasionally, standing on the first-floor landing, he would look up the stairs to the next storey and wonder what lay up there, but the thought never went any further than that. James did not wish to get ahead of himself.

Apart from scraping and sanding and plastering and painting, he did almost nothing worth the trouble of remembering. The long, dull winter slowly transformed itself into a dull, wet spring, and James slowly transformed the first floor into a perfectly white replica of the ground floor.

Then one day, as he was putting the finishing touches to the ceiling of the first-floor landing, he noticed something odd: a tiny, faint grey stain on the wall next to the staircase. At first, thinking this was just a smudge of dirt, he wiped it with a cloth. If anything, however, this only darkened and widened the stain. Irritated, he painted over it.

An hour later, when he returned from eating lunch, he discovered that the paint had dried strangely, in a kind of crisp bulge. James touched this and, to his horror, it crumbled and peeled away – not only in the small circle he had repainted, but in a huge streak covering half the wall. And underneath the crumbled paint he found neither white primer nor white plaster, as he had expected, but a long, dark, mottled, brownish stain, with a kind of triangle on top. When James stood back and squinted at this, he had the disturbing sensation that the stain was shaped like an arrow, and that it was pointing up to the attic floor.

He put his head in his hands. All his hard work, ruined like this. If only there was some way of erasing these stains *for ever*, he thought. How much happier and more free I would feel then . . .

To distract himself, he decided to go for a walk outside. He hadn't breathed fresh air in months, he realised; perhaps the paint fumes were going to his head and he was seeing things. Perhaps the arrow only existed in his mind. Reassured by this thought, James put on his coat and was about to open the front door when he noticed that it was blocked by the pile of letters. Down on his knees, he picked the envelopes up one by one and, studying each in turn, threw them into a plastic bin-liner. He had nearly finished when he came to a pale-blue envelope. There was something familiar about this envelope. His name was typewritten on the front, and below it his old address in Amsterdam; this had been crossed out, as had his parents' address. The stamp was postmarked November; evidently it had taken nearly four months to reach him.

He opened the envelope. Inside was a typewritten letter, headed TOMAS RYAL ASSOCIATES. 'Dear client,' it began,

> Our records show that you have yet to purchase a new supply of LWZYYY34-C, your personalized anti-allergy medication. As we explained to you during your induction session, you are of course free at any time to discontinue your medication, but to do so carries certain **very severe risks** which need to be discussed in person so that you can be advised on the best methods of coping with the inevitable side-effects and complications arising from the decision to end treatment. Be warned: if

you do not control your allergy, it may return – and **the longer you delay, the more you will suffer**. Contact your local representative NOW to discuss ways of reducing your torment. Prices for a full consultation begin at £1,000. If, however, you have simply forgotten to renew your subscription, then all you have to do is . . .

The rest of the page consisted of various payment options. James skim-read them, searching for the sender's name, but the letter was unsigned. Then he dropped the letter to the floor and stared into space, his mouth open.

VI
THE BLACK BOX

It was quarter-past ten the next morning when James entered the park. He checked his watch twice to make sure. Today, he told himself, I am not going to let time slip away from me. I am going to keep a tight grip on reality.

It was a grey, damp day, the clouds like stains on the sky. He walked along the path towards the large white building. From the outside, he noted, it was as he remembered it: five storeys high, several hundred metres wide, very few windows. When he arrived in the lobby, James told the woman on reception that he wished to speak to Dr Lanark.

'Your name please?' she demanded.

'James Purdew.'

The receptionist nodded and pressed a few buttons on the computer keyboard, then spoke into the headset. 'Dr Lanark, there is a James Purdew to see you in reception.' A pause, her face blank, then: 'Very well, Dr Lanark, I will send him down now.'

James felt shocked by how easy all this was. Was he really going to talk to Dr Lanark? Was he really going to find out the truth? He followed the woman's directions to a lift. He pressed the call button and the doors opened. As before, he pressed the lowest button. When the doors opened again, he found himself in an empty white corridor, with a set of double doors at one end. He walked through the corridor, past white, unnumbered doors on either side. James was surprised: he had thought that his memories of the underground laboratory had been mere hallucinations, dreamemories, yet here everything was, just as he had remembered. As he walked, the corridor curved slightly, and James had the faint, creeping impression that the floor was sloping gently downward. When he stopped still and tried to verify this, he found he couldn't be absolutely sure, but the further he walked, the more obviously the corridor seemed to curve and slope.

There was no one else around, and the only sound was the low buzz of the ventilation system. James counted the double doors as he moved through them. One, two, three, four. How big *is* this place? James wondered fearfully as he continued. And was it his imagination, or was the lighting in the corridors growing gradually dimmer? He felt sure that when he had first emerged from the lift, the neon striplights had been burning brightly; now, however, they were barely more than nightlights.

Finally, he heard voices further along, so he walked in that direction and stopped outside a half-open door. He knocked softly and said 'Hello?'

'Enter,' said a man's voice.

James stepped into the luxurious parlour. This both comforted and disconcerted him: the former because the parlour was almost exactly as he recalled it – a generous fire burning in an open hearth; three leather armchairs positioned round a low wooden table; on the table a crystal decanter filled with amber liquid and three empty glasses – and the latter because, in his memory, the parlour had not led directly on to the corridor. He stepped into the room and saw a small man sitting in one of the chairs. The man looked up and James saw his face, which was small, pale and unremarkable. 'Ah, Mr Purdew . . . do you remember me?' the man asked.

'Vaguely,' James replied. 'You're Dr Lanark, aren't you?'

'That is a name I have used in the past, yes.' He smiled patronisingly. 'It is not, of course, who I am, any more than "James Purdew" is who you are. One should never put too much trust in names. But you recall my face?'

'I think so. It's difficult to say from when or where, though. I'm pretty sure you taught me in university, but I also think I've dreamed about you recently. There were two of you.'

'Indeed?' Dr Lanark looked amused, then studied the papers on his desk. 'So how long is it since you stopped taking the medication?'

'I . . . I don't know. Several months, I suppose.'

'Hmm. I imagine it's been a difficult time.'

The doctor's tone was cool and matter-of-fact. James, trying to act likewise, simply nodded.

'You've suffered hallucinations?'

'Yes . . . I think so.'

'Any dreamemories?'

'One or two.'

Dr Lanark nodded, and murmured as if to himself, 'Only to be expected. So . . . do you remember what happened?'

Up until this moment James had been regarding the interview with a sort of casual curiosity, as though it were happening to someone else; now, suddenly, he felt nervous. This was, he realised, the moment of truth. So . . . *did* he remember what had happened? Cold fingers tightened around his heart and he said, 'Some of it.'

'You stopped short, then? You chose not to remember?'

'I suppose so . . . yes.'

'You do realise that, soon, you will no longer have any choice in the matter?'

'But what if I . . . ?'

'It's too late, I'm afraid. I could give you a stronger dose, of course, to try to reverse the effect, but the risks would be very high. You might end up losing more than the targeted area. And if we chose to erase now, you would probably lose the last ten years as well.'

James thought of Ingrid, and shook his head. 'I can't do that.'

'No. I quite understand. It must have come as a shock when you realised you had forgotten those years?'

337

'Yes . . . although I felt like I knew already, in a way. It was more like it had just . . . slipped my mind.'

'Really?' Dr Lanark smiled with alarming enthusiasm and began writing furiously on one of the papers. 'The technical boys will be delighted.' James said nothing. When the doctor had finished writing, he looked at James with a serious expression and said, 'You do understand, of course, that the memories were never truly lost? The medication you chose was an inhibitor, not an eraser; thus the need for it to be taken continuously. We did discuss other options when you . . . do you recall any of this yet?'

'Bits and pieces,' James admitted, looking around the office. 'I didn't come here, though, did I?'

'No, that meeting took place in our previous premises. You've been back there quite recently, I believe.' There was a sly look in the doctor's eyes as he said this.

A suspicion flickered in James's mind. 'You mean . . .'

'Harrison Lettings, yes. Associates of ours. I'm glad to say that T.R.A.'s financial position has changed for the better since those days. What's the matter, Mr Purdew? Your face appears to be turning green.'

The doctor wasn't joking. James was beginning to feel nauseous. It was the memories returning – scores of them coming back to life at the sound of Dr Lanark's voice, his words, these hints of a forgotten past – but James didn't know that then. 'I feel unwell,' was all he said.

The doctor poured some armagnac into a glass and passed it to James along with a single triangular grey pill.

'What is it?'

'Just something to calm you down. I'm afraid the next few days are going to be rather traumatic for you, Mr Purdew. This will help reduce the pain and the nausea.'

James eyed the pill suspiciously, but in the end he accepted the doctor's advice. He swallowed the pill, then took several long sips of the *digéstif*. Moments later his chest felt warm, his mind calm. He sighed, closed his eyes, and when he opened them again, the office seemed to have grown darker. There were two candles on the low table, and no other light at all except for the fire in the hearth. James had the curious feeling that time had passed without his knowing. Was it day or night? He walked over to the window, which was concealed by a Venetian blind, and pulled on the drawstring. Oddly, it seemed to move upward, and yet no window was revealed behind, only a Venetian blind. The *same* Venetian blind. Puzzled, he tried twisting the plastic tube to make the slats move into a horizontal position, but that didn't work either.

'You can't see out of the window,' a woman's voice explained, 'because you have never seen out of the window.'

James turned around: it was Dr Lewis. She was sitting in an armchair next to Dr Lanark, her stockinged legs crossed provocatively. For some reason James thought of a storeroom cupboard in an Australian post office. 'I don't understand,' he confessed.

'Hmm. You never were one of our more gifted students,' Dr Lewis said sarcastically.

'What we are showing you is a reflection of the past,' Dr Lanark explained. 'In the past you never opened the blinds, never saw outside. For that reason, you cannot do so now.'

'So what *is* out there?'

Dr Lewis sighed impatiently. 'Why are you so interested in the view?'

'I don't know,' James admitted. 'Because I can't see it, I suppose.'

'We can't tell you what is outside,' said Dr Lanark, 'for the same reason that you can't see it yourself.'

'So you can't tell me anything I don't already know?'

'On the contrary, we can. Because what you have experienced and what you remember are not the same thing,' Dr Lanark said. He, James could tell, was the more patient of the two. Already Dr Lewis was tutting and muttering about having her time wasted. James wondered if she were angry with him; after all, he hadn't returned her phone calls. He sat in the chair opposite hers. She crossed her legs, revealing a glimpse of suspenders, and said, 'Surely you must have some more pertinent questions you would like to ask us. We haven't got all day, you know.'

James didn't respond because his mind was suddenly filled with a memory of Dr Lewis sucking his penis. It was a spectacularly vivid memory: he could feel her hair, slightly wiry, on his bare abdomen, and see her lips, pushed out and misshapen, as they slid up and down the shaft of his erection. He blinked. Dr Lewis was staring at him expectantly, her face severe, her lips held tightly together. Evidently she had just asked him a question, though he had no idea what it was. 'Sorry,' he began, 'I was just . . .' His words trailed off. She raised an eyebrow and James blushed.

'Mr Purdew, your sexual fantasies are no concern of mine, but there is really no point in us being here if you are not going to be able to concentrate for more than half a second at a time.'

'Sorry,' he repeated.

'We are here to help you, if we can,' said Dr Lanark. 'Now think carefully . . . there must be some questions you would like us to answer.'

James thought about this. The doctor was right, of course. For the past eight months his life had been little more than a series of questions without answers. He had come to H. in the first place, desperately seeking clues to the truth of his past. He had been so curious to fill the gap in his memory that he had abandoned everything: his girlfriend, his job, his friends, his future. For long weeks at a time he had thought of nothing but uncovering the secrets he guessed to be hidden in the labyrinth of his mind, of finding the key that would open the black box. And yet, recently . . . since the turn of the year or thereabouts . . . his desire to know – his hope of remembering – had come to seem a perverse, almost shameful emotion. Now, the desire, the hope, had transformed itself into something else. It had turned itself inside out, or perhaps only rotated on its axis to reveal its other, darker side. The hope, James saw now, was also fear. He did not want to know. He did not want to remember.

'No, I don't have any questions.'

Dr Lanark smiled and sighed. 'Amnesire.'

'Pardon?'

'Amnesire. It's a word I coined myself. It means the desire to forget, or – as in your present case – the desire not to remember. Strange, isn't it, that no word already existed for such a strong and common emotion. Most people, I believe, are amnesirous. We forget because we wish to; because we need to. For the majority of people, the majority of the time, the process of forgetting is automatic. We do it every day and don't give it a second thought. It is as natural, and as necessary, as urinating, excreting and exhaling. And imagine if you didn't do *those* things! For certain people, at certain times, however, this process stops working. Something happens: something so large, so dark, so unforgettable, that their view of the present and the future is obscured. Instead of looking at the world through a window, they find themselves looking at a mirror – a fairground mirror if you like: distorting, enlarging, turning the mundane monstrous – so that they cannot see around or ahead at all, but always and only behind. We set up T.R.A., Dr Lewis and myself, because we wanted to help those poor, tormented souls. We wished to facilitate forgetting in those who had lost the instinct.'

'Very interesting,' James yawned, 'but what has all this got to do with me?'

'You were our first customer,' said Dr Lewis.

'First *patient*,' Dr Lanark corrected.

'When you came to us you were suicidal, so in a sense we saved your life. Not that you've ever shown any gratitude . . .'

'To be fair, Dr Lewis, he didn't actually remember.'

'Well, he remembers now, doesn't he?'

Dr Lanark looked at James curiously. 'Do you?'

James nodded. 'It's coming back . . .' Panic rose in his chest even as he spoke. 'I don't want it to come back.'

Dr Lewis rolled her eyes. 'As Dr Lanark has already made clear, this is no longer something over which you have any choice. Really, it's your own fault for going with the inhibitors in the first place. We told you erasure would be safer . . .'

'My dear, let's not go over all this again,' said Dr Lanark, giving his colleague a reassuring squeeze on the thigh. 'The point is, Mr Purdew, that in the next few weeks or days or perhaps even in the next few hours, you are going to be overwhelmed by memory. You are like a man stranded on a beach; a man who, because of exhaustion or injury, cannot climb the few yards to safety, and who is now simply lying there, waiting for the tide to return. And it is drawing close, believe me. Soon, very soon, the waves will break over you, crash down on you; they will pull your inert body out to sea, where it will sink, down, down, down into black water, endlessly deep . . .'

'Stop!' James gasped. 'I get the idea. So what can I do?'

'You must prepare yourself.'

'How?'

'First you must find a dark and silent place in which you can be alone. You will need to concentrate fully, so it has to be somewhere secret; somewhere with no telephone or radio or television.'

James thought of the cellar he had glimpsed from the cupboard under the stairs, and nodded. 'I think I know a place like that.'

'Good. You will need a notebook and some pens, and enough food and drink to last you a week, possibly longer.'

'That shouldn't be a problem.'

'When you are settled and calm and you've had a chance to empty your mind, you should open the black box. It is vitally important that you do this *before* the memories return. You must understand that the memories, when they return, will feel like chaos – like sad, dark chaos – and without some basic narrative structure into which you can fit them, they will almost certainly sweep you away. That, I am afraid, is the price you pay for the long-term inhibition of memories. It's like building a dam: one little crack, the tiniest leak, and the entire structure is in danger of collapse.'

'As you were warned at the time of your treatment,' added Dr Lewis.

All this talk of water was making James thirsty. He took a drink from the glass of brandy. The warm buzz calmed him down. He tried to think logically. 'The black box. You mean I should read my diaries?'

'Not necessarily.'

'Then what am I supposed to . . .'

But Dr Lanark wasn't listening any more; he was looking at his watch. Dr Lewis had already put on her coat and was standing impatiently by the door. 'You must excuse us, Mr Purdew,' said Dr Lanark. 'We have an important meeting with our patron in a few minutes.'

'Your patron? Who's that?'

'*Our* patron, Mr Purdew. Not only mine and Dr Lewis's, but yours as well.'

'Uh . . . I have a patron?'

'Indeed. Whose house did you imagine you had been living in for most of the past year?'

James started. 'The man in the black coat? He's behind all this?'

The two doctors looked at James as though he was an idiot. 'He hasn't exactly made a secret of it,' said Dr Lewis. 'Really, for someone who fancies himself as a private detective, you're not very sharp, are you?'

'But who is he?'

Dr Lanark stared at James in silence, his face unreadable in the flickering half-light.

'Oh, let me guess. You can't tell me because I don't already know . . .'

'No, it's not that,' Dr Lanark replied. 'It's just that you wouldn't believe me if I told you.'

'Try me!'

'He will reveal himself to you when he believes you are ready.'

'Why not now?' James shouted. 'Let him show himself . . .' He was angry, tired of these games, desperate to know. And yet, at the same time, he couldn't help feeling a little relieved when Dr Lanark shook his head.

Dr Lanark showed James to an emergency exit and, in return for a thousand pounds in cash, gave him a small silver-coloured key, which James put in his pocket. They shook hands, said goodbye. James opened the door and found himself out in the park, at the rear of the large white building. The sky was turning dark, and there were drops of rain in the air. He turned to ask Dr Lanark one last question, but the door had already closed; it was too late.

Glancing at his watch, James discovered that it was quarter past eight. He wondered where all the time had gone. Numb with exhaustion, he began the long walk through the park to the bus stop. I stood at the window, watching him go.

He put the black box and the black notebook and the white notebook into the rucksack, along with a couple of biros. Then he went to the kitchen and packed as much tinned food and bottled water as would fit. After that he went to the cupboard under the stairs. He bent down and opened the little door. As before he saw darkness, smelled damp ashes, felt cold air on his skin. He put his feet through first and found solid steps leading down. After taking one last breath of untainted air, James entered the cellar and closed the little door behind him.

The darkness felt thick, and heavier than normal air; like something that, if he kept breathing it, would fill his insides, line his lungs; like something in which he might drown. A torch, he thought, that is what I need. But as far as he knew there wasn't a torch in the house. And the shops had already closed. He could wait until tomorrow morning, of course, but what if the memories came tonight? No, it was no use: he would just have to deal with the darkness as best he could.

He took a few deep breaths and squatted down so he could touch the step on which he stood. Cold smoothness met his fingertips. The steps were made of stone, and slippy with moisture, so he descended with extreme slowness and caution. There were nine steps – he counted them – and then he was standing on a different surface. It was noisier, less stable. James crouched down and discovered pebbles. He stood up again, and it was at this point that he noticed a chink of non-darkness in the black air that surrounded him. It wasn't light exactly, just a point of dim orange that illuminated nothing else. It was in front of him, the distance incalculable, and it appeared to be in the shape of a tiny circle. James's first thought was a lit cigarette end, but it was too still, too unvarying for that. And besides, who else could be down here? James didn't like to think about that, so – legs bent low to the ground, hands waving eagerly before him – he concentrated on finding his way around the cellar.

He sat on a narrow bed, looking out into the almost absolute nothingness and telling himself where everything was: saying it over and over again so that soon he imagined he could see each object, each wall, each corner of the room in which he sat. For some reason, he thought of Tomas Ryal and his theory of solipsism. What if this were the true nature of the world? What if he only saw buildings and trees and other people because he had spent his life telling himself they were there? Normally such an idea would have intrigued James, but down here in the darkness it seemed too believable, too disturbing, so he put it from his mind.

The cellar was, as far as he could tell, the same shape and size as his ground-floor bedroom, which must, he thought, lie directly above. Strangely, the bed on which he sat, though low and narrow like most of the other beds in the house, was freshly made, with ironed sheets, a plump pillow, and a heavy, feather-filled duvet. James did not give any thought to what this might mean; he was simply glad of the comfort. In any case the real source of his wonder was not the bed, but the periscope.

That was what he called it anyway. In reality it was just a hole in the wall – a crack, he supposed, caused by the same subsidence that gave the floor of his bedroom a slight tilt – but, despite the lack of mirrors and right-angles, it performed the same function as a true periscope. He had found it by walking towards the orange circle. When he touched it he had found this gap in the concrete wall, just wide enough to fit his thumb, but not quite wide enough for two fingers. Feeling inside with his index finger, he learned that the aperture widened as it went along and that it rose upward at roughly 45 degrees. Curious, he put his eye to the opening and was amazed to see the silhouette of the chestnut tree, lit from behind by a streetlamp.

He felt tired, but he knew time would pass very slowly down here if he simply lay in the blackness and waited to fall asleep, so he decided he ought to do something. It was then that he remembered the rucksack. He unzipped it and began removing objects – tins, packets, bottles – and arranging them on the floor by the bed. When all the food and drink had been dealt with, he was left with the black box and the notebooks. He thought of opening the black box, but it seemed too big a step to take. He did not feel ready. And what good were books in the dark?

He had an idea. He moved the bed close to the wall and held one of the notebooks beneath the periscope: in the middle of the dark page a faint amber shape appeared, illuminating a single word. The word was *Ingrid*.

When James woke up he noticed a pinprick of brightness in the gloom. He crawled to the bottom of his bed and put his eye to the opening. To his surprise, he saw a beautiful and tiny world; no more than an inch in diameter, yet as real-looking as the world he had known before. In this tiny world the light had an innocent, early-morning milkiness that painted in heartstopping detail the top of the iron gate, part of the white van, the middle section of the chestnut tree and, in fragmented glimpses through its hundreds of budding leaves, the brickwork and silvered windows of the house across the road.

The view was so fresh, so vivid, that James considered the possibility of living in the cellar, not only for the next few days but for the rest of his life. After all, he had never felt such an intense love for the world while he'd actually been part of it. But just then he caught a stray scent from outside. A gust of wind must have blown it through the crack in the wall. Enraptured, he put his nostrils to the opening and sniffed greedily at the tunnel of cool air: earth, grass, tarmac, nectar, bacon, tea, petrol fumes . . . He felt a sudden, urgent need to be free.

First, though, he had to open the black box – and wait for the memories to come. The idea made James anxious. He tried to imagine the pain he would feel, and then he tried to stop imagining it. This must be how women feel just before they give birth, he thought, except that what they are bringing into the world is new life, the future, whereas all I can bring is reflections of the past.

He would open the black box later, he decided. In the meantime, it was important to keep busy. James didn't know why he felt this, but he was convinced it was true. He did some exercises on his bed – press-ups, sit-ups, leg-raisers – counting each repetition out loud. The sound of his own voice was reassuring. When he had finished the exercises, he thought about what else he could do. He drank some water from a bottle and ate a tin of olives. He stared through the periscope. The seconds were so slow, down here. He lay on the bed, closed his eyes and listened. The silence was absolute. He could feel it regathering in the darkness around him: an immense and hungry silence, patient as hell.

Finally, James picked up the black notebook and started reading. The words told the story of his life in Amsterdam, living with Ingrid in her apartment. A year ago; a lifetime before. As the words passed before his eyes, each one lit up in a little oval of leaked daylight, his mind filled with pictures of this abandoned past. He saw Ingrid sleeping, her face blank and innocent; he saw her naked body, with its lovely curves and hollows; he saw the street below their balcony, bright and empty at dawn; he saw a tall glass of cold beer, its crisp shadow on a chrome tabletop; he saw the surface of the canal, gleaming multicoloured in the dusk. As he saw all this, his heart contracted. How happy he had been! What a fool he was to walk away from such a life! He read on, nostalgia transforming these ordinary memories into visions of a lost paradise.

In the words, time passed too quickly. It slipped away. He came to a sentence he had written in August, a few days after Ingrid left – *'Is happiness nothing more than the sum of its absent opposites?'* – and realised that, unknowingly, he had asked the right question and arrived at the wrong answer. In a sense, he saw now, it was true: happiness *was* nothing more than the sum of its absent negatives. In order to be happy, James understood, one must have not only life, warmth, food, freedom, comfort, health, company, sleep and sanity, one must also think, every day, of the imminent, everpresent danger of losing these gifts; one must see, feel, breathe the perpetual possibility that one could be dead, cold, hungry, enslaved, in pain, ill, lonely, insomniac or mad. No wonder happiness is so rare, thought James: it is fucking hard work.

At this point James closed the black notebook and put it down on the bed. He couldn't bear to read on; to watch his former self decline, by degrees, to the point where he finally became his present self. He put his eye to the hole in the wall and watched dusk fall in the tiny world of the periscope. The white shell of the parked van turned a deep pink in the gloaming while the windows in the house across the road melted into golden pools, their calm surfaces occasionally rippled by the movement in wind of the branches of the chestnut tree, its new leaves shining in a thousand glorious, irrecoverable shades of gold and green. Slowly (and yet too quickly) the colours faded and the van, the tree and the house existed only as shapes in a blue mist, illuminated and silhouetted by sodium light. It was astoundingly beautiful. Breathtaking, James thought, but then the double meaning of that word made him suddenly, horribly aware of the staleness of the air in the cellar.

He took a few deep breaths, but couldn't seem to get enough oxygen into his lungs. His head was spinning and he felt nauseous. He put his mouth to the hole and tried to suck the night air from outside. It tasted cool and good but the supply was no more than a trickle, and now fear was making him breathe even faster. He looked around him at the threatening, invisible room and saw his own death staring back. Afraid that if he lost consciousness he might never regain it, James tried to stay awake. He pinched his skin and pried apart his drooping eyelids. Each breath, each waking moment, was an act of will; a rebellion against the room's dark embrace. Stay awake, stay alive till morning, James told himself. In the morning you will open the black box . . . and after the memories have returned, you will escape this place . . . you will breathe again the air outside . . . you will see . . .

His thoughts dissolved into pictures. Paradise lost. The soft anaesthetic of nostalgia. His breathing grew calm. Some time in the middle of the night, his tiredness overpowered his fear. James lay back in bed and drifted slowly into sleep.

Down, down, down he slid, into the deepest sleep he had ever known. At first in the dream he seemed to be walking through the same tunnel as before, except that now there were no eyeholes, no lights; only the darkness and the walking. Beneath his feet, the ground sloped upwards. Above his head, the damp earth ceiling grew lower and lower, until soon he had to walk with his back bent, like an old man, and soon after that he had to crawl on all fours, like a baby, and soon – though it seemed to take ages – he had to creep on his belly, like a snake. Narrower and narrower the tunnel grew, and now he could taste the damp earth in his mouth as he moved: he was *eating* his way through it, becoming part of the airless earth himself, disappearing into total blackness.

Just as he felt sure that he was dying – that this was his death dream – James spotted a tiny light ahead of him. He guessed that it must be the tunnel's end, far far away in the distance, and this possibility, however remote, filled his heart with hope. Onward he slithered, onward he crawled, onward he crouched, onward he walked, for days, weeks, months, years, the tunnel growing wider and higher all the time, but the tiny light for some reason remaining tiny. Suddenly he found himself in a dark room, with four invisible walls and an invisible bed. He reached out and touched the source of the light – the light he had imagined, hoped, believed was the end of the tunnel. It was not much wider than his index finger. It was the periscope, and this was the cellar, and James was awake.

He put his eye to the opening and watched as the sun rose over Lough Street, as leaves and windows sparkled, as shadows grew blacker and shorter, disappeared and reappeared on the other side, grew longer and greyer again, as windows and leaves glowed yellow pink red and faded to blue, as the tiny world grew dark and was illuminated by moon and lamp, and as the first peek of sun extinguished them and the earth began another revolution. He watched as the moon shrank from sphere to sliver and grew fat and bright again; as the leaves on the tree uncurled and turned vivid green, dark green, patchy yellow, deep orange, blood red, as they fell one by one and gathered in dry heaps through which children kicked and played with conkers, as the rain came down and turned the leaves to mulch, liquid brown, and the branches of the tree held their pose, naked, and sagged slightly under the brief weight of snow; as the skies above the house broiled grey and low and the snow became hail became sleet became rain and the thin slick-blackened branches, so dead-looking, grew miracle buds which blossomed and were scattered and revealed green tips and it was spring, and he watched as the earth began another orbit of its sun. Years passed; he grew thin and old, and his memories of life before the cellar turned faint, watery, unreal, lighter than air . . . He lay in bed, his eyes open to the darkness and let the images float haphazardly through his mind, all of them weightless and meaningless and beautiful.

It was at this point that I entered the cellar.

James opened his eyes and crawled to the end of the bed. Looking through the periscope, he noticed that there was a black van parked next to his own white van. Suddenly he was impatient to escape the cellar. For some reason James felt sure he was in the wrong place.

Carrying the black box in one hand and the black notebook in the other, he climbed the steps, opened the little door, crawled into the cupboard under the stairs, and from there walked to the kitchen. He put the kettle on and went into the garden, where he stood for a while, feeling the gentle sun on his face, breathing in the scents of nature, listening to the birds. Then the kettle started screaming and he went inside.

He made a pot of coffee and a bacon sandwich and ate breakfast under the apple tree in a state of bliss. Or rather it would have been a state of bliss had James's subconscious not kept interrupting it with unwelcome, unsettling memories of his dream. Feeling that he would not be able to stop thinking about the dream until he had written it down, James put his mug and plate in the sink, opened the black notebook, and wrote the following:

I had a strange dream last night. In the dream I was lying in bed in the cellar, awake, when I heard a noise. I sat up and saw a man sitting calmly at the end of my bed, looking through the periscope.

The odd thing was, even though the cellar was in darkness, I could see him perfectly clearly, as if he were sitting in broad daylight. That's how I know it must have been a dream.

I knew who the man was, although he looked different from all the other times I'd seen him. He wore a pale blue T-shirt and jeans, not his usual black coat, and his left arm was in a plastercast. His hair was slightly longer too. Even so, I felt sure it was him.

I cleared my throat and he turned towards me. He smiled with his lips, but his eyes were curious, penetrating, as though he were looking at me for signs of something. His face seemed familiar and I said so.

'Yes,' he said, 'although in fact you have never seen this face before, and it'll be quite a long time before you see it again.' I was about to ask him how he could possibly know that when he continued: 'I've seen your face, though. I remember it well.'

I recognised the sound of his voice and yet at the same time it was utterly alien to me. Listening to it gave me an unpleasant feeling.

'Who are you?' I demanded.

He turned his attention back to the periscope. 'You wouldn't believe me if I told you.'

'Try me.'

'I am Malcolm Trewvey.'

'A middle-aged scrabble obsessive, you mean?'

'I am Tomas Ryal.'

'A non-existent Czech philosopher.'

'I am Martin Thwaite.'

'A fictional character in a Victorian detective story.'

'I am all these people, but those are not my real names.'

'No? What's your real name, then?'

'James Purdew.'

'That's a coincidence,' I said sarcastically.

'I can prove it to you if you like,' he answered. 'I'll tell you things about your life no one else could possibly know . . .' He went on to list the names of my oldest school friends, the addresses of various houses in which I've lived, my mother's maiden name, my earliest memory, and the details of an embarrassing incident that happened on my eighth birthday.

By the time he finished speaking, I had become angry. 'You've read my notebooks!' I shouted.

'That I can't deny. I was reading them the other day, actually. They're among our more fascinating diaries.'

'Our?'

'My name is James Purdew and I was born on the 8th of July 1973. I am thirty-five years old; next month I will turn thirty-six.'

Now I knew why his voice was both intimate to me and strange: it was my own voice, but not my own; it was the voice I only ever heard on tape-recordings, just as his face was the face I only ever saw in photographs, only older than mine: more lined and tanned.

'Impossible,' I insisted.

'Don't you remember when you were young, wanting to meet a slightly older version of yourself; someone who could hold your hand and guide you through the maze?'

I stared at him. Was he mocking me? 'That was just a child's fantasy,' I said. 'And anyway, it's April, not June.'

'For you, yes. For me, it is eleven o'clock in the morning on a bright, hot day in June and I am sitting in the summer kitchen of the house in . . . ' – he hesitated, as though weighing his words – 'the house where I live now.'

'I'm dreaming,' I said, relieved. 'This is just a dream.'

'Yes, you are dreaming me. And, at the same time, I am dreaming you, although I am awake. I'm writing a book about you, you see.'

'A book about me?' I laughed. 'What's the story?'

'Well, it begins with you breaking your ankle on the stairs to Ingrid's apartment . . . '

'Oh, very funny. How did you break your arm, by the way?'

'I was playing tennis and I slipped. The court was damp.'

'I don't even play tennis,' I objected.

'You'll start later this year.'

'Right. So why do you walk with a limp?'

For the first time, his self-assurance faded and he looked almost

354

bitter, as though his vanity had been wounded. Then, forcing a smile, he said, 'Well, actually, that is your fault.'

'My fault? How do you work that out?'

'When the doctor took your cast off, he told you that you'd need physiotherapy. Remember? But you never went . . .'

'No . . . I forgot.'

' . . . and as you get older, the joint will stiffen. And you will limp, slightly. Most people don't even notice it.' There was a silence. He put his eye to the periscope again. 'What a lovely night,' he murmured.

I couldn't think of anything to say. Or rather I could, but I was afraid the answer to my question would not be what I hoped.

Unnervingly, he seemed to read my mind. 'Don't you want to know what you'll be doing five years from now?'

'I thought you'd just say you couldn't tell me.'

He looked at me with a kind of awkward tenderness. 'I can't tell you any details,' he said, 'but don't worry, you've already reached the lowest point.' He put his hand out to touch my shoulder; instinctively I recoiled. He smiled sadly. 'My advice is to forget about the future: just try to live each moment as it happens.'

Another silence. Presumably he thought I was digesting this hackneyed slice of wisdom, but in truth I was beginning to realise something: there was a hole in the logic of his story. 'So do you remember this happening to you when you were thirty?' I asked.

A look of surprise flashed briefly across his face before the trade-mark knowing smile reappeared. 'Who ever remembers their dreams?'

'True, but you said you'd read my notebooks recently. Wasn't this mentioned in there?'

'No,' he replied. 'It wasn't.'

Our eyes met. I looked away. I couldn't bear his gaze; it was like being outstared by a mirror.

Oh, and there was another thing. He told me I was in the wrong place, that I had to go up to the attic. But I'd already figured that out for myself.

James closed the black notebook and picked up the black box. Then he walked upstairs towards his fate.

I opened the notebook and read what he had written. It was funny how different his memory of the conversation was from mine. Several times he misquoted me, and it was notable that whenever he came out on the losing side of an argument he simply omitted all mention of it. And yet, despite his flaws and those flashes of hostility, I felt sorry for my younger self. He had been through so much, and there was more yet to come.

By the way, I lied about the description of the dream not being in the notebook: it was and is. But human beings have to believe that the future is unwritten, otherwise they do not feel free. I myself had a dream recently in which I talked to a grey-haired, suicidal version of myself. But it was only a dream.

Carrying the black box, James climbed the first flight of stairs. The second storey was as perfectly white as the first. He stood on the landing, admiring all that he had achieved. And then, with mounting dread, he turned and looked at the dark arrow pointing up the next flight. Above him, all was grey, stained, filthy; wallpaper peeled and stairs creaked; a cold draught blew from who knew where. Slowly he ascended.

At the top landing he reached inside his pocket and touched the key that Dr Lanark had given him. Then he opened the door to the attic room. This, he knew, was where Ian Dayton had killed himself. He had thrown himself from the window of this room to the garden below. The only question now was why.

There was nobody in the room. James walked a few steps further in and listened, but all he could hear was the sound of his own breathing. He surveyed the room's furniture: a bed, a table, a wardrobe, a bookshelf. Lots of dust, of course, but nothing remarkable or untoward. He walked towards the window, which was open. From there he stared down at the familiar vertiginous view of the sloping roof, the apple tree, the shining grass, and the small stone grave marked with two letters that were, from this height, unreadable.

James sat down on the floor below the window, with the black box between his legs. It was time: already he could feel the wave moving towards him, the memories returning. He took the key from his pocket and inserted it into the lock. A turn, a click. He opened the lid. Inside he found three diaries, all bound in black vinyl, the years embossed in gold lettering on the front. He picked them up, one by one, and then he put them aside. The truth, he sensed, was not in these diaries, but elsewhere. And there, at the bottom of the black box, he found what he was looking for. He picked up the first sheet of paper and began to read . . .

CHAPTER 6

Months have passed during the writing of these Confessions, and I am in darkness now . . . it is bleak December, in the year of our Lord 1893, and the memories of that sad affair are ever-more distant to me. Already the details are fading, and yet, as they are all I have, as I am their only hope for posterity, and as nothing remains for me but to confess before I die, I will attempt once more to return to those days. Yes, ladies and gentlemen, I will perform a conjuring trick. I will attempt what the theologians and scientists tell us is impossible! I will, without the aid of any gleaming machine, with nothing but this dense mass of tissues, veins, fibres and electricity that is my brain, project myself *back in time* – and, once there, I will try, as best I can, to finish this story before I myself am finished.

First, however, I must beg your flagging patience, dear reader, for one moment more before the tale is resumed. It is time for me to reveal my true identity. My name is not Martin Thwaite. Or rather, though that is the name I go by now, it is not the name I had when the events of this story took place. Ivan and Angelina, Sarah and Dr Lanark, they all knew me by a different name. In their eyes, and in the eyes of the law, I am John Price – and it is no longer worth the trouble of concealing this fact. What I am writing, after all, is not a penny-dreadful fiction, but a true and frank confession of real events. You must believe that, reader, even if, in certain places, the cataclysm that I am about to describe must, by its very nature, strain your credulity.

~~~

I landed in Portsmouth on the morning of the third of May and made my way directly to London. By the time I'd deposited my bags in the room I had rented, it was evening, and I was hungry. I walked to The Green Man and ordered broth and ale. After dinner I traversed the familiar streets of Mayfair, the evening sky turning from white to pale pink to star-sequinned turquoise while the façades of the houses on either side grew steadily haughtier and grander. I approached the door of 21 Luff Street and even went so far as to place my hand on the lion-headed knocker; but as I did so a memory flashed into my mind – of Angelina's face, the day she told me she was a married woman – and my heart began clanging like a tocsin. At the same time, Gerard Ogilvy's vague, insidious accusations whispered again inside my ears, and I took a step backwards. The mansion reared up above me, alien and impassive. Somewhere inside those brick walls was she: kisser of my lips; stroker of my skin; breaker of my heart. A kind of nauseous apprehension gripped me and, without any further thought or calculation, I retreated across the road to that silent doorway in which I had spent so many nights. The action was both automatic and reassuring. It was with a new calmness – the natural detachment that accompanies routine – that I settled in place and began my watch. Only once I was there did I begin to rationalise my actions to myself: just a precaution, my mind murmured; nothing more sinister than that; all being well, the two of you will be in each other's arms before the night is over. O, slaughtered hopes! O, rightful fears!

She emerged, alone, at nine o'clock, and my heart leapt at the sight of her. I could not believe that she was, after all that time out of my sight, apart from my life, beyond my knowledge, still breathing, existing, and still so astonishingly, woundingly lovely. How I wanted to call out to her then, to wave and cross the road, to see her face light up with surprise and love . . . but I did not. Something in me – some part of me, hidden until that moment; a darker, colder, more suspicious me – stilled my arm and silenced my voice. And instead of greeting Angelina, I began to follow her, twenty yards behind, a furtive figure in the shadows; a detective.

I immediately observed that her route had changed – we were not heading south, but rather northeast – and so had her bearing. Whereas before Angelina had walked with the bizarre, unerring calm of a sleepwalker, now she looked more . . . excited? nervous? awake? happy? More *herself* is what I thought: as though her personality, on those previous nocturnal walks submerged under layers of hypnotised somnolence, was now alive and present at the very surface. This observation perturbed me, so I forced myself to stop thinking altogether and simply to follow her.

In the distance she turned right and I hurried to catch up with her. As I turned where she had, I found myself in a courtyard. I have been here before, I said to myself, though as yet I couldn't remember when or in what circumstances. Even so, the familiarity was powerful, distracting. By now the gibbous moon was shining down and everything looked unreal, like a stage set. I hardly noticed as Angelina stopped outside a door, unlocked it with a key, and entered, closing the door behind her. Numb with apprehension, I walked in her footsteps. It was the same building; it was the same door . . . could this really be a coincidence? My heart was pounding now as I stood outside the entrance to the house in which I had once lived for several weeks. The window on the third floor was lighted, the curtain drawn.

As I stood in the silent courtyard that night, watching their silhouettes move behind the glowing curtain and then join with darkness as the lamp was extinguished, I felt myself divide in two. On the surface, the young boy trembled, his eyes tearing. How could they do this to him? Surely it could not be true. There must be some other explanation. But beneath him, in the depths, a new me was stirring: a cold Mr Hyde, growing like a malignant tumour from the heart of warm, innocent, foolish Dr Jekyll.

Hyde had expected such a turn of events all along, and now it had happened, he felt vindicated. Vengeance would be his, he swore. Angelina Vierge and Ivan Dawes would pay for their betrayal.

～～～

For the next hundred hours, I wandered London, shadowing Angelina. I remember very little about those days and nights, except that they were sleepless and that, by their end, I saw everything through a fog of exhaustion. All my memories and emotions from that time are compressed into two images.

The first image is of the view through the living-room window of 21 Luff Street. I had followed the two of them to her house early one morning, after they had spent the night at his apartment. They went through the front door and I walked around into the back garden. That wide lawn, with its single apple tree, instantly cast a spell of maudlin nostalgia over me, but it was as nothing to the vision that greeted me as I stood at the window of the living room and, hands cupped at either side of my eyes, breath steaming the glass before me, stared into that sore-familiar space, at the Chesterfield settee and the lionskin rug and the grandfather clock and the low Indian table and the dear little fireplace and, close by it, the battered old armchair where I used to sit, where I sat so many times, so many happy mornings just like this one, as Angelina, then mine, made tea in the servantless kitchen, humming some popular tune low under her breath and I could hear the too-slow ticking of the clock's pendulum and see the low gold sunlight coming through the window, filtered by the branches of the apple tree, illuminating cobwebs and dust in the air, and I sighed and lay back, eyes closed in absolute happiness, remembering the bliss of the night just gone and seeing the future unroll in endless simulations of this perfect moment, just as he, Ivan, was doing now.

The second image I am not sure is even a memory at all. Perhaps it is, I don't know. It feels too symbolic to be true, and yet it has the vividness of something genuinely seen. If so, it must have occurred at a similar time on a different night. This is what I remember: It is five or six o'clock in the morning, the dark hour before dawn, and Ivan and Angelina have just left his apartment. He is walking her home. Using the wire from a pipe-cleaner, I have unlocked his front door and entered his room, which is familiar to me from my time here as an invalid. The air is warm and smells of her. The sheets on the bed are ravelled. Before I start to search the room for incriminating papers, I walk to the window and look down, to check on the lovers' progress. And there they are, like a distorted reflection of another memory. The scene is blue, as it was before, and they pass beneath a lamppost, hand in hand, their silhouettes melting into darkness as they exit the penumbra of gaslight. And then, entering the next pool of light . . . she leans her head on his shoulder and he puts his arm around her back. I stand, staring, in disbelief. (Jekyll's heart breaks in two. Hyde sniggers.) Does she remember, as this happens? Does she think of me, and that moment when we said good evening to the young constable? But no, of course not, for she missed the second part of that memory. She was probably falling asleep, exploring her own private dark-nesses, or awake and fretting the edges of her guilt, while I walked back the way I had come and the senior police officer moved for-ward threateningly and the constable placed a hand on his elbow and said, 'It's all right, sergeant, I know this gentleman. He's just walked his fiancée home.' Of course the memory would mean nothing to Angelina; it probably no longer even existed inside her mind. It was mine alone, and would die with me. (And oh, the bit-ter sorrow that simple insight provoked in me! Even now, I strug-gle to comprehend and accept its self-evident truth.)

It was early the next morning that I confronted Ivan. I knocked on his door, certain he would still be abed. I myself was in desper-ate need of sleep, but I knew it would not come to me until I had seen his face, until I had asked him all those questions, the answers to which I feared I already knew. I banged and banged at his door. Finally he roused himself and opened it. Oh, the joy in his eyes when first he saw me! It was not faked, I am sure of that. His heart was filled, above all, with love for me and happiness at my return. It was only when he noticed that my own face remained closed and clouded that his expression changed; only then that I was able to read in it the emotions I sought: guilt, shame, fear.

'John! I am so glad to see you. Come in . . . did you just return from Australia? I heard from one of your former colleagues that you had gone. You look well, if somewhat tired. What is it? Are you ill? John, why do you regard me so?'

My voice came as if from icy depths. 'I have seen you . . . the two of you.'

'John, I . . .' The blood had drained from his face by now. 'Please come in, I . . .'

'You do not deny it, then?'

'How can I? But John, it's not how you imagine.'

'When did it start?'

'Before you even knew her, that's what I mean. Listen, sit down, I will tell you the whole story.' I remained standing, my face impassive, as he recounted the history of his liaisons with Angelina Vierge. As dearly as I wished to disbelieve him, his story chimed in with that of Gerard Ogilvy to such a degree that either they must have been in cahoots or, more likely, the story was true.

This is, as far as I recall, what Ivan said to me: 'I didn't lie to you, before, when I told you that I had loved her, but there was more to it than I mentioned at the time. When I first met Angelina, I was eighteen and she was nineteen. It was at a party, among rich friends. Back then, she was engaged to a Frenchman called Laurent de Silva. He was living in his own country at the time, and they saw one another only occasionally. I was quite an, um, experienced eighteen-year-old and I could see in her eyes that she was not quite the young innocent she appeared to be. There was a sensual hunger in those eyes that belied her name, her bearing, the conventionality of her words. At some point that evening she stared at me unwaveringly for several seconds, her face expressionless, then, without a word, turned on her heel and walked upstairs. I think I was the only one who noticed her go. The people around me were drunk and laughing. I watched her, from the corner of my eye, climb to the first-floor landing and open a door. As she entered, she turned back to look at me – only for a second – and then closed the door behind her. Nothing had been said, not even hinted, and yet I knew without a shadow of a doubt that she wished me to follow her. After making some excuse, I went upstairs and joined her in that room. You can guess the rest, I'm sure. Oh John, I'm so sorry. I tried to warn you, all those years ago, do you remember? I told you she was bad for you; that it would be best for you if you forgot her. I'm sorry, I tried, perhaps not hard enough . . .'

His eyes were filled with tears now and he looked suddenly older, more frail than I had ever seen him. I felt no pity.

'Are you going to marry her?'

'Marry her?' He almost laughed then. 'No . . . no, I am not going to marry her. You see, for a long time, between us, it was . . . only sex. I fell in love with her, but never dared reveal it to her. What she liked in me was my . . . depravity. Any hint of sentiment and I would have been discarded, I felt sure. Her fiancé, De Silva, he was a good, kind, considerate fellow – as was Ogilvy, later – but Angelina didn't want goodness, kindness or consideration; indeed, at certain times she despised those qualities and longed precisely for their reverse. What she desired in me was badness. It is somewhat different now, that's true. She thinks she loves me, but I know what she is . . . I mean to say that Angelina's feelings are somewhat like the wind. They . . .'

'Destroy everything in their path?'

' . . . change all the time. Oh John, I am truly sorry. Are you leaving now? Please don't go. Stay, and let us talk. Our friendship is more important to me than any . . .'

I could listen no more to his lies. I turned around and walked away from him, back to this bare, lonely room, where I did not even undress before collapsing on to the bed and plunging into a black and oceanic sleep.

❧

When I woke that evening, the momentary amnesia came as a blessing. As soon as I remembered, I felt myself falling into the void. The conversation with Ivan Dawes: I had not dreamed it; it was true. He and Angelina had been sleeping together . . . for years. Perhaps even during the months of bliss? But no, I could not despoil the only Paradise I had ever known. I could not believe our love had been sullied by that . . . I cannot believe it, even now. The point was, however, that I had lost her. And lost him, too. And, in some deeper sense, lost myself. I was in Hell.

Naturally I sought oblivion. I went out drinking in Soho. Those pubs . . . their names are erased; they exist only as a blur of faces and bodies. I drank so much beer that I could barely even walk. And yet, oblivion remained out of reach. I *remembered*, in spite of my inebriation. Reeling from the last pub, I threw up in a sidestreet – I recall a woman's voice scolding me for the mess in her doorway – and, some time later, found myself walking towards the Thames.

The water looked blacker than the night sky, and gave off its usual stench. It is not so much a river as a gigantic chamber pot: all the shit of London flows through it. Corpses too. How many floating suicides and murder victims are dredged, bloated and blue, from its poisoned current? And how many more are never found? Suddenly I was aware of myelf as an insect, a tiny speck, lost in the vast labyrinth of this Babylon, this city of horror; I looked up at the sky, the stars hidden by the ugly pall of smog that we – mankind – have smeared above us, and shivered. Even if God existed, he would not see through that foul cloud. He would long ago have abandoned us to the fates we deserve. It was then that I saw the brute truth: I was alone; no one cared for me; my existence was of no consequence at all. Self-pity rose within me like the tidewater, its surface decorated with scum. What was the point of continuing to exist? I asked myself. I was drunk, it is true, and yet I was sober enough to think clearly, to see clearly. I do not believe I have ever seen the world so clearly as I did that night.

After some time musing thus, I made the decision to kill myself. That was the core of the idea, I swear: to end my own agony; to exit the labyrinth at last. And yet, even then, in my deepest despair, I could not forget (and certainly not forgive) the two people whose actions had, as I saw it, driven me to this state. Ivan and Angelina. I searched in my pockets and found my old detective's notebook and a pencil. Ripping a page from its binding, I wrote the note quickly and unthinkingly, almost as if it were being dictated to me. When it was finished, I undressed, leaving the note folded neatly in one of my shoes, and dived into the black water.

My God, it was cold! Instantly the current took me. I am not a particularly strong swimmer, and I knew it would not have been long before the river's monstrous mouth swallowed me under as it had swallowed so many other poor souls. All I had to do was remain in its centre, out of reach of either bank, and the success of my suicide would be guaranteed. But, oh, I was a coward! At the crucial moment, when I felt the inevitable pull towards nothingness, some animal instinct rose up in me and cried out 'No!' Like a frantic child, I swam as hard as I could towards the northern shore.

When I reached land, naked and shivering, I felt no relief; only the same blank despair I had felt before. And yet I knew now that I could not do it. I was not man enough to choose oblivion, no matter how fervently I wished for it. It was in those dark moments, climbing the embankment and wondering where I was and how I could get home without being seen, that I remembered my clothes. They were miles away now, I calculated. It would be quicker and easier to go straight home. And I was exhausted and . . . and yes, a part of me (you know which part) saw in this chance circumstance the possibility of revenge. As far as the world knew, I was now dead. When they found my clothes and that note the next morning, what other conclusion would they draw? The police would have no choice but to interview Ivan and Angelina; thus the lovers would discover my death, and their part in it. What torments would they suffer then? What remorse, regret, what agony! And, sweetest of all, I would no longer be John Price. That worm, that sad fool, he was dead now, and I could assume whatever identity I wished: I could be a new man.

Thus it was, on that freezing, frightened return to my room, that I was born for the second time. The name I took by chance: I was passing a row of terraced houses somewhere in Farringdon when I noticed a letter protruding from a letterbox. I pulled it out and glanced at the addressee: Martin Thwaite.

For a couple of days I was ill and could not leave my bed. By the time I was well enough to haunt my enemies, they already knew the 'truth'. I could see it in the sadness of their bearing, the absence of laughter, the solemn expressions. With what satisfaction I watched them mourn me; each flicker of regret in their eyes was like an explosion of happiness in my heart. I was disguised, of course, as I haunted them. Sometimes I was able to stand so close – as they ate dinner in a restaurant, or walked in a park – that I could hear the words they spoke. True, I never actually heard them mention my name, but I felt sure I could detect the undertow of guilt, of sadness, in those brief, enigmatic conversations.

Soon, however, monstrously soon, they returned to normal. They began to laugh again, to smile, to hold hands and kiss. Barely a fortnight had passed since my tragic demise, and already they were over me. They had put it behind them. They had forgotten. I could not believe their callousness. Was that all my life had been worth to them? My first love and my closest friend. I had killed myself because of them, and yet twelve days later they could go to a tavern, tell jokes, enjoy their meal, make love, sleep? Outraged, I began to plot my revenge.

Thus it was that on the evening of the first of June 1893 I removed my disguise, dressed in my own clothes, powdered my face and hair so that they gave off a kind of dusty white glow, and walked to Ivan's apartment. Silently I entered. I walked past Angelina, lounging on the sofa; she did not even look up as I moved behind her. In the kitchen Ivan was pouring whisky into two glasses and muttering to himself. I stood still and watched him. He was only three feet away from me. I did not make a sound. By chance he turned towards the window and there, reflected in the glass, he saw the ghost of his friend John Price. Oh the scream that parted his lips! The sweet music of breaking glass! As Angelina ran towards him, begging to know what was the matter, I slipped away, unseen. My work there was done for the night, I thought. The next evening I would surprise him in the park, or as a distant face at the theatre ... I could haunt him for years like this. I could be his Banquo.

I slept well that night. The next day, curious to see what impression my prank had made on the conscience of my former friend, I walked to his apartment. As there was nobody there, I then took the familiar route to Luff Street. It was early afternoon and the day was hot and cloudless; I could feel sweat streaking the powder on my face. From the pavement outside number 21 I heard the pop of a champagne cork. I crept around the side of the house, through the unlocked gate, and into the sun-dazzled garden. And there they were: Angelina and her silver-spoon cronies, sitting on the grass around a blanket, eating and drinking and laughing. They were having a *picnic*, those monsters! This threw me into such a rage that I almost revealed myself there and then, but something made me hesitate, and in that moment I had time to remark the fact that Ivan was not part of the company. Angelina, I noticed, kept looking up, somewhat distractedly, at the attic window. I looked up myself and saw that it was open. Thus I guessed where Ivan must be. I myself had slept several times in that attic room: it was a guest room, rarely used, and Angelina used to sneak me up there occasionally when there were servants around. What he was doing up there now, in the middle of the day, I had no idea, but it seemed a good opportunity for a haunting, so I entered the house through an open ground-floor window and began to climb the back stairs.

I have such a strangely vivid memory of climbing that staircase; in my mind it is intimately connected to the staircase in that house of ill repute, the first night I ever saw Angelina unclothed: the sights, the sounds, the sudden dizziness, the way I had to stop for a moment and blink, confused to when and where this was occurring. What I was experiencing as I climbed up to the attic was undoubtedly a flash of déjà vu – a sudden, unwilled reminder of the moment this whole dark adventure had begun – though I find it difficult not to believe, in retrospect, that it wasn't also a kind of premonition. My chest was filled with fear as I ascended. You, o reader, more rational perhaps than I, may counter that such visions, such glimpses into the future, are no more than misremembered emotions, and in the cold light of logic I cannot argue with you. But how, then, do we explain the corresponding sense of déjà vu I experienced that first time, on my way to the naked Angelina? How explain the sense of doom in my young chest then, if not by speculating that, somehow, the labyrinth of time had, by some wild chance, closed in on itself and I had seen through to another moment of my life – *this* moment – that I had sensed the end as I embarked at the beginning?

At any rate, after a dizzy spell when I had to stop and breathe deeply before remembering where I was and what I was doing, I climbed the remainder of the staircase. At the door I stood still and listened. Silence. He must be asleep, I told myself. I tried the door and, finding it open, I entered.

Ivan was sitting at the desk by the window, his face side on to me, writing something in a black notebook. His expression, in contrast to the picnickers outside, was sombre and concentrated. The air in the attic room was hot, motionless, heavy, and Ivan wore only his underwear as he sat there, writing what, though neither of us knew it at the time, was his suicide note. I did not say a word or make a sound. I only stood still, in the shadowed doorway, and watched. A minute or so later, he sighed, and leaned back in his chair, fountain pen still held between his fingers, and it must have been then, from the corner of his eye, that he saw me. He did not turn to look at me, only groaned and held his face in his hands. It was enough, I decided. The last thing I wanted was for him to realise that this ghost was nothing of the kind, but a corporeal being. Swiftly, silently, I departed the room and tiptoed down the stairs. To my satisfaction, as I descended, I heard Ivan weeping and repeating my name.

I reached the ground floor and escaped through the open window without being seen, and it was only as I stood outside the house's stern façade, wiping the damp powder from my face with a handkerchief, that I heard that indescribable sound. Indescribable, I suppose, because it was not so much the sound I noticed – was there a sound, or is that merely my ghoulish imagination filling in the blanks in memory? – as the silence that followed. It was during that long and awful silence, before the inevitable screams and moans, that I began to flee, knowing in my heart the truth whose verification, in black and white, I was to discover the next day, when I saw the announcement in a newspaper.

The truth: that Ivan Dawes had called my bluff. That, in the game of human whist we had been playing, he had trumped me. That, while I had only pretended to kill myself, he had truly done so.

∽∾

The days that followed have left no trace. In the main, I suppose, I slept and drank: in my room, the curtains drawn, the lights extinguished. Anything to blank out what had happened. And yet, it always came back to me. The word 'guilt' is so small, so meaningless; it cannot possibly sum up what I felt, which was enormous, devouring. Oh, it is pointless even to try and express all this! I know what I went through; I know also how richly I deserved it. No punishment could ever be enough.

But the world is not like that. People are not like that. Our memories, by virtue of their porousness, save us from the Hell of existence. Just as Ivan and Angelina were laughing and fucking within two weeks of my 'death', so I was able, if not to smile, at least to hope, to desire, to see through the vast dark cloud of mourning and self-hatred to the possibility, however remote, of redemption. In short, I began to daydream of Angelina. I remembered her: how it had been between us. The way she had made me feel about myself; the way she had drawn out that surprisingly large, colourful soul from my shy adolescent shell, and made me live. The almost telepathic closeness we had shared. The laughter, the tickling, the whispered gossip. It had not always been intense and serious, I recalled. My romanticism and my nostalgia had elevated the idea of her to some divine, impersonal status – frozen her image and stuck it atop a plinth – but the truth was that she was a real human being, with flaws, needs, desires of her own; the truth was that we had been friends. The two of us were suffering now, for, if not exactly the same reason, then something very similar. Perhaps, perhaps, we could be of comfort to one another. Perhaps together, we would suffer less than we did alone. Perhaps – and here, I confess, my starving imagination got the better of my common sense – we could fall in love with each other again, put everything back in its right place; could defy the laws of physics and metaphysics and

371

actually turn back time. Of course we could not summon Ivan from the grave, but in some deep recess of my heart I was glad about that. Ivan, I told myself, had been the serpent. Now he was slain, there was no reason why the two of us could not recreate Eden.

In my defence, I was very weak at this point. Physically, I was close to collapse. I had some money left, but no will to go out and spend it on food; no appetite to swallow anything but water. And, like a man crawling across the desert floor, I began to see mirages ahead in the distance. The possibility of resurrecting my love affair with Angelina was the largest and most vivid of these. It was ludicrous – contemptible, even – but it also, I think, rescued me from the grave. Without the hope and desire that the memory of her inspired in me, I would probably have let myself starve to death that summer.

Instead, I began to eat, exercise, sleep, gain strength. A week or so after the idea first entered my head, I was well enough to walk to her house. That evening, I merely stood and watched. I'm not sure why; a combination of habit and cowardice, I suppose. I remember seeing a surprising amount of activity in the house – servants coming and going, carrying pieces of furniture, framed pictures and so on – but in my serenely hopeful state, I did not realise what this frenzy portended. It was only the next afternoon, when I screwed up my courage and actually knocked on her door, that I learned the truth. It was the maid, Jeanette, who told me. She recognised me, and her eyes flashed shock, horror, pity. 'Reports of my death . . .' I began, but she did not smile. Eventually, when she had calmed down and accepted (if not comprehended) the fact of my continued existence, I got it out of her that her mistress was leaving the country that very day. She could not tell me where Miss Vierge was going – 'I don't know myself, sir, it's all very hush-hush' – but she did let slip that Angelina had already left the house. Clearly distressed and confused, she said, 'Please sir, you didn't get this from me, but . . . if you rush, you might catch her before she leaves. I heard the cook say that she's taking the three o'clock train from Victoria.' I looked at my watch – it was quarter past two –

then quickly nodded my thanks to Jeanette, and ran as fast as I could.

By some miracle, I saw her, stepping down from a hansom into the crowd, and caught up with her at the entrance of the station. Perhaps she was merely numb, so deep in grief that nothing else could touch her, but it occurred to me afterwards that Angelina looked less shocked by my resurrection than her maid had done. Her face was pale, it was true, but her eyes barely flickered at the sight of me; almost as if she had been expecting such a sudden reappearance; almost as if she had never believed that I was dead. It was ten to three by now, and I knew she was in a rush to reach the platform, but she didn't complain when I held her still by both shoulders and begged her to listen to me. Her servants came over and looked at me threateningly, but Angelina just told them to put the bags on the train and await her at the platform. When they had gone, she looked at me. Around us, people pushed and shouted, but it was as though we were inside a bubble. My memory of that moment is oddly similar to my memory of the time we sat and talked at the café in Regent's Park – the way time pulsed slowly; the way we seemed cut off from the rest of the universe – except that, in mood, they are polar opposites: our first conversation and our last conversation; the beginning and the end. As her grey eyes swallowed me up, I realised that I no longer knew what to say. The words in my head evaporated, and I just stood there, biting my lip.

'You look nervous,' Angelina said. There was compassion in her voice and eyes. I don't remember how I replied. Indeed, I remember almost nothing of that conversation, except that the sound of her voice and the look on her face opened me up, and that words came flooding out of me. I think I tried to explain to her how much I loved her, how much I missed her, how no one else in the world had ever made me feel the way she did. I said I wanted us to be together again, but first there was something I had to confess. And then I told her what I'd done. The hauntings. I confessed that I was his killer.

Do I remember a tear in her eye, or do I only imagine it there now? She was silent for a few moments and then she told me, in a calm, deliberate voice, how much I had meant to her. Only fragments of

373

those words have stayed in my memory. I don't know why. Perhaps the emotion I felt blurred them all? Perhaps I wasn't really listening, but going over in my head all the other things I wanted to say to her? In any case, I can recall no more than a few phrases: 'You were like a drug to me: the more I saw you, the more I wanted to see you . . . I have never told anyone else the things I have told you, and I doubt that I ever will . . . Nothing will ever harm my memory of our time together; that will remain sacred . . .'

I heard all this and a wind of exhilaration and ecstasy blew through me, and yet, deep down, I knew that something else was coming. Something bad. Those final words reverberate within me even now.

'But, John, what you've done . . .'

She didn't need to say any more. The earth opened up and swallowed me. The flames of shame incinerated me.

I nodded, trying to dam my tears. She turned and walked towards her platform. For several seconds, I just watched her, my heart breaking. I would never see her again. Finally, just before she went through the ticket gate, I ran after her and called her name. She turned and I saw that she was crying, the tears rolling, unstopped, down her cheeks. I said her name again. She took a few steps, until she was standing close to me, then leaned up and whispered something in my ear. At the same wretched moment, a steam whistle shrieked, and one of her words was lost in the blur of noise. How many times have I relived that moment, trying to hear what she said, but always part of the line is missing.

'I really . . . . . . love you.'

In more optimistic moments, I hear the word 'do' above the train's scream. At times of depression, of course, what I hear is 'don't'. Now, after all these months, having thought about it over and over, I am almost convinced that what she said was worse than either of these. Worse, because it opens up the one wound that can never heal: regret. What Angelina said, I believe, is:

'I really *did* love you.'

I dreamt of her last night. It was a beautiful dream. Normally my dreams of her are horrible – she disappears into a crowd as I run, desperately, failingly, after her; or she hates me, or is coldly indifferent to me; or she is kissing someone else, or worse – but last night's was different. It seemed more real. It was as though Angelina herself had made a guest appearance in my mind; returned for one night only to end the torments, calm the waters, remind me of the unblemished memories she herself has of us. In the dream we were in a cable car, travelling up some snow-covered mountains. There were other people around us in the cable car, but we took no notice of them. We were inside our bubble: the two of us sitting close together on a little leather bench; her leg brushing mine; her head leaning lightly on my shoulder; and she was talking away cheerfully, confidentially, like she used to do, while through the windows of the cable car we watched the white mountains rise into the clouds. It was into the clouds we were going, or so it seemed to me. Higher and higher, until the mountains were far behind, the earth too, and all the other people. Until it was just the two of us, and whiteness.

I do not believe in Heaven, but it did occur to me, when I woke this morning, that my dream was a vision of Paradise; a kind of afterlife of the soul; an eternal dreaming, where hopes and fears melt away and all is relief. My reason tells me such sweetness can last no longer than it takes the brain's electrical impulses to stop functioning, but even if I only dream of her for a minute or two, after dying, is that not better than remaining pointlessly alive in this dry, hard, Angelinaless world, with only my heartache for company? Before this dream, I had been resolved to die, but afraid. Now, I no longer feel afraid. I am ready. There is only one episode left to record.

❧

After I had watched Angelina run to the platform and disappear into the train; after I had watched the train pull away from the station and felt my poor heart crushed beneath its wheels; after that, I went out into the streets of London and wandered in a daze. I drank a few pints, but not much: just enough to soften the pain. I may have fallen asleep in a doorway; I can't remember. What I do recall clearly is buying a loaf of bread just before dawn and over-hearing two women in the bakery talking about the 'terrible train crash' the previous evening. I knew instantly it was her; that she was dead. After that, I remember walking through Regent's Park with the loaf, still warm, tucked beneath my arm. I was hungry, and had intended eating it myself, but when I came to the café where Angelina and I had first talked, and noticed the ducks on the pond, I decided to feed them instead. A sacrificial offering, somehow.

As I stood at the edge of that dark, calm water and began tearing pieces from the loaf and throwing them – watching the white arc through blue into black – I realised that it was over. I was the only person on earth with any memory of the tragedy; with any memory of the joy that preceded it. It was, I saw, my responsibility to tell the story as best I could. To confess, before I killed myself. After all, I was already a dead man in the eyes of the world; it would only be a small step to finish the job. I thought all this while feeding the ducks and, as the sun rose through the trees by the edge of the pond, I felt a kind of strange relief, a lightening. Having made the decision to confess, having sentenced myself to death, the weight of the guilt was lifted from me. I was free.

That was the end of June: six months ago, almost to the day. Six months. Twice as long as my stay in Paradise.

Heaven and Hell. They are, I have discovered, real places. And they have nothing to do with death.

No, death is what comes after. Death is what comes next. I open the window and look down to the garden below. It is time. Good-bye indifferent world.

POSTSCRIPT

As this ink in my hand attests, I am still alive. Several hours have passed, and I have stood at the open window, staring down, willing myself to jump, but . . . I couldn't. Fear again? Mere cowardice? I must plead guilty. And yet, it was more than that, I believe: something finer, or at least less despicable. It is a beautiful morning, and as I stood there with the garden swimming vertiginously below me, I felt the sunlight on my skin, I saw a cat curled up on the grass next door, I heard the birds singing from the treetops, and some animal pleasure rose up inside me. If it was fear, then it was the fear not of pain or hellfire, but simply of no longer existing. The choice between sun and no sun; between air and no air; grass and no grass. Being or nothingness. What kind of choice is that?

Now, if only I could wipe away the last three years, like chalk marks from a blackboard, I think I might almost be happy. If only I could *forget*. But only time can make the memories fade, and even then not entirely. In a hundred years, perhaps, science will have developed some fantastic means of erasing or suppressing the unwanted past, but for now, in this dark century soon ending and in the century to follow, I have no choice but to live on in a world befouled by stains. Oh well. The window to the next world is always open. I must remember that. Somewhere she is waiting for me, in the eternal dreaming of the soul. Until then, I must steel myself, become cold and invulnerable and unthinking like all the others, and re-enter the labyrinth.

James finished reading, then looked out of the window. He wiped the tears from his eyes. That was it, he thought. That was what had happened. For the first time, he understood that *Confessions of a Killer* was simply *Memoirs of an Amnesiac* under a different title, in a different genre. It was the unwritten chapter – Chapter 3 – the blank at the heart of his life story. Only it wasn't blank; it was in code. He also knew that he had written it himself, even though he could not remember having done so.

Obviously these were not the *facts*, but they were something more important than facts. They were the truth. He could read the diaries, of course, and discover all the facts, but he had a feeling he would only be disappointed. Besides, there was no need to read them because the wave was coming. Any moment now, his memories would return. Oddly, the prospect no longer filled James with dread. Even guilt and regret are better than nothingness, he thought. Even being a killer is better than being nobody.

And at the very moment that he thought this, the wave broke.

During those few seconds of revelation, James remembered *everything*. It was as though a million butterflies swarmed out of the black box. They flew around his face, briefly filled the room, and then poured through the open window and away, never to return. This took only seconds, though to James it seemed like years had passed. Afterwards, he was left with only the vaguest impression of what he had seen. And yet, during the moments when the butterflies were before his eyes, he saw every single one; not as a blur of colour, but in impossibly perfect detail.

He stood up and looked out of the window. Below him the garden was shining in the sunlight. A single butterfly flew in crazy circles near the apple tree, then disappeared. James took a deep breath: the air smelled of earth, grass, tarmac, nectar, bacon, tea, petrol fumes. He noted with relief that the buzzing sound in his head had now stopped. A moment passed. I stood behind him, watching, curious. I could feel the thoughts moving through his mind. He felt sorry for Ian, and for Anna, and for James. She was alive, of course, he knew that now, just as he knew he would never see her again. As for Ian . . . well, who knows why people kill themselves? No suicide note can ever tell the whole story.

And the third person? For the first time in his life, James Purdew saw the young James Purdew not as some ur-version of himself, but as a stranger. Another being. Poor him, James thought. If only I could go back in time and whisper words of comfort and wisdom in his ear. If only I could hold his hand and guide him through the labyrinth. But time travel only happens in books, James knew. In real life, you are always marooned in the present, always alone. Then he turned around and looked me in the eyes. And slowly, almost unbelievingly, he smiled. And began to laugh.

In that moment, I ceased to exist. I had thought I was dreaming him, but when he started laughing, I understood that he was dreaming me.

For the briefest of instants, my mind is a blank. I know the details of the present moment: I am climbing a bright, wide staircase; the air is warm, close, sour-smelling; my right temple aches. But none of these facts gives me any clue to where or when this is happening, or even to my own identity.

I stand still, breathing heavily, and a hundred vague staircases swim together in my memory. Have I been here before? It looks familiar, but then a staircase is a staircase. That smell reminds me of something, though. What is it? Drying blood. Warm sweat. Human faeces. I listen closely and hear the faint hum of traffic; someone coughing from behind a door. A drop of sweat trickles down my forehead and into my eye. It stings. I blink. And, in the time that it takes for my eyes to close and reopen, it all comes back to me.

Reality. The present. My self.

Relieved, I begin climbing the stairs again. Halfway up, I hear a harsh, urgent, familiar sound. I start to run, taking the steps two at a time. Near the top, I miss my footing and almost fall. My right ankle hurts a little, where I broke it once before, but luckily there is no damage done.

Still the sound continues, high-pitched and imperative. I open the door and see Ingrid, naked and unconscious on the bed; next to her, twisted up in blood-stained sheets, is something small and purple-skinned and alive. Instinctively I know what it is. The consequence. The solution to the puzzle. The real mystery: mysterious reality. The blank page upon which I, time, the world will soon, ineffaceably write. The exit of one labyrinth and the entrance to another.

Full of hope and full of fear, I walk towards the screaming child.

Thanks for the memories . . .

Tim Adams, L'Ancien, Adam Ant, Beverly Armin, Mr Ashton, Pedro Calderon de la Barca, Joel Barish, John Franklin Bardin, Anna Barsby, Richard Bates, Rafael Benitez, Tibor Bejczy, The Black Bull, Jorge Luis Borges, Lee Brackstone, Jane Buttery, Mr Buxton, Jonathan Cainer, La Cantina, Nick Carraway, Adolfo Bioy Casares, Rupert Christiansen, Jean-Baptist Clamence, David Clarke, The Coach & Horses, Lisa Cull, Kenny Dalglish, Richard Davies, Arthur Conan Doyle, Ingrid Drijver, Alicia Duffy, Greg Dulli, Olivier Durette, Stéphanie Durette, Mr Earnshaw, Claire Eddison, Sandra Elissen, Barbara Ellen, Nathalie Esterbrook, Jane Ferguson, John 'Scottie' Ferguson, Field Mill, Robert Forster, Jean Fourcade, Lizzie Francke, The French Horn, Alex Games, Christian Gaze, David Godwin, The Golden Frier, Yakov Petrovitch Golyadkin, Mrs Gretton, The Gunmaker's, Luke Haines, Charles Hammond Jr, Matthew Hatton, Paul Hedley, Mr Hill, Peter Hobbs, Victoria Hobbs, Phil Hogan, Rachel Hunt, The Hutt, David Icke, The Infinity Bar, Vicki Jagello, Andrew Jaspan, L. B. Jefferies, Philip Johnson, Mary Keane, John Kessel, Nastassja Kinski, Philip Larkin, Alexander Lennox, Lexington Avenue, Lisa Litchfield, The Little John, Vanessa Lodi, The Lookout, Simon Lumsdon, Alexander Luria, Vanessa Matkin, Richard Manley, Eric Maycock, Carol McDaid, Grant McLennan, The Mint, Mitch's, The Mitre, Eiji Miyake, Bill Montgomery, Chris More, Josephine

Morley, Daniel Morvan, Jaime Mullerat, John Mulvey, Simon Murch, Herman Mussert, Lucy Neville, Sylvia Nofsinger, Jeremy Novick, O'Hanlons, Toru Okada, Will Oldham, The Olde White Harte, Steve Ovett, Lucy Owen, Richard Papen, Margaret Parkes, Martin Paul, John Peel, The Pink Palace, Pliny the Younger, The Polar Bear, Ford Prefect, Dan Pritchard, Qfwfq, Thomas De Quincey, Daniel Quinn, James 'Malcolm' Reilly, Gareth Rigby, Rock City, Antoine Roquentin, Steven Rose, The Roundhouse, Tomas Ryal, Mr Ryder, Oliver Sacks, Saint Augustine, Daniel Schachter, Michel Schmitz, Niquette Schmitz, Clare Sears, Rebeka Shaw, Leonard Shelby, The Sherwood Ranger, Karen Smart, Gavin Smith, Mark E. Smith, Dawn Sobota, Diana Spencer, Neil Spencer, Bruce Springsteen, Geoffrey Sonnabend, The Station, Anna Stead, Robert Louis Stevenson, Jocelyn Targett, Keith Taylor, Margaret Taylor, Matthew Taylor, Milo Taylor, Oscar Taylor, Patricia Taylor, Paul-Emile Taylor, Duncan Thaw, Wendy Timmons, The Tower, Dave Lee Travis, Trie FC, Clare Tryon, Jennifer 'Breg' Tryon, Lucy Tuck, Mary Ann Tuli, Nicholas Urfe, Paul Vanags, Anja Vendrig, Jorrit Verweij, Michael Vignal, The Vodka Bar, Stephen Wakeland, Burhan Wazir, Mr Webster, The Wherehouse, Mr White, Murphy Williams, Jonathan Wilson, Willy Wonka, Valentine Worth, Nicola Wyatt, Steve Xerri, Ye Olde Trip to Jerusalem, Tora Young, Zhivago's.

And to everyone and everything else that, in one way or another, influenced this book, but whose names (or existence) I have forgotten . . .